'A compulsively readable what-if story... Enfield brilliantly conveys how claustrophobic and trapped the four main characters feel as events spiral out of control... A surprising page-turner with an extraordinarily haunting conclusion.'

Mail on Sunday, Novel of the Week

'Dramatic... captures perfectly the consequences of different parenting styles.'　　　　BBC Radio 4 *Woman's Hour*

'A compelling read, with a constantly evolving plot that kept me hooked to the end, as well as a vivid, detailed and funny picture of the life of two modern families.'

William Nicholson

'Lizzie Enfield has a great talent for mirroring all our lives through those small moments that make up a whole. She has a wonderful forensic style in which ordinary details are used to create extraordinary stories. Her writing reminds me of Anne Tyler's.'　　　　Araminta Hall

'A highly provocative and thought-provoking novel... a superb examination of one of the most contentious of recent issues, exploring both sides of a morally ambiguous coin and the wider impact of the decisions we make.'

We Love This Book

'Lizzie Enfield is a writer with a gift for conveying the intricacies and subtleties of relationships between family and friends. Her dialogue is perfectly pitched, and her storytelling thought-provoking and nuanced. *Living With It* explores an emotive issue with insight and care.'　　　　Sarah Rayner

Lizzie Enfield

Living With It

Myriad Editions

First published in 2014 by

Myriad Editions
59 Lansdowne Place
Brighton BN3 1FL

www.myriadeditions.com

Reprinted 2014

3 5 7 9 10 8 6 4 2

A CIP catalogue record for this book is available from
the British Library.

ISBN: 978-1-908434-47-0

Designed and typeset by Linda McQueen, London
in Sabon LT

Printed and bound in Sweden
by ScandBook AB

For my parents

Not your sort of book,
and you don't have to read it

Ip dip do
Cat's got the flu
Dog's got the measles
So out goes you

Traditional playground rhyme

WEEK ONE

Isobel, Saturday

'I thought you knew?'

The way Sally said it made it clear there was something I ought to know, something that everyone else knew and presumed I must also be aware of. And she looked around the room and lowered her voice, not wanting to be heard before delivering those four words in a questioning tone, making me feel anxious about whatever it was I was supposed to have knowledge of but didn't. Not just then.

There ought to be a word for being in a state of unknowingness: for waking up in the morning and going about your life, thinking everything is quite normal, when something has already happened which will change everything.

I read once about a woman from New York who was staying at a spa in some exotic location, destressing or detoxing or one of those things New Yorkers do, when 9/11 happened – and this woman missed it. She'd signed the 'no external interruptions' box in the spa's list of requirements for her stay. Her suite was in a block without television, radio or wi-fi. No newspapers were delivered to her door. So it was only twenty-four hours after the event, on September 12th, when she walked across the complex to the treatment rooms and one of the other guests heard her say 'I've got an appointment for an Indian head massage' in her unmistakable accent and cried, 'Oh, my God! Are you from New York? I'm so sorry. It's just so terrible...' that she was alerted to the fact that the world she lived in had changed.

Blissfully unaware was how I was this morning, but the words are not the right ones. They don't come close enough to describing just how free I was, without knowing the thing that Sally would tell me a few hours later in the day.

We were all in upbeat mode.

It was what Vincent would call a 'pink' morning, with his strange synaesthetic tendency to ascribe colours to moods.

I was surprised when he first did it.

'I don't like Wednesdays,' he said over breakfast one morning. 'They're yellow.'

He was busy seeing things in the remains of his cornflakes, another Vinnie peculiarity. 'There's a Fiat 500 driving across the desert,' he'll say, adjusting some minor detail of the image visible only to him with his spoon, pushing milk-soaked flakes about slightly, as if to sharpen up the picture. Or, 'there's a deer drinking from a stream,' and sometimes 'a butterfly flapping its wings'. He's like an ancient astronomer, picking out hunter's belts from random stars. He sees things clearly that the rest of us must also try to see. 'Oh, yes!' I'll admire the soggy orange mush as if the butterfly wings are equally visible to me.

The colours thing felt slightly different.

'What do you mean, they're yellow, Vincent?' I asked him.

But his answer was not illuminating. 'They just are. Thursdays are a bit brown and Fridays are purple.' He carried on eating his toast before adding, 'Like Gabby.'

'Like Gabs?'

'Yes. She's purple, Daddy is silver, Harvey is green and you're sort of wood-coloured.' He pointed to a shelf.

'Beige?' I was insulted. If Eric was silver, why couldn't I be gold? I'm his mother, I should be gold.

But I was intrigued by the way my youngest son's mind works. And this morning it was on sparkling form.

'Why are you making that face, Vincent?'

4

I was putting lipstick on, using the hall mirror, before we left, and I could see him reflected behind me, his cheeks bulging in a peculiar way.

He disappeared into the living room without saying anything and re-emerged carrying a piece of paper.

'I AM TRYING TO BREAK THE WORLD RECORD FOR HAVING A MOUTHFUL OF WATER,' it read. 'I'VE HAD IT SINCE I CLEANED MY TEETH. PS DON'T MAKE ME LAUGH…'

It made *me* laugh – a heartfelt, happy, 'full of the joys of family life' laugh.

Eric laughed too, when I told him and showed him the note, before tucking it in the pocket of my cardigan, where I would later discover this reminder of that moment, before I knew, before any of us knew.

'Will Ben and Maggie be there?' Gabriella asked as we found seats on the train.

'Can we move up a bit, Gabs?' I nudged Vinnie forward and nodded towards an empty peanut packet, left lying on the table.

Harvey has a nut allergy. I don't think it's as severe as the ones you hear about, when people can die simply from breathing in the dust from a discarded packet, but I don't want to take risks. He hasn't had a reaction for a long time, and that makes those around him forget that he has one and behave as if it's gone away. Sometimes I feel that I'm the only one watching out for him. If even his fifteen-year-old sister, who is caring and sensible and really looks out for her younger brothers, nearly sits him down in front of a peanut packet, how can I trust anyone he spends time with to make sure he avoids contact with them? It's a constant anxiety, when he's at school or with friends.

'Sorry, Mum.' Gabs moved on up the carriage, casting around for five seats. 'Here?'

'But I need a table,' Harvey rejected her choice. 'I need to finish the cake.'

About five minutes before he left, Harvey had decided he would make Anton an origami birthday cake. It was an ambitious project. One that required several sheets of paper, more than five minutes and a flat surface.

'You sit there, then,' his older sister said, nodding towards a spare seat by a table. The other three were already taken. I'd thought it would be nice if we could all sit together for the twenty-minute journey along the coast from Hove to Lancing, but Harvey took the vacant seat, keen to get on with his creation.

It was rare that we all did things together these days and I was surprised Gabriella had opted to come. She prefers to spend time with her friends, and the fiftieth birthday of the husband of one my old university friends would usually make her run a mile. But she had been keen to come with us to Anton's.

'I'd like to see everyone again,' she'd said, when I'd mentioned the invite.

By 'everyone' she'd meant the group of friends we'd been with for ten days in France, during the summer: Yasmin, who had been a fellow student of mine, and her husband, Anton; Sally and Paddy, who also went to the same university and who own the house in Gascony where we stayed at the beginning of August; and Ben and his wife Maggie. I'd lived in the same halls of residence as Ben. I met him on my first day and later I would meet Eric, Ben's oldest friend, through him.

Initially Gabriella hadn't been keen to come on holiday, but we weren't going to leave her at home despite her protests of 'everyone else's parents let them' and 'but there won't be anyone my age there'.

Anton and Yasmin's son, Conrad, is just over a year older than Gabs. When she was born, we were all still living in London and I'd hoped Yasmin and I might spend time together. Apart from Sally, who had got pregnant in the midst of her finals, none of my close friends had children yet. But I'd found Conrad slightly disconcerting. I wasn't sure why at first. He never looked at me or smiled, and he took no interest in Gabs, or in anything really.

When Gabs was just over a year old, Conrad's slight strangeness got a label. He was autistic. It was a terrible blow to Anton and Yasmin, who were by then expecting their second child, Mira.

'There's a poem,' Yasmin once said to me, 'called "Welcome to Holland", about raising a child with a disability. It likens it to thinking you'd booked a holiday in Italy and finding out you're going to Holland instead.'

I'd understood what she meant. She still had a child, whom she loved very much, but he was not the child she had envisaged, and the journey with him through life was going to be very different from the one she and Anton had anticipated. And so was our friendship. Conrad and Gabs never became the close childhood friends I had once thought they might. When Yasmin and her family moved to the south coast, several years after we had moved to Brighton, it was so that Conrad could go to a local special school. By that time my kids had their own lives, and I had mine too, albeit one tightly bound up with the children. We did meet up, but only occasionally. It was always difficult. Conrad was always difficult. Gabs and he did not communicate. Harvey and Vincent were scared of him.

The holiday in France was the first time we had all spent any length of time together, and effectively Gabs was right: she was on her own. But she had suddenly seemed to grow up and had got on well with all the adults, especially Maggie, whom none of us really knows that well.

'Will Ben and Maggie be there?' she asked again, as we settled on the train.

'And Iris,' Vincent said, opening the can of Coke Eric had bought him and spraying it across the seat.

Iris is Ben and Maggie's baby daughter. Gabs had got on well with her too. She's always been good with younger children. I suppose it comes from being the eldest.

'I'm sure they will,' I said, with a confidence that turned out to be entirely misplaced. 'Vinnie, be careful.'

I thought they would be there because it was Anton's fiftieth and it was rare for them to have a party. Socialising has never been easy because of Conrad.

I thought they would be there because we all left France in the summer saying, 'See you again at Anton's fiftieth!'

I thought this too because, even though Ben hadn't responded to my text asking if they were all going, I presumed he was just busy.

Ben and Maggie had been home again by the time Iris went down with measles. I knew how scary it must have been because it was scary for me too, seeing Gabs so ill. And I knew that Iris could only have caught the virus from Gabs while we were away. But it was over now. They were both fine. Their immune systems were probably stronger for it.

And anyway, our friendships, mine and Ben's and Ben's and Eric's, go back so far that I imagined that any bad feeling there had been at the time was is in the past.

I am wrong.

Vincent is out playing football in the garden with a couple of other kids, watched by a small group of adults. It's early November, but the temperature is mild. I am not sure where Harvey has got to and Gabriella is hovering at the edge of the living room, looking as if she wished she hadn't come. Again, there's no one here her age. I know she wanted to chat to Maggie and see Iris too. Gabs seems to get on better with Maggie than I do. I think it's because they are both musical and also, when we were away, Maggie must have been grateful that Gabs was willing to spend hours entertaining the baby.

'Are Ben and Maggie not here yet?' I say to Sally, watching Gabriella sitting, bored, on the other side of the room.

'I don't think they're coming,' she says. She sounds strained, but I think nothing of it.

'Oh. I thought they'd be here,' I say.

Sally's look tells me there's a reason they are not here and she feels put on the spot because I don't know and she's going to have to be the one to tell me.

Or maybe I read too much into the way she looks at me.

'Don't you know?' she asks.

'Know what?' I say, my 'pink' mood starting to evaporate.

'I thought they'd have told you,' Sally says, and she's looking around now, perhaps for a means of escape.

'Told me what?' If there is such a thing as premonition, I feel it then: that whatever she says next is going to be bad.

'This isn't really the place.' Sally is looking away, at Anton, who is circulating with a bottle. She won't catch my eye.

'Sally?' I force her to.

We've known each other over twenty years.

We've always been completely at ease in each other's company.

What is it she's not telling me?

'It's Iris.' She lowers her voice and this time looks straight at me. 'She was very ill after the holiday.'

I knew this. 'But she's better.' I'd spoken to Ben since and he'd reassured me that Iris was fine.

'Yes, better.' Sally takes a sip from her glass. Then another. 'But…'

'But what?'

'I thought you knew?' Sally says. 'She's deaf now. Completely deaf in both ears.'

I've only drunk half a glass of champagne but the room starts to swim before me.

'You'd better sit down,' Sally is saying, and again, 'I'm sorry, I really thought you knew.'

'I think I need to go to the bathroom,' I hear myself saying, and then Yasmin is there too.

'Are you OK, Bel?'

'She didn't know,' Sally says to her. 'I thought she would know.'

9

'What's up, Bel?' Eric has found me – has honed in on my distress from where he was standing, just outside in the garden.

'I'm just not feeling very well.' I look at Sally, willing her not to tell him, not yet.

'Oh, love.' Eric is concerned. 'I hope you're not coming down with something. Anton said Maggie's not well either.'

Eric does not seem to catch Sally and Yasmin exchanging glances. I do.

'I feel a bit sick.' I stand up and head towards the bathroom.

'Shall I come with you?' Eric asks, and I try to smile.

'No, I'll be fine, I'm sure.'

He looks worried, but Yasmin steps in. 'I'll take her. I think we've got some anti-nausea stuff in the medicine cabinet.'

We pass Conrad's room as we walk across the landing to the bathroom. He's sitting on his bed making the strange moaning noise he makes, the way some people hum under their breath. He hates large gatherings. They make him stressed, anxious and angry.

I pause to look in and see that Harvey is in the room with him, kneeling on the floor, using a large book on Conrad's bed as a table, on which he is folding his origami.

I'm not entirely surprised he ended up here. The origami began on holiday. I bought a kit, as I wanted the boys to spend time doing something other than playing on their iPods. Harvey took to it immediately – unsurprisingly, as he loves making things – and Conrad developed a fascination with watching him and a fondness for the miniature paper creations that resulted.

But I am surprised that Harvey sought sanctuary in Conrad's room. Conrad is not the sort of child whose company you'd seek out, or with whom you'd be likely to find sanctuary.

I walk past.

Yasmin is ahead of me now, opening the door to the bathroom. I push past her in a sudden hurry, sit down on the

10

edge of the bath and take a deep breath. Yasmin stands by the washbasin.

'I suppose everyone thinks it's my fault?' I say.

I want Yasmin to say something comforting, but she remains quiet. Or rather she looks away, and says nothing, which is not quite the same as remaining quiet. It's more like not saying what she actually thinks.

And that speaks volumes.

So, I answer my question myself. Of course they are blaming me. How can everyone *not* be blaming me?

'Are you feeling a bit better now?' Yasmin says, looking at me again.

'Not really,' I tell her. 'But I'll be fine. I just need a minute.'

'OK.' Yasmin moves to leave.

Of course she wants to get back to the party. I know that. She's the host. But at the same time I feel there's something else, something she isn't quite saying. I put my hand into my pocket, searching for a tissue because I think I might start to cry, but instead my hand finds Vinnie's note. Was it only a few hours ago that we were full of the joys of family life?

I start to cry.

I know that if Ben has not told me himself then he must be angry with me. And I'm beginning to feel sorry for myself, because I know people are going to judge me.

Ben, Saturday

'Where are you going?' Maggie asks. 'You haven't finished your coffee.'

She's just made a pot.

'I'm going to empty the dishwasher,' I tell her.

'But it hasn't finished its cycle.'

'It has. I just heard it beep.'

'That was the washing machine,' Maggie says, too patiently.

'What's that supposed to mean?'

'It doesn't mean anything. All I'm saying is there is no point you jumping up to unload the dishwasher because it hasn't finished its cycle. It was the washing machine which beeped.'

'You're implying I don't do enough around the house,' I snap. 'Because I can't tell the difference between the particular beeps our various household appliances make.'

'I'm not implying anything of the sort, Ben. I'm just saying that the dishwasher hasn't finished. Jesus...' She bites her metaphorical lip.

'What?'

'Nothing.'

Iris, who's been sitting in a chair that clips on to the table, rolling wax crayons over a sheet of paper and seeming happy enough, suddenly emits one of her horrid high-pitched screeches.

'You're pissed off with me now,' I say, ignoring our daughter.

'I'm not,' Maggie replies, but of course she is. Why wouldn't she be? I am tetchy and irritable and taking it out on her. 'Look, Ben, if you need to be doing something, then by all means unload the washing machine and hang the washing up. All I asked was if you wanted to finish your coffee.'

'Well, clearly it's time I acquainted myself b-b-better with the household appliances.' I curse myself for stuttering, riled by the stupidity of the argument but determined to have it anyway. 'Where's the laundry basket?'

'By the back door,' Maggie says, wearily, getting up herself, lifting Iris out of her chair, even though she's stopped screeching and returned to crayon-rolling.

Maybe we should have gone to the party. I'd wanted to make a big angry statement by not going, but Yasmin had just seemed to accept it when I'd phoned to tell her we couldn't make it – and why. 'Of course, I understand.'

Her reaction was disappointing. Too understanding and sympathetic. No outright condemnation of Isobel. No real sense of shock at what had happened. No 'Jesus, that's terrible' or stunned silence. She was the first of our friends to hear the news and I'd wanted her to be outraged. I didn't want a measured, 'That's awful, Ben, I'm so sorry.'

I suppose I should have expected it. Deafness, to her, with crazy Conrad for a son, is probably not that bad. Maybe she stopped herself saying, 'That's great, Ben. She's deaf, not autistic. Lucky you. Get on with it. You'll learn to live with it.'

Paddy was more shocked, when I told him, but the old group loyalties are still there. Sympathy for Ben, but we're not going to condemn Isobel outright because she's our friend. Why not, though? She's in the fucking wrong. It wouldn't have hurt Isobel if Paddy had said as much, and it might have helped me.

So we're at home, knowing some of our friends will soon be glugging wine all day, marking a milestone in the traditional way. And it's getting to me, not really doing anything while elsewhere life is going on.

'Will you watch her while I take a shower?' Maggie asks. She's put Iris on the floor of the kitchen now, in front of a shape-sorter.

13

'You know I will,' I say, as I drape wet clothes over the laundry maid.

She doesn't need to ask me to watch my own daughter. She knows I could watch Iris all day. Her every action still captivates me. Her infant beauty bowls me over. I just can't stand that when I say, 'Hey, pumpkin!' she no longer turns to look at me and smile. She just carries on with what she's doing, and if she gets bored, which seems to happen increasingly quickly, then she starts to cry.

Our post lands on the floor of the hall mid-morning. There's a lot today: mostly junk, a few bills and a subscription magazine for Maggie. The letterbox has a brass flap on the inside to keep cold air out, and every time a letter is posted through it makes a loud clanging sound, followed by the 'phut' as the piece of post hits the floor. It's a noisy process, and today it culminates with 'Alan with an ampersand' ringing our doorbell.

We call him this on account of his Christmas card. We had no idea what our postman was called, until he sent one last year. Even when we opened it, it took us a while to work it out. 'Happy Christmas from &lan,' it read.

'Oh, it's Alan!' It dawned on Maggie first.

I still wasn't convinced. 'Alan with an ampersand?' I asked.

From then on our post was delivered by 'Alan with an ampersand', just as one of Maggie's old boyfriends, Iain, was always referred to as 'Iain with two eyes', differentiating him from other Ians we knew, who were Cyclopes.

Our doorbell is loud and insistent. It makes you jump if you've not heard it before; in fact it makes me jump now, even though I already know Alan with an ampersand is on the other side, struggling to push something through. I'd thought he might give up and ring the bell.

But Iris, sitting on the floor chewing shapes from the sorter she's apparently 'too young' to master, doesn't react at all: not to the clanging, or the landing, or the insistence of the bell. She just carries on exploring the red triangle-shaped block with her tongue, as if it were a lollipop rather than a bit of wood painted in primary-coloured non-toxic paint.

And I feel like snapping at her now, 'Can you really not hear?' – the way old people whose hearing is going start snapping at everyone around them for mumbling, refusing to admit they have a problem, making it everyone else's.

I stomp to answer the door, glancing back at Iris to see if she notices. I want her to be fooling us. Is she too young, I wonder, to have decided to pretend to be deaf, just to annoy us? Of course she is. But it doesn't stop me thinking or hoping it, or wanting to jolt her into hearing by yelling at her.

I open the door and Alan with an ampersand says he has a parcel for Maggie, although he calls her Mrs Bisseker, because that's what it says on the parcel. It's wrong because we are not married, so officially she is Ms Bisseker.

'More books,' I say, feeling an irrational need to explain why we've been having so many parcels lately. It's not really any of Alan's business and I doubt he cares. But I want to impress upon him that we are not simply shopping and making his mailbag a little heavier than usual, but also improving ourselves, or rather improving our knowledge about our daughter's condition.

That's been Maggie's response: to read as much as possible, as if knowing about it will make it easier to handle. She can spend whole hours on the National Deaf Children's Society website, when she's not on Amazon finding books.

I suppose she's right: the more we know, the better. But my response is different. I'm angry, because it's so fucking unnecessary. I'm furious that this has happened to our beautiful baby girl and I'm furious with Isobel, because it's her fault.

Maggie cautioned me against calling her as soon as we found out. 'It's not going to help.'

She was so calm, but these things hit people in different ways. I knew she was upset too. She hasn't picked up her trumpet in days and that's unheard of. She used to play all the time, but it's been quiet in our house since we found out. Too quiet. A quiet only punctuated by the doorbell.

'Maybe someone else should tell her,' Maggie said. 'She needs to know, I agree, but maybe she needs to hear it from someone else and get her head round it before you actually speak to her.'

Sometimes Maggie can be so understanding I almost can't stand it. It makes me want to shake her and work up a bit of the rage that I feel, just as I want to shout at Iris, tell her to stop closing her ears to the world and react to a sound.

I actually thought, when we went to the hospital two weeks ago, that the trip was just a formality: a reassurance for anxious parents whose children had had a previous spell in hospital; a box that NHS staff needed to tick on the records of kids who'd had measles. *Have they been in for a follow-up appointment?* Check. *Did they take their children to be checked over by an audiologist?* Check.

'She's just not as responsive as she used to be.' Maggie was more anxious, especially when the GP referred Iris to the hospital, saying something about 'ruling out deafness'.

But I still thought that was all we were doing: ruling deafness out, not having it confirmed. I hadn't even thought I needed to go with them, but Maggie had insisted. 'I don't want to be on my own if there is anything wrong.'

'I'm sure there isn't.'

After Iris had come out of hospital before, we had both done the whole internet thing, even though the doctors had advised against it. I'd looked up the effects of measles and the possible complications. Again and again the online reports had stressed that these were 'rare'. My older brother had measles, and he was and is fine. Younger, I'd had a jab and been immune to the few weeks' unpleasantness that the virus brought with it.

Iris had been ill too – horribly, alarmingly ill. I never wanted to see her so poorly again. But she'd recovered quickly and seemed fine.

She was sitting happily on Maggie's lap, looking about the room exactly like a child who was engaged with the world, when the consultant spoke.

'Your daughter appears to have suffered Sudden Sensorial Bilateral Hearing Loss.'

'What do you mean?' Maggie and I both said this at once.

What I was actually thinking when he said this was, *Why can't they use plain English when they tell you something?*

I tried to catch Maggie's eye. I wanted to raise my eyebrows in a way that conveyed *Isn't it daft, the way they talk?*

But Maggie was ahead of me. 'You mean she can't hear?' she translated. 'And that it happened suddenly? Will it return?'

'Well, there are things that can be done.' The consultant looked from me to her. 'But I'm afraid the damage appears to have been caused by the virus your daughter contracted earlier this year. Her hearing won't return naturally, though of course it is possible for her to have hearing aids and – '

'Hearing aids?' I suddenly linked the plural with the 'bilateral' from the consultant's earlier sentence. 'You mean she's lost the hearing in both her ears?'

'It would appear so,' the consultant said, tidying his notes into a pile, as if delivering this bombshell was a natural conclusion to this particular consultation.

I think someone must have passed the news on to Isobel by now. Or they will soon. Fuck knows how she'll react. Will she be shaken out of her smug 'I work so hard at being the perfect parent' mode and feel as terrible as she should? Or will she dredge up some list of selfish justifications for landing this on us?

'Are you regretting not going to the party?' Maggie is washed and dressed and on the money. She has scooped Iris off the floor and is talking to her, even though she can't hear a word. 'Do you think Daddy would rather be getting drunk at a party?'

Maggie curls her hand into a C shape and tilts it towards Iris, as if drinking. Already she has bought a book on signing and is communicating with our deaf daughter in a way neither of us ever imagined. I am still obstinately resistant. What about hearing aids? What about implants? I am not willing to consign her to this other world.

'This came for you.' I ignore Maggie's question and hand her the parcel. 'Another book.'

'Yes, another book,' Maggie replies. The standoff continues. She could put a stop to it, if only she'd share some of my anger.

It's not that she's entirely accepting. There have been tears, lots of futile 'what if's, defiantly questioning, 'Why didn't she tell us it could be measles?' 'Why do you think the kids weren't vaccinated?' But she's more focused on working out how we're going to cope than on pointing the finger.

So she's a better person than me. So what? I think as I hand her the parcel containing what I suspect to be more books on deafness: *Coping with Deafness*, *Living with Deafness*, *Coping with a Deaf Child*. There are hundreds of books on the subject and Maggie seems determined to work her way through all of them. Well, at least the ones about children. There are books on living with deaf parents or siblings, on working with deaf colleagues. There's even one – and I'm glad it's out there because when Maggie found it, searching on Amazon while Iris was napping after that hospital visit, she called me over and we laughed – called *Living with a Deaf Dog*. I thought it was a spoof when she showed it to me.

'*A deaf dog enjoys life just as hearing dogs do,*' Maggie read from the description of the book. '*He still has his fine nose and his eyes, which are far more important faculties to a dog.*'

'Is it for real?' I asked, sounding strangely American to myself, wondering if an American wrote the book.

18

'I think so.' Maggie read on. '*This invaluable book will help owners of deaf and hard-of-hearing dogs not just to accept their loyal companions for what they are, but also to establish a closer bond as they help each other find new or adapted ways to live together.*'

'Do you think deaf dogs have hearing people trained up to react for them?'

Maggie laughed, not at my lame joke but at the fact that the author had a deaf Dalmatian called Chocolate. 'It seems a bit cruel to confuse the poor dog by calling it chocolate when it's black and white,' she said.

'Well, it can't hear her,' I replied and Maggie laughed at my joke, this time.

But it pissed me off, that I'd made the joke and that she'd found it funny. It seemed cruel. I pointed this out. 'Do you think we'll start making jokes about Iris?'

Maggie stopped laughing and started to cry.

Isobel, Saturday afternoon

At what point would I have had to act differently for it to have made a difference?

That's what I keep asking myself, as I close my eyes on the train back home, trying to block out the world and focus on what I've just been told. Eric still thinks I'm not feeling well. I think he thinks I drank too much.

'Why don't you have this seat, Bel?' he says. 'I'll sit over there with the kids. You could maybe try to sleep.'

'Thank you.'

I am grateful for the thinking space, for the chance to ask myself 'what if', and, because we've just been with the same group of friends, I keep going back to the time when we were last all together and wondering how things might have played out differently.

When I was a child, our family holidays always had a particular day to look forward to, a day that was imbued with some sort of expectation and mystique – a day we'd save for the end of the week so that even while we were away, doing the thing we'd been looking forward to all year, there was still something else, something better, to anticipate.

In our case it was getting the ferry to Padstow. These were the days when Padstow was a very touristy fishing village in Cornwall but not yet a place of foodie pilgrimage. The excitement lay in waving the flag from the other side of the estuary to let the ferry that traversed the narrow point know you were there, then the ten minutes chugging through the often choppy water, rewarded with a few hours wandering round gift shops and eating ice cream.

It was the one day of the holiday when I didn't have to swim before being allowed a cornet – a peculiar rule of Dad's. Pleasure was not just to be taken; it had first to be earned by swimming in the freezing Atlantic. The rule only applied to myself and him, but it is a rule I still use with my own offspring. 'Why don't you go on the trampoline before we have cake?' 'Don't you want to come for a walk before lunch?' 'Why don't we save the sweets until after the water park?' I am a chip off the old block.

Mum was allowed to stand on the shore, holding towels, ready for when we got out. But she still got her raspberry ripple cone. She was an adult already. There was no point in Dad trying to instil an element of toughness in her.

Or perhaps she already knew she was ill. I did not.

There was no trace of Rick Stein in Padstow then; no scattering of artisan bread shops attracting Notting Hill habitués. Nevertheless Padstow was always held up as the thing we would do when the weather was good, or when all the other fun had been had and could only be topped by this pinnacle of holiday outings.

Paddy and Sally, at their house in Gascony, had created a similar ritual: a thing that at some point we would all do, when we began to tire of lying round the pool and buying oysters in the 'disgusting' shacks. Harvey coined this phrase for the *dégustation* sheds where you could taste oysters. He thought disgusting was more apt, given the delicacy on offer. 'Why on earth would anyone want the world to be their oyster?' he would remark, every time Eric threw a slippery morsel of mollusc to the back of his throat and pronounced that it was. 'If your world has got to be a fish, why can't it be battered cod from Jenny's fish and chip shop?'

The thing Paddy and Sally had spent the weeks whipping up enthusiasm for was a trip to the Dune du Pilat. 'One day we'll go and climb the biggest sand dune in Europe,' Paddy had promised early on. Harvey and Vincent were closer to frenzied excitement than enthusiasm.

'I'm in training!' Vinnie had been rushing up and down the stairs of the house daily, ever since the outing had been outlined. 'Should I bring all this?' he'd ask, laying out an array of items for this 'expedition' on his bed.

Preparation was well under way before Paddy even decided on the date, and by the time the weather was slightly cooler and we'd tired of lounging we were all looking forward to the change of scene as much as the boys were.

But by then Gabriella was really quite ill. Her cough was worse; the slight temperature she was running was higher; her eyes were sore and she seemed listless.

'Should I bring my torch?' Vinnie was winding up his battery-free flashlight and directing it at various spots on the wall. I feared the anticipation of the Dune du Pilat might prove more exciting for him than actually climbing it.

'Do you know it has a volume of sixty million metres cubed?' Paddy was further heightening the anticipation with hard facts, on the morning we finally got ready to go.

'I'm worried about Gabriella.' I was the one to pour cold water on the boys' excitement. 'She's not well enough to come and I think I ought to stay with her.'

'No, come, Mum, please come!' Vinnie stopped darting and flashing and began pleading. 'Harvey wants you to come too. Don't you?'

He looked at Harvey, who simply shrugged. I suspected he was not bothered either way. Harvey has always seemed a little more Eric's child, I'm not sure why. Perhaps because he's the first boy, or because Eric makes an effort to make sure he doesn't get lost in the family by being in the middle; or maybe because they are just more similar. Harvey is certainly more easygoing than Gabriella or Vincent, and if I had continued to say I couldn't go with them to the dune he'd have accepted it, whereas Vincent would probably have carried on insisting I come too.

'Yes, come, Bel. She can stay behind if she's not keen.' Eric clearly thought Gabriella was suffering from teenage lethargy, nothing more serious.

But I was concerned. 'I just don't think it's a good idea to leave her by herself.'

'Why not? She's fifteen!' Ben, too, clearly thought I was being over-anxious.

'Actually, I think I'll stay here.' Maggie unwittingly became the deciding factor. 'It sounds like quite a climb, even without trying to carry a baby, and I'm happy to stay put.'

'Well...' I was torn between wanting to go, to be with the boys to see their triumphant faces when they reached the top of this giant sand dune, and wanting to keep an eye on Gabby.

'That's settled, then,' Paddy was anxious to get going and Maggie said she was fine, staying with Gabs.

'It's probably just a summer cold,' Ben said.

But there was something else – a slight uncertainty, preying on my mind. Earlier in the week, before Gabriella had begun to feel unwell, she'd been down to the lake to call her boyfriend. Sam had not returned any of the texts she'd sent since we'd been away and she was clearly worried that a few days' absence was enough for him to lose sight of her and move on.

'He's really ill!' she'd said to me when she came back, clearly relieved rather than worried by the cause of his silence. 'He's got measles.'

'Really?' I'd tried to sound casual. 'Well, I'm sure he'll be fine in a few days.'

Gabriella had seemed happy enough again, but when she started to get ill it was there, the question slowly forming in my mind. Was it measles? What were the symptoms? She didn't have a rash, so it was probably just a cold.

No one except Eric and I knew she'd not been vaccinated. Why would they? It wasn't the sort of thing that came up in conversation.

So it was there, in the back of my mind, when I left her with Maggie and her nine-month-old baby – the thought that it was

23

possible Gabriella was going down with measles, and that, if she was, I should be the one staying to look after her.

And that I should tell Maggie, even it was only a possibility and I was wrong.

But I pushed the thought from my mind, worrying that I was worrying too much.

And even if I'd known then what I found out today, would I have been able to do anything that changed how things have panned out?

I imagine myself insisting on staying and, if I'd been there, Gabriella would not have got up and sat Iris on her lap and played with her while Maggie made them all lunch.

Would I have said then, 'Look, there's a chance she has measles. If you're worried about it, we should keep them apart?' Perhaps Ben would have insisted on driving into town and finding a French doctor, demanding that Iris have the measles vaccine there and then, even though it was a little early.

But I didn't do, or say, any of those things.

'Are you coming, then?' Harvey asked, tired of my indecision.

Vincent was buzzing around me. 'I'm doing a waggle dance,' he informed me. 'It's something bees do to let the others know where the honey is.'

I laughed, as I tend to whenever Vinnie opens his mouth. 'Well, if you're sure, Maggie,' I said, because I wanted to be with him, with all the others. I wanted to get out of the house and drive somewhere. I wanted to see this big sand dune, I wanted to earn my picnic lunch by climbing it, and I wanted to watch the boys scamper up and roll and slide down again, laughing, happy and carefree.

So I went with them, and set in motion a sequence of events that I can't reverse.

Ben, Saturday afternoon

By mid-afternoon, I really wish that we'd gone to the party.

I keep checking my watch, thinking, they'll all be there now; they're probably having lunch now; maybe they are thinking about going home again; maybe someone's told Isobel about Iris and she's...

Then, I think, she's what, exactly? I'm not going to find out because we're not there. Maybe we should have gone and then I could have told her myself, seen her face, seen how she reacted. We could have had an angry confrontation. We might have ruined Anton's fiftieth. It might have been worth it.

It wouldn't have been fair, though. Not to Anton.

It's driving me a bit crazy, being at home.

It's three-thirty. Iris is having a nap and Maggie is reading her new book.

'I think I might go for a walk,' I say.

Maggie looks up. 'Good idea.'

We're still a bit out of kilter. I think it's Maggie's fault for being so calm. She doesn't really seem to have noticed.

'Where are you going?' she asks, not bothered that I am not waiting for Iris to wake so that I can join them when she takes her out in the buggy.

'Nowhere in particular. I just want to get out of the house,' I say, and offer a grudging, 'Is there anything we need?'

'I don't think so. I'll take Iris out when she wakes.'

'Do you want me to wait, then?'

'No, it's fine. You go now.'

I don't know if she means that it is fine or if she's pissed off and would rather I waited, but I don't hang around to find out. I grab my coat and keys and head off in no particular direction.

The way Paddy went on about it, it was like something out of *Lawrence of Arabia*. All the time we'd been there, he'd been promising us that one day we'd take a drive, venture into the wilds of cultivated, second-home-dominated Gascony and climb the Dune du Pilat. 'One day we'll go and climb the biggest sand dune in Europe,' he kept promising. And, on the day we eventually set off to conquer it, he was bombarding us with facts and figures.

'It's five hundred metres wide and nearly three kilometres long.' He was behaving as if he'd built the fucking thing himself, with a bucket and spade. 'And it's a hundred and ten metres above sea level.'

'What's that in old money?' I asked. It didn't sound that high, although it turned out to be a tough climb in the summer heat.

Maggie wasn't sure whether to come or not, and by the time I was halfway up I thought her deciding against had been the right decision.

'That's about three hunded and sixty feet,' Paddy converted for us and, looking at Conrad, added, 'So if we took a step every second we'd be up there in six minutes, but it's a bit harder than that.'

Conrad ignored him and Anton muttered under his breath, 'He's not a fucking mathematical genius.'

I knew this was the first time Yasmin and Anton had been on a holiday with other families, and Anton was almost as wary of people's reactions to their gangly autistic teenage son as Conrad was of the rest of us. Paddy was the worst, in all honesty. I mean, he was the host and he's a mate and he meant well, but he was clearly expecting some sort of *savant*, and had decided to welcome Rain Man into his holiday home. When he actually got a strange, surly, non-communicative, angry teenager (OK, so that makes him sound normal and without being rude I can only say he's not fucking normal), Paddy decided to ignore this and carry on as if it was Rain Man he was trying to enthuse with the proportions of his great big sandcastle.

It was the first time we'd been away with other families, too – new to children, new to the shared family holiday – and it was driving me a bit mad myself. It was like living in a shared house or student accommodation – apt, as we'd all been students together, but irritating, and starting to get to me by Dune Day.

'Oh, no!' There was drama in the way she said it. 'Who finished all the chocolate spread?'

Isobel had asked this over breakfast and Maggie had confessed she'd given it to Iris the evening before, with a banana, for her pudding. 'I'm sorry,' she'd apologised – unnecessarily, I thought. 'There's a jar of Nutella in the cupboard?'

'It's for Harvey,' Isobel had retorted. She was making him toast. 'He's got a severe nut allergy.'

'Oh, yes. I'm so sorry,' Maggie apologised again. 'I didn't think.'

'There's jam,' I'd said.

'Harvey doesn't like jam,' she'd retorted, and I'd bitten back my urge to say 'chill' the way the kids at school do, in their pared-down, text- and social media-influenced language. I ask my students their opinion of Beckett and they say, 'Like.' I read them a hilarious passage and rather than actually laughing they say, 'Lol.' It infuriates me.

So I didn't tell Isobel to chill. Instead, I raised my eyebrows at Maggie, who shrugged, as if not particularly bothered.

Later, when we were all getting ready to go, Isobel's children were somehow still central to the proceedings.

'Ben, would you mind shoving this lot in the car?' Sally had asked me, nodding towards a steadily growing stash of picnic food.

'Ah, the female imperative,' Paddy had joked. 'Sally uses it all the time. "Would you mind" meaning "Do it – or else".'

'And Paddy… would you mind buttoning it and trying to get everyone out of the house?'

'I'm worried about Gabriella,' Isobel had announced in a way that served to dampen the general air of excitement, especially from her boys. 'She's not well enough to come. I think I ought to stay here with her.'

'Are you coming or not?' Vincent sounded slightly miffed.

Isobel always seemed to be fussing about one of the kids, but it was usually Gabriella or Vincent. Harvey just got on with it, while the others had ways of demanding her attention.

Eric seemed to note the slight tone of pique in his voice.

'Yes, come, Bel,' he had urged Isobel. 'She can stay if she's not keen.'

'I just don't think it's a good idea to leave her by herself.'

'Why not? She's fifteen!' I snapped.

But Maggie was more understanding. Jesus, if Maggie wasn't always so understanding, maybe things would be different now.

'I think I'll stay here,' she said. 'It sounds like quite a climb, even without having to carry a baby.'

'Well…' Isobel looked undecided but Paddy made the decision for her.

'That's settled, then,' he said, and began heading towards the door.

I picked up the bags of picnic stuff I was under instructions to take to the car.

'It's probably just a summer cold,' I said to Isobel, expecting her to look annoyed with me, but she didn't. She looked anxious, hesitant still, as if she really was worried about Gabriella. I'd thought she was fussing, at the time. Now, I realise, she knew.

She fucking knew.

I think I may have said this out loud, as I walk past an office which until recently I'd thought was a café. It popped up a few months ago, on one of the roads just off the High Street, and brought itself to the attention of passers-by with a lot of lime-green, grey and oak. I didn't really pay it much attention; it looked too hip, whatever it was. I just happened to notice that it had two or three tables in the window and the next time I walked past there were people sitting at them drinking coffee. It seemed safe to assume it was a café.

It's only today, when a woman standing outside appears to notice me talking to myself and hands me a flyer, also lime-green and grey, that I realise it is a solicitors' office. *Miller, McDonald and Magnusson*, the flyer reads, in bold serif font. *Specialist compensation claims and personal injury solicitors.*

'England, Scotland and Norway?' I say to the leafleteer. I don't really expect her to respond, other than with a blank look; I'm just amusing myself with a banal observation. That's what Croydon on a Saturday afternoon does to you, especially when you are me and in a bad mood.

But she smiles and puts out her spare hand, the one that isn't clutching the flyers.

'Hedda Magnusson,' she says.

'Like Hedda Gabler?' I ask, again expecting her to look blank.

My expectations are based on stereotyping. Hedda is very blonde indeed. Hedda is handing out leaflets outside what I had hitherto thought was a green and grey café. I am not expecting her to be a cultured Norwegian lawyer.

'Yes.' She nods. 'My great-grandmother was a friend of Ibsen's. I was named after Hedda Gabler.'

'Oh, well, that's a coincidence,' I find myself saying, and this time she does look blank, which is fair enough. 'I played Tesman, Hedda's husband, in a production a few years back,' I explain, realising that this isn't actually a coincidence at all really. It's just a thing.

29

'You're an actor?' she asks, her face showing just a trace more interest, the way people's faces do when you've said something that makes them think you might be more interesting that they first thought you were, while trying to disguise the fact that they presumed you dull in the first place.

'Used to be,' I said. 'I teach drama now.'

'That must be an interesting job.'

'Yes.'

I hate it. It's not what I wanted to do. But failing to make it as an actor is one of the many disappointments life has thrown my way.

'Well, if you ever need a solicitor...' she says.

And that could have been it – the end of the conversation, the turning point in my frustration-relieving walk. I could have said, 'Thanks, bye,' and gone on my way...

'What were you doing all that time?' Maggie is sitting at the computer when I get back. Iris is balanced on her lap, rolling a pen backwards and forwards across the desk, as Maggie trawls the NDCS website – for what? Information? She must have gleaned nearly all there is from it already. Hope? I didn't see much of that on the site when I last looked.

'You've been gone much longer than I expected.' She doesn't look up when she says this.

'Did you take Iris out?'

'Yes, just round the block. I thought you'd be back sooner.'

It's hard to work out if this is an accusation or just a comment. 'I lost track of time,' I say. I've no idea if she'll be more annoyed if I tell her. So I don't. I don't tell her I made an appointment to see Hedda. I don't tell her we might be able to sue Eric and Isobel for the damage to Iris. I decide there is no point in talking about it, until I've found out if it really is possible. But it makes me feel better knowing it might be.

I can't just accept this and do nothing.

Isobel, Saturday evening

The news is on but I'm not really watching it. Eric is, taking it all in before *Match of the Day* begins. I'm just letting it wash over me, trying to find the right moment and the right way to say what I have to tell him.

'What if it's not the worst thing that could happen to you?'

There is a debate on the news about rape, and I look up because what the woman is saying catches my attention.

I've missed the peg, the reason they are discussing this. When I look at the screen I see a well-known feminist writer, sitting alongside the 'not the worst thing' woman, and she is giving her a hard time.

'How can you say that – ?' the writer begins.

'I'm not diminishing the crime,' the woman cuts across her. 'I'm just saying that there are other things, murder for example, or the rape and murder of one of your children, which could possibly be construed as worse.'

I agree with her, now. When I was the same age as the young feminist writer, I might have argued as forcefully as she is doing now. She is still in that state of unknowingness. She has no idea how having children changes your view of the world.

I realised, as soon as my children were born, that the worst thing that could happen to me now was something happening to them. All the fears of the past – being raped, killed, becoming ill, losing someone close to me – began to recede. They gave way to a whole new set of fears: that any of those things might happen to one of the children.

And now I have a new scenario: something happening to someone else's child and being partly to blame.

'You still don't look well, Bel.'

Eric is still in the state which I think 'unknowingness' is not a good enough word to describe. Some weeks later, I will hear, discussed on the radio, a condition known as 'epistemic uncertainty' – an uncertainty based on things we could know in principle but we don't in practice – and I wonder if this is the state I was in.

But now, back home after the party, Eric is still pleasantly drunk, both from alcohol and company. He went to a different party from the one I went to, and spent it thinking Ben and Maggie weren't there because Maggie was unwell, a bit worried that I was sick too, but not unduly so.

'Maybe there's some sort of bug going round. Why don't you go to bed? I'll tidy up down here.'

The boys are in bed and Gabriella is in her room, doing whatever it is she does up there for hours on end – a combination of schoolwork, Facebook and listening to music seems to be the sum of it.

'It's not a bug. It's something I found out at the party; something I need to tell you.'

Eric is switching from news to *Match of the Day* mode. He's taken up his position on the sofa: feet on the coffee table, glass of wine beside them, remote in hand. Saturday evening is when he is most relaxed at the moment. Eric works as a sub on a popular tabloid newspaper, and, since we came back from holiday, he's been working on the features desk. This means no early starts, no late nights and no working weekends but the best of it is Saturday evening. No work the following day, taking Harvey and Vincent to football and tennis and all the other Saturday running around done, and the prospect of a lie-in and an empty day ahead. Throw in the imminent prospect of footie on the TV and this is probably the best bit of his week.

'Are you going to watch the football with me?' he'd asked Harvey earlier. He likes having a son to share it with, and Vincent, though he likes to kick a ball around, is not interested in watching it.

'I'm tired today, Dad,' Harvey had replied, and I could see that Eric was a bit disappointed. Shouting at the TV, telling the linesman he made a wrong decision, is clearly more fun when you've got a twelve-year-old boy to back you up.

So I feel bad that I am about to disappoint him further and spoil his favourite part of the week.

Eric is relentlessly positive, but deep down I think he hates his job. He finds comfort in the odd moment – a joke shared with a colleague, the occasional pat on the back from the editor – but he's not doing what he wanted to do. His aspirations to be an investigative reporter fell by the wayside, given the need to support a wife and three children. 'Making sure chip wrapping is accurate' is how he jokingly describes his job, but it's not far from the truth. His news is largely whether the women in the Cabinet have put on weight or what they are wearing. A major headline could be the prime minister snapped going for a swim on a holiday – hold the front page! It's not exactly groundbreaking investigative journalism.

If I'd found a way to go back to work, after the children were born, he'd probably be doing something less well paid but more rewarding now. But he never complains, always tells me I'm doing a great job with the kids, and reassures me he's happy enough doing what he does.

So he doesn't deserve what's coming, and I wonder if I should wait till the morning.

But the boys will be around then, demanding and distracting. I need to tell him now.

'What's up? Is someone ill or something?'

'Yes, sort of.'

He puts the remote down and gives me his full attention. 'It's not Maggie, is it? Is there something serious?'

I can imagine what he's thinking when he asks this. He'll be feeling concerned, and worried for Ben, the man he's known since they were eleven and to whom he's been a loyal friend ever since. He'll be putting two and two together – the fact that Ben and Maggie were not at the party and my 'funny turn' – and making five. Or maybe four and a half, because he's on the right track. He's just got the wrong family member.

And he'll be thinking that, if Maggie is ill and it's serious, it's unfair because Ben has been on his own so long and only just recently, after meeting Maggie and having Iris, seemed to be really happy for the first time in his adult life.

And Eric hates unfairness. He doesn't have the 'life's unfair so we shrug and get on with it' gene. He wants to make it fair. That's why he wanted to be a campaigning reporter and put the world to rights. That's why he'll already be thinking about what can be done to make Maggie better, if she's ill, wondering if maybe his paper could highlight whatever failings in the NHS might contribute to her not making a full recovery.

'It's not Maggie.' I don't know what to do except come straight to the point. 'It's Iris. She's deaf.'

'Oh, no, that's terrible. But it's not the worst thing,' Eric says, his optimistic streak coming immediately to the fore. 'I mean, she could have hearing aids, or cochlear implants if it's really bad, or learn to sign.'

'You don't understand – ' I begin, but Eric is still in full flow.

'It can't be that bad because she seems, well, such a responsive baby; maybe it's only partial. It's not the end of the world, Bel, though it's rather touching that you feel so cut up for them.'

He puts out his arm to draw me to him and kisses me and I wish he weren't in this state of unknowingness. Or I wish that I were too, and this moment of kindness from the man I love could be as reassuring as he means it to be. But I have to break it – the moment.

'No, Eric, listen to me.'

'OK, sorry.'

'Iris wasn't deaf when you last saw her. She was fine. There was nothing wrong with her hearing.'

I pause because knowing what I know is one thing, saying it out loud quite another. I wonder now if Eric has an inkling. He's a phenomenally bright man. His mind works in leaps and bounds. I imagine it's computing now, making the connections, reaching the conclusion without my having to actually tell him, but it appears I am wrong.

'What happened?' he asks.

'It was having measles that caused it.'

There, I've said it, and I start to let it all out. 'She's completely deaf in both ears, no hearing at all, not any more. She was perfectly healthy before and now she can't hear a thing. And it's my fault, Eric. It's all my fault.'

Eric removes his hand from my shoulder, as I feared he would, and looks hard at me. Now I can almost hear the computing going on, although he says nothing. The silence is unbearable. Why can't he reassure me? Why can't he say, 'It's not all your fault. You mustn't blame yourself.'

'Say something, please.'

'I don't know what to say.' He picks up his glass and drains it, as if it were a beer not a large red wine.

Because Eric can't reassure me, I start trying to reassure myself. 'I should never have left Gabby alone with Maggie and Iris that day we went to the dune,' I begin. 'It was just that the boys wanted me to go and Maggie said she was happy – '

'Jesus Christ, Isobel!' Eric interrupts me. 'Is that where you think the fault lies? It wasn't the fact that we left her that day that led to this. It's because you didn't have the kids vaccinated. I told you it was ridiculous not to.'

I am taken aback. 'That's not fair!'

'Isn't it?'

'No! We discussed it at the time. You knew my concerns. It's not like I kept them from you. We went over it all.'

'But it was your decision,' Eric says.

'How can you say that?' I'm beginning to feel angry.

'Because it's true.'

'But we discussed it when Gabs was little. You knew I was worried about it. You knew I'd decided not to take her. You can't go along with decisions I make about the kids and then blame it on me when things go wrong.'

'I didn't "go along with it", Isobel.' Eric raises his voice, something he rarely does. 'Yes, we discussed it. I knew you were worried. I told you I thought you were wrong. I told you everything was being blown out of proportion and there was nothing to worry about.'

'But you said it was up to me in the end,' I shout back. 'You accepted it. That's the same thing.'

'The same thing as what?'

'As going along with it.'

'No. It's different.' Eric adopts a calm and reasonable tone, which makes me feel like hitting him. 'I brought back fistfuls of information from work assuring you that the MMR was perfectly safe, but you chose to ignore it and listen to the hippy mums you hung out with instead.'

'Oh, don't be ridiculous. They're not hippies. They were just parents too, and I hung out with them because I had small children and no one else to be with. You still have no idea what it was like for me, when they were little. You just went off to the office every day, as usual. My life changed completely, and while you were worrying about whether someone had put a comma in the right place I had to make difficult decisions about our children, and sometimes the only people I could go to for advice were other parents. And anyway, it wasn't just "the hippy mums I hung out with". You know how much coverage there was in the press at the time. Everyone was worried about it.'

'*I* wasn't.' Eric is so self-righteous when he wants to be. '*I* had my own opinion, which I told you, often enough. You refused to hear it. The only opinions of mine you want to hear are the ones you've already told me first.'

'Oh, for fuck's sake. What's that supposed to mean?'

'That half the time, especially where the kids are concerned, you only ever ask my opinion if you want yours validated.'

'I do not. That's so unfair.'

'You do, Isobel. You bloody well do. If I have a different view from yours, you never want to hear it. You always think you're right.'

I'm livid with Eric now but I've backed myself into a corner. If I go on insisting he's wrong and I'm not, I'm doing what he says I do.

'You know I've always had strong opinions,' I say, taking a different tack. 'It was one of the things you used to like about me.'

'You used to have strong opinions about things that mattered,' he replies.

'And our children don't?'

'Of course they do. You know that's not what I mean.'

'Then what do you mean, exactly?'

'I mean that I told you I thought the MMR thing was all a lot of fuss over nothing. I told you the scare would all blow over and I thought our kids should have it. But yes, you're the one who looks after them on a daily basis. So I let you make the decision not to vaccinate them. That doesn't mean I agreed with you.'

Eric glances briefly back at the TV. There's a report from Afghanistan. 'Can you imagine what a woman in Afghanistan would say?' he continues. 'A woman who probably has to walk across mountains for two days to get to a vaccination clinic, risk being raped by the Taliban on the way and then pay a fortune for the privilege when she gets there. Can you imagine what she would say if she heard that all we have to do here is walk to the end of the road at an appointed time and yet people choose not to?'

I sigh. 'We've already had this discussion.'

We've had it several times. When he rushed off to the local doctor in France to get the boys immunised immediately.

Again after we heard Iris was ill, and on various occasions since, when there's been stuff in the news about measles outbreaks.

'And that just proves my point,' he says.

'Is that all you've got to say? Your best friend's baby is deaf and, yes, we are partly responsible for that. Does that make you happy? Because it *proves your point*?'

'Of course it doesn't make me happy, Bel. Don't be so fucking ridiculous. Christ knows how Ben and Maggie must be feeling. I'm just saying I told you it was selfish not to have the kids vaccinated. It was bad enough seeing Gabs get so ill, and then hearing about Iris too, but now this!'

'*Selfish*?' I am furious again now. 'Selfish to try to protect my kids – no, *our* children? You think I was being selfish when I spent hours agonising over whether to have them protected against one form of illness but put them at risk of another? You think I was doing that for myself?'

'That's not what I meant!'

'Then what do you mean, Eric? What exactly do you mean?'

'I mean the decision wasn't just about our kids, was it? It was about the wider public good.'

'You are so fucking smug sometimes,' I spit. 'It's all very well worrying about the wider public good, but when it's your own children you think of them. At least, I do.'

'And look what happens when you do,' Eric says.

'And look what might have happened if I'd done exactly what you wanted,' I counter. 'It's all very well with hindsight to tell me I was totally wrong, but at the time I was really worried about the link between MMR and autism.'

'There is no link.'

'But at the time, Eric. At the fucking time, I thought there was. I thought there might be. Virtually the only other parent I knew before I had Gabs was Yasmin, and she had Conrad, and you know what? – Conrad scared me. I didn't know if I could have coped with a child like that. I didn't know if *we* could have coped with a child like that. I didn't want to do

38

anything that might put my lovely daughter at risk of turning out like that.'

'So instead,' Eric begins, and I think to myself that if he says 'you put someone else's child at risk' out loud, even if that's what he's thinking, I might just throw something at him.

But he stops mid-sentence and begins again. 'How long have you been there?'

And I realise Gabriella is standing in the doorway, hovering, and I too wonder how long she's been there, how much of what I said she has heard. The look on her face tells me it was all of it.

'Gabs,' I say. 'Come and sit down.'

'I don't want to sit down,' she begins and, while Eric appears lost for words, she lets out a torrent. 'See what you've done? It's all your fault! And it's my fault too, because you let me get ill and you let me play with Iris when you knew what might be wrong with me.'

'Gabs, I didn't – '

But she won't let me get a word in.

'You knew. You knew the risks. You must have done. You know this stuff. Everyone does, for fuck's sake.'

Normally I'd pull her up for using bad language, but it doesn't seem appropriate now. She continues, 'It's all out there. I've looked it up. You let me get ill. For some weird reason you thought you wouldn't protect your own daughter from a disease that everyone else in the world wants to be protected from. And...'

She pauses, almost deliberately, as if to emphasise what she is about to say next.

'And you let me play with Iris and now – now...'

She stops and waits for me to say something.

'Gabs, I didn't think – ' I begin.

'No!' she shouts at me. 'You didn't think, did you? You never do.'

Ben, Saturday evening

Sometimes Eric texts me before *Match of the Day*. It's our male way of keeping in touch. I look at the texts Maggie gets from her friends sometimes and wonder how they find the time. Busy women – the lead violinist in her orchestra, for example – will send texts as long as *War and Peace* – letters, in all but the means of delivery.

'We're just keeping in touch,' Maggie will say, if I comment on the plethora of beeps coming from her phone.

Sometimes members of her orchestra even seem to text during performances. 'There's a very slow section with no horns,' Maggie will say, if I question the acceptability of doing this.

I guess the Facebook messages, the text missives, the phone calls, all make her feel she's not missing out on anything while she's on maternity leave – which has now been extended owing to Iris's condition. She hasn't actually seen many of her colleagues since she stopped touring, but she knows exactly what goes on in all their lives, whereas I could go to the pub all evening with mates and come back knowing nothing about theirs.

'How's Moira?' Maggie will ask, if I've been for a drink with Matt Green, head of maths, one of the few teachers at school I count as an actual friend.

'I'm not sure. I didn't ask,' I'll tell her, and she'll roll her eyes, exasperated.

'What did you talk about, then?'

'We were too busy moving beer from the table to our lips to talk,' I'll reply, which is partly true.

I can drink with mates without going over the minutiae of their lives. We pass the time of day, but never seem to elicit any of the facts which women regard as salient. I don't feel the need. If I don't see Eric for months on end, but he sends me the occasional text asking, *Are you watching the match?* I feel as if we are in regular contact. I know he's watching the match. I know he's OK. He knows I am. We just cut out the chatty crap in the middle. *You watching the match?* means, 'Hi, Ben. It's Eric here. I'm just settling down after a long week at work to watch the football. The kids are all fine. Bel's good. How's everything with you. Fine too? That's great. I do think about you, even though I don't get in touch to let you know. I hope Liverpool win.'

We don't need all that extra information. It's implicit.

But today, I check my phone as I plonk myself down with a beer, half expecting there to be something more, something longer – a missed call, even. Because they must know by now – Eric and Isobel. They've been at a fucking party all day, while Maggie and I have been sitting at home, not feeling celebratory or up to seeing anyone because we've got a deaf daughter and the last time we saw them all she could hear perfectly.

I thought one of them would call, text, say or do something. But my phone is, as usual, devoid of social activity, unlike my partner's.

'I'm going to have a bath and go to bed now,' Maggie says, putting down the 'Family' section of the *Guardian*, which she's been holding but not reading. She reaches to pick up *How to Live with a Deaf Child* from the floor beside the sofa.

'Why don't you just get some sleep?' I say to her. I'm irritated that she keeps reading the bloody books, but I try to disguise it as concern. 'You look really tired.'

'I probably will,' she says, taking the book with her anyway. 'Will you turn everything off?'

'Yes,' I reply.

I always do. I tend to go to bed later than Maggie at the moment. Her nights are still broken by Iris waking, so the nightly routine of switching off lights and making sure the back door is bolted falls to me. I never forget, but Maggie always reminds me. Perhaps it's like the texting with her friends. She needs things to be said, even if I think they are understood.

But right now I am the one who needs things to be said. I need Isobel and Eric to say something. Their silence is laden with bad intent and, if they don't break it, I'm going to force them to.

I pick up the remote and switch the TV on. There's ten minutes of news left and the newsreader is informing me that a date-rape case involving a footballer has just been thrown out of court. The woman who had accused him had lied about the fact that she'd been stalking the footballer for months, mostly via Facebook and Twitter but also in person, hanging around in the clubs and bars he was known to frequent.

There's a brief studio interview afterwards but I'm not really listening. I keep checking my phone, angrily. Why aren't they fucking contacting me? Have they got nothing to say?

Then my attention swings back to the television. 'The number of reported measles cases in the area is now reaching dangerous levels, health officials are warning,' says the newsreader. 'And parents whose children have not been vaccinated are urged to do so as soon as possible.'

A reporter is now doing a piece to camera from a small village in Wales. He's standing outside a building which he says is the local primary school.

'The headmaster here has asked parents to provide evidence that their children have been immunised before admitting them to school this week in a move aimed at preventing the spread of the disease,' he says.

The film cuts to the headmaster. 'This is a small community. I know many of these children well. Some of them have been seriously ill. In some states in America children must be vaccinated against certain diseases before they enter school. I think it's sensible to insist on the same here, given the numbers of very young children we are now seeing falling seriously ill.'

I pick up my phone and begin tapping furiously into it.

Are you watching the news before the match? Have you seen the report on this measles outbreak in Wales? Did you enjoy the party today? Did anyone tell you that Iris is deaf? Oh, and btw it's your fault. How are you? Everyone well I hope? Do you think Man United will score?

I look at the message and my finger hovers over the Send key.

But I delete it.

If I don't hear from them, I've got a meeting with a solicitor in two days.

I still haven't mentioned this to Maggie and I'm not going to, not until afterwards, but I do feel guilty when I go up to bed, after the match, and she's still awake.

'I thought you'd be asleep by now,' I say, as I climb in beside her.

'I was worried about you,' she says. 'You seem a bit distracted. I know you would have liked to go to the party.'

'It's not that,' I tell her.

'Do you want to talk?' she asks.

'No,' I say, but I feel a huge rush of tenderness towards her for noticing and for asking.

'Do you want anything else?' she asks, and I realise that she is not wearing the T-shirt she usually wears to bed; and as I pull her towards me and feel her skin next to mine, although I am tired, although we are both tired, I want to forget everything, even if it's only temporarily. I want to hold on to those few moments when everything is right with the world.

Isobel, Sunday morning

When I wake up I can hear Vincent singing on his way to the bathroom and this morning I wish he wouldn't. I wish he'd tiptoe and close the door quietly behind him. His relentless singing usually makes me smile, but today it just reinforces the awful mess that's beginning to unfold.

I stayed awake until the early hours, the hours the Spanish call the *madrugada*, a word that captures the sort of menacing wretchedness you feel when you are unable to sleep and is so much better than our word, 'dawn'.

Hearing Vincent sing makes the nauseous feeling rise up inside me again. It's the way your body reacts to feeling bad about something. Guilt and fear both seem to affect the stomach directly. It had only stopped when I finally fell asleep.

Of course Vinnie doesn't know what's going through my mind. It's just another normal day, as far as he's concerned.

'And she's climbing a stairway to heaven!' His musical taste is wide-ranging but his lyrics are lacking in accuracy.

'Buying.' Harvey likes to get things right. 'It's *buying* a stairway to heaven.'

We've woken on more than one occasion to the sound of this particular argument.

'No, it's climbing!' Vinnie will insist, but he doesn't really care.

'Buying.'

'Climbing,'

'Buying.'

'Buying doesn't make sense. You can't buy a stairway that would reach all the way to heaven.'

'You can't climb one either, because it's a metaphor, nit-brain.'

Why do children have to argue all the time?

I remember saying this out loud once when the boys were working themselves up over nothing in the street and one of our neighbours was trying to ask me about planned changes to parking. It wasn't a question. I only said it to try to indicate that I couldn't really give her my full attention because there was a fracas over a toy car going on and if I didn't intervene soon it was going to develop into full-scale war.

But this woman said to me, 'Often it's because their emotional needs aren't being met.'

I was furious. They were arguing about a toy car, for heaven's sake. What right had she to say that?

'Boys, let's go inside,' I said.

'Don't let her get to you, Bel,' Eric said later, when I told him about it. 'Don't let the boys get to you, either. Let's have a drink.'

Eric was just back from work, still basking in the post-laboural glow of a day in the office, a day in which he achieved something more satisfying than trying to stop two small boys hitting each other.

He didn't get it.

What if she was right and the boys did fight so much because their emotional needs weren't being met. Whose fault was that?

Mine, was the obvious answer. I was the one at home with them, trying to do my best but somehow failing them; failing to make them get along, failing to get Harvey to eat vegetables, failing to help Gabriella with her maths homework... failing to do well at the only thing that I actually did now.

I wanted to be a good parent. That was what I set my mind to. I wanted the natural birth, the breastfeeding and the sugar-free, weapon-free upbringing. And I wanted to do it well, because that was all I was doing.

In the fug of this morning, Eric has forgotten my latest and most serious failing. He rolls over in bed, as he usually does, spooning me in his embrace, slipping his hand under the top I wear in bed and cupping my right breast. On working days this is simply a moment of comfort before the alarm forces him up, into the shower and on his way to London. At weekends it's often a precursor to sex. I feel him begin to harden against me.

Will it help, I wonder? Will the silent, frosty 'I need to get my head round it' treatment of the night before, after Gabby had gone to bed, give way to something more conciliatory and forgiving, supportive even?

'What time is it?' His eyes move swiftly from me to the radio alarm clock beside our bed, as if he can't bear to look at me, and I feel him go limp as he rolls away.

'What's up?' I ask.

He doesn't reply but sits up in bed, rubbing his eyes.

'Eric, we need to discuss this properly,' I say, raising myself up beside him. 'I don't know what to do. I feel I should do something but I don't know what.'

'Not now, Bel,' Eric says irritably. 'I've only just woken up.'

'Do you want a coffee?' I ask.

'No,' Eric says and he swings his legs over the side of the bed and reaches for his dressing gown. 'I think I'll go for a run.'

We can hear Vinnie now, still singing, accompanied by the rush of water as he goes to the toilet. It's all so urgent with him first thing. Wake, hit the floor, crash out of bedroom and into bathroom, pee and head downstairs, all the while singing away at the top of his voice, as if the whole house is one giant shower.

But this morning I am tired and frustrated, and Eric's coolness is forcing me to keep going over the sequence of events. What if I'd done this, or this, or not done this? It was a pointless conversation I'd been having with myself the past eighteen hours, because the damage is done. I need to talk about what to do now.

Maybe when he gets back from running Eric will be calmer and more clear-headed.

I wish, as I wish on an almost daily basis, that Mum were still alive. And Dad too – he would have had practical advice, but Mum would have helped just by being here. I wish she'd been around to meet Eric and I wish she'd been here when the children were born. It's different, mothering when your own mother is gone. It's more than a subtle difference. It's huge.

I see friends traipsing off to the park, toddlers and grand-parents in tow, sometimes looking a little stressed, as if however long their parents have been visiting is beginning to take its toll. And I think to myself, 'You don't realise how lucky you are. You have no idea how difficult it is being presented with this enormous challenge and having no one to refer to.'

Even Maggie, who was forty-five when Iris was born, still has her own mother, Ruth. I met her when we first went to visit the new baby, a sprightly eighty-something who had control of the kitchen, making coffee and preparing lunch so Maggie didn't have to do anything. But, more than that, she was just *there*, reassuring Maggie that she was doing everything right. Maybe that's why Maggie has always appeared so relaxed with the baby in a way that I never was with any of mine.

If Mum were here now, I know she'd give me some sort of reassurance that what I did was not such a terrible thing – the reassurance Eric can't give me.

If she'd been here when the children were born, maybe I would have felt less anxious about them.

'She's absolutely fine. You're doing a great job.' I can almost hear her saying it. But I never did. She died long before she had the chance to meet her grandchildren.

47

Eric is in the bathroom now and I go downstairs to make coffee. Gabriella is already in the kitchen. It's early for her to be up on Sunday. Harvey must still be in bed.

'Hello.' I try to sound cheerful. 'You're up early.'

'I couldn't sleep,' she says, sitting at the table, a cup of coffee already on the go.

'You should have stayed in bed,' I say. 'Had a bit of a lie-in.'

'It didn't feel right just to be lying around doing nothing,' she says, accusatory.

'Oh,' is the best I can think of.

'Yes, "oh",' she mimics.

'Do you have anything planned today?'

'I might go and see Sam later.'

'Right.'

I put the kettle on and try to think. Gabriella has been spending a lot of time with Sam, since they've been going out together. It's only been a few months but they seem close. He comes to our house, they go into town together and at weekends she often spends evenings there. Sam's the youngest in his family so regularly has the house to himself. Cue gatherings. Not parties exactly – they are a surprisingly sensible group of young people, Gabriella and her friends. So I try not to worry too much about what they get up to. And I'm not sure that she and Sam are getting up to anything much yet.

'I don't want to be a grandmother,' I said to her, in the early days.

'Mum. I'm not like that,' she said, sternly. 'And neither is Sam.'

I left it at that. I didn't say, 'But all boys are like that,' which was what I thought. But I felt I would know, somehow, if something changed, if their relationship moved up a gear.

Turns out I was worrying about the wrong thing. *What if she gets pregnant?* should have been *What if she gets measles?*

I never thought about that until the horse had bolted.

'Are you going into town with him?' I ask her now.

'Maybe. I don't know. We haven't really got any plans. I just wanted to talk to him.'

'Right,' I say as I busy myself with coffee and a cafetiere. 'Are you going to mention to Sam about Iris being deaf.'

'Yes. Of course.' Her tone is challenging.

'Listen, Gabs – ' I begin.

'What?'

'Maybe it's not a good idea to tell Sam, not just yet. Maybe we should talk about it first, you and I?'

'What is there to talk about?' she replies, standing up, ready to leave the room if I try to go down this route.

'I just don't want you to think that any of this is your fault,' I say.

'No. It's yours.' I've never heard her sound so forthright and blunt. Gabs has always been polite and well-mannered, even to us. 'But I'm still involved, aren't I?' she continues. 'And Sam is too.'

That's what I'm worried about – what she might say to Sam, how he might feel. He had measles first, so the chain of events involves him too. I don't know his parents. If I did, I might call them, before she went over there.

'I just think maybe you need a bit more time to think about it all,' I say. 'I think we all do. It was a shock, hearing about Iris. For you and for me and Dad too. A terrible shock. I think we need a bit of time to let it all sink in.'

It was a shock when I found out I was pregnant with Gabriella too. It happened too quickly, too soon, and it took me by surprise, even though I'd come off the Pill, thinking that at some point in the not too distant future we might start trying.

Of course Eric was delighted, when I told him after a day at work when I'd been feeling really sick and had bought myself a test kit on the way home.

'That's wonderful,' he said, eyes all shiny with happiness. 'We're going to have a baby!'

49

It wasn't at all what I'd imagined that moment would be like, though. And I had imagined it, often. In my mental scenario, Eric's words were the same. 'We're going to have a baby,' he would say, and come over and hold me, and we'd stand there for a bit, enshrined in our happy moment. Schmaltz, I know, but it would have been better that way than the way it actually turned out. Because the words were right, but the way I reacted felt all wrong.

Eric didn't understand this at all. How could he? I didn't understand myself really.

I think it was partly the shock. But it was also the huge change that was about to come over me. I didn't feel ready for it. I didn't know anything about being a mother, and I didn't have a mother to ask.

'You must be so pleased,' people kept saying to me, kindly, in their congratulations, and I'd smile back and say that I was and try to look pleased.

But I felt like crying, most of the time.

Dad was delighted when I told him.

'If it's a girl, we're thinking of calling her Gabriella, after Mum.' I could see his eyes growing moist, although he was from the generation who never cry.

I wished I could be happier myself. But I was filled with anxiety throughout the pregnancy, unable to enjoy it because I was too worried about all the unknowns that came with it.

It's a total wonder to me how Gabby entered the world so calm and smiley. Given the way I was when I was pregnant with her, I'd have expected her to be a total infant nervous wreck, not quite so serene and self-contained.

But she's agitated now.

'So what are you going to do?' she says, as I set my coffee down on the table and she prepares to leave the room.

'I don't know, Gabs. I need to talk to Dad about it.'

On cue Eric comes down the stairs and goes straight out, without coming into the kitchen first. He slams the door behind him as he sets off on his run.

'He's angry with me at the moment.' I say to Gabby.

I don't know if this is a wise admission.

'He's not the only one,' she snaps.

'I know, and I'm sorry you feel that way, and I'm sorry you feel caught up in it. But none of this is your fault, Gabs.'

'I was the one who was ill. I was the one who made Iris ill. It might not be my fault I was ill but I still passed it on.'

She turns and marches out of the room and up the stairs, still uncharacteristically stroppy.

'What's that coming up the stairs, is it a monster?' I hear Vincent singing from the landing.

'Out the way,' Gabriella says.

'No, it's a Gabster,' Vincent sings, and he carries on singing his own mutated version of the song by The Automatic as he comes down the stairs.

'Vinnie. That's enough,' I say as he comes into the kitchen.

'Why?' he asks, blissfully unaware but sensitive to something being wrong. 'Is everyone a bit green today?'

Ben, Monday morning

'Why didn't you tell me before?'

Maggie is not angry. She's miffed. This is her way. She never really gets angry, just upset and a bit hurt which, ironically, makes me angry. 'Same thing,' I've taunted her, on occasion, but she always maintains it's not.

It frustrates me because sometimes I need to have a full-blown, let-it-all-out angry session, and Maggie never responds in a way that makes that possible. Rather she retreats into her own thoughts. 'I didn't want to upset you,' I say, which is partly the truth. The other part is that I didn't want her to try to talk me out of it, which I know she is going to do now.

There's been a whole thirty-six hours in which I could have told her about my encounter with Hedda, in which I could have told her I have a meeting after school today, in which I could have told her I am thinking about suing Isobel and Eric.

I have thought of pretty much little else since I came back from my walk on Saturday afternoon. But I haven't shared my thoughts with my partner. So she could be angry if she wanted to. But she's gone for quietly miffed, which is having the effect of making me cross. And, if I let it show, she'll have the moral high ground.

'I wasn't going to say anything until I'd had the meeting.' I try to make myself sound considerate. 'I didn't want you to have to worry about it unless anything came of it.'

'You should have told me. I don't like the idea of it. It seems all...'

'What?'

'I don't know. Unhelpful? Wrong? I don't get it. I spent the whole day yesterday trying to get my head round the various options for Iris, and unbeknown to me you spent your whole day thinking about how to get back at Isobel.' Maggie says this with defiance, daring me to contradict her view of my motives.

'That's not fair.' I rise to the challenge but Maggie turns away, busies herself with the banana which will form the basis of our daughter's breakfast, refuses to give me the satisfaction or something.

She had a bad night. Iris was fretful. She had to get up and go to her several times, and ended up sleeping in the spare bed in the room with her cot. She does this so that I can sleep through the night. 'You have to work all day,' she always says. 'It's more important that you sleep. And anyway, in a funny way, I rather like it when she wakes.'

Maggie misses being called by Iris during the night. Now that Iris is a bit bigger and more mobile Maggie doesn't get to hold her as much as when she was tiny, and she relishes the chance to sit with her in the dark, soothing her with her touch and presence. I thought she was joking the first time she said it, but, no, she actually misses being woken in the night.

But she looks tired this morning. Her eyes are smaller and her skin is sallow. And I'm still angry, as I have been for two weeks now, in no mood to be placated by anyone, not even by my partner.

'But what on earth do you hope to gain?' Maggie asks.

I've told her I have a meeting with a solicitor, which I arranged when I went out on Saturday, and that I will be later home from school than usual. And I told her why.

'I'm doing it for Iris's sake and yours,' I say.

'How?' Maggie is still in her dressing gown, and she's tugging at the ends of the cords in frustration.

'B-because we might need things for Iris that we can't afford, or special schooling or something.' I stumble over the B;

the stammer I have successfully managed to rid myself of still creeps back at times when I feel under pressure.

Sometimes it alerts me to the fact that I am under pressure before I've even realised it myself.

'We don't know that yet.' Maggie is beginning to look tearful but this just makes me feel more angry, not with her but with Isobel, always with fucking Isobel. 'And you're not even stopping to think about Iris, to find out exactly how it's going to affect her – us. We need to find that out. We have to discover what her future is going to be like – what we need. I keep making phone calls, trying to make appointments, trying to find out more. And rather than helping me you are just pursuing your own separate... vendetta.'

'That's not true,' I say, because that's how you react, especially to someone telling you a home truth that is not particularly palatable. 'Aren't you the least bit angry?'

'Of course I am.' Maggie doesn't raise her voice but her tone is vehement at least. 'Do you really think I don't "mind" every bit as much as you do? But a legal battle sounds so draining – and what about the cost?'

'It's a "no win, no fee" thing,' I trump her.

'Even so.'

'Even so what?' I sound childish, even to myself.

'It's not going to be a quick and easy process, is it?' Maggie points out. 'I don't want you, or us, to have to waste our energy pursuing something which may get us nowhere, when we need it to deal with Iris.'

'It could help us with Iris,' I say.

'Will it?' Maggie asks. 'Do you really think you have a chance of winning this case? Or are you just trying to put the frighteners on Isobel and Eric?'

I say nothing. I'm not sure, not at this point. And Maggie is right: my primary motive is not to get whatever little bit of money we might be able to screw out of them. It is to get back at them.

'There are other ways,' Maggie says, looking at me now.

'What do you mean?'

Iris starts to cry; the deep sleep she'd finally fallen into in the early hours, when Maggie was too tired to get back to sleep, has finally broken. In the past Maggie would have been able to say, 'Now you've woken Iris,' but no longer.

Our raised voices don't disturb our daughter any more.

We both know this as we stand, staring at each other across the few feet of kitchen space which suddenly feels like a yawning chasm.

'I'll see you later, then.' Maggie pulls her dressing gown cord tight around her again and goes upstairs to get Iris.

'I'm doing this for Iris,' I say to myself, pushing the standoff with my wife to the back of my mind as Hedda ushers me into her *über*-office.

I'd already guessed what it would look like and I was right: lime-green walls, big oak desk, grey leather chairs. The floor is some sort of black lino, which throws me slightly.

I'd noticed also, while I was sitting outside in the café area of the office, that all the staff wore suits of the same grey cloth.

I'm not sure if blending in with the décor is a good advertisement for a lawyer. It makes them look a bit too style-conscious. Maybe they think they look efficient.

Hedda certainly seems efficient.

'So, you wish to pursue a claim for damages against a third party for injury caused to your baby daughter by their failure in a duty of care towards her?' She phrases this like a question, but I feel she is laying out exactly how it could work legally, if we go ahead.

'Yes.' I nod.

'And, just to make sure I have understood what you told me correctly, let me again go through the circumstances which led to the damage to your daughter.'

'Iris,' I say. Calling her my daughter makes her sound like a legal party, not my beautiful, sunny baby girl.

'Iris. What a lovely name.' She looks up and smiles at me. 'And your wife's name?'

'Maggie. Not a name many people would call their child these days.'

Hedda looks confused. 'Why not?'

'Thatcher wasn't exactly popular,' I say.

But she has no time for quips. 'You went with a group of friends on holiday to France at the start of August this year?'

I nod.

'Your daughter, Iris, was then just nine months old. And she was a healthy baby?'

'Yes,' I say. 'Apart from the odd cold, she'd never been ill and she was very easy.'

'But during the course of your holiday she was exposed to the measles virus?'

'Yes. Gabriella got ill towards the end of the fortnight. She's the daughter of one of our friends, Isobel B-Blake.'

I pause, partly because I have trouble getting her surname out – Bs have always been a problem – but also because it feels strange referring to Isobel by her full name – referring to her as Isobel, even. I've always called her Bel, except when I was angry with her.

'And you believe your daughter picked up the virus herself as a result of direct contact with Gabriella Blake?'

'Jordan,' I correct her. 'Isobel is married to Eric Jordan but she never changed her surname. The children have his name.'

She notes this down.

'The place we were staying was isolated,' I tell Hedda. 'And comfortable. The others went into town quite regularly but Maggie, my partner – we're not married – she always stayed at the house with Iris.'

'For the entire duration of the holiday?'

'Well, she went for walks down by the lake and into the woods but, as I said, the house was very comfortable. It had a pool and places to walk nearby and our hosts looked after us very well. Maggie was... well, she was very tired when we arrived and Iris was in a routine she didn't want to get her out of. She was happy just to stay put and relax.'

'Thank you.' She scribbles away for a while and I fall silent.

'So what exactly is the position, legally?' I ask when she's finished. 'Can we do anything?'

'Yes. I think so.' Hedda has that Scandinavian delivery that gives nothing away. 'We know that Iris's deafness was caused by having measles. As long as we can prove that the measles was caused as a direct result of contact with Gabriella Jordan, and that Ms Blake knew that she was contagious at the time but failed to warn you, then there is a case to be answered.'

I nod. 'And you think we can win?'

'If I didn't, I wouldn't be taking you on.'

'But, if we don't, you'll have taken me on for nothing?'

Part of me is uneasy with the 'no win, no fee' element of the deal. It doesn't seem right for Hedda to put in the hours if she isn't going to get anything out of it, although we don't have the means to pay a solicitor, so this is the only way we can proceed.

'There are no precedents, but I think we have a case,' Hedda says, and unless I'm mistaken the even level of her voice has upped a gear to 'slightly excited'. I look around the office, taking it all in: the lime-green, the grey, the young Nordic solicitor. I suppose that, for her, working in a colour-co-ordinated office is not enough. She also wants to make her mark, and here is a case which might help her do that.

'There might be some publicity, Mr Deakin,' she says, confirming my thoughts. 'Would you and your partner be happy with that?'

I nod, because nodding seems less untruthful than saying yes. Maggie isn't happy about my being here in the first place. But maybe if I talk it all through with her she'll come round.

'So, tell me how you first met Mr and Mrs Jordan.' Hedda flips the page of her notebook and sits poised again. 'I mean Ms Blake and Mr Jordan.'

Isobel, Monday evening

'Hey, Gabs. You look like Johnny Depp!' Vincent scuttles out of the living room and bounds upstairs, pausing momentarily to comment on his big sister's appearance.

I can see what he means – it's the eyeliner – but I wouldn't dare say so myself. It must be hard, trying to be a young woman when you have a brother six years younger. I was spared the indignity of siblings pointing out I'd overdone the blue eyeshadow when I was that age.

She gives him a look and hovers in the hallway.

She's ready to go to orchestra. She plays the French horn in the youth philharmonia. She has a musical gene that I don't; Eric's mother used to sing and play the piano so I imagine it comes from his side. He still plays guitar a bit, the way men do.

A few weeks ago, I came in and found them all jamming together. Harvey was on the piano, Eric strumming, Vinnie singing and Gabs playing the odd riff on her French horn. 'I feel like an outsider in my own family!' I joked, but kind-hearted Vincent clearly felt I needed to be included.

'Mum, you could play...' He paused, stumped by what I might be able to contribute to this musical ensemble. Then he had a brainwave. 'The shaky egg!' Everyone laughed, and a few days later a track came up on the CD player in the car, on which a shaky egg was being played. 'Mum! You can play along,' Vinnie urged me. So, as Eric drove, I began shaking my imaginary shaky egg in time to the music, or so I thought.

'You're not even shaking it in time,' Gabriella said.

'No, you're not,' Harvey agreed, laughing. 'You're supposed to shake it on the beat.'

I shrugged; clearly my musical ability was so poor that I could not even keep time with an imaginary shaky egg.

'You should have lessons,' Harvey said, and Gabs laughed.

It was funny then, but now it seems all wrong again. Why do I, a woman with very little musicality, have three such musical children? Why does Maggie, a supremely gifted professional trumpet player, have one who can't hear at all?

Today has been fraught and I was glad of it. I helped out in Vinnie's classroom this morning. 'Are you coming to help with the slow readers?' he asked me first thing, pleased that I'd be at school and never the least bit hesitant to label himself a slow reader. If anything, he's proud of it. 'I'm a slow reader,' he said, smiling happily, to the supply teacher, when she asked why some of the class had a different reading book.

I thought he was dyslexic when he started school and couldn't read, but apparently not. He takes everything in and he writes well; he just seems to find reading difficult, partly because he gets hung up on the way the words look. 'Hippopotamus is just amazing,' he will say, screwing his eyes up 'so that the Ps pop!'. He gets so drawn into the pleasing aspects of the way the letters look that he forgets to plough on with the sense.

Sometimes Vinnie leaves notes on my pillow. When he was younger they were mostly grateful jottings. *I love you*; *That was nice cake, Mum*; *Today was a pink-ish day*.

They started when Ben sent him a pack of Post-its for a present.

We'd been to lunch with them a few days earlier. This was before Iris was born but after Ben had met Maggie. He wanted us to meet her too.

Somehow Ben got on to the subject of things which had been invented by accident. Crisps – that was what started it. They gave the kids some before lunch.

'Did you know crisps were invented by accident?' Ben asked. 'A chef in America got so cross when someone complained that his chips weren't cooked enough, he got more potatoes, chopped them up really thin and deep-fried them to death. Then gave them to the customer.'

'What did he say?' Vinnie loves Ben's stories.

'He loved them, just like you do!'

How they moved to Post-it notes, I don't remember, but Vinnie was taken with the tale of the scientist trying to invent really strong glue and inventing really useless glue instead.

'It was only useless to hold something that really needed holding together, though,' Ben explained. 'Then he realised that, if you wanted to be able to stick something just a bit and then unstick it again quite easily, it was actually very useful glue. Very useful indeed, in fact, for sticking little bits of paper on to things and being able to unstick them again later!'

The pack of yellow oblong Post-its arrived a few days later and Vinnie began writing me notes.

Lately they've become more critical. Last week I found one, stuck to the switch of my bedside lamp. *My packed lunch was not very nice today. Did you forget I like orange cheese best?*

This afternoon he stuck one to my teacup. *Why is everyone being grumpy today? You are too, Mum. Be nicer!*

I smiled at the last line, but felt sad that he'd picked up on the atmosphere in the house. Gabs was still quietly fuming.

'Did you do anything today?' she said, pointedly, when she came back from school.

'I've been helping in Vinnie's class.'

'That's not what I mean,' she retorted.

I knew that, but I changed the subject while she made herself toast. 'How was school today?'

'Fine.' She was non-committal as she spread Marmite on two slices of granary before picking up her plate. 'I'm going to my room.' Now she is down again and about to go out.

'Are you off to orchestra?' I ask. 'Have you got enough money for the bus? I'll pick you up after.'

'Yes,' she says, still hovering and doing the thing she does when there is something she wants to say – saying something completely unrelated first. 'Mr Coles has grown a moustache,' she says.

'Ughhh,' I replied.

'He looks like a Seventies porn star. Alfie told him.'

I wonder how Alfie knows what a Seventies porn star looks like. 'What did he say?'

Mr Coles is the school music teacher. He also conducts the city orchestra. He's one of those teachers they regard as less of a teacher, more of a friend, and the sorts of conversations they have with him seem to stray into dangerous territory.

'He said – ' Gabby swishes her hair in imitation of the teacher's longish locks ' – Alfie, if I'd ever seen a Seventies porn film I am sure the star would look like me!'

I laugh, even though I don't really feel like laughing. I'm just glad that Gabs is talking to me and being friendly again.

But of course it's leading up to something. I just fail to spot the signs, as I usually do, if she needs money or wants to do something she knows I won't be entirely happy about. 'You look nice today. Can I go to an all-night party, Mum?' 'I'm changing my sheets. Shall I do the boys' beds too? Could I have £20 for new shoes?'

But today, just now, I regard what she's saying as a peace offering to me.

It isn't. It's simply stalling.

'I'd like to go and see Ben and Maggie,' she says, her tone now confrontational and no longer friendly.

'I don't know, Gabs.'

I've been thinking of nothing else, but I haven't got any closer to working out what to do. Should I call Ben? Email him? Try to arrange to go and see them myself?

Maybe Gabriella thinks she can breeze in, all full of fifteen-year-old charm, and everything will be OK but it won't be. I know Ben too well. I can imagine how he feels towards me, and I don't imagine it's warm.

'Why not?' Gabriella asks.

'You know why not.'

'So are we just not going to speak to them any more? We need to say something, Mum. You have to do something. You can't just not do anything.'

I know. I just don't know what to do.

'You're going to be late for orchestra,' I say.

I've said the wrong thing. Gabby is fuming again, picking up her instrument case and crashing it into just about everything she can on her way to the front door. She slams it so hard that a photograph hanging on the wall in the hall drops to the ground and the glass breaks.

'What happened?' Harvey is standing at the top of the stairs, lured from his room by the crashing and the smash of the glass. 'Mum, are you OK?' he asks, touchingly.

'Yes, the photo just fell off the wall when Gabs closed the door.'

'Stroppy cow.' Harvey grins and I smile despite myself, glad of his temporary allegiance. 'I said hello to her at lunch today, 'cos she was sitting by herself looking all moody, and she told me to eff off.'

'Did you have an argument?' I ask.

Harvey and Gabriella usually get on well enough, though, being the middle child, Harvey chops and changes his allegiances. Sometimes he and Gabs seem closer on account of being at the same school together; at other times he and Vincent will be boys together. Often he seems closer to Eric than to either of his siblings or to me.

'Shall I help you, Mum?' he offers.

'No, stay there,' I say to him as he comes halfway down the stairs. 'You've got bare feet. I need to get rid of the glass. I don't want you to get hurt.'

'Well, you've got bare hands,' he points out as I pick up a piece of shattered frame. '*You* might get hurt.'

'I'll be careful,' I say, and think that any hurt the broken glass may do will only be skin-deep.

Ben, Monday evening

I told Hedda that I met Isobel on my first day at university.

I didn't tell her that I also fell hopelessly in love with her and carried on feeling that way for years, even though it was never fully reciprocated. I haven't even told Maggie, although I think she suspects. It might be female intuition or maybe just the fact that Isobel has never been wholly welcoming towards her. They've always seemed wary of each other. I think everyone noticed it on holiday, even before Gabs got ill.

When I arrived at university, Isobel was outside on the terrace of the building that would be our home for the first year, pulling a large rucksack and several holdalls from the back of a car – a new car, I noted. I arrived with less stuff than Isobel but with sackloads of chippiness. I was convinced I would be the only person there who'd been to a comprehensive school, the only person whose parents couldn't drive me because they didn't have a car, the only person who wanted a revolution.

'How exactly do you plan to bring about a social revolution by playing Hamlet?' Isobel asked me, some time later, after I'd got to know her. 'Or getting a part in *Crossroads*?' She was studying politics and she'd spent a year in India, working in an orphanage, both things she thought would better equip her to change the world.

If we hadn't been living in the same block of university accommodation, I might never have spoken to Bel. The chippy me took against her, as she stood on the pavement surrounded by stuff and talking to the tall, slim, grey-haired, striking-looking man who I assumed and later confirmed was her father.

She was striking too. She had her father's physique and long, dark brown hair with a slightly reddish tinge. Her clothes all looked long, too: long skirt, long top thing and long necklace. The only items of clothing that skimped on material were her shoes, which were flip-flops.

'I'm really going to miss you,' I overheard her say as I looked for the entrance to G-block, my home for the next year. It sounded like a prison and it looked a bit like one, too. The building was constructed of breeze-blocks and no one had thought to plaster or paint them on the inside. The rooms were like cells, each with a bed and a desk and a washbasin. The only thing missing was bars.

'Will you be OK without me?' I heard her say to her father.

She was well-spoken and she irritated me. Rich daddy's girl, I thought, disliking her for having the arrogance to think her father might not manage without her.

'I'll miss you, Bel,' he said, putting his arms around her and just standing there, holding her, in a way neither my mother nor father would ever hold me or had ever held me. 'But I'll manage. I managed when you were in India. It's no different.'

So she's a hippy as well, I snorted to myself, and made my way up the breeze-block stairs to find my room.

I was doing my party trick that evening when she appeared, hovering nervously at the door of my room. I'd left it open in a friendly and inviting way and a couple of other blokes from down the hallway had taken up the invitation and were now seated on the bed.

'Do you play the guitar?' one had asked, nodding towards my acoustic propped up against the wall.

'A bit.' I hoped to sound as if I was being modest, whereas in fact I was being truthful. I did only play a bit. But I had one or two tricks, which usually impressed.

64

'What can you play?' the other bloke asked.

'I'll show you.'

I picked the guitar up and tried to manoeuvre myself into position, which was harder in my cell than it had been in my bedroom at home. There, I had a kind of big squishy old armchair that sagged everywhere to accommodate the guitar. In the room, I had to half lie on the bed. Of course I could have sat on it, if I'd been going to play the guitar normally, but I was out to impress.

I put the guitar behind my head and began playing 'House of the Rising Sun', contorting my arms to make the chords and strumming with difficulty. It was something I'd taught myself one afternoon when I was bored. I'd mastered the song with the instrument in regular position then decided to try it another way. It impressed the friends I'd done my A-levels with and later, when I was trying to make it as an actor, naively I thought it might come in useful. They always asked at auditions if there was anything else you could do: sword-fighting, scuba-diving, that sort of thing – something that might give you the edge in a Bond movie. I thought maybe being able to play the guitar behind my head would be useful. Looking back on it, I must have looked like a pretentious twat, although if anyone had said as much I'd have told them I was being ironic.

Isobel looked confused at first when she looked into the room, as if she couldn't work out who was playing. Then she saw me and smiled this huge, beautiful, friendly smile, and I more or less immediately dropped all my earlier preconceptions and asked if she was going to come in.

It's odd now because, even though she has three children, I never think of Isobel as motherly. But I did then. Not like my mother, or any of my friends' mothers – more like some sort of fantasy mother, the kind I would have liked to have, waiting at home when I came back from college, to be introduced to my friends.

Isobel instinctively took people under her wing. By the end of that first evening she must have had at least seven people back in her room, waiting to be fed. She thought we should eat before going to the freshers' disco.

Somehow, in between saying goodbye to her father and appearing at the door of my room, she'd unpacked all those bags. Her room didn't look like a cell. It was actually inviting. She had posters on the wall, cushions on the bed, a beanbag on the floor, and the black surface of the desk was lined with books. Next to it was a smaller table that she must have brought from home, covered with some sort of Indian throw and stacked with plates and cutlery.

I only had one of everything. Isobel had at least ten. She must have been planning to cook for friends, even before she arrived. And she did, that evening and on numerous subsequent evenings. Soup and pasta mostly; the odd curry and quiche too. She made it all seem so effortless, looking after everyone.

So if you'd asked me back then who, of everyone I knew, would be the most natural mother, I'd have said Bel without hesitation. But when she had Gabby she surprised us all. She seemed on edge, unsure what to do, harassed by having to deal with just one other person. I didn't get it.

Maybe Isobel didn't know what to do because her own mother died so young.

'Is that your dad?' I asked her, pointing at a photo in a frame on the desk. 'I saw him dropping you off.'

'Did you?' She looked really surprised that I'd seen her, as if she'd have expected me to introduce myself there and then. 'Yes, that's my dad.'

And then, either because she wondered if I'd overheard her talking to him or just to spare me and the rest of the crowd sitting around on her floor forking pasta off china plates from Habitat the embarrassment of asking something awkward, she told us.

'My mum died a few years ago and I'm an only child. So it's just been me and him at home for the last few years.'

Beautiful, capable and tragic, I remember thinking.

I wouldn't admit it to anyone then, but I was scared of going to university... terrified really. I didn't think I'd fit in, didn't think I'd be as clever as everyone else there, didn't know if I could act, even though I was studying drama, wondered if I'd make any friends, thought I'd miss home.

I was a giant bundle of anxiety, but meeting Isobel made me feel calmer, safer and less anxious, for a short time anyway. Then I began to fall in love with her, began to believe that she really could change the world if she wanted to, and mine too.

Well, she's changed it now, and I'm not prepared just to sit around doing nothing.

'We lived in the same hall,' I told Hedda. 'We met on the first day and we've been friends ever since. She met her husband through me. He was my best friend from school.'

I made it all sound so grown-up, so comfortable, so civilised and easy.

But it wasn't, not for me, and I want to make it as uncomfortable as possible for Isobel now. Why should I be the one who always has to suffer?

Isobel, Monday evening

'Where is everyone?' Eric asks, when he comes in from work and finds me sitting at the kitchen table, inert, thinking, looking at the photograph in its glassless frame.

It's a picture of Gabby in her first Christmas play. She was a snowflake because school plays never touch on religion these days. When I was at school we did the classic traditional Nativity story every year, so that by the time we reached secondary school at least a quarter of the girls had had a chance to play Mary. But our children are only dimly aware what the Nativity is.

This particular year, when she was chosen to be 'chief snowflake', I don't think Gabriella was aware what snow was either. She used to think those polystyrene packaging chips were snow. It didn't snow down south until she was at least twelve. But all the time she had spent watching *Pingu* had given her a feeling for it, and I had been so proud when I pushed the shutter on my camera as she stood up, all dressed in white, and said, 'I am going to keep coming every day until New Year.'

I was as proud of her then as I am now, when I go to watch her play the French horn in her school's Christmas concerts.

'The boys are watching TV,' I say to Eric, getting up, trying to look busier. 'And Gabs is at orchestra. I have to go and pick her up in a bit. Dinner's in the oven. We'll have it when we get back.'

'How is she?' Eric asks. I sense the subtext.

'Fine,' I reply, ignoring it.

'I'll go and pick her up if you like,' Eric offers.

'No, it's OK. You've only just got in.'

'I don't mind, really. It will give me a chance to talk to her.'

'I wish you'd talk to me,' I say.

Eric avoided me most of yesterday. After his run he took Vincent to the park to play football. They stayed out for ages and came back at lunchtime, at the same time as Harvey, who'd been out with friends and returned with a battered abandoned supermarket trolley.

'Harvey, what are you doing with that?' I'd asked.

'I'm going to make it into a chair. Dad, will you help me?' he'd replied.

And so I lost any chance to speak to Eric all afternoon to a spate of ingenious product design, which required his assistance.

The end result was impressive. Between them they'd managed to cut off the front so it resembled an Eames-style wire chair, with wheels. Harvey had slid it to and fro across the kitchen as I prepared dinner, outlining his ambition to become an industrial designer. He is gifted at art and design technology and he might have been on to something with the chair, but at the time I was resentful that his master plan had occupied Eric for what little time I might have been able to monopolise him – although I knew it was good for Harvey to do stuff with his father. Somehow Vincent and Gabriella always seem to demand more of my attention and Harvey just gets on with things. So it makes me feel a little better when he manages to claim more of Eric's time than the others.

But, however much fun they had had together during the afternoon, Eric was uncommunicative towards me over dinner last night, and every time I tried to broach the subject that was always on my mind he kept repeating, 'I need time to think.'

'I don't know what you want me to say, Isobel,' he says now.

'Anything,' I say. 'Anything is better than this silent with-drawal.'

Eric shrugs.

'Eric, can't you see that I feel terrible? It's all I can think about, Iris being deaf. I wish I could change things. But I can't. I need you to talk to me,' I plead.

'I'm sorry, Bel,' Eric says. 'I don't know what to say. I know you feel bad, but what can I do about it? I just wish you'd thought it all through in the first place, because then things would be different.'

'It doesn't help,' I say, frustrated that all he is willing to do is keep going over the past. 'In hindsight I wish I'd done things differently, of course I do, but at the time – '

'I just wish you'd listened to me. If you had, none of this would have happened.'

'Oh, for Christ's sake, Eric, this isn't getting us anywhere. Yes, you were right. I was wrong. But I took a decision I thought was right at the time. If you were so convinced I was wrong, you should have taken the kids to be vaccinated yourself.'

'Yes? And how would you have felt if I had?' Eric laughs in response.

'I don't know,' I snap.

'You'd have been furious with me. You used to get angry if I so much as gave the children a chocolate biscuit. You'd behave as if I was poisoning them.'

'No, I didn't,' I protested, but he was right. I did regard their sugar-free early years as one of my greatest parental achievements. Sugar-free, nut-free biscuits were my peculiar speciality; I always had a tin full of them. There was no need for Eric to offer them his chocolate digestives, yet he did.

'Isobel. You knew exactly how I felt about the MMR. I tried to bring you round. I tried to make you see sense.'

'As I said, if you really felt so strongly about it, if you really thought there was a serious risk to any of the children from not being immunised, then you should have done something about it.' I was damned if I was going to be held solely to blame. Eric knew I didn't want to have the kids vaccinated and he'd accepted that, at the time. He has to share some of the responsibility, surely?

'What could I have done? Be like that bloke who fell out with his wife? The man who took his ex to court to force her to have their kids vaccinated?'

'No, of course not,' I say. When I'd heard about it in the news I was chilled by the lengths that man had gone to, to make his point.

'My loyalty was to you,' Eric says. 'I knew you were shouldering the bulk of the childcare.'

'Bulk?' I'm laughing now. I'd done pretty much all of it, when they were young. It was my choice, but I still wanted Eric to acknowledge the amount of work I'd put in.

'Yes, I knew you were shouldering the bulk of the childcare, and so I thought that, out of respect for the job you were doing, I should allow you to make decisions.'

'Jesus Christ, you can be infuriatingly smug, Eric,' I retort.

'Well, there's no point trying to talk, then, is there?' Eric replies, looking at the clock. 'I'll go and get Gabs.'

He picks up the car keys, leaving me to go over and over things in my mind. It gets me nowhere. I wonder if there is anything I can do to help Ben and Maggie and Iris. I wonder if they will ever forgive me. I wonder if Eric will, or Gabriella.

I wonder how the unfolding events will affect us all: Eric, Gabriella, Ben, Maggie and the rest of our friends.

And I wonder how it will affect me and Ben.

It was towards the end of the spring term. We'd been to a gig in the Student Union. I can't remember what the band was. I only remember it was a high-octane, high-energy evening. We'd been dancing throughout, and we were hot and high when it ended.

'Let's go for a walk,' Ben said. 'Before we go back.'

So we headed off around the lake before going to my room, as we usually did at the end of the night. Ben bought little more than bread and beer from the Student Union shop, and only had one plate, one mug and one set of cutlery in his room, whereas I had a kettle, a toaster and jars of peanut butter, Marmite or cheese spread to go with the toast we invariably needed by the end of an evening.

I liked Ben from the start. He was funny and interesting and I felt at ease with him. He was easy to talk to, kind, and he made me laugh. I was really glad of his friendship, especially in that first year when I could have easily been lonely: missing home and the friends I had there, missing Dad, and still grieving for Mum.

And I still missed Deepak too.

Ben had asked me about him when he nosed through my photographs early on. 'You're so fucking right on and dungarees,' he'd said. 'Working in an orphanage and screwing the local doctor.'

'What's that supposed to mean?' He could wind me up when he wanted too.

'Right on – politically correct,' he said. 'Dungarees – a feminist.'

'And how does what I did in my gap year fit in with your theory?' I asked, secretly flattered because that was exactly how I wanted people to think of me.

'Right on, because you were saving the world by rescuing orphans while at the same time making it clear that you were not just some patronising posh white girl who needed India on her CV by sleeping with one of the natives. And dungarees because you loved him and left him and probably broke his heart in the process.'

'And is that your definition of feminism?' I asked.

'Nope – just wearing dungarees is enough to qualify as a feminist in my book!'

Ben was still flipping through my photo album. I knew he was trying to get a rise from me. So I ignored him, and tried to ignore his further questions too. 'So, this Deepak – what was he like?'

'He was nice, kind, interesting – a doctor. What more do you need to know?'

'Well, there must have been a bit more to him than that if he charmed his way into your bed.'

'It was a holiday romance, that's all.' I half wished I'd not told Ben I'd had a relationship with him. But he said I'd given it away when he asked who the tall, dark, handsome stranger in the photograph was. 'Deepak,' I'd replied, thinking my tone was neutral. 'He was a doctor in the village. He came to run a clinic at the orphanage once a week.'

'So were you shagging him?' Ben had asked.

'Why do you ask?' I'd wondered what in my reply had given it away.

'So you were!'

I'd brushed it off as a holiday romance, but in reality I'd fallen heavily in love with Deepak and not known, until months into our relationship, that he was married with three children and another on the way. I'd thought when he came to the orphanage at the end of the week that he lived in the countryside with his parents... presumed when he asked me if I'd like a drink one evening that he was older than me but equally free and single. I had never for a moment, when he came back to the small room on the edge of the orphanage courtyard that was mine, imagined that he had a wife and children to go home to.

I'd thought the secrecy and the not staying the night were to protect me. I hadn't been sure how the elderly expat English Christian woman who ran the orphanage would react to her foreign charge having a relationship with someone, and on the premises at that. I'd had no idea, until Deepak did not attend the clinic one week 'because his wife has gone into labour', that I had done anything wrong.

And even though I was in the wrong only unwittingly, I still felt that I had done something terrible and deserved the heartache I felt when I realised I'd had an affair with a married man. I felt every bit as guilty about it as I would have had I known at the time.

I tried not to think about him after that, but I still missed him, missed being loved by a man, even if he had not really loved me as I thought he had. But, in the absence of the relationship I'd had with him, I was glad of the warm and affectionate friendship I had with Ben.

So when, that night after the gig, he collapsed next to me on the beanbag and put his arm around me, I thought this was just another typical ending to another typical night out. We'd eat toast, drink orange juice, Ben would tell me the bass player was slightly out of key and I wouldn't have a clue if he had been or not. Then Ben would go back to his room to sleep.

But on that particular night, when Ben put his arm round me, he pulled me closer to him.

'Isobel?' He sounded suddenly serious.

'Yup!' I was not.

'You are the most amazing, kind, clever and beautiful woman and I want to kiss you,' he said.

'Do you, now?' I was still treating it as a bit of a joke.

'Yes,' he said. 'I've wanted to kiss you since day one and I think I'm going to now.'

There was a split second then when I thought, this is all wrong, we're just friends, I don't even fancy him, it wouldn't be fair to Ben to let this happen, and various other thoughts along those lines. But alongside them I was thinking, why not? I haven't kissed anyone for the past six months. I like Ben. We get on well. Maybe it would be nice to kiss him. We're good enough friends for it not to matter.

Again, I was naïve. If you are in your late teens, you've been out drinking and dancing, you don't have to get up in the morning and you start kissing someone a foot away from a bed you have access to, the chances are you will end up in that bed with them.

So, of course, we did. Then, and the following evening, and again and again for a few months, until I realised it had to stop.

It was the morning after Ben had spent the entire night in my room.

Previously, he'd gone back to his. It made sense. The single beds were narrow, almost impossible for two people to actually

74

get any sleep in, and Ben had his own identical bed just a few doors away. Plus in my mind – and probably in Ben's too, considering what happened next – it kept things fairly casual. We slept together because we were both young and single and we liked each other and we wanted sex. But that night Ben said he was too tired to move, and when I woke in the morning he was already awake, propped up on one elbow, looking at me.

'Morning,' I said, rolling away from his gaze because there was something in it that made me uncomfortable.

'Come here,' he said, rolling me back towards him, holding my naked body against his and pushing my bed hair from my eyes.

Then he said it.

'I love you, Isobel.'

And that was when I knew we had to stop.

'I don't, I can't...' I couldn't find the right words. 'I'm really fond of you, Ben. I love you as a friend but...'

It's hard not to hurt someone who has just told you they love you, when you are telling them that you don't.

'You should have made it clearer earlier,' Yasmin said to me when I told her afterwards. She seemed to think I'd been remiss: that I'd somehow led Ben on, made him think I felt more for him than I did. But I'd thought we both knew it was friends-with-benefits.

Of course things were strained after that, for a bit. It was a little awkward, but Ben seemed OK. We were still friendly, even if I didn't ask him back to my room so much any more – friendly enough for him to ask if Eric could stay in it, when he came to visit on a weekend I was going home to visit Dad.

Friendly enough for me to say, 'Sure.'

Ben talked about him a lot: Eric Jordan, his friend from school. Eric whose parents had encouraged Ben more than his own: to try to get into acting, to go to university, to be the person he wanted to be.

Eric was at Cambridge reading history. Ben always said that I'd like him, but we'd never met. I'd never seen Ben in the holidays. He went back to Nottingham, I went home to Sussex, and Eric had never come to visit Ben at UEA, even though it wasn't that far and he had a car.

It felt a little weird letting someone I'd never met stay in my room, but I tidied it up before I left, changed the sheets, and locked away in a drawer anything I deemed too personal for a stranger to stumble across.

My room looked so untouched, when I returned, that I wondered if he'd changed his mind and cancelled the trip, but Ben said they'd had a great weekend, divided between showing Eric around Norwich and the campus and the Student Union bar.

Eric was 'quite good-looking, well-spoken and very interesting', according to Helen, another friend on the same corridor. 'And,' she added, 'he seemed quite interested in you.'

'How so?' I asked.

'He saw the picture of you in India in your room and asked how long you'd been there and what you were doing,' she told me. 'And he looked at your books and wanted to know what you were studying. And at your 'Support the Sandinistas' mug and asked if you were a genuine revolutionary or just another student hung up on a cause!'

'What did you tell him?' I asked.

'I didn't get a chance,' she replied. 'Ben filled him in a bit then went off on some story about something that happened when they were at school together.'

'So when do I get to meet the famous Eric?' I said to Ben later. I wasn't really bothered one way or the other. I was curious to know what the friend he talked about was like, but that was it.

'I'm not sure that I want you to meet him, Bel,' Ben said, suddenly going all quiet and serious.

'Why not? He's your best friend. I'm your close friend. Why don't you want me to meet him?'

'Don't make me spell it out,' he said, raising his voice a little.

That was when I realised I'd been naïve to assume that everything was fine and cool between us.

Ben, Monday evening

'Eric is your best friend,' Maggie says, calmly but with meaning.

There's a stage direction for you. *Once more, calmly but with meaning.*

'I know,' I reply.

I don't have that many people I would count as good friends, just a handful that I've retained from various stages of my life. Eric is my oldest.

We are stacking the dishwasher, after the meal during which I recounted the details of my meeting with the solicitor. Maggie knows now that Hedda thinks it is possible we could sue Eric and Isobel. I want to go ahead, but Maggie isn't so sure.

'You could lose him,' she says, taking a dishwasher tablet from under the sink and slipping it into the dispenser. 'And Isobel.'

'I don't care,' I reply.

'Really?' Maggie asks. 'We've got a deaf daughter, Ben. We're going to need friends. You're going to need friends.'

'I've got other friends,' I say, although none I could count on the way I used to think I could count on Eric and Isobel.

'You could lose them too,' Maggie continues. 'You don't know how people will react, if you sue your best friend and your...'

She pauses, and I wonder, as I often do, just how much she knows about Isobel and me. She knows we went out together briefly, of course, a long time ago. The only reason Isobel is still in my life, I've told her, is because she's married to Eric. But you know what women are like. Sometimes they know more than they let on. Sometimes they know stuff, even though no one has told them.

'His wife,' I finish the sentence for her.

'If you go ahead, people will take sides. You may not be able to count on their support, and we're going to need all the support we can get. Our daughter is deaf.' She repeats this as if I don't know, as if I don't think about it virtually all the time.

'I know that! That's why I'm doing this,' I say, then correct myself. 'That's why I'm thinking about it.'

'Is it?' Maggie challenges me. 'Is that really why you're thinking about it? Do you think that is the best thing to do for Iris?'

'Ultimately, yes,' I reply.

'And you're not just doing it to...' She pauses again.

'What?' I think I know what she's thinking but I want her to say it out loud if she is.

'I'm going to check on Iris.' Maggie closes the door of the dishwasher and moves past me to go upstairs, leaving me with my thoughts.

I had this idea that it would all stop when I went to secondary school. The *B-B-B-Ben*-ing, the *Are you having a b-b-b-bad day*-ing and the *Cry b-b-b-baby*-ing.

I convinced myself, during the summer holidays, of three things. One, that the stammer I had had since I was very young would miraculously cease; two, that, with the worst of the bullies going to a different school, the ones that were left would lose interest in taunting me; and three, that the boys and girls I'd never met before would find my slight speech impediment endearing rather than something to take the piss out of.

My conviction didn't last beyond the first day. Why is it, I wonder, that so often people stammer over the letter their name begins with? I was fine with Deakin, but the shiny new comprehensive I attended didn't call people by their surnames, unlike the grammar school it had replaced. Had I been a few years older, I might have been spared the relentless bullying that having to say 'Ben' incurred.

But on day one the geography teacher highlighted my inability to speak by asking me both my name and the capital of Germany and I was already exposed, ripe for the ribbing which would inevitably follow.

It wasn't bad at first. It was a big school. We were at the bottom of it. The people who would emerge as the cruellest were still taking stock. Others were keen to make friends.

But a few weeks into the new term a boy called Matthew (why wasn't I called Mike? I had no problem with Ms either) decided the way he was going to make friends was by getting the rest of the class to join him in a game. This involved asking me questions to which the answer always began either with a B or a P.

I tried to take it in my stride, laughing with them and turning his game into one of my own – a game of coming up with an alternative word.

'What type of bread is that?' Matthew would ask, pointing at my sandwich.

'Wholewheat,' I was the point-scorer, as far as the rest of the kids were concerned.

'What colour school jumpers did you have at your old school?'

'Navy.' I was a walking Thesaurus.

'How were you out in cricket today, Ben?'

'B-b-b-bowled.'

I think, because he was always jocular and I tried to remain so too, Matthew actually thought it was all good-natured. They didn't know how much I hated being unable to say things, or that I cried myself to sleep most nights.

Three weeks into term Eric arrived, all blond and shiny and confident and exotic because of it. Exotic too because he was three weeks late for the start of a new term at a new school and the school seemed to have given him dispensation to do whatever it was he'd been doing before he arrived.

'I've been with my family in Rio,' he explained. 'My dad was at a conference there and they said he could take the family. It was too good an opportunity to miss.'

'What does your dad do?' someone asked.

'He works for a think tank,' Eric answered, as if we'd all know what a think tank was.

Of course nobody did, but nobody admitted it either.

'He used to be in politics,' he added, either to casually let us know who his dad was or to give an inkling to those that didn't know what a think tank was.

I looked at his exercise books, stacked on the desk next to mine. A boy who arrived three weeks late into term had no choice about where he was going to sit; he got to sit next to the stammerer, whom everyone else avoided. Eric Jordan, he'd written on the front and it all began to fall into place. The late start, the trip to Rio, the father who used to work in politics... his dad must be Ralph Jordan, former local Labour MP and social reform campaigner.

Of course Ralph Jordan would have a son who didn't mind sitting next to the class stammerer – not only didn't mind but told the others, in such a way that he didn't alienate himself or me by doing so, to ease up on the teasing. And his mother was a drama teacher, who helped me learn not only to act but, more importantly, to speak.

I sometimes wonder, if Eric hadn't been at the same school, how my life would have turned out. If we'd not been friends, I'd never have met his mother who somehow made me take myself out of the words I was saying and just say them. 'To be or not to be.' I still remember the thrill of saying that for the first time, unimpeded by errant Bs. I never imagined that by the time I was in the sixth form I'd be the lead in *Hamlet*, centre stage, in front of a hall full of pupils and parents, to-be-ing and not-to-be-ing without a care in the world. Nor did I ever think I'd go on to do drama at university and try to forge a career in acting.

That ambition failed, but, for me, even to have the ambition felt like a huge achievement.

And of course he got me interested in politics too, which led me to UEA and Bel.

I wonder what I would have done, if he'd gone to the grammar school on the other side of the city?

One of the many 'what if's in my life. What if I'd not persuaded Maggie to go on holiday with my friends? What if Isobel and Eric hadn't come? What if Gabby hadn't got ill? Would we still have a healthy hearing baby, or would another 'what if' have stepped in to fulfil our fate?

Maggie was forty-five when Iris was born, high risk for Down's syndrome. We didn't have the tests, even though we knew this, because we weren't going to get rid of this child, were we? Perhaps we were always meant to have an imperfect baby.

I know it's not PC to say that. I wouldn't actually say it to anyone, although I wish I could. But that's what I feel. We had this perfect child, and something came along and spoiled her.

And what if I'd not asked Isobel if Eric could use her room, that weekend when he came to stay? He was interested in her then, I could tell. Of course he wanted to meet her.

And, when they did meet, whatever secret hopes I still harboured that Isobel might actually have more feeling for me than she was letting on were dashed. They looked like they were together, within minutes of my introducing them.

'Oh, Bel, this is Eric.' I tried to sound casual when she knocked on the door of my room, and I tried to feel it when she came in and sat next to him and started talking and they carried on, as if they'd known each other for ever.

If you can see two people connect, I saw it then. It hurt, of course, when they slowly started getting together – just letters at first, because there were no mobile phones or emails. Then he came to stay again and I knew it wasn't really me he wanted to see.

He told me when I walked back to the station with him.

'Ben, I've asked Isobel if she wants to spend the weekend with me in Cambridge.'

I don't think I disguised very well the fact that I felt as if I'd been punched in the stomach. I was privately furious with him. Why did Eric get to have it all? He had the place at Cambridge, the right-on dad that would have made him a magnet for half the women at UEA. He was good-looking and could have had his pick of virtually any woman. Why did he have to decide that Isobel was the one he wanted?

But Eric didn't know how I felt about her, and I wasn't about to tell him.

That was the point at which I stopped sharing with Eric. Up until then, we'd talked a lot. But then I realised there were some things I'd never be able to share with him.

I'd never be able to tell him how hopelessly in love with Bel I'd been and still was, even though I knew it was largely unrequited. And I've never told him, or anyone, what happened afterwards.

Isobel, Tuesday evening

'E!' I can hear the irritation in my voice, although I am trying to convey urgency.

Eric is still playing his cards close to his chest. 'Did you talk to Gabriella?' I'd asked him, after he brought her home from orchestra last night. 'Did she say anything?'

'Not really,' was all I could get out of him.

'Eric!' I use his full name this time.

He's back early. We have a parents' meeting later at Gabriella's school and we would have been in plenty of time, had Eric not decided to shower.

'It smells of burning rubber in here,' he'd said, as if the smell of the kitchen necessitated his washing.

'Harvey's been melting vinyl.' I gestured towards the work surface where a row of mini bowls were cooling. Harvey had made them from a selection of EPs he'd picked up at a market a few weeks earlier. He'd spent the hours after school heating them in the oven then shaping them into misshapen bowls. It was his design and technology homework.

'Cool,' Eric said, looking at them, forgiving the smell if his creative son had caused it.

'Not yet,' I'd joked, trying to lighten the mood, but Eric had ignored me and gone upstairs to the bathroom.

Harvey is helping Vincent with his homework now.

'I have to write a list of as many nasty things people call each other that I can think of,' Vincent announces, taking his blue homework diary from his Simpsons rucksack.

'I'll help,' Harvey offers, and I smile at the obvious appeal the task has for him.

'What subject is this for?'

'PSHE.' Vinnie grins, clearly relishing it as much as his older brother.

'Prick,' Harvey dictates, sitting next to him. 'Blockhead...'

'I don't think you can have "prick",' I interject. I'd never have let Gabriella get away with saying the word when she was nine, but it's harder with the boys. They're exposed to everything much earlier by virtue of having older siblings.

'Does that mean he can't have "wanker" either?' Harvey challenges.

'Harvey!' I try to convey warning in my tone.

'Gay.' Harvey doesn't question this time. He just points at the page, indicating Vincent should write it down. But he glances sideways at me, in anticipation of an admonition.

'You shouldn't use "gay" as a term of abuse,' I oblige, but my heart is not in it.

All I am thinking about is Iris's deafness. What can I do? The damage is done. I can't undo it. I can try to explain myself. But I know Ben is not always receptive to my explanations.

I've hurt him before – unintentionally, but hurt him nevertheless. I've been thoughtless towards him, but Ben can twist thoughtlessness into deliberate intent.

'Pig, idiot, blobfish.' Vinnie's terms of abuse are less crude than his brother's.

'Dickhead, condom face, the C word.' Harvey knows better than to actually say the word.

'Don't write that down, Vinnie.'

'Darling,' Vinnie says, a note of triumph in his voice.

'That's not rude, egg-brain,' Harvey insists.

'It is.' The childish anger Vinnie hasn't quite yet learned to control, especially where his brother is concerned, creeps into his voice.

'"Darling" is a term of affection, peewit,' Harvey laughs at Vincent. 'You say it when you love someone, Tinky Winky.'

'Not just.' Vincent's voice is quivering. 'Mum says it to Dad when she's cross with him!'

I adjust the lid on the saucepan, clattering instead of reacting, and Eric appears. I look at the boys, wondering if they are aware of the tension between us. They must have noticed. They are old enough to spot the difference between kind and considerate, and merely civil. And Gabriella is picking fights at every opportunity, keen to show what she thinks of me.

I remove the pan of pasta from the hob and begin spooning it on to plates for the children.

'Can I have pesto?' Vincent asks.

'Not today,' I say.

'Why not?'

'Because Harvey's not allowed it and we're about to go out.'

Vincent still gets tetchy about not being able to eat things with nuts in himself, unless I'm there to supervise. But I can't risk it. Harvey can't remember the last time he ate a nut and what happened. I'm worried that, now he's reached the age where he thinks he's invincible, he may not take his condition seriously. He may be tempted to try something. I want to be there if he does.

'OK.' Vincent accepts it, this time. 'Is it nearly ready?'

'It is ready,' I say, as Eric appears and echoes me.

'Ready!' He makes it unnecessary for me to call 'E', 'Eric' or 'darling' – or anything else.

'Is Gabriella all right at the moment?' her English teacher, Mr Gill, asks us. 'She seems a little distracted.'

'Distracted' is one of those euphemisms that could cover a whole range of behaviours.

'Does she?' I ask. 'In what way?'

'Well, she usually contributes to the class a lot. She's one of the most able in it. I can usually rely on her to answer a question and get the others to take her lead. But today she seemed to be somewhere else.'

'She's probably just tired.' Eric jumps to her defence. 'She's been working quite hard.'

'Yes, of course,' Mr Gill says. 'It was only today really. As a rule she's a huge asset to the class.'

'That's great.'

'And Harvey is too,' he adds, as if making the connection suddenly between Gabriella and her younger brother. 'Did he show you the poem he wrote about Marmite?'

'No,' I say, and am then surprised when Eric responds.

'Yes, it was very funny.'

'It was brilliant,' Mr Gill continues. 'Really brilliant. Shakespearian in style and epic in quality.' He goes on to wax lyrical about Harvey but my mind is wandering. I'm worried about how everything is affecting Gabs. I need to talk to her, make her realise it's not her fault, make sure she doesn't let it affect her school work, not this year, when she has GCSEs.

'Who are we seeing next?' Eric asks as we stand up after our allotted ten minutes with the English teacher.

I look at the list Gabriella handed me earlier. 'Mr Coles.'

It's a bit of a bunfight, parents' evening at this huge comprehensive school, the mums and dads of three hundred children all milling about in the school hall and its surrounding classrooms, trying to find the teachers their offspring have made them appointments to see. People miss their time slots; queues begin to build behind the desks of the core subject teachers. We've gone home before having missed one or two of our allocated slots.

But we see Mr Coles. He tells us he thinks Gabriella could get into Oxford or Cambridge to read music if she wanted.

'But obviously the next stage is A-levels. Has she thought about where she wants to do them?'

'She's not decided yet,' I say, and Eric is unusually quiet. 'Do you really think she could get into Oxford or Cambridge?'

'I do, if she keeps working as hard as she does and continues playing at the level she is – quite easily if she wanted to,' he replies.

'That's very encouraging.' I smile and I look to Eric to say something, but he is looking around as if anxious to be gone. 'Well, thank you,' I say to the music teacher, standing up.

'Are we done?' Eric asks, and I know what he's thinking because it's what I've been thinking too. Gabriella's musical ability no longer seems the blessing it once did; instead it's a thing which underlines the terrible position Maggie and Ben find themselves in.

'What do you think I should do, Eric?' I say to him in the car as he fixes on the road. 'Should I call Ben? Or write?'

'I found another elderly lesbian professor the other day,' Eric responds. 'But I didn't send it.'

This is game which Eric and Ben have been playing since their twenties. They spot pictures in the newspaper of men who, as they've got older, begin to look more like 'elderly lesbian professors' (the sexism is not lost on me). Sometimes emailing each other pictures is the only contact they have with each other for months. But it seems to serve as communication.

'He's told some of the others,' I say. 'So he must know that we know.'

I want Eric to say that he will call him, take the responsibility at least for that first move. I want him to see how the land lies and find out if any contact from me will be welcome. I want him to speak to his oldest friend, for God's sake.

I take my phone out of my bag. 'I'll just text Gabs to make sure everything's OK at home.'

'Why wouldn't it be?' Eric mumbles, but he's concentrating on the road.

I send a brief message to Gabby. Then another to Ben.

I'm so sorry to hear your news, I write. *Is there anything we can do? Please let me know. Bx.*

I stare at it for a while. It doesn't say it all, but I think it says enough for now – enough for a text, anyway. I press Send.

A few minutes later, my phone vibrates in reply.

It's from Gabs.

Fine, is all it says, brief and to the point.

Ben, Tuesday evening

What time will you be back?

I read the text from Maggie as I wait for the next set of parents to pitch up to my desk in the school hall.

On paper, I don't have that many appointments. The kids make them themselves, but sometimes the parents decide to stop anyway, if they catch a teacher without a queue.

Last appointment is at seven-thirty, I text in reply, and stare at my phone as the message sends. I keep staring at it. I can't quite believe that I have heard nothing from Isobel.

'Mr Deakin, do you have a moment?' An anxious-looking woman wearing a strange jacket that looks like a fake sheepskin rug comes up to my desk. 'I've not got an appointment, but I wondered if I could have a quick chat.'

'Sure.' I nod at the empty parent chair and I think to myself that the jacket must be hot. It's very stuffy in the hall. It's clearly some sort of fashion thing, but it seems faintly ridiculous to be wearing it in here.

'I'm Alice Penwarden's mother,' she says. 'Gina.'

'OK, Gina,' I say, trying to think who Alice Penwarden is.

'You don't actually teach her,' Gina says.

'Ah.' I wonder why she wants to talk to me, then.

'Alice has Miss Effingham for drama,' she tells me.

'She's here tonight,' I say, nodding to the desk where Julie Effingham is sitting chatting to a bloke with a beard.

Gina leans forward and lowers her voice. 'Yes, well, it's you I wanted to talk to.'

'Well,' I say, and brace myself for some sort of confrontation I'm not in the mood for, 'if you've got a complaint about Miss Effingham, it's not me you should be speaking to.'

'Oh, it's not a complaint,' Gina assures me before adding, 'not exactly.'

'What, then?'

'Well, it's just that Alice is very gifted, at acting – she's been going to classes since she was five,' she tells me, and I struggle to maintain my politely interested face. I can't stand these parents. The ones who think their child is a genius and want to make sure we are absolutely certain of it too.

'I'm sure she is,' I say.

'She is.' Gina smiles, oblivious to my sarcasm. 'And yet she keeps being overlooked for school productions. I've spoken to Miss Effingham about it before, but – '

'I'm sure if Miss Effingham is aware of her talents – ' I interrupt her, but Gina cuts in right back.

'Well, she doesn't seem to have taken it on board,' she says, her voice rising slightly. 'And I wondered if you could do anything about it.'

'I'm not sure exactly what you want me to do?'

'You could speak to Miss Effingham and make her aware you think Alice should have a role in your next production.'

'But I don't think Alice should have a role,' I say, smiling. I am irritated, but I try to keep it pleasant. 'I don't even know who Alice is.'

I don't think I've been rude – I think I've been fairly reasonable, actually – but Gina Penwarden behaves as if I've told her her daughter is incapable of auditioning for even the back end of a pantomime horse. 'Well, really,' she says, pushing her chair back and standing up. 'I'd expected more.'

I bite my tongue because I am tempted to shout after her. The urge to scream 'What? What did you expect?' is almost overwhelming. In fact I want to go after her, take her by the scruff of her stupid jacket, pull her back to the chair and make her sit down and listen to me.

I want to say to her, 'Listen, Alice Penwarden's mother. I'm sure your daughter is very talented and she probably could, or possibly even should, have a part in the next school play. I don't know because I don't even know who she is. And quite frankly I don't care. What I do know about your daughter is that she can hear and she can speak, and if the fact that she doesn't get the starring role in the school production is the greatest of your worries then you're lucky.'

I don't do that. I take out my phone again, wondering if, while I was commiserating with Mrs Penwarden about her poor, talented, overlooked daughter, it has crossed Isobel Blake's mind to commiserate with me about my damaged, deaf one.

She must know by now, for fuck's sake. She's probably at a parents' evening herself right now. They are taking place today up and down the country. I'd have expected her to text, call – send an email even – anything... something. But nothing – that's weird. There's never not been anything.

I saw less of Isobel on a daily basis in our final year but I still saw her a lot. She shared a house off the Unthank Road with Yasmin and Siobhan. Siobhan is based in Africa now. Three years of development studies put her on a fast track to save the world. I'm not exactly sure what it is she does but I know it's worthy. That makes me sound more cynical than I actually am. I liked Siobhan and she's doing what she always wanted to do, which is more than can be said for the rest of us.

Anyway, I lived a few streets away, sharing a house with Paddy and Sally and a boy called Tom. I've no idea what happened to him.

So we still hung out together a lot: walked to campus together, popped round for coffee, that sort of thing. Isobel still cooked a lot. If I was ever in danger of going hungry, she could always be relied on to feed me.

We even went to Cambridge together once, to see Eric, which was weird. I left early, left them to it, but it was OK. We got on OK. Our friendship was still strong. But as the end of our final year loomed I began to wonder what would happen to us all when we went our separate ways. All of us, but me and Isobel in particular. I knew we'd lose the particular closeness forged from simply spending so much time together.

There was a lot going on at the time: exams, job interviews, parties, getting rid of stuff we'd accumulated, because we were going to move out of the places we were keeping it. I saw Bel here, there and everywhere but not really on her own, not to sit and chat till the small hours, as we used to, until she dropped by one evening when no one else was around. Paddy and Sally had gone down to London to look for a flat there together. They needed to find somewhere as Sally was heavily pregnant by then. Tom was out, so I had the house to myself and was enjoying the space, when there was a knock at the window and I saw Bel standing in the front garden, miming at me to get off the sofa and open the door.

'Busy?' she asked.

She could see I wasn't.

'Very!' I replied.

'Hungry?'

'Yes.' As soon as she asked, I realised I was, but as usual there was very little in the house to eat. 'But the cupboards are bare.'

'Aren't everyone's?' she said. 'It feels odd, doesn't it, knowing we're all going soon? Do you want to come back to ours and I'll cook?'

'No,' I said. 'I'll cook. Stay here and I'll pop to the corner shop and get some food.'

'I'll come with you,' Bel said.

And we walked to the shop in a strange semi-awkward silence and she hovered while I bought some pasta and splashed out on mince and a tin of tomatoes – and a bottle of wine. 'It's an occasion,' I said, taking it out of the carrier bag, when we were back at the house.

'Is it? What occasion is that, then?'

'I'm cooking for you, for starters,' I joked, but then I felt more serious. 'And this could be the last time we sit and have a meal together, here anyway. We move out in a week, and after that...'

'What?'

'I don't know.'

I opened the wine and poured her a glass. That seems like a normal thing to do now. But we were students, it was a gesture, and it was not lost on Isobel.

'We'll still see each other, Ben. Cheers!'

'It won't be the same though, will it? Cheers. We're moving on. You'll be in London. Eric too. I don't know where I will be. I haven't got beyond taking some of this lot back home.' I gestured at the stuff I'd begun to pile up in semi-organised stacks – books, LPs – everything except clothes and my single plate.

I was busying myself with the rest of my meagre shop when Bel got up and came over to me. 'I'll miss you, Ben,' she said, slipping her arm around my waist.

She could have done that as a simple, easy gesture, a way of saying, 'Look, we'll always be close,' but I took it as something more.

I turned round towards her, so we were no longer standing side by side in that 'Love Is' cartoon pose, but facing each other, close.

Isobel could have stepped away, but she didn't.

So I kissed her.

She could have stopped me, but she didn't. She put her glass of wine down and she pulled me to her, close enough that she could feel me hardening against her. And we carried on kissing as I moved my hand inside her shirt, across the warmth of her skin then down inside the waistband of her jeans and on to her buttocks.

Only when I moved my hand further still and stopped kissing her mouth and began kissing her breasts instead did she pause. 'We shouldn't be doing this,' she said as I moved my hand around to the front of her jeans. 'I'm with Eric. He's your best friend.'

I stopped then, stood up and looked at her.

'I won't tell him,' I said, looking into her eyes because I wanted her more than ever before, because I was fearful now that this was the end for us, whatever it was that 'us' had morphed into.

I expected her to protest a little, but all she said was, 'Can we go to your room, then?'

She closed the door behind us and I yanked the curtains shut.

'Ben...' She paused by the door and I thought then that she was going to stop, but she came over to me. 'I just wanted to say goodbye.'

Briefly I wondered if she meant that that was all she'd come round for – literally just to say goodbye, not to say goodbye like this. But I didn't ask her; I just pulled the T-shirt I was wearing over my head and began fumbling with the buttons on her blouse.

She put her hands over mine and again I wondered if she was having second thoughts. But what she was stopping was my button-fumbling, just so she could take her shirt off, deftly, as deftly as she removed her jeans and knickers. And she was standing in my room naked and beautiful and so fucking desirable I wondered how I'd got through the last couple of years, screwing other people when I still wanted her.

I didn't undress myself then, not immediately. I wanted it to last as long as possible because, unless things changed, it was going to have to last me a long time – like, for ever.

To this day, that is the only time I have ever come at the same time as the woman I've been with. She may have faked it, of course, but I don't think she did. So yes, to this day, that time with Isobel, the time when we shouldn't have slept together but we did because we both knew we were about to go our separate ways, has always been a sort of stupid benchmark.

Afterwards, I wasn't sure if I was glad to have had the

experience or sad because she made it clear it wasn't going to happen again.

'Why?' I asked her afterwards, as we lay together for a few minutes before she said she ought to go.

'Because I ought to go home,' she replied.

'No, I mean why now, Bel? Why after all this time? Why when you and Eric seem so close?'

'Because I do love you, Ben,' she said. 'Just not in the way you want me to. And I wanted to have something between us to hold on to.'

'We had something before,' I said.

'You know what I mean,' she replied, sitting up and shifting to the edge of the bed, picking her clothes up off the floor. 'You promise not to tell anyone else, ever?'

'I promise,' I promised, and I meant it.

She knew what she wanted and it wasn't me, but I was glad to have had that evening, even if it meant living with cheating on my friend; even if it meant knowing how it could have been, knowing that it could not be.

But I began to resent her for it, soon enough.

My phone beeps in my pocket and I take it out and see her name attached to a message in my Inbox.

I'm so sorry to hear your news. Is there anything we can do? Please let me know. Bx.

'Fucking hell!' I say out loud, and feel a deep fury. Is that all she's got to say? *Sorry to hear…* It's not our fucking news. It's news about something she fucking caused. Yes, Isobel Blake, there was something you could have done which would have avoided all this. But you never did it.

I type *FUCK YOU* into my phone to vent some of the anger I feel, and save it to the Drafts folder. I'm not going to give her the satisfaction of any sort of reaction, until I hear what the solicitor has to say.

Isobel, Tuesday evening

I switch my phone off when we get home, to stop myself checking for a reply from Ben. I know that if I heard it vibrate I'd be tempted to pick it up immediately. But I need to concentrate on Gabriella, relay to her what her teachers have told us.

Sometimes I hate the fact that we are all electronically tagged now, like offenders on probation. I remember when I was first asked to carry a pager for work and respond if someone paged me; it felt like a huge violation of my freedom. Now I could be contacted at the weekends and in the evenings. Even then, at least I could say I was nowhere near a phone, if I didn't reply immediately. Now, I've got my mobile with me all the time and check it constantly, mostly in case one of the children needs me.

'Where's Vinnie?' I asked when we got home.

Harvey and Gabriella are playing Scrabble in the kitchen. 'Watching TV,' Gabs says. 'We're playing Scrabble.'

'In French,' Harvey says, looking up.

'French?' Eric asks.

'I've got a test tomorrow,' Gabs says. 'I wanted to practise.'

'I'm checking the words,' Harvey says, patting a French/English dictionary, an old one of Eric's, which is on the table beside the board.

'Is *coït* a word?' Gabriella asks.

'Yup.' A smile crosses Harvey's face as he flicks through the pages of the dictionary and finds the answer. 'It means sex.'

'Ha!' Gabriella lays down her letters triumphantly. Only then does she ask, 'What did my teachers say?'

'They all say you are doing brilliantly,' I tell her. 'You work really hard. You are polite and you engage with the class.'

Harvey snorts.

'Mr Gill mentioned you too, Harvey,' I tell him. 'He was very impressed by a poem you wrote. I'd like to see it.'

'It was just a stupid poem,' Harvey says.

'What did he say about me?' Gabriella asks.

'He said you were doing brilliantly too,' I tell her. I don't tell her that her English teacher mentioned she was distracted.

'Can we stop playing now?' Harvey asks, distracted himself now that we are home.

'OK, Gabriella agrees. 'Thanks for the game, Harves.'

'S'OK,' he mutters, getting up and leaving the room.

'Did you see Mr Coles?' Gabriella asks me.

'Yes, of course. He said you're on course for an A-star in music. He thinks you might even get into Cambridge if you keep up at the level you're at. All your teachers said that if you keep up the good work you should do really well in all your subjects.'

I know it is important for Gabriella to hear this. It's the thing that will make all the hours she's going to have to put in over the coming months worthwhile – knowing her teachers and Eric and I are pleased with her.

'You're the model pupil, Gabs,' Eric reinforces this.

'And thanks for looking after the boys,' I add. 'Was everything OK.'

'Yes, fine,' Gabs says. 'There's some pasta left over in the pan.'

Later, when the boys and Eric have all gone to bed and Gabs is up in her room, I switch my phone back on again.

I have one new message.

But it's not from Ben.

How are you doing? It is from Sally. *Hope all OK. Give me a call some time. Xx.*

Is it too late to call now? I reply.

No, Sally pings back. *Paddy's staying in London tonight. I am watching rubbish TV.*

I press the Call Sender button and wait a few seconds before Sally answers.

'Hello. Hang on a sec. Just going to switch the TV off.'

There's a pause and then I hear my friend's voice again.

'Hi, Bel. How are you?'

'I'm OK,' I say, wearily. 'The last few days have been a bit difficult.'

'I did wonder. Have you been in touch with Ben?' Sally asks.

'No. I've texted him but he hasn't replied.'

I realise how lame this sounds, when I say it.

'Have you tried calling him?'

'No. I thought… I don't know if he'll want to talk to me. I thought I'd wait and see if he responds. And I don't really know what to say, either. What can I say?'

'Maybe you'd know if you spoke to him?'

'I don't know. I've just got no idea what he's thinking. It's a terrible thing that's happened and I feel responsible, naturally. But I don't know what Ben thinks. Does he blame me? Does he hate me?'

'I don't know,' Sally says. 'Yasmin spoke to him, before the party, and she said he was just very matter-of-fact. He told her they'd had some bad news, what it was, and said that they couldn't face seeing people, not just yet.'

'People, or me?' I ask.

'I don't suppose they can face seeing many people just now. Yasmin said she found it hard, after they had the diagnosis with Conrad. You probably remember?'

'Sort of,' I say.

I remember Yasmin telling me and feeling a mixture of sympathy and relief. Sympathy for her and Anton because it was such a terrible thing for them to have to cope with, but relief because at the time, having so little experience of children, I'd wondered if all children behaved like Conrad as they got older. He was alternately sullen and withdrawn or violent and angry, throwing tantrums which I knew went with his age but which seemed so extreme. 'Terrible twos,' Yasmin used to say, and shrug, when he threw himself down on the floor, burying his face in the carpet and howling. Something he still does even now.

I used to laugh it off with her, but when I looked at my sunny, smiley Gabby I couldn't quite believe that hitting two would bring about such a total character change. When they found out that Conrad was autistic, it made sense. His behaviour wasn't normal. Conrad was different – and there was the horrible possibility that something had made him like that.

'What else did Yasmin say?' I ask Sally.

'Just that, really. I think she only had a very brief conversation with him.'

'No, I mean about me,' I say, though I realise I am putting Sally in an awkward position. 'It's just, at the party, when I'd just found out, she seemed...'

'What?'

'I don't know really. She didn't really say anything. I just sort of expected...'

I pause because I don't really know what I expected. I could hardly deserve sympathy for my predicament when both Ben's and hers are so much worse.

'I tried to call Ben earlier myself,' Sally changes the subject. 'But he didn't pick up and I didn't leave a message.'

'When was this?' I know I have no right, but I feel a bit put out. I'd thought when Sally texted me she was concerned for me, for how I was feeling. I know she probably is, but now I think she's playing go-between.

'Earlier this evening...' Sally paused. 'Listen, Bel. I know this must be difficult for you and I just wanted to say, I don't blame you. I know how hard it is making decisions that affect or might affect your children. But I can see that from Ben's point of view...'

'What?'

'Well, just that his child is deaf. He might not be feeling very forgiving. Not yet, anyway.'

So maybe she's not the go-between.

'What do you think I should do?' I ask. 'I just keep going over things in my head and I don't get anywhere. Eric is being very distant and won't really talk. Gabs seems upset but she won't talk either. I don't know how Ben is and I'm worried about him, obviously. But I don't know what I can actually do.'

'Maybe you should try to call Maggie?' Sally suggested. 'Maybe during the day, while Ben's at school.'

'I don't know,' I say.

But I think about it later, after I've finished talking to Sally, as I'm plugging my mobile phone into the charger and find a Post-it note tacked to the socket.

Cheer up, Mum ☺ Vincent has written on it, and I smile.

At least it's not critical, not like the one he stuck to the metal headboard of the bed in the room Eric and I were sharing with Gabriella at the house in France. She said she was too old to camp out with the boys in the hut in the garden, but I was surprised she preferred to share with us. It meant she had very little privacy and neither did we.

As it turned out, it probably spared the boys from getting ill too.

Why are you being so mean to me and Maggie? Vince had written in thick black felt tip, which somehow made the note look more menacing and less friendly than his usual sticky notes.

I wondered if Gabs had seen Vinnie come in with the note, before she'd finally and fitfully fallen asleep. Her breathing sounded so laboured, I could hardly bear to listen to it.

And I wondered if anyone else had noticed that my relationship with Maggie was difficult. I tried to cover it up, hide my feelings towards her as best I could. But if Vinnie had noticed, then surely everyone else had too?

I shouldn't have shouted at him earlier in the evening, but by then I was really quite worried about Gabby, and the incessant drone of his remote control car was beginning to get to me. He was playing with it on the terrace below our bedroom window, motoring to and fro across the terracotta stones, manoeuvring around and occasionally bumping into flowerpots. Gabs had been trying to sleep, but had woken when I went to see how she was. She was hot and coughing a lot, and what had been a slight concern was becoming a distinct possibility.

I knew Sam had measles. I knew she'd been in close contact with him before we left. And I could see a feverish flush, which could easily be the beginnings of a rash, starting to spread across her body.

'I've got a terrible headache,' she told me, and I was beginning to get one too, from the anxiety. I was worried about Gabs, worried that the boys might get ill. And, of course, I knew Gabby had spent the previous day in close proximity to Iris. If I was worried about Gabriella, who was a fairly robust fifteen-year-old, God knew how Maggie would feel if Iris got ill.

'I feel like everything is pressing in on me, Mum,' Gabriella moaned. 'It really hurts.'

'Where does it hurt?'

'Everywhere. I just want to sleep but I can't.'

I felt completely powerless, and guilty too, seeing her lying there in pain, unable to do anything to alleviate it.

That was when I'd shouted at Vincent, opening the window and letting my anxiety out with some of the heat. 'Vincent, will you stop that now!'

He had looked up, surprised, at my voice, not knowing it was anxiety not anger and not directed at him.

'Switch that car off now.'

He hadn't argued. He'd just shrunk before me. He'd picked the car up and flicked the off switch and stood there, staring up at me, confused and unsure.

I could understand why Vince had felt aggrieved, but I wondered what had made him say I was being mean to Maggie too, and whether the others had noticed. If they had, did they think it was because I was jealous of her and Ben?

I'd asked myself the question because it took me by surprise, the feeling of suppressed anger I'd started to feel around Maggie. Was I, after all these years, jealous that Ben had finally found someone he seemed really happy with? There had been a time when I'd been flattered that he still seemed a bit hung up on me. I'd liked having Ben around. He was like the brother I never had. Maybe I'd have felt jealous if a doting brother suddenly had had his attention diverted by a new partner and baby.

But I liked to think I was not quite that petty or mean-spirited.

So why, every time Ben and Maggie came down to breakfast together, cooing over their baby as if they were the only people ever to have one, did I feel so resentful?

I kept asking myself that, and I think I know why.

I was jealous of Maggie. But not because of the way she was with Ben. Because of the way she was with the baby. In fact I was jealous of everyone there, and the way their lives had turned out.

Everyone else seemed to find it all so simple. Even Yasmin with her big unruly autistic teen, lashing out and screaming and refusing to co-operate, seemed to find it easier than I ever had.

And Maggie, who had had her first child aged forty-five, was a completely natural mother.

'Will you go back to work, Maggie?' someone asked her at dinner one evening.

'Yes, I'm planning to, when Iris is a year old,' she replied. 'Maybe just a bit of teaching at first. I'm not sure how easy it will be to tour, and I still get the odd bit of session work.'

'Did you know it's Maggie playing that trumpet that they play when a Ryanair flight arrives on time?' Gabriella asked everyone excitedly.

'Really?' Eric was suitably impressed.

'Yes. Da da, da da! That's me!' Maggie laughed. 'I played Brückner with the European Symphony Orchestra, which is very difficult, but what impresses everyone most is the Ryanair trumpet!'

'Babies don't get any easier just because they're a year old. If anything they need their mother more as they get older,' I said, creating an awkward hush which made me wish I'd kept my mouth shut.

'Isobel just says that because every time there's a chance she might go back to work she decides to have another baby!' Eric joked.

Another time I might have taken issue with him about how looking after children full-time was not exactly a piece of cake, but on this occasion I kept quiet.

'Why did you say that about kids not getting easier?' Eric asked, angrily, as we cleaned our teeth and undressed for bed later that evening.

'I didn't mean anything by it,' I said, avoiding Eric's look in the mirror.

'You keep having little digs at Maggie, Isobel.' Eric only ever calls me Isobel if he's angry. 'I just don't get it. What have you got against her?'

'Nothing,' I protested. 'And I don't keep having digs at her.'

'You do.' Eric runs the tap and wets his toothbrush before smearing it with paste. 'It was like the breastfeeding thing you said earlier.'

I knew exactly what he was referring to. Paddy had been going into the village and I'd asked him to pick up some paracetamol at the chemist for Gabs. Maggie had asked if he could get some more formula milk too. 'Did you not breastfeed at all?' My remark had been unnecessary and laden with the horrible self-righteousness of someone who had fed all her children for over a year.

'Why did you say that?' Eric asked, holding his toothbrush in mid-air.

'I didn't mean anything by it. I was just asking.'

'Just asking, the implication being that she'd somehow failed for not breastfeeding.'

'No,' I said to Eric. 'The implication being that at least I managed to do that.' I know it's not important in the great scheme of things, but when you are a full-time mother it becomes more so. I wasn't achieving anything outside of the home. Feeding my kids, to me, felt like a major achievement. Why should Maggie, with her career as a professional musician and her perfect baby, with whom she seems so at ease, also be successful at breastfeeding? Why can't I at least have that?

I said nothing and I brushed my teeth in silence, humiliated that my irrational feelings towards Maggie were so obvious. Eric had noticed, and Vincent. He was right, when he'd scrawled his message on a Post-it and left it for me to find before I went to bed.

Ben, Tuesday evening

Maggie has gone to bed early. She's exhausted and so am I. Parents' evening usually takes it out of me. But I sit on the sofa, watching rubbish TV, staring at my phone, looking at Isobel's message again and noting that I have a missed call from Sally.

It's probably too late to return it now. I wonder if she's spoken to Bel. They've always been close, but Paddy is more 'my' friend. We were on the same drama course, although Paddy couldn't act, a fact which served him well in later life. He began writing instead, and took a play he'd written to the Edinburgh Fringe. It sparked interest from Channel 4, which commissioned him to write a drama series; Paddy, the son of a miner from Sheffield, set up his own production company to make the programme and he's never looked back. He made a fortune. The boy done good. Their kids went to private school. They lived in a huge house in Highgate until they sold that and moved to a slightly smaller one in the country, not far from Brighton, and bought their French place with the leftover dosh.

I think they've seen a bit more of Eric and Isobel since they moved. I wonder if Sally's seen Bel since Anton's party... whether she knows how she reacted to the news and what she's planning to do about it, if anything. I wonder, if she knew, whether Sally would tell me what goes on in the Blake/Jordan household. Would she tell me what impact the news had had on Isobel?

The afternoon things began to unfold, Isobel had yelled at Vincent.

We were lying by the pool, the three of us plus Iris, who was sitting in an inflatable boat, filled with a few inches of water and a handful of origami penguins. Harvey had made them earlier in the day and given them to Iris. Funny kid.

'They'll just get soggy if she puts them in water,' Maggie had said.

'They're penguins,' he'd replied, and sloped off, slightly embarrassed by the gesture.

Vincent was on the terrace near the house manoeuvring a remote control car that he'd found in a cupboard earlier in the day. 'I remember Chris doing the same thing,' Paddy said, watching him driving the toy, which had belonged to his son. 'They grow up so quickly.'

He looked from Vincent to Iris, splashing happily, and I followed his gaze, letting mine rest on my daughter, so perfect in her tiny swimming costume, picking up a cup and pouring water over her paper penguins, focused on the task and apparently oblivious to the drone of Vincent's car and the occasional cracking sound as he ran it into a flowerpot. It seemed almost impossible that she would one day even be Vincent's age, let alone grow up and leave home. I watched her, wanting to freeze the moment, keep her like that as long as possible. But it was broken by Isobel, leaning out of her bedroom window and yelling at her son.

'Vincent, will you stop that now! Switch that car off now.'

She sounded unreasonably furious. Vincent started and shrank, picking up the car and switching it off without argument.

'It's probably the menopause,' Paddy said, and I laughed, but Maggie shot me a look.

Vincent ambled over, dejected.

Paddy sat up. 'Fancy a diving competition, Vince?'

The laziness had been driven out of the afternoon by whatever was eating Isobel. I wondered what it was as I stood up and caught sight of her turning away from the window and disappearing into the upstairs room. She seemed to have been on edge for the past couple of days. She kept making snarky remarks towards Maggie, making comments about breastfeeding because Maggie wasn't, asking her if she planned to go back to work and implying that if she did she might somehow be neglecting her child. What did it matter to Isobel if Maggie went back to work or not?

And now, maybe she won't be able to. It's unlikely, in the immediate future anyway. There's too much else to think about: how we learn to communicate with our child, what we are going to do to try to combat her lack of hearing, who could look after her if Maggie does want to tour again.

I wanted to tell Isobel to fuck off and leave my wife alone. But of course I didn't. I couldn't. Instead, when we went upstairs after dinner and Maggie began to undress, with the lights out so as not to disturb Iris who was sleeping, I stood behind her and told her to wait. 'Let me do it,' I whispered in the dark as she began unzipping her dress.

Maggie didn't say anything. She held up her arms as I lifted the dress over her head and then stepped closer as I undid her bra.

'I love you, Maggie,' I said quietly. 'Don't let Isobel get to you.'

Then I knelt down and removed the rest of her underwear, kissing her until she stopped me and we moved on to the bed.

'I love you too, Ben,' she said, afterwards. 'We're OK, aren't we?'

'We're more than OK,' I said.

Isobel, Wednesday morning

'Goodbye, then.' Eric is still pissed off with me.

We've already had the discussion we've been having for the past few days.

I am sure, because I know Eric, that he must be feeling guilty too, but it seems to manifest itself as antagonism towards me.

'What are you going to do?' he asks.

'What can I do?' I ask back.

'Contact Ben,' he says.

'I've texted and he hasn't replied.'

'Then call him.'

I need to discuss what to say with someone first. I need Eric to help me. He is refusing.

'I'm having lunch with Sally today,' I tell Eric as he heads for the door and the early train to work. 'I spoke to her last night, after you'd gone to bed.'

'Well, that's really proactive,' he says, and leaves.

'At least someone's willing to sit down and talk about it,' I shout after him.

I switch on the radio to fill the silence. There's a report on the news about ostrich farmers going bust during the recession.

'I didn't even know there were ostrich farms in England.' Harvey joins me in the kitchen, opening the fridge as soon as he's through the door, in desperate pursuit of food. 'Are there any bagels?' he asks.

'Not in the fridge,' I say.

'Ham?' He's still looking.

'On the middle shelf?'

'Cheese?'

'You're hungry this morning!'

Harvey grunts, pulls ham and cheese from the fridge and heads towards the bread bin. 'Do you want something, Mum?'

'No, thanks, love.' I don't have the stomach for a huge breakfast at the best of times. I pour myself a coffee, the dregs left in the cafetiere Eric had made for himself, and sit at the table, keeping out of Harvey's way while he busies himself with his breakfast. The radio is a drone in the background, but suddenly the words jump out at me.

'... growing concern over the number of reported cases,' the radio newsreader is saying. 'Ministers are urging parents whose children have not been vaccinated to attend the additional clinics that are being set up around the city.'

'Oh, yeah, Joe's going today,' Harvey says.

'Where?'

'To have his jabs.' I hadn't been aware he was listening. 'I told them we had ours in France.'

'Are any of your other friends having them?' I ask, wondering if Harvey is aware of the controversy over the MMR vaccine. It was only when Gabs got ill that we'd rushed the boys off to the local French GP and asked if they could be immunised, hoping they'd spent so much time outside that they'd not already caught it from Gabby.

Harvey takes very little notice of what goes on in the world, but he has half an ear to the radio now.

'A GP at the centre of the recent epidemic said some people had been invited to get their children vaccinated with the MMR jab fifteen times,' says the radio presenter. 'Joining me now to discuss this is Dr Ailsa Millington...'

'Some,' Harvey says in reply to my question. 'Alfie might be, I think.'

He tucks into his bagel.

'Immunisation levels among ten-to-eighteen-year-olds have fallen to such low levels in the area that it is only a matter of time before there is a widespread outbreak,' Dr Millington is saying. 'Parents who have still not had their children vaccinated are being grossly irresponsible.'

'That's what Sean's mum said about you.' Harvey looks up.

'When did she say that?' I feel piqued to think people are talking about me behind my back, although I suppose I knew it was likely.

'When I went round last week,' Harvey says, his nonchalance disguising a certain gleeful curl around the corners of his mouth. Clearly hearing another parent bad-mouthing your own mother gives a boy a certain sense of satisfaction.

'What did she say exactly?' I don't really want to know but I can't help myself.

'She said you were grossly irresponsible.' Harvey grins, his mouth loaded with ham and cheese, and I look away. 'Declan brought a note back from school about measles and I told her Gabs had it while we were on holiday and she went off on this rant.'

Declan is Sean's younger brother.

'And what did you say?'

'I asked what school Declan was going to next year.'

'I mean what did you say when she said I was grossly irresponsible?'

'Nothing.' Harvey takes another bite of his bagel.

'The region has a large vulnerable age group,' the doctor on the radio is saying. 'It's only a matter of time before we start seeing deaths.'

'*She's* grossly irresponsible for not having a net around her trampoline,' I counter Sean's mum's accusation, even though she's not here to hear me, even though she has every right to say what she said – just not to my son.

'Bloody hell, Mum. That was years ago,' Harvey says. Clearly he remembers the incident too. He must have been seven or eight when he went to play with Sean after school and fell off their trampoline on to the decking. He hurt his arm. I thought he'd broken it, he made so much fuss. I rushed him up to Casualty and they took a look but said it was just badly bruised. But I still had a go at his friend's mum for not watching them while they bounced, even though I knew you couldn't watch kids all the time. I berated her, too, for not having a net round the trampoline.

To be honest I've never really liked this particular mother, but I was forced to keep up a semblance of friendship for the sake of Harvey's friendship with Sean. However, now they're both in their second year at secondary school and surrounded by other friends, I feel less compelled to accept the invitations to the 'impromptu drinks' which still arrive by text every now and then.

Sorry, we're not around that evening, I will lie in reply, exercising my right not to *have* to be friends with her, now that the boys are no longer so thick.

She is, no doubt, glad to be shot of me too.

'What if it had been worse?' I'd said to her at the time of the trampoline incident.

'But it wasn't,' she'd replied. 'You're overreacting.'

In hindsight, I was, but at the time I really thought Harvey had seriously injured himself. Not everyone had trampolines in their back gardens then. Google Earth wouldn't have revealed half as many black holes in between terraced houses as it does now. Sean's house was one of the first places that the boys got invited to bounce at, and, when Harvey fell, I couldn't help feeling that his mother was to blame.

And now it's her to turn to call me grossly irresponsible.

Ben, Wednesday morning

'The current measles epidemic is slowing down, but too few young people are protected against the disease,' a newsreader says as I switch on the radio.

It's early. Maggie and Iris are still asleep. I am in the kitchen making breakfast. The radio's just background noise in the quiet of the morning. My thoughts are elsewhere, but it grabs them.

'Unless there is a significant take-up in the vaccination rate there will be more large outbreaks of the disease,' the newsreader continues. 'Six new cases were reported yesterday, and public health officials are predicting more.'

I listen attentively as I wait for my toast to pop.

'Parents whose children have not been vaccinated are urged to attend the additional clinics that have been set up around the city.'

A discussion follows. A doctor is explaining how some parents have been invited to attend vaccination clinics up to fifteen times but have still not done so.

'Does that surprise you?' the interviewer asks, which is a variation of the question Hedda asked me when I met her on Monday.

'Were you surprised that Ms Blake had not had her children vaccinated?'

'I was surprised when she told us Gabriella had measles,' I told her. 'I didn't think anyone got it any more. And Maggie was worried, naturally. We both were.'

Actually at the time, if anything, I was more struck by how odd it was, to have measles. I'd thought it had more or less disappeared.

'And yes, it did surprise me,' I said to Hedda. 'Isobel was always so principled. It was the sort of thing I can almost hear her sounding off about.'

'Sounding off?' Hedda asked.

'Going on about, making a point,' I explained. 'I mean, it wasn't an issue then. But, if it had been, she would definitely have had a view.'

Everyone had strong opinions when we were at university. It was a place for idealists, radicals and people who wanted to change the world. Isobel was one of them. And I thought she would, too, because she was clever and energetic and she really thought that all it required was a bit of effort and organisation.

She wasn't overambitious in her plans. She didn't want to bring about world peace or end apartheid single-handed, although she did her bit. She just wanted to change things a little. 'If my mother had lived twenty miles away she might have survived,' I remember her telling me, and I thought it was the saddest thing. 'She was denied the drugs that could have saved her because the health authority where we lived wouldn't pay for them.'

At the time, Isobel was holding forth, to a room full of people all engaged in sitting around and changing the world with their chatter. She had their attention. 'How is it right that, if you live twenty miles apart from someone with exactly the same kind of cancer, one of you gets a life-saving drug and the other doesn't?'

I thought Bel was so beautiful when she was passionate about something – and she always was, when she was younger. Now the only thing she seems to get worked up about is whether the kids have had enough fruit to eat.

I know we've all grown up a bit, and our priorities have changed, but I never expected Isobel to shift so much.

'And your wife?' Hedda asked me. 'She was angry that Ms Blake had not had her children vaccinated?'

'Yes, she was.' I nodded. 'Angry because our baby was at risk of getting ill, especially as Maggie had never really wanted to go on holiday in the first place.'

'Why was that?'

'Is all of this relevant?'

'It could be. I need as much background information as possible,' Hedda explained. 'If this case gets to court, it would be the first of its kind. We are testing the water.'

She looked up from her notebook and there was a shine to her eyes that wasn't there before. I think it was zeal. Hedda wants this case, not because it might make a difference to Maggie and me, but because she wants to trailblaze.

'There have been a couple of similar cases in the States,' she told me, twisting her white-blonde hair around her finger, an unconscious gesture that seemed to help her concentrate, 'where people have sued successfully for deliberate infection with HIV. This is different, harder to prove, but if we are to prove it I need to know as much as possible about the relationship between all the parties concerned.'

She's well suited to being a trailblazer. I can imagine her on the television news, talking to reporters, briefing them on the steps of the courthouse before we go in to hear a judgement, if that's how it works.

'Maggie didn't know the rest of the party as well as I did,' I told her. 'And she wasn't really that keen to travel with the baby.'

'Why was this?'

'No reason, really; she was just happy to stay at home.'

'But you decided to go anyway?' Hedda asked.

'Yes, I wanted to go. I felt I needed a holiday – teachers always do by the end of the summer term – and I wanted my friends to get to know Maggie, and Iris too.'

This was what had driven the decision for me. I'd wanted to show off my wife and my baby. I'd wanted to show them that I was one of them now, settled and happy. I'd wanted them all to get to know Maggie.

The unspoken worry had been Isobel.

I knew they were wary of each other. I'd never told Maggie how I used to feel about Bel but, although she never mentioned it, I think she was somehow aware. She was curious, when we first met, about why I'd never settled down. I think she suspected that there was someone, somewhere in my past, whom I had not quite let go of, someone who had stopped me from moving on. And, when she'd met Bel, I think she'd known it was her.

Isobel, Wednesday lunchtime

'*Grazie mille*.' The waiter retreats after we've ordered a couple of glasses of wine.

We're in an Italian restaurant on the seafront. It feels a bit too lavish today. When Sally suggested coming down and meeting me for lunch, I'd thought that we'd have a sandwich in a café, but Sally had insisted we come here. 'My treat,' she'd said.

She is more decadent than I am. She can afford to be. That's not to say she isn't generous. She is – always was. Even before Paddy started to make money and she had a baby and was not working, it never stopped either of them sharing what little they had.

'I love that expression,' Sally says. 'Italian is such an effusive language. "Thanks a lot" is the nearest we get to *grazie mille*!'

'Gabriella and her friends seem to say "thank you sooo much", which is almost the same.'

Sally laughs. I set down the menu and put my reading glasses back in their case.

'That's a novel specs case,' she remarks.

'It's one of Harvey's creations.' I smile, seeing the case, which is now familiar to me, through Sally's eyes. It's made of a juice carton, a Tetrapak – a Polish one that he bought from one of the increasing numbers of Polish supermarkets that have sprung up to keep up with the increasing numbers of Poles in Brighton. So it's adorned with interesting graphics which I can't interpret, and various red and green fruits. It must have been a mixed fruit juice before it was drunk and the carton folded and glued into a funky spectacle case.

'He ought to sell them,' Sally said examining it. 'It's a clever concept.'

'He's decided he wants to be an industrial designer,' I tell her. 'He keeps coming back with bits of junk and turning them into something useful. He now sits at the dinner table on his newly created supermarket trolley chair.'

'That's great,' Sally replies. 'He's obviously got a real flair for design. You could tell with all those origami figures he made on holiday.'

'Maybe,' I reply, proud of Harvey's emerging talent. 'He's got a friend whose father designs drain covers. I think he's inspired him.'

'Well, I suppose drain covers are necessary, but I think Harvey could probably go further. He's a bright lad and a credit to you.'

'Thank you,' I say, grateful.

'And how are your other talented children?' she continues. 'More importantly, how are you?'

'Not great,' I tell her, beginning to feel slightly better now that I'm with someone willing to sit down and talk to me.

'I'm really sorry about the party,' Sally says. 'I mean, the way I told you about Iris. I just presumed you would already know.'

'No.' I shake my head. 'I'd spoken to Ben a couple of times after the holiday. I knew Iris had been ill. But the last time we talked he said she was OK again.'

'I should have realised. He called and spoke to Paddy, after they'd had the diagnosis. I don't know why I thought he would have told you. I can see it would be difficult. He probably expected us to pass the news on, then.'

'Did he ask you to?'

'Well, it's possible he asked Paddy, but if he did he never relayed it.'

The waiter returns with two glasses of pinot grigio and a bottle of sparkling water.

'Thank you,' I say.

'Thank you sooo much,' Sally adds, then, to me, 'Cheers.'

'Cheers. Thanks for calling, Sally. Thanks for coming down.' I take a sip of my wine and look around the restaurant. 'It's good to see you, but this all feels a bit wrong. It seems too normal.'

'Do things feel abnormal?'

'Yes, they do.' I put my glass down. 'I can't stop thinking about Iris being deaf and stressing about all the "what if"s, wondering what I should have done to make things turn out differently.'

'It's no good thinking like that now.' Sally does her best to be reassuring.

'But I can't help myself. I know why I did things at the time, but now of course I wish I'd acted differently. I wish I'd never left Gabby with Maggie and Iris that day we went to the dune, but I wanted to be there for the boys.'

'It probably wouldn't have made much difference.'

'It might have.'

'Maybe, but Gabs had measles and we were all sharing a house. I don't think you need to beat yourself up about going on the outing.'

'Meaning I should be beating myself up about not having had her vaccinated?'

'I didn't say that, Bel. You had your reasons. I respect that.'

'Do you? No one else does. And wherever I turn there seems to be something to remind me of that.'

'What do you mean?'

'I suppose it's just that you become more aware of things when you're caught up in them. I switched the radio on this morning and they were talking about the measles outbreak in Wales, warning parents to do get their kids immunised. It felt as if they were admonishing me directly.'

'I know what you mean,' Sally says. 'But it's like you said: you just start noticing things more. Paddy came home from work on Monday saying the ticket inspector was deaf and he hadn't realised and, I don't know, they had some kind of exchange before he saw his hearing aids and then felt bad.'

'What does Paddy think?' I ask.

'Well, he was a bit embarrassed, I think, but he mentioned it more because he said he'd just started noticing that there are a lot of deaf people around.'

'I mean about Iris.'

'Well, he thinks it's very bad news, of course. It's going to be hard for them. And it's sad because... well, because Maggie's not likely to have any more children.'

'Would that make it better?' I ask.

'I don't know. It's just, if it's your only child, it seems worse somehow,' Sally replies.

'And a whole lot worse if you know it could have been avoided?' I say. 'Is that what you mean?'

'That's not what I said.' Sally bristles at my tone. 'I'm not saying it's your fault. Iris could have picked up measles elsewhere.'

'But she didn't, did she?' I reply. 'I've been going over and over the circumstances in my mind, trying to come up with any possible scenario in which Iris did pick it up elsewhere, and, believe me, I've tried very hard, but I can't. We were at your house for two weeks, Sally. Maggie and Iris never left the place. The only person Iris came into contact with was Gabriella.'

'Even so, what were the chances that she would become deaf? It's unusual. It's unlucky. You never could have foreseen that she would lose her hearing.'

'The chances are high enough in a baby.' I sigh. 'I should never have left Gabriella in the house with them on the day we went to the dune. I should have stayed and looked after her myself.'

'It does no good to keep torturing yourself, Isobel. We've all done the same. I remember making Chris wear a hoodie when we went away once because he had chicken pox and we didn't want to cancel our holiday.'

'It's not the same – '

'It is, though. I knew the airline wouldn't let us fly if they noticed his spots, I knew it posed a risk to other passengers, but I did it all the same. You didn't even know Gabs had measles at the time. Don't be so hard on yourself.'

'No, but...' I begin.

It was true, I hadn't known for sure, not until the doctor confirmed it, but I'd had my suspicions. No, I'd had more than suspicions; I can admit that to myself, but not to Sally.

'It's such a terrible thing to happen, to Iris,' I continue. 'I feel responsible. Eric clearly thinks I'm responsible too, and Gabby. I don't know what to do.'

'I feel partly responsible as well,' Sally says. 'Because it was at our house.'

'But you were just looking after us all. It's nothing to do with you.'

'All the same...'

'But it's not the same, is it? I just wish there were something I could do, some way of turning the clock back.'

'And would you?' Sally asks.

'What do you mean?'

'If you had the time back, would you have acted differently? Maybe it's not helpful to think that you would. Maybe you wouldn't.'

'I would if I knew what I know now.'

'But you didn't, Isobel.'

Sally pauses to butter her bread and I realise I am not the slightest bit hungry.

'At the time, when you decided not to have Gabs immunised, there was all that stuff in the news about the dangers, about the risk of autism,' Sally continued. 'Conrad had just been diagnosed. If I'd been in your shoes, maybe I'd have done the same.'

'Would you?' I doubt it somehow. Sally is so much more practical and far less emotional than me.

'I'd have been seriously worried about it, yes. If I'd had my kids later and all the stuff about the MMR had been in the news I might well not have had them vaccinated either, though I'm sure Paddy would have put his foot down.'

'So Paddy does think I was wrong?' I don't really want to know, but I feel I have to.

'Well, you know what Paddy's like.' She looks away, which tells me what I need to know.

'He thinks I'm a "bloody emotional fool"?' I say, mimicking his Sheffield accent.

'Actually...' Sally begins, then hesitates.

'What? You might as well tell me. I'm aware people are going to make judgements. Jesus, it was bad enough when we came back from holiday and other parents found out Gabs had had measles. I got the full range of dirty looks and bitchy comments in the playground at the start of term. I still do.'

'Well, yes, if you really want to know, Paddy does think you were "bloody daft", but he doesn't just blame you,' she says.

'I was the only one who didn't have my kids vaccinated.'

'But you weren't, were you? Eric is their father. I told Paddy you were feeling terrible and Eric was refusing to talk to you and he said he thought he was just as much to blame. I mean if anyone is. It's not all your fault.'

'That's not what Eric seems to think,' I say, grateful that, even if Paddy does think I've been irresponsible, he's not laying it all on me.

'What does he think?'

'Well, I don't really know because we haven't talked but, judging by the way he's been behaving towards me, he thinks it's all down to me.'

'But you must have made the decision together, to not have the kids immunised?' Sally asks.

'Not exactly,' I try to explain. 'We talked about it at the time and Eric could see I was worried and tried to reassure me that there was nothing to worry about.'

'But he didn't convince you?'

121

'He tried to, but in the end he let me make the final call.'

'So he has to share some of the responsibility for the outcome of that call.'

'I don't think that's how he sees it,' I say, wishing he did. It would still be hard to come to terms with the sequence of events, but it would be a whole lot easier if Eric were with me.

'Ben and Maggie must really hate us,' I change tack.

'They probably don't feel that warm towards you at the moment,' Sally concedes, as the waiter comes back to take our order. 'But maybe they just need some time. I can't believe there will be any lasting fallout. You've always been so close, you and Ben.'

'Not always,' I say, unsure how much Sally suspects.

Sometimes you think you have secrets, and then discover that everyone else knew them all along. Sally's known me almost as long as I've known Ben, longer than I've known Eric. I sometimes think she knows, even if it's only subconsciously, about me and Ben. I think she's probably guessed. But maybe she hasn't. Maybe she doesn't want to know.

Sometimes life is easier if you remain in a state of unknowingness.

Ben, Wednesday afternoon

'Do you want tea?' I ask.

I've made a pot, which feels like a prop, something Maggie and I need between us when we 'talk'.

I came home from school earlier than usual, which is possible on a Wednesday because I don't teach the last period. Maggie and I have earmarked the time to discuss what we're going to do. It's the first time, since I met with Hedda on Monday, that we've had a chance to sit and talk properly. And we both know that even this discussion is likely to be broken by Iris.

Maggie has been strapping her into the baby bouncer that hangs in the doorway between the kitchen and the hall. It keeps her happy for longer than other things. Sometimes she can bounce and make noises, watching us, for a good twenty minutes.

Iris smiles now as Maggie pulls a chair up to the kitchen table and sits at right angles to me.

'So what did you tell the solicitor?' Maggie asks, as I pour her a cup of tea. 'How did you leave things with her, at the end of your meeting?'

'That I'd discuss it with you.'

'I wish you'd done that before you made the appointment to see her.'

'I told you, I didn't know if there'd be anything to tell. I didn't want to distract you. You've got enough on. I didn't want to give you extra stuff to think about if there was no point.'

'Exactly,' Maggie replies.

'Exactly what exactly?'

Iris makes a horrible deep-throated sound and we both turn to look at her. There's nothing wrong. She's bounced herself round so she's facing away from us, that's all, but it's set her off grizzling. Maggie goes over to the doorframe, twists the bouncing thing round so she's facing us again. Iris stops the grizzling noise but she's still wearing the grizzly expression.

I'm quietly pleased with her for being in this mood, even if it disturbs our chance to talk. She's illustrating why I have to do something; making the point that she's not the same as she was before. She's not how I want her to be. She wasn't always easy, but this inability to engage is different and I don't like it. I know it's not her fault but I find myself getting irritated with her anyway – not now, when I want to use her irritability to suit my own ends, but generally. *Just be how you used to be, Iris*, I want to say to her.

I could say it. She wouldn't hear me. So it's irrational to think that if I articulated this in her presence she would mind. But it's not the sort of thing you should say out loud anyway. I can't even say it to Maggie. She's angry too, obviously, but more accepting.

It's something no one tells you, the great unspoken rule and the elephant in the room – if you have a disabled child, you can't actually say to anyone that you hate the fact that they are. You have to learn to live with it, just as the doctor said. It's not what my mum would have called 'the done thing', to tell anyone that you find having a child who can't hear a thing and doesn't respond because of it slightly freaky. You can't tell your friends that the frustration she clearly feels herself also drives you to distraction. You're the grown-up in all of this. You're the one who has to cope with it.

But it might be a whole lot easier if you could just say to every single person you met, 'My daughter is deaf. It's a fucking nightmare. It makes her grouchy and irritable most of the time and she's going to have to learn sign language or have implants or something. It's a fucking mess and it's not fair. We didn't deserve this.'

It might be a whole lot easier if I could just say to every Tom, Dick and Harry, 'I never even wanted children in the first place and now, not only do I have a daughter, I have a deaf one at that. There's irony for you.'

It's ironic also that I think if it wasn't frowned upon to say these things I might feel a tiny bit better, but it is, so I can't. I have to pretend it's a terrible thing, yes, but it could have been so much worse and we're coping, thank you very much. But the truth is, I'm not.

I can't just accept it and get on with it. So if getting a solicitor to rattle Isobel's cage helps me then I'm going to do it, even if Maggie is not keen. It's better than saying to my partner, who I really love, 'I never wanted a child in the first place and now look. How do you think that makes me feel?'

'So what would happen first, if we decided to go ahead?' Maggie stresses the 'we', as if it's very doubtful that she will give the go-ahead herself.

'She would send a letter of action to Isobel and Eric, basically outlining our case.'

'Which is?'

'That they had a duty of care to our child but effectively they allowed Iris to be infected, by not telling us they knew Gabby had measles. Therefore they are consequentially responsible for the damage to her hearing and we are seeking damages for costs incurred by having a deaf child.'

'You sound like a solicitor yourself,' Maggie says. 'And then what happens?'

'She waits for them to respond,' I say. 'They'll need to get a solicitor themselves. Their solicitor will probably deny it at first. They will write a lot of letters and eventually we will reach a settlement, or we'll take them to court if we don't.'

'It sounds as if it will all take ages, be stressful to us and may not get us anywhere.' Maggie can only see negatives.

'At least we will have done something.' I want her to try to see this from my point of view. 'At least *I* will have done something.'

'There might be something else we could do,' Maggie says, thoughtful.

'Such as?'

'I don't know. I just wonder if there's another way of making a point. If that's what you want.'

'It's not just that,' I say. 'There are financial implications too. You don't know if you'll be able to go back to work. Iris is going to need extra equipment, specialist schooling, stuff like that.'

'But Eric and Isobel don't have very much money,' Maggie points out. 'Even if your solicitor does manage to screw some out of them, it's not going to amount to much. Is it really worth all the stress?'

'But there's the principle as well.' I try to appeal to Maggie's sense of right and wrong but she is distracted by Iris, who begins to cry again. 'Shhh, shhh,' she says, turning to the door and raising her fingers to her lips, making a sign everyone knows, not just people who've started to read books on sign language.

'Eric and Isobel haven't been in touch. We haven't actually heard anything from them,' I remind Maggie.

I didn't tell her about the text from Isobel. It made me too angry and amounted to nothing.

'I know.' Maggie walks over to the bouncer and lifts Iris out of it. She puts her on her knee but Iris struggles to be free so she sets her down on the floor, where she seems momentarily happy to sit and chew the table leg.

'By the way, Sally called earlier,' Maggie says.

'Really?' I also hadn't told Maggie she'd tried my mobile too. 'She called here?'

'Yes.' Maggie gives me an odd look.

'What did she say?'

'She just said she was sorry we hadn't been at the party as she'd been looking forward to seeing us and finding out how we were – that sort of thing.'

'And what did you say?'

'I said we were OK and you'd call her yourself some time.'

'Is that all?'

'Well, obviously, we had a longer conversation. I told her a bit more about how Iris was. But I got the impression she wanted to talk to you, although she must have known you wouldn't be back from school. I said you would call her when you were.'

'She must have spoken to Isobel. Did she say?'

'No.'

'No, she hasn't spoken to her, or, no, she didn't say?'

'No, she didn't say, Ben.' Maggie is beginning to sound tetchy. 'She said she phoned to ask how we were. She didn't say anything about Isobel.'

'Alright.'

'If you want to know what Isobel thinks, why don't you call her yourself?' Maggie confronts me.

'I don't give a fuck what she thinks,' I say.

'Obviously you do.'

'What's that supposed to mean?'

'Nothing,' Maggie replies as Iris begins to wail.

It's a horrible, high-pitched, off-key wail. It sounds like the cry of someone who can't hear it. If they could, even though they were crying to attract the attention of their parents, to try to make them do whatever it is they want doing for them, they couldn't possibly bear to listen to it themselves. I wince, and Maggie picks Iris up and heads towards the hall.

'I'm going to take her for a walk,' she says, pulling the buggy out from its corner by the coat rack and yanking Iris's coat from it. 'Do you want to come?'

'OK.'

We can walk and talk. It might be easier that way.

'It's not that I don't want to do anything,' Maggie says as we stroll up the street. 'I'm just as angry as you are. I'm just worried that taking legal action might not be easy for you. For us. We'll get bogged down with solicitors and court action, when we need to concentrate on other things. And I'm worried that you might regret it, if you go ahead.'

'What do you mean?' I am pushing the buggy so I can't hold Maggie's hand and I wish I could. I want to feel that she is with me, even if she isn't. 'I want to shake them up, Maggie. I want to force some sort of response from them. I want them to realise that what they did was irresponsible and wrong.'

'So do I,' Maggie says, bending down to pull a blanket from the basket underneath the buggy and tucking it in around Iris. 'I'm just not sure that this is the way.'

'I can't think of any other ways. Can you?'

Maggie is silent, preoccupied with tucking.

'Can you?' I ask her again.

'They're not my friends.' Maggie looks at me, briefly, then away again. 'It's different for me.'

I'm not exactly sure what she means by this.

'When Sally called today,' she says, 'it was nice of her and everything, but she's not the person I would go to, if I needed someone to talk to. I've got my own friends. So it doesn't really matter to me what your friends think – but it might matter to you. Does it matter to you what Sally would think if you told her we were going to sue?'

'I didn't want any of this,' I say, my voice rising vehemently. 'I didn't want Iris to be deaf, obviously. I didn't want to be put in a position where I'm even considering taking legal action against two of my oldest friends. I feel so powerless. But we are in this position.'

'I know.'

'I have to do something and I can't think of anything else to do. Can you?'

Maggie says nothing.

We walk home in silence and I wonder if she does have another plan, something she's not telling me.

'It will be worse for you, Ben,' she says, finally as we near our house. 'They're your friends and you could lose them. Not just Isobel and Eric: the others will take sides. Are you prepared for that?'

I nod. 'It's not just us – ' I begin to say. I have a rant prepared, but I don't need to go on.

'OK.' Maggie bends down to unbuckle Iris. 'Tell Hedda to send the letter to start with. Let's see how they react.'

Isobel, Friday morning

It's like the aftershock from an earthquake, I imagine. You think it's stopped, that the worst is over, and then there's another quake and the ground beneath you shifts again.

I know that Eric is looking at me, but I don't know what he's thinking. Can he see that I'm freshly shocked and upset? Is he going to ask what's wrong? If I tell him, will he try to reassure me? Or will he give me the silent, accusing look, the look that says this is my fault entirely and that everyone's suffering because of it?

If I'm honest, I was beginning to get used to it – the fact that Iris is deaf, that I am partly to blame and that this was going to affect us all. For the first few days after the party, I thought about nothing else, but I actually woke up this morning and went through all the usual motions without doing so.

Then the post arrived.

I'm trying not to react visibly, not in front of the children. I'm standing by the work surface in the kitchen, away from the breakfast table, the opened letter in my hand, its contents hammering away at my mind, nudging my body to still, quiet nausea.

It's noisy in the kitchen; too noisy to think properly.

The radio is on but no one is listening to it. Vincent is playing the piano, tucked into the alcove behind the breakfast table. He's singing too, an Adele song. His unbroken nine-year-old voice hits the high notes with such an innocent clarity, it makes me want to cry.

The song is about being scarred by love. Vinnie gives it his all, oblivious to the rest of us, imbuing the word 'despair' with meaning, even though this is not an emotion he can have known in his brief life.

I am the one who feels it now.

'Nice tune, Vinnie, aka Liberace.' Harvey pushes his shopping trolley chair back from the table, gets up, and brushes against Vincent as he walks past. It could have been accidental, the body contact, but Vincent's hand abandons the chord he was playing and slaps Harvey.

'Get off!'

'Ow, that hurt!' Harvey's voice is exaggeratedly camp, clearly implying it didn't.

'Stop acting like twats,' Gabriella says, annoyed that their spat is disturbing her toast consumption.

'Harvey,' I say, and he looks at me, expecting further admonishment, but I haven't the energy or the will.

If Eric had brought the post in, he would probably have put the letter straight in the recycling. Apart from the odd bank or credit card statement, he never gets letters. Neither do I, really. Everything important is communicated by email and the rest is junk but I still open that, just in case.

The letter I am holding now gave nothing away. A DL envelope revealed my typed name and address through its cellophane window but nothing more. I'd never have guessed it was from a solicitor, nor what it contained. It took me a while to work it out. The wording is not clear. Eric would have a field day with the language, if he was minded to. But I imagine he also will be too stunned by the contents to start going on about grammar and use of words. I feel as if I've been punched in the stomach.

At last Eric reacts.

'Right, you lot.' He raises his voice so he can be heard above Vincent, who's back, rolling in the deep. 'You need to leave in five minutes. Go and get your stuff.'

Harvey goes. He was on his way anyway. Gabriella's finished her toast and is stacking her plate in the dishwasher.

131

She looks at Eric, questioningly; wanting to know if she too has to make herself scarce or is exempt, on the grounds of being older.

'Gabs...' Eric says.

She shrugs, resigned to leaving the room, but Vinnie's still singing.

'Vinnie,' Eric says.

'Mmm hmmmm?' Vince doesn't look up, but he stops playing long enough to let his dad know he's open to an instruction.

'Scoot!' Eric gives it and Vincent obligingly swivels round on the piano stool and runs upstairs to clean his teeth, still singing about his scars leaving him breathless.

'What is it?' Eric asks. 'Who's the letter from?'

'A solicitor,' I say.

'Why? Has someone died?'

I feel like saying 'a part of me', but instead I hand it over with the words, 'Your best friend's solicitor.'

I say this because this is Eric's problem too now, even if he tried to make out it wasn't before.

I also say it to test Eric's loyalties.

'You mean Ben?' Eric asks.

'Of course I do,' I say, and watch as he screws up his eyes, trying to focus without his reading glasses.

His emotions are barely perceptible as he lets the information sink in, but something about him changes. It's like watching a sand-timer, as each grain of sand slowly filters from one side to the other, hardly appearing to change, yet nevertheless effecting a complete reversal.

The sand in the timer appears to have all filtered through now, allowing other emotions to occupy the space inside Eric's head.

'Fuck,' he says, and I want to hit him because that doesn't tell me anything.

'What a fucking mess,' he says.

I already know that.

'Fuck, Isobel,' he repeats. 'It just gets worse.'

'I know,' I say, angry that he is still angry and still seemingly determined to point the finger at me. 'Why's he doing this?' I say, trying to deflect it. 'Why would Ben do this to us?'

'You don't think he has reason?' Eric asks, looking at me, accusing again.

'I know he must be furious and upset. But he knows none of this was deliberate. What good will come of getting solicitors involved?'

'But he doesn't know, does he?' Eric says. 'He doesn't know that you didn't mean to harm his child, because you haven't spoken to him. He doesn't know you're sorry, because you haven't told him.'

'Jesus Christ, Eric!' I snap. 'I can't believe you're doing this again.'

'Doing what?'

'Turning it all on me. Making it all my fault. Not being able to find one reassuring thing to say to me. Not even offering any practical advice?'

Eric looks at me. 'You haven't done anything, Isobel. For the last week, since you found out that Iris was deaf, you haven't done anything to let Ben know that you're sorry. You haven't asked if there is anything we can do.'

'I texted him. He didn't reply. I didn't know what more to do and you've not exactly helped.'

'What did you want from me?'

'You stand there accusing me of not doing anything, of not asking if there's anything we can do, of not letting him know we're sorry, but you haven't done any of that for me,' I retort. 'Have you got any real idea how terrible I feel? Have you got any idea how much I wish things were otherwise? You come and go, behaving as if I'm wholly in the wrong, when you know full well that if you felt so strongly about the kids not being vaccinated at the time you could have insisted. And you haven't done anything yourself since we found out about Iris, either.'

133

'I've been busy,' Eric says. 'I have to get the bloody train up to London and work all day in a shit job before getting it home again, while you do whatever it is that you do.'

'Is that what this is about?' I ask him. Is Eric angry with me because I never went back to work? Does he think I sit around all day at home doing nothing?

'It's about taking action, Isobel. You used to do things, but you just keep letting stuff happen. It's not about what you've done, it's about what you've not done.'

'For Christ's sake, Eric. Why don't you just drop the "everything is your fault" stance and do something yourself?'

'And what might that something be, exactly?' he asks. 'Go and see Ben myself and tell him how sorry we are that we never got round to having Gabriella vaccinated because you were worried at the time and then when all the fuss had died down you just forgot? Tell him that you're sorry Iris is deaf but during the past week you never got round to telling him that?'

'If doing nothing is the worst thing to do then, yes, you should have taken action. You can't just say it's all my fault for doing nothing, when you've done nothing yourself.'

'You put me in an impossible position,' he says, highly agitated now. 'Ben is my best friend. You are my wife. I feel for you both.'

'Do you?' I snap back. 'You haven't given any impression that you've thought about what I'm going through right now.'

'I've thought about virtually nothing else,' Eric says, slightly calmer. 'I've thought about how you must feel, and I've thought about how Ben and Maggie must feel.'

'And you think I haven't?'

'I don't know. I don't know if you really have. But if I'd been Ben and there'd been nothing from us, no real gesture, then I think I'd have been driven to do something like this.'

'Seriously?' I can't quite believe Eric is saying all of this. 'Sometimes, Eric, I don't think I know you any more.'

'Well, maybe that's because you've changed!' he says angrily. 'You used to be a fighter.'

I'm stunned by this outburst. I don't know quite how to counter it. I know I've changed, of course I do, but things are different. We have a family.

'I've changed because we have three children, Eric. I've changed because I opted to look after them myself. I don't go up to London every day and talk politics and current affairs with other like-minded people. I'm here at home with the kids, combing nits out of their hair and making sure they've done their homework. Of course I've changed, but that doesn't make me a bad person.'

'I never said that, Isobel. I'm...'

He pauses and, for a moment, I think he's about to say that's he's sorry. Instead he says, 'I'm going to be late for work. I'll talk to you later.'

'Should I call Ben today, then?' I ask, as he picks up his jacket. I'm not going to be accused of failing to take action again.

'Not yet,' Eric says. We may need to get a solicitor ourselves. We'll talk later.'

And, with that, he heads for the front door.

'Fuck them both,' I say to myself, meaning Eric and Ben. 'This is getting ridiculous.'

Ben, Friday morning

'See you later, beautiful,' I whisper, as I bend over her cot and kiss my sleeping daughter before I leave for work.

I don't need to whisper in order not to wake her but my brain is hard-wired to. It's what you do around the sleeping: lower your voice so as not to disturb them.

Iris is so peaceful when she's asleep. The contrast between sleeping and waking is greater now. Her deafness makes her fractious during her waking hours. When she's asleep, I can almost forget. I inhale her baby scent as I hover after my kiss, hoping to breathe in some of her peacefulness, because I am feeling agitated this morning as I get ready to head off to school. I keep thinking, I wonder if the letter has arrived yet. I wonder if they've read it.

And it makes me feel a bit sick, if I'm honest, that the shit is about to hit the fan. I know it's what I wanted but, still, I can imagine how I'd feel if that letter landed on my doormat. My heart would sink, my stomach would churn, I'd be fucking angry at whoever asked a solicitor to send it. I want Isobel to feel all of that. I had to go ahead and send it. I don't want her to forget.

'I'll do it today,' Hedda had replied yesterday when I saw her again. 'They should receive it first thing tomorrow morning.'

But now that it is tomorrow morning, well, my feelings are mixed.

So, although I really ought to go to work, I stare at Iris for a bit longer – to remind myself why I'm doing what I'm doing,

I suppose, or just to remind myself that I do love her, despite the deafness.

'Did you always want to have children?' Hedda had asked me in that meeting on Monday, and I'd toyed with telling her the real answer or one which might give more weight to the 'case'. I wondered if a judge would be more sympathetic if I said that I'd always wanted to have children. It would add an extra layer of pathos to our plight, if I was a man who had always wanted children but had never met the right woman and, when I finally did, the only child we were ever likely to have was damaged in a terrible way.

But I didn't always want to have children.

'Not really,' I'd told her, truthfully.

People often assume that, as I work with them, I must like children in general. But I don't. I didn't go into teaching because I always wanted to work with children; I went into teaching because I had desperately wanted to be an actor but failed in that ambition. Teaching drama, showing off in front of bunch of eleven-to-sixteen-year-olds, was a substitute. A poor substitute.

I like some of the kids, but not many of them, and I don't like children *per se*. They have to earn my grudging respect or admiration. Damian O'Flaherty, a boy in my GCSE year group – I like him because he's bright and a good actor and a bit off the wall.

'What's your English set text?' I asked him last week. I knew it was one of two books, *Of Mice and Men* or *To Kill a Mockingbird*.

'*How to Kill a Mockingbird*,' he'd replied, 'and the sequel, *How to Cook a Mockingbird*. It's a best-selling cookery book.'

'And what recipes does it include?'

It was a throwaway remark, but he took out his phone and showed me a document: 'Our list'. It was inventive. 'Owl's Liver Twist (Dickens)', I read. 'Sautéed Wings of a Dove (Henry James)', 'Pan to Fry Quails (Chaucer)?'

I laughed. 'Very funny.'

'You haven't seen the best one yet, sir,' he said, scrolling down the page and showing me 'Robins in Le Creuset'.

It took me a few moments to see what it was.

'That is brilliant. Is this what you do in your spare time?'

'Me and Emma Johnson have been working on it,' he said, shrugging as if all teenagers whiled away their hours playing literary word games.

So I liked Damian and a few others, but most of them were just grist that passed through the educational mill, teens I had to try to teach who were generally not particularly interested in what I was trying to show them.

And at the moment I'm finding the bright, engaging ones problematic too, because they embody a young adult life my daughter seems unlikely to lead. I resent them for that.

'I never really thought about it seriously, until I met Maggie,' I told Hedda on Monday.

'Go on.'

'I'd had a few previous relationships with people who wanted children, but I was sure I didn't. So they foundered.'

'Right.' She made a note.

'To be honest I was pretty sure I did *not* want to have children,' I carried on. 'When it came up before, with a couple of previous girlfriends, it became the deal-breaker, even though at the time there'd never been a deal in place.'

'What do you mean?'

'There were a couple of women I was going out with, and we weren't even planning to settle down and live together or anything, but the subject of having children came up. When I said I didn't want any, they said they didn't want to be with anyone who didn't want to have any. So the relationships ended, amicably enough. I'm sure they found people who did want kids and settled down.'

'So what made you change your mind?' Hedda asked.

'I met Maggie, for starters,' I told her, although a child had still been far from my mind when I had. Part of the attraction of Maggie, on paper, had been that I presumed she didn't want them either. She didn't say anything about it either way in the information put up by the dating agency; I just presumed because of her age – forty-three when we met – that if she had ever wanted them she was past that point.

And when we met in person the attraction was Maggie herself. She was beautiful, clever and talented, and I loved being with her. I'd been doing the dating agency thing for a while and I'd always found it a bit of strain. You have to perform to a certain extent on a first date and, even though I like performing, I don't like it when the part I'm playing is myself.

But with Maggie, even on the first date, I felt comfortable, the way I used to feel with Bel. When Bel and I first met, we were easy in each other's company. Sometimes she'd come into my room and ask if she could read while I was writing an essay, and I liked just having here there. Even if I said nothing and carried on working at my desk while she lay on the bed, I liked her being there.

But when you go on a date you have to fill the silences, and of course more often than not there are lots to fill. But with Maggie there were silences which, rather than thinking of as awkward moments, I thought of simply as breathing spaces, time to reflect on what had just been said or what might be suggested next.

She felt right to be with. She was the first person who had felt right since Isobel, so right that even before the date was finished I was saying to her, 'I'd really like to see you again – soon, if you'd like?'

'Yes,' she'd replied. 'I'd like to see you again too. Soon.'

I felt so happy when I went home that evening. And we met up again soon after, and, after that, as often as Maggie's touring schedule allowed. She went on a tour of Switzerland a few weeks after that first meeting, but we spoke on the phone every day. And I thought about her all the time. I was amazed by the fact that, after twenty-plus years of trying to find the right woman, it could all seemingly fall into place.

I was almost expecting something to go wrong: for Maggie to suddenly reveal that she thought Hitler had had a viable plan when he'd set out to create the master race or to tell me she was a convicted serial killer. But she never did. She just kept amazing me with her kindness and generosity, her humour, her talk and herself.

Then, one evening, when Maggie was just back from a few days playing in Lucerne, I had my first 'oh, shit' moment.

I'd been so looking forward to seeing her. I'd tidied my flat, been shopping, bought flowers and wine, cooked a nice meal, and she'd told me all about the concerts she'd been playing in and the concert hall in Lucerne – apparently it's one of the best in the world – and the boat trip they'd taken across the lake.

'It all sounds lovely,' I said.

'It was,' she said. 'But I missed you.'

And I leaned across the table to kiss her, not for the first time that evening, but for longer.

'Pudding?' I asked, when we broke apart.

'Let's go to bed first,' Maggie replied.

So we did. The perfect end to a perfect evening, until I removed the condom I'd used and found that the end was split – a tiny, almost imperceptible split, but a split nevertheless.

The week after Maggie's period should have come was excruciating. And the day Maggie came round to my flat for dinner, and brought with her a pregnancy test, was hellish. But the moment she came out of the bathroom and burst into tears was a bizarre relief. At least we knew now, and I didn't feel as bad as I'd thought I would. 'You want to keep it, don't you?' I asked her, just to be sure, and she nodded as she stood there, yards away from me, in floods of tears.

'I'm sorry,' she said, through them. 'But yes, I think I do.'

And that was when I knew.

I stepped over the distance between us and took my sobbing girlfriend in my arms, kissed her, held her, stroked her hair, tried to calm her, so that I could tell her.

'It's OK, Maggie. I do too. We'll have this baby together.'

'You don't have to,' she said, pulling away slightly so that I could see her beautiful face, streaked with tears. 'I know we haven't known each other that long. I know you never wanted children. I know this isn't what you wanted.'

'It wasn't, no,' I told her truthfully. 'But it is now.'

And that was true too. If Maggie hadn't wanted to have the baby then, sure, part of me would have been relieved, but I'd have wondered, too, what it would have been like, this child of mine. And now I knew that this woman, with whom I felt more at home than I had with anyone for years, was carrying my child, I wanted to know what it would be like. I was filled with a sudden strange sense of certainty and purpose. I was going to have a baby.

'I want to have this baby, Maggie,' I told her again and again. 'I want to be with you and we're going to have a baby together. Everything will be all right. I promise.'

And, for a while, I was right.

'When Iris was born,' I said to Hedda – and had to pause because I found myself becoming slightly tearful remembering the moment.

'Go on, please.' There was something about the way Hedda said 'please' that invited me to try to tell her exactly what I'd felt.

'It was like every good emotion I'd ever felt in my life, all rolled into one. I hadn't expected it, either. I'd thought it would take me a while to love the baby. I knew that I would but initially, when it was just a baby, I wasn't sure. But as soon as I set eyes on her I was completely overwhelmed with love. She was just the most perfect thing I had ever seen. I didn't want anything to change that.'

I stopped because I knew if I went on I would start to cry.

Hedda said nothing. She too, I found, could make a silence seem like a breathing space.

'But it did, didn't it?' I said, with an edge to my voice, a harshness that made Hedda shake her head and look away.

Isobel, Friday, later

Vincent's beaming face has been the only thing that's cheered me today.

'Are you helping with the slow readers?' he asked excitedly when Eric left to catch his train to London, his parting shot being, 'You'd better look into finding a solicitor.'

'I'm in Vinnie's class this morning,' I'd replied, and Eric had said nothing. But Vincent's clear excitement at the prospect of my helping made me feel loved.

Vincent has what the school calls 'additional literacy needs'. They make every effort to ensure no one feels they are less able than anyone else. The different sets are graded by shapes rather than ability. There are Squares, Diamonds, Rectangles, Triangles, Ovals and Circles: groups into which the children are divided by ability, but labelled so as to make them think it has nothing to do with that. But they all know which groups are which. Some of these children may not read as well as others, or barely at all, but they are not stupid. Vincent knows that the Squares and Diamonds hardly need to pause for thought to grasp the meaning of the words on the page, that they can read adult books by themselves and extrapolate information from the history sheets the teacher hands out. And he is well aware of the fact that words, to him, appear a strange mishmash of shapes, making him a 'slow reader'.

When you add in his strange synaesthetic tendencies, you begin to wonder what he does see on the page. ' "Laugh" is such a muddy word,' he said to me this morning, making me laugh myself.

When they first began to emerge, Vincent's reading problems were a cause of tension between Eric and me. I wanted to find a reason.

'I think he might be dyslexic,' I said to Eric one evening after sitting on his bed reading *The Very Hungry Caterpillar* for the umpteenth time, knowing that when I asked him what the caterpillar ate and he said 'apple' it was the picture not the A-P-P-L-E that dictated his answer.

'He's not dyslexic. It's just taking him a bit longer than average to get there,' Eric replied. Eric read with him too. He was aware of the problems Vincent was having, but less concerned about them.

'I think we should take him to see someone.'

'We've spoken to his teacher about it, Bel. It's not uncommon for boys of his age to be a bit slower to grasp the concept, but he will get there in the end.'

'But what if we could get him extra help and get him there quicker?'

'By sticking a label on him for the rest of his life? How is that helpful? Vincent is a bright kid, we know that. He's starting to read, albeit slowly. He's getting extra help and the teachers don't think he is dyslexic.'

'But what if they just haven't realised?'

'They know the signs. They're trained to look for them,' Eric insisted.

'But if we took him to see someone we'd know for sure.' I wanted there to be a reason why Vincent couldn't read as well as Gabs and Harvey. We read to them all in bed every night. I'd read to Gabs as soon as she was old enough and carried on until she began reading for herself, while Eric read to Harvey in his room. Then I started reading to Vincent, but for some reason he was slow to grasp the skill himself.

But Eric and the teacher were right. He's getting there now.

'You know how Paddy says "laff" not "larf"?' Vincent asks, as I sit in his circle of Circles. I have just pointed to the word and didn't expect any of them to recognise it instantly. I'm amazed that Vinnie was the first to do so.

'Yes, he does. It's his northern accent.'

'It actually looks more like "laff",' he goes on. 'The A and the U like that. It should be "laff" not "larf".'

I am so pleased with his progress that I forget about the letter, until I go to the staff room and notice a copy of the local paper lying on the coffee table. I can't bring myself to pick it up. I can glean enough from the headline: 'Boy, 15, Dies of Measles', and underneath a picture of a teenage boy in school uniform. It isn't a uniform I recognise but this is the local paper, so the boy must be from somewhere hereabouts.

And then I see one of the classroom assistants, catching me looking at the headline, and I look away because I don't want to be drawn into conversation. But it's too late. 'Didn't your eldest have measles?' she asks, her tone critical.

'While we were on holiday,' I say, as if this somehow mitigates the circumstances. In fact it made them worse.

'Yes, I heard,' she says, and I wonder who she heard from. 'It's terrible, isn't it?' I think she is talking about me, I think she is saying that I am terrible for letting it happen, but I realise she is nodding towards the newspaper.

'Yes. It's awful,' I agree.

'It's probably not the first and it probably won't be the last,' she says, and repeats, 'It's really terrible.'

I make my excuses and leave, her criticism ringing in my ears, even though it is unspoken.

The local swimming baths are not far from the school and I usually spend an hour or so doing laps, between finishing helping in Vinnie's class and picking him up after school. When I'm standing in the shower afterwards I hear my name said, tentatively, as if the speaker is not sure it's me.

'Isobel?'

'Hannah?' I know it's her: my questioning tone is surprise, because I haven't seen her for years. I didn't even think she lived in Brighton any more.

'How bizarre, I was just thinking about you,' she says.

'Were you?' It's a bizarre-enough encounter anyway.

If we'd met in the street, we probably would have kissed, but here in the showers, with Hannah covered in shampoo, we just stick our heads out slightly from under the flow of water and talk.

'I thought you'd gone away.'

'We did,' Hannah tells me. 'We've been living in Spain. We've only been back a few weeks.'

'And already you're back in the swim of things.' The pun is unintended, but it was in this pool that I'd first met Hannah, when Gabby and Hannah's daughter Rosa were just a few months old. We were both part of a group that regularly attended baby swimming classes. And by a part I don't just mean I went and met them at the pool and took our children to the class together; I mean I felt I belonged to that group of women.

At the time, I was no longer part of the team at work, no longer part of the throng of people who got up early every morning, took the tube to work and spent all day doing a job. I needed to be part of something else. And that was what I became part of – a baby swimming group.

The classes were held in the baby pool. It was heated to temperatures so warm it felt like getting into a bath and, for the babies, back into the womb. In it they seemed utterly content to be swished and swirled around the water, to be splashed and even to be dunked right under, before happily being lifted back to the surface.

'Babies don't fear the water until they're older,' the teacher said, and she was right. Gabriella had seemed more contented in the water than anywhere. It was one of the few places I'd felt truly relaxed with her, in those early days.

The other women became my colleagues, the people I worked with at being a mother. And they were women who, like myself, were determined to 'work' at it. These women had all had good jobs. Now they were determined to apply their high standards of efficiency to raising their children. They were women who persisted with breastfeeding even if their nipples were cracked and bleeding and it caused them physical pain. These were women who pureed organic carrots at midnight rather than pollute their babies' tiny bodies with chemicals they might encounter in a jar. These were women who read about and researched every latest trend or notion in child-rearing, discussed it among themselves in the changing rooms, and believed the opinions they formed were generally right – especially Hannah. I didn't think to question any of this. Nor did any of these other highly intelligent, reasoned and reasoning women, because we all wanted to belong.

Hannah had also believed that vaccinations were unnecessary – all of them: the risks outweighed the benefits; they were to blame for the rise in asthma and allergies; they were actually harmful to a child's immune system;, they were in fact a government conspiracy to coerce mothers in a way I was not entirely clear about. When the MMR scare had started, it had seemed to give weight to her view.

'Do you fancy a coffee when you're dressed?' I ask Hannah now, picking up my goggles and shampoo from the floor before heading for the changing cubicles.

'Sure, it would be great to catch up. But I can't be too long. I need to be home by three-thirty.'

'That's fine,' I say, and feel almost happy as I towel myself dry and dress. If anyone is sympathetic to the situation I find myself in now, it will be Hannah.

'Jesus, that's awful. You must feel terrible,' she says, as we sip a drink the dispenser claims is coffee from plastic cups, at a table overlooking the pool. 'I mean, that's just so unlucky.'

'It's not, though, is it?' I say to her. 'It's not just bad luck. It is because we didn't have our kids vaccinated. It could have happened to any of us.'

'Oh, I did have mine done,' she says, breezily, as if she's forgotten that she was the one who expressed the strongest views against it.

I'm completely taken aback. 'When?' I ask.

'Before we went to Spain,' she says, smiling. 'We did a bit of travelling in Africa first so we gave them the lot. They still have a lot of measles in Africa. Kids die of it. It's terrible.'

'Really?' I am annoyed now and can't think of anything else to say. Hannah had been so adamant that it was unnecessary.

'Yes.' She sounds almost smug. 'It had all blown over by then anyway, the MMR thing. It would have been daft not to.'

I want to knock my cup of coffee over and let it spill on her lap. How can she sit there, so calmly, and lecture me on the stupidity of not vaccinating my own children, when she was the person who'd made me feel I shouldn't in the first place?

But of course she's right. I was stupid. I didn't have to go along with what she thought just because I wanted to be part of the group.

'I have to go now,' I say, nursing my injured pride. 'I've got to pick my son up from school.'

On my way I call Sally. I'm still livid with Hannah and even more so with Ben. The more I think about it, the more extreme his action seems.

'Fuck,' Sally echoes what Eric said earlier. 'I can't believe it. What are you going to do?'

'I don't know, Sally. The letter only came this morning. We haven't really had much time to think about it.'

'What does Eric think?'

'I don't know,' I repeat. 'Whenever I try to talk to him he just keeps going on and on about my not having had the kids vaccinated in the first place. He won't move on. I'm beginning to hate him for it. '

'He must feel bad, Bel. Ben is his best friend. You know what Eric's like.'

'I thought I did, but I'm beginning to wonder. He's usually more practical. He can usually see both sides too, but he just seems to be putting all the blame on me. Even when we got the letter, it seemed to be me he was angry with, not Ben.'

'It must have been a hell of shock to find out he's planning to sue. I feel a bit sick myself.'

'Of course it was. He's Eric's oldest friend. I don't think they've ever fallen out over anything. But I just don't get what Ben thinks he's playing at. I mean, why didn't he speak to us first?'

'Did you call him?'

'No,' I admit. 'I was sort of waiting for him to get in touch. I did text him and he never replied.'

'And you didn't call Maggie either?'

'No,' I say. 'Do you think she put Ben up to this?'

'I don't know,' Sally says. 'It doesn't really seem the sort of thing either of them would do.'

'I just don't get it.'

'It's hard.'

'It's impossible, Sally. I mean, of course now I wish I'd done lots of things differently. But it's not as if any of this was deliberate. Everyone is behaving as if it is.'

'Everyone?' Sally asked.

'Well, people. I had a bit of a run-in in the staff room this morning too.'

'What sort of run-in?'

'Nothing really. Just a pointed comment. And then I met this woman who...' This was a longer conversation than I had time for. 'Well, it doesn't matter. It just seems that everyone I try to talk to thinks it's all my fault, and I really don't know what to do.'

'Maybe you should speak to Yasmin?' Sally suggests. 'You could ask her advice. I mean, I know it would be better if you could sort it out between yourselves, but if they've already got a solicitor and they've started proceedings maybe you need to talk to someone too?'

'I suppose I could,' I say.

'It might help you. If you spoke to Yasmin, she might at least be able to give you a clearer idea of the legal position.'

'Mmm – I could give her call at home. Although she'll be tied up with Conrad.'

'You don't sound sure.' Sally picks up on my hesitancy.

'It's just that...' I begin.

'What?' Sally asks.

But I don't answer because I am not quite sure what the answer is. Perhaps I was being oversensitive, but at the party, when I found out, when Yasmin took me up to the bathroom, she didn't say anything, so maybe that's it: I'm not sure that she will sympathise with me, so I'm nervous of asking for her help.

'It doesn't matter, Sally,' I reply, trying to sound a bit brighter. 'I'd better go now. I'm just about to pick up Vincent.'

'OK,' Sally says. 'But if you need to talk...'

'Thank you,' I say, as I hang up.

Ben, Friday, later

I check my watch in the middle of a lesson and think, they must have read the letter by now.

Funny how one thing replaces another in your thoughts. I can't stop thinking about the legal action now, and that means I think a bit less about Iris being deaf.

I wonder how long it will take them to respond to the letter. 'We'll follow it up if we don't get a response within a week,' Hedda had said to me.

It seems too long. I want an immediate reply.

I'd been through the timings of everything with Hedda in her office. 'Let me just go through this again,' she'd said, even though she'd written everything down and questioned me, as we went along. She is nothing if not thorough. 'It is very important if the case is to be successful.'

I nodded.

'Are you absolutely sure that Isobel Blake had knowledge that her daughter was infectious when she left her with your wife and baby at the holiday house in France?'

I nodded again.

'You are certain?' she pressed me.

'Yes,' I tell her. 'I am certain.'

I didn't realise it at the time, but when we started piecing the events together afterwards we knew she must have known.

'And she did warn you that there might be a risk to your child of having prolonged contact with her daughter?'

I shook my head this time.

'Mr Deakin?' Hedda asks, and I realise she needs me to say it.

'She never said anything at the time. When she came back from the doctor and he had confirmed that Gabriella had measles she told Maggie that she'd known there was a lot of it about. She knew some of Gabby's schoolfriends had been ill and she knew that she had spent time with them, especially with Sam, her boyfriend – a great deal of time – before they went away.'

'So you think she knew that her daughter's first symptoms of illness were measles?'

'If she didn't know for sure, she must have had a pretty good idea. Isobel is not stupid, far from it. She knew the symptoms, she knew Gabby had had contact with people who had the disease, and she knew she hadn't been vaccinated. She must have known that it was the most likely cause of Gabriella's illness.'

'So when she asked if she could leave her daughter, who was too ill to go on this outing, with your wife and daughter, you are certain she knew she was putting your child at risk of catching this highly infectious disease?'

'She knew. She must have known,' I said, and then to myself, because I didn't want Hedda to write it down, *but she never fucking mentioned it*. Not until she came back from the doctor with Gabriella the following day.

I had felt a bit more relaxed when Isobel took Gabby off to the doctor. Her fussing over the kids, not just Gabs when she started to get ill but all of them generally, was beginning to get to me.

I'd taken a brioche out of the bread bin a few days beforehand, only to be asked by Isobel to put it back.

'Ben, would you mind leaving that? Harvey hasn't had anything to eat yet and he can't eat croissants, as they are more likely to have come into contact with nuts.'

I had felt like contesting both these statements. A, Harvey was sitting at the table with a half-eaten bowl of cereal in front of him and it wasn't Goldilocks who'd been at it, and B, I was fairly certain that croissants were no more likely to have come into contact with nuts than brioche rolls.

What Isobel meant was that Harvey didn't really like croissants, and as there was only one brioche roll left but plenty of the former she thought it perfectly reasonable that it should be set aside for her precious son, rather than eaten by me. But she'd never have said outright, 'Could you not eat that because they are Harvey's favourites and that's the last one, so I'd rather he have it than you!'

And she'd been doing her ridiculously even-handed routine with the boys just before that. Harvey and Vince had both drawn a picture and wanted to know which was best. I reckoned Vincent's was definitely the best but, rather than just saying this, she had pointed out the various merits of both drawings. Which wasn't good enough for either of them.

Vincent had picked up a cereal packet from the table. 'Let's make a sunflower out of cereal and see which is the best!'

I'd laughed because Harvey had only just told him his picture looked like a potato and he'd retorted, 'My teacher says the artist who went mad and cut off his ear painted people to look like potatoes.'

'Van Gogh,' Isobel had said.

Clearly Vincent was warming to a theme – or would have if the removal of the cereal packet had not sent Conrad, who'd been sitting there staring at it, apparently oblivious to anyone else in the room, into a crazy disturbed fit. He let out this horrendous scream, threw himself from his chair on to the floor and began crying. Suddenly this huge sixteen-year-old boy was lying on the floor, hammering it with his fists and sobbing like a toddler.

It was disturbing to watch.

My first thoughts were ones of sympathy, for Yasmin who had to try to calm him, and for Conrad himself. What must it be like to be him? I wondered. What demented world did he inhabit, that things like that caused him such distress?

Iris was still upstairs in our room with Maggie at the time, so any disturbance the scene might have caused her didn't really come into it. Vincent, though, was visibly shocked and upset. 'Sorry, sorry. I'm sorry,' he said, putting the cereal packet back. But it was too late. The damage was done.

'Yes, sorry,' Isobel said. But she didn't look sorry, and I don't think she was. I think she was pissed off that Yasmin's crazy son had upset her sane ones.

So I was glad she'd had to take Gabriella to the doctor.

Maggie and I were lying by the pool. Iris was in her inflatable boat under a sunshade and we could see the boys and Conrad's younger sister Mira a little way away, attempting to climb a tree, probably relishing their mother's absence too. There was no one to spoil their fun by saying 'Be careful', 'Don't go too high', 'I think you should come back down now'.

Conrad was in his room and Yasmin had earlier dragged a sun-lounger away from the pool to a quieter part of the garden, where she was reading. Perhaps everyone wanted time to themselves.

'I'm going to take a walk down to the lake.' Eric emerged from the kitchen where Paddy and Sally were still seated at the table, sharing a quiet cup of coffee. As the hosts they were the ones doing the lion's share of interacting. They didn't seem to mind, but, as I turned my head lazily in the heat and caught sight of them sitting quietly, I reckoned even they too had probably had enough bonhomie for a while and wanted to stay where they were, not talking or doing, just being.

Eric paused close to where we were lying. His sentence had been a statement, but his hesitancy in setting off suggested a question.

'Enjoy,' I said, freeing him from whatever obligation he felt to ask if we wanted to join him.

He glanced briefly at the boys but said nothing and left. 'Peace at last,' I said when he was out of earshot.

'Is it starting to get to you?' Maggie asked, as she lay on her lounger trailing one hand lazily in the shallow water of Iris's boat, engaging with her in the most languid way possible.

'A bit.' I reached out my hand and took her free one, holding it across the space between us. 'You?'

'I'm OK,' Maggie said, squeezing my hand. 'It's nice to have a bit of time on our own, though. I might take Iris for a swim.'

Iris loved the water, but she got a bit overwhelmed when the pool was crowded. It was a reasonable size, but the weather was so hot, and there were so many of us staying, that it filled up quickly.

'I'll come too,' I said, sitting up and scanning the boys and Mira in the distance. I imagined it wouldn't be long before they got hot and came back to cool down.

'Hey, Iris, shall we go for a proper swim now?' Maggie bent down to our splashing daughter.

'Ba.' Iris splashed in response and Maggie scooped her out of her inch of water and carried her to the steps of the pool.

I followed, but we'd hardly been there two minutes when the boys and Mira ran over, hot, covered in bark and grime, and jumped into the pool. Harvey began thrashing up the pool, doing a sort of clumsy butterfly, a stroke far too strenuous to be named after an insect that flutters so unobtrusively. He was making huge waves, dislodging the water so it splashed over Iris's face and she began to cry.

'Boys!' I adopted my teacher's tone. 'A bit less boisterous. You nearly landed on Iris.'

'Sorry, Ben,' all three chorused at once, but the energy they brought to the pool was still making the water choppy.

'Just calm down a bit!' I raised my voice again, enjoying being able to tell them off in Isobel's absence. I'd lobbed a few gentle 'keep the splashing down' remarks in the boys' direction before, in their mother's presence, and heard her muttering,

'It's a holiday,' as if I had no right to say anything that might spoil their fun.

'Sorry,' they chorused again.

'Shall we go to the lake?' Harvey showed his displeasure at being told off by suggesting they remove themselves from the presence of one irritating adult. 'We can swim later.'

'Good idea.' Mira shot me a look as they clambered out over the side and ran towards the path which led to the lake, bumping into Eric as he returned from his walk. There was a brief exchange between them and Eric approached us by the pool just as a car crunched on the gravel to the side of the house and the sound of doors clunking told us that Anton, Isobel and Gabriella were back.

Eric went to greet them. 'How is she?' I heard him say, but couldn't catch whatever it was Isobel was saying in more hushed tones.

I watched them walk round the side of the house and go in, and a few moments later I could hear their voices coming from the direction of the bedroom they shared with Gabriella. They were raised, as if arguing, but I couldn't catch what they were saying.

It was later, a little while after Maggie had gone into the house with Iris to get changed out of their wet swimming things and I went to find what was keeping her, that I found out what it was.

Isobel, Friday afternoon

'Do you want something to eat, love?' I ask Gabs, who is just in from school. 'I got some scones from the baker earlier.'

I bought them as a peace offering but Gabby rejects it.

'I'll get something,' she says, opening the bread bin and taking out a stale loaf. She cuts herself a slice, defiantly.

Vincent is eating slices of apple with chocolate spread. It's the only way I can get him to eat fruit. 'How was school today, Vinnie?' she asks.

'Yellowish,' he says, licking his finger clean of chocolate spread. 'Mum came in to help.'

'Right.' She closes the bread bin again. 'And what are you going to do now?'

'Nothing,' Vincent says cheerily.

Gabriella seems to think he needs pointing in the right direction. 'Do you want to borrow my ukulele?'

Vincent's been teaching himself to play, and sometimes the instrument walking from her room is a source of tension. But today she seems keen for him to go and take it.

'Maybe,' he says, getting up. 'Thanks.'

'It's under my desk,' Gabs tells him, as he leaves the room. Then she asks me, 'What's going on?'

'What do you mean?'

'The letter you got this morning. Obviously there was something in it. What was it about?'

'Well, it was...' Gabs has taken me by surprise. 'It was...'

'What?'

156

'I need to talk to Dad about it first,' I try.

'Was it from Ben?' she asks, more attuned to the momentum of the past week than I realise.

'No, not exactly?'

'What does that mean?' she says sulkily. 'If it wasn't from Ben, who was it from?'

'I'll tell you later. I just need to talk to Dad first.'

'Why am I always the last to know anything?' she demands, starting to get agitated. 'You never tell me anything! I have a right to know. I know from the way you're behaving that it's got something to do with Ben and Iris. Maybe you should tell me. Maybe I could do something. Maybe if you'd thought to tell me I'd never been immunised I could have done something about it.'

'It wasn't your decision – '

'Why not? You could have at least told me and let me do what I thought best when I was older. People talk about it at school, you know. Other kids know they've not had jabs. First I know of it is when that French doctor turns round and tells me I've got the fucking *rougeole*.'

'Gabs, don't speak to me like that – ' I begin, but she's already leaving the room and heading up to her bedroom, just as Harvey comes in from school.

'Hi,' he says, looking chirpy.

'Hi, love. How was football?' I ask.

'Yep. Good. I'm starving.'

'There's scones,' I offer.

'Great.' Harvey enthuses where Gabriella had scorned the offering. He plonks himself down at the table, clearly expecting me to get them for him. I oblige, tired of Gabriella making me feel as if I have failed her; I can at least keep Harvey happy by feeding him.

Eric was furious when we came back from the doctor in Biscarrosse. 'I told you at the time that it was irresponsible but you wouldn't listen.' His voice was raised. 'Jesus. I might have known something like this was going to happen.'

We were in our bedroom and Gabs had gone back to bed.

'Keep your voice down, Gabs is trying to sleep,' I said, but I was more worried about the open window and Ben and Maggie, who were by the pool, being able to hear us.

It hadn't taken long for the French doctor to pronounce that the cause of Gabriella's illness was '*la rougeole*'. My French isn't good, but it's good enough to know that sounded red and rashy. 'Measles,' he'd confirmed.

'Measles?' Gabby had asked. 'How come I've got measles?' She'd sunk down in her chair in torpor, breathing heavily.

'You must have caught it from Sam,' I'd told her, gently, but I knew that was not what she was asking.

'What else did the doctor say?' Eric asked. 'Is she going to be OK?'

'Yes, he just said she needs paracetamol to ease the temperature and something for the cough but otherwise just to let it take its course.'

'And how long is that?'

'Possibly around two weeks, as long as there are no complications,' I said.

'Well, let's hope there aren't, for your sake.'

'That's not fair, Eric. Don't you think I feel bad enough already? Don't you think, seeing how ill Gabby is now, that I wish I'd done things differently? It doesn't help, you rubbing it in.'

'What about the boys?' Eric asked, quieter but not exactly contrite.

'He said they may have picked it up from Gabby already,' I told him, 'but that we could take them in for jabs anyway if we wanted, although it will take a few days for immunity to kick in.'

'I'll do that this afternoon, then,' Eric said, clearly needing to distance himself from my decision and show he was the one who did the sensible thing.

'They might be OK,' I said, hopefully. 'They've spent so much time outside. They've hardly been in contact with Gabriella.'

This was true. The house was big, but with all of us it was splitting slightly at the seams and, rather than sleep on our bedroom floor, the boys had opted to sleep in the summerhouse at the bottom of the garden. I suspect it was this physical separation from Gabby when she was most infectious that stopped them getting ill.

'But Iris has.' Eric put into words what I already knew, what was worrying me almost as much as the state Gabriella was in. 'Gabs spent the whole day with her when we all went to the dune.'

'I know that.'

And I already knew, even before the doctor asked if she'd had contact with any 'vulnerable groups', that babies were more vulnerable to the disease and that Iris was too young to have been vaccinated herself yet.

'You have to tell Maggie,' Eric said, laying the responsibility on me once more.

And Maggie was just as angry as Eric when I told her.

There was a bit of awkwardness, anyway, when I knocked on the door of her room. I think she must have expected me to be Ben and she came to the door only half dressed, wearing her knickers and holding a T-shirt up to her chest. 'Sorry,' I said, catching her embarrassment. 'I just needed a word.'

'OK, you'd better come in, then,' Maggie said, but she looked uncomfortable.

'Shall I wait out here for a minute?'

'No, it's OK.' She turned away from me and slipped the T-shirt over her head as she walked back towards Iris, who was on the bed, and took a pair of shorts off the end. 'We were just getting changed,' she said, stating the obvious as she slipped them on.

Really there was nothing for either of us to be embarrassed about. But I think we both felt it. I was curious in the way

159

you are sometimes when you catch another woman naked, especially if it's a woman who is sleeping with a man you once slept with.

So we weren't exactly off to a good start, and the exchange didn't get any easier.

Iris was sitting on the bed, wrapped in a hooded towel, smiling and 'chatting'. 'Ba ba ba ba,' she was saying. And then she added some of those other incidental sounds that babies that age make, which so perfectly mimic the way people speak that it almost sounds as if they really are talking, just not in a language that anyone but them understands. Although their mothers pretend that they do, and in a way they do, intuitively. They get the gist, as you do when you have a few words of French and the person you are speaking to is well disposed towards you.

'Do you want to sit down?' Maggie moved a pile of Ben's discarded clothes from a chair so I could sit somewhere other than on the bed with the two of them. I'd already disturbed the intimacy of the moment. I don't suppose she wanted me intruding on it any further than the chair by the dressing table.

'Thank you.' I sat, as invited.

'Baaa, baaa.' Iris was all smiles.

'Oh, you do, do you?' Maggie was too.

'I love the way they sound as if they're talking, before they actually do.' I was acutely aware how peripheral I was to the scene.

Iris began another unintelligible monologue and we both laughed.

'I'm sure it makes sense to her.' Maggie appeared to relax a little.

'I'm sure. She probably thinks it's us who are talking nonsense.'

'Which most of us do most of the time.'

Because I was hypersensitive to the news I was about to deliver, I wondered if Maggie was having a go at me.

'It's all part of them learning to speak...' I began, but I could hear myself sounding too like the expert mother, adopting the tone which Eric had pointed out made me sound as if I was undermining Maggie.

'How did you get on at the doctor's?' Maggie asked.

'Well, the thing is...' I stalled and then began to gabble. 'Apparently there's quite a lot of it around at the moment. Here, in the area, and at home as well. One or two friends of Gabriella's from school have had it. So she's been exposed quite a bit...'

'To what?' Maggie brought me to the point.

'Measles. The doctor says she has measles.'

'Poor Gabby,' Maggie said slowly, as if she was saying what she thought she ought to say first, while at the same time allowing the implications for her, for Iris, to sink in slowly. 'No wonder she's been feeling so poorly.'

'Ba ba?' Iris appeared to be questioning her mother's visible change of spirit.

'I kno-ow.'

Maggie picked her up now, drew the towel tighter around her and held her, protectively, while she spoke to me. 'It's highly contagious, Isobel.'

'I know that, unless you've been immunised. Has Iris?' But I knew she was too young; the jab was routinely offered at thirteen months. But some people did have it earlier, sometimes, if they were travelling somewhere where they might encounter the disease...?

I was clutching at mental straws.

'No!' Maggie's voice rose and then she lowered it, as Iris twisted round to look at her, alarmed by the hint of anger in the word. 'And presumably neither has Gabriella!'

'No.' I shook my head.

I should have kept quiet and simply apologised for putting Iris at risk. I should have made it clear then how bad I felt. I should have told her that Eric would drive her to the doctor in Biscarrosse, as he was planning to take the boys.

I could have said almost anything and it would have been better than what I did say.

'Often they have antibodies from the mother to ward things off in the first year, especially if...' I realised, as soon as I got near the end of the sentence, that I could not finish it without adding insult to injury.

Maggie finished it for me. 'If they've been breastfed? Is that what you were going to say, Isobel? Jesus fucking Christ.'

I'd never heard Maggie get angry before, not even the odd snappy word spoken to Ben, the way people do, not unkindly, just the way they take out their irritations with the world on the people they love most.

'I'm sorry. I'm really sorry, Maggie.'

'You must have known all along that that was what was making her ill. You must have had an idea. If you knew some of her schoolfriends had had it and you knew she wasn't protected, why didn't you say something? Why didn't you take her to the doctor sooner? Why didn't you warn me? You knew yesterday that she probably had measles and you left her here with me, let her play with Iris knowing how infectious it is, knowing Iris would get ill.'

'I'm sorry. I didn't think.'

'No, you didn't. Jesus Christ, Isobel, what were you thinking? You're an intelligent woman. It's a serious disease.'

'Not always. I know lots of people who had it as kids.'

Iris had started crying now, clearly distressed by the argument playing out in front of her. I said nothing more and Maggie took a deep breath, as if to calm herself so she could deal with her crying child. 'I know, sweetheart. I know.' She began rocking Iris slightly, focusing on her, looking up at me only to say, 'I want you to leave now.'

Reliving this scene, I wonder, not for the first time, whether Maggie is behind the solicitor's letter. It just seems too out of character to have come from Ben. I mean, no matter how angry he's been with me in the past, we've always come to terms with the way things are between us.

But Maggie has never really seemed to like me, and it's nothing to her if we fall out. I can't believe Ben would risk losing either of us, even after what's happened.

'Can I sit down?' I ask Gabriella now, and even with my own daughter I feel a bit apprehensive about sitting on the edge of her bed with her.

'So what's going on?' Gabs sits on the end and pushes herself as far back into the wall as she can. She couldn't create any more distance between us unless she went through the wall. Her position speaks volumes. I am not quite sure what to say.

'The thing is,' I begin, 'the letter this morning...'

'Yes?'

'Well, I haven't talked it through with Dad properly yet and I need to do that, and we need to find out a bit more, so, if I tell you, do you think you can not talk to anyone else about it, until I have?'

'That depends,' Gabs says.

'Gabs, please. You're right to be worried about it. That's why I've come up to talk to you. But I don't want to worry the boys, not yet, not if I don't have to. The fewer people that know what's going on, the better.'

'What is going on, then?'

Gabriella looks at me and I take a deep breath.

'The letter was from a solicitor,' I tell her. 'A solicitor who's acting on behalf of Ben and Maggie. They want to sue us for, well...'

I stop speaking because I realise I have to be very careful how I phrase this. I don't want Gabriella to feel she is in any way to blame, but I know she feels responsible.

'Because Iris is deaf,' I tell her. 'They want us to help pay for some of the costs they might incur from things like special equipment, schooling, that sort of thing. That's what the letter was about.'

'But why don't they just ask us?' Gabby asks. 'How much money do they need?'

'I don't know yet,' I tell her. 'And I don't know why they've gone to a solicitor, either.'

'What are you going to do?' Gabriella asks.

Same old question, for which I have the same old answer.

'I don't know,' I say, and I can tell from the way she looks at me that, once more, I've not given her a satisfactory reply. 'We might have to speak to a solicitor. But we'll try and talk to Ben first. I'm sure we can sort this mess out among ourselves.'

I try to reassure her, but I'm not so sure myself.

WEEK TWO

Ben, Saturday morning

'Couldn't you just switch your phone off today?' Maggie says irritably. She has invited friends for lunch. One of her colleagues – maybe a former colleague, if she can't go back to work. She thought it would distract us, when she asked Lola and her husband and child, but now, after a disturbed night, after a disturbed week, I think she wishes she hadn't.

'Sorry.' I put my phone in my pocket.

It's still on and I will keep checking it. I'll try to pretend it's just another Saturday, if that's what Maggie wants. But it isn't. It's beginning to feel a bit like last Saturday.

They must have got the letter by now, and I want a reaction. Just like last week, when I knew that Isobel and Eric would find out Iris is deaf, and was expecting to hear from them.

'What time are Lola and Joe coming? What can I do to help?'

'They said about one. They'll have George with them too. I've got some fish to cook for lunch. I wonder if I should get some fish fingers or something for him, just in case he doesn't like it?'

'Do you want me to go and get some?' I am compliant. 'I could take Iris with me. Maybe we could go to the park for a bit on the way home, while you start on lunch, unless you want me to stick around and help.'

'No.' Maggie softens. 'It would be good if you could take Iris down to the shops. And maybe you could pick up some more wine on the way back?'

'Sure,' I say.

We haven't seen anyone for a while. Plenty of wine is a good idea. We need to have some fun. I know I'm not exactly relaxed at the moment. We don't want our friends to walk into a house of gloom and anxiety.

Isobel was different the first time I went to see them, after Gabriella was born. I expected her to be preoccupied with the baby, tired, all those things, but essentially the same Isobel. She wasn't.

She was pissed off with me for starters, for not having visited sooner. Gabs was about six months old when I did. I'd sent a card and flowers and I'd phoned Eric and congratulated him. But I hadn't actually been to see them, hadn't actually set eyes on the baby.

I hadn't realised it was a big deal. I was busy at the time. I had two jobs, one as a barman at a pub in Soho, and a shit job doing market research on Oxford Street; and an agent who got me auditions for parts I never got.

I had no idea that while I was getting on with my life I was also building up the impression in Isobel's head that I was snubbing her, not until Eric called.

'Are you planning to come and see us, ever?' he asked and it was the 'ever' which suggested pique. In it was an indication that I had been remiss in not visiting them before, and I'd better get my ass down to Brighton and take a look at this bloody baby.

So I arranged to go down on a Saturday.

I was invited for lunch, but when I arrived Bel was still in her dressing gown, sitting on the sofa feeding the baby, and lunch was clearly a long way from even being thought about, let alone served.

Eric let me in and I have to hold my hands up to finding it all strange, them being parents – not least the spectacle (yes, I know 'spectacle' is not the PC way of describing it but that's what I felt at the time) of Isobel beckoning me over to the sofa, where she was stranded, unable to get up because the baby, which was much bigger than I anticipated, was stuck to her breast.

I know now this sounds immature, male, not very 'new man', but it made me feel uncomfortable seeing women breastfeeding, especially when the woman was Isobel. Her dressing gown was open and her breast was so exposed it was difficult – well, difficult for me anyway – not be slightly transfixed by it. To make matters worse, when I bent down to kiss Bel, the baby stopped sucking and turned to look at me.

So, just as I bent down, to kiss Bel, I was suddenly face to face with her nipple, which was larger, darker and more erect than the last time I'd been been so close to it.

'What do you think of her?' Isobel asked.

'She's beautiful,' I said, unsure what else to say.

'Do you want a drink?' Eric offered, and I was grateful for the diversion.

'I could do with a coffee,' I said, imagining this was a fairly simple request.

'I'm afraid we're out of coffee,' Eric replied, and he and Isobel exchanged a look. 'Tea?'

'Great.'

'I'll make it, and then I'll just pop to the shops to get a few things.'

'And, when she's finished feeding, would you mind keeping an eye on Gabs while I have a shower and get dressed?' Isobel asked.

'Sure,' I said, although I didn't feel at all sure.

Eric came back with a cuppa and soon after that I was left literally holding the baby while he went out to buy lunch and Bel got herself washed and dressed. She couldn't have been more than about ten minutes but it felt like a long time. I had no idea what to do, other than shake a toy rabbit with a plastic stomach that contained beads at her and hope she didn't cry.

After pasta with a pot of sauce from their local corner shop, Isobel said she was going to feed the baby again, then rest.

Eric suggested we go to the pub. Or rather, he asked Bel if she would mind if we did. The female imperative tense.

'I'll have my phone with me. You can text when you wake up or if you need me,' he said, reassuring her in a way that suggested we were going on an expedition up Mount Everest, rather than to the end of the road for a pint.

'So how are things?' I said when we were ensconced in the corner of the Open House.

'To be honest, it's not that easy.' Eric took a sip of his beer.

'I can imagine,' I said, although in truth I couldn't. I had no idea. I wondered how difficult a baby could be.

'She's a gorgeous baby,' I added. 'And Bel looks really happy.'

'She is. She's amazing. Honestly, Ben, you have no idea what it's like. I never thought I could love anyone as much as I love Gabriella, and Isobel's devoted to her.'

I could sense a but.

'But?'

'I don't know, really. I mean, Bel's great with her. She can hardly bear to be parted from Gabs and she is coming on really well. But sometimes she seems to get everything out of proportion.'

I nodded, although I wasn't sure what he meant.

'I came back from work the other day…' Eric lowered his voice, although there was hardly anyone in the pub. 'Gabriella was asleep in her cot and I was hoping Isobel might have been able to get us something to eat. I know that sounds old-fashioned.'

'Not really.' Isobel was at home with a baby all day. Eric went up and down to London and did a full day's work in between. Hoping for a meal at the end of it all wasn't some sort of throwback to the Fifties; it was reasonable.

'I know it sounds odd, but you kind of need to eat when the opportunity arises, and Gabs being asleep was an opportunity. But Isobel hadn't done anything about dinner.' Eric paused before adding, 'Which was fine. I'm happy to make something for us both when I get home.'

'Go on.'

'Well, I was back a bit earlier. I'd rushed because I'd spoken to Bel during the day and she was upset. Gabs had hurt herself.'

'How?'

'She had a bit of a scratch, near her eye. It wasn't that bad, but Isobel thought it was her fault. She'd been changing her nappy and the phone rang and she picked Gabs up off the floor a bit too quickly and caught her head on the side of the bathroom cabinet. Her face did look a bit sorry.'

'Accidents happen.' I couldn't see the big deal.

'That's what I said, but when I got home Bel was in a sort of frenzy. She didn't even register that I was there at first. She was cutting up bits of sponge and taping them to every edge she could find: the corners of tables, the tops of chairs, even round the banisters on the stairs.'

'Why?' I didn't get it.

'It was crazy really. She said she was just trying to stop her from getting hurt again but half the stuff she was covering, Gabs doesn't even have access to anyway. I mean, she can't even crawl or anything.'

I was unsure what to say.

'I tried to remonstrate with her. I told her that life was full of risks and she couldn't protect Gabriella from everything, and she just said something like, "Well, I'm going to do everything I can to try," and then burst into tears.'

'It all sounds a bit strange.' I ventured as much of an opinion as I dared. It sounded downright weird really.

'She wouldn't stop, either. She was tired and hungry but she carried on while I cooked dinner. She was wrapping torn-up bits of sheets around the door handles by the time it was ready.'

'And later?'

'She calmed down a bit. I made her eat and then Gabs woke up and needed feeding, and by the time she'd finished she was so tired that she went to bed. The next morning she was a bit more sanguine, shrugging and saying she'd gone a bit over the top and removing some of the padding!'

'So, it was just a one-off?'

'I think so, but...'

I waited.

'She's so over-anxious, Ben. I don't know if it's normal or maybe there's something more to it. She doesn't seem to find it as easy as I'd have imagined. I'm worried that maybe she's got some sort of postnatal depression or something.'

I offered something along the lines of, 'Maybe she should see someone?' But I don't know if she ever did. I don't know if Eric really wanted her to. At the time, I think he just wanted to talk.

And almost on cue, as I am thinking this, as I'm putting on my coat and getting the buggy out ready to wheel Iris to the shops, my phone vibrates in my pocket, and I take it out and identify the caller's number.

It's Eric.

'Hello.' I try to sound neutral.

'Ben, it's Eric.'

'I know.'

'Listen, is this a good time to talk?'

'It's a bit late,' I say.

'Do you want me to call back later?'

He doesn't seem to get it. 'I meant I thought you would have called before now.'

'I know, Ben, and I should have done. It's just – well, I'm really sorry about what's happened with Iris. It's terrible news and I'm so sorry and I know that we are partly responsible...'

'Then why didn't you call?' I ask. 'Why didn't you call me when you found out? Sally called last week. Other people have called or emailed or written. I kept waiting to hear from you or Isobel. But nothing. Why didn't you do anything?'

'I'm sorry, Ben. Believe me. I wanted to call, but...'

'Then what stopped you?'

'I was angry.'

'*Angry*? Why were you angry?' I raised my voice and Maggie, who was in the kitchen, came to the doorway holding Iris and looked at me questioningly.

'Eric,' I mouthed to her.

'I was angry with Isobel,' Eric said. 'I know I'm responsible too. I do know that. But I was angry with Isobel. I know I should have called you as soon as I heard, and I'm really sorry I didn't, but I wanted Isobel to do something.'

'Well, she didn't.' I don't count her text.

'I know, and I'm sorry that I didn't either,' Eric says, and then waits as if he wants me to say something.

'If that's what you called to say, I'm about to take Iris out to the park,' I say, adding, 'She gets bored easily now.'

'Sorry,' Eric says again. 'Should I call back later.'

'No, we've got friends coming for lunch.'

'OK,' Eric replies, and that's it. He hangs up.

'What did he say?' Maggie asks.

'Nothing much.'

'He must have said something.'

'He said he was sorry about Iris and he was sorry he hadn't called before,' I tell her.

'And have they got the letter?'

'I presume so,' I say. 'I guess that's what prompted him to call. But he didn't mention it.'

'Why didn't you ask?'

'I don't know.'

It's true. I'm not sure myself why I said so little to Eric. I've been wanting him to call, but when I heard him on the other end of the line it was Eric, and I don't argue with Eric. This is really between me and Isobel. I think Eric knows that too, and that's why he said so little.

Isobel, Saturday morning

'What did he say?' I ask Eric as he comes in from the garden and puts his phone in his pocket.

It's Saturday morning. Eric came in late last night, tired and hungry and keen to go to bed, but we talked briefly first, and he said he'd call Ben this morning, before we did anything else. He went into the garden because the house is too full of children. But we have the kitchen to ourselves when he comes back in.

'Not a lot,' he says, closing the door to the garden.

'But he must have said something?' Eric was hardly gone two minutes, but still.

'He sounded angry.'

'Obviously, but what did he *say*?'

'Really, he hardly said anything. I said I was sorry that I hadn't called and he said he was too. And angry. Angry that neither of us had been in touch. And then he said he had to go.'

'So he didn't say anything about this letter.'

'No.' Eric is fiddling about with the kettle and now it's me who feels angry – with him. I wonder if there is something he's not telling me.

'But did you ask him?'

'Ask him what?'

'Why they sent the letter?'

'We know why, don't we, Bel?' He turns round to face me now. 'It was all there in writing, clear enough.'

'But I thought that was why you were going to call him. I thought you were going to try to find a way round all this.'

'It was. I did. But he didn't want to talk.'

'So you just left it?'

'I didn't just leave it. I phoned him and I apologised for what's happened – for our part in that. One of us needed to do that, and you never did. You've had a whole week and you haven't done anything.'

'I didn't know quite what or how – ' We've been through this. Our lives are beginning to feel strangely Groundhog Day-ish. The shock of finding out has worn off, and the discussions we keep having are becoming increasingly familiar.

'I didn't say anything about the letter. Ben didn't say anything. He was about to go out with Iris.'

'So will you call him later?'

'I asked him, but he said they were having friends round.'

I try not to let my fury at his unsatisfactory answer show. 'And so you left it like that.'

'Yes, I left it like that, Bel. He's my oldest friend, for fuck's sake. I phoned him and he made it very clear he didn't want to talk to me. How do you think that made me feel? What was I supposed to say?' There's an edge to Eric's voice and it's not anger. I think he's upset.

'I'm sorry,' I say, going over to where he's standing. I put my arm out to touch him but he moves away.

'Don't, Isobel,' he says. 'Just don't.'

'I don't understand – ' I begin.

'What don't you understand? What was I supposed to say to him? Sorry that your daughter's deaf and that we caused it and I know that life's going to be harder for you and Maggie but we can't do anything about that so could you call off the solicitors? Sorry that Isobel never bothered to get in touch herself but she was busy helping the boys with their homework?'

'Oh, for God's sake, Eric. You know I just thought it might be easier if you spoke to him. He is, as you keep pointing out, your oldest friend, and I, as you also keep pointing out, am clearly the one in the wrong. You could have told him all that. You could have slagged me off behind my back.'

'Is that what you think I'm like?' Eric asks, infuriating me further with his ability to retain some form of self-righteousness no matter where an argument leads. 'You think I'd call him just to start slagging you off?'

'That's not what I meant?'

'Then what did you mean?'

'I just feel sometimes that your friendship with Ben is more important than our marriage.'

'That's ridiculous,' Eric responds. 'Especially given the way you and Ben are sometimes.'

'What do you mean?' The words are out and I wish I'd not asked them. Does Eric know more than he lets on?

'That you've never quite managed to let go.'

'That's ridiculous,' I protest – perhaps too much. 'Ben was a good friend to me when I first met him. I met you through him. I probably would have lost touch, if it hadn't been for your friendship.'

'You really are more self-centred than I ever would have thought,' Eric says, and I am too stung to reply. 'You must have known that Ben had a bit of a thing for you. He adored you and I never blamed you for not feeling the same way, but you must have been aware of it. Even after we were married, until he met Maggie he was still hung up on you – and you let him be.'

'Well, if it bothered you so much – ' I begin.

'It did bother me, yes,' Eric says, and I begin to panic. 'It bothered me when I first met you because I could tell how he felt, even though he never said anything. He knew I liked you, he never said anything that suggested he wasn't happy that you and I got together, but I know that must have hurt him.'

'I knew that too,' I say, not willing to allow him to portray me as totally insensitive.

'Then you should have let him go sooner,' Eric says. 'And yes, maybe I should have done something too. Maybe I would have been a better friend to Ben if we'd seen less of him, but partly...'

'Partly what?' I ask, curious and fearful too.

'You,' he said simply.

I say nothing, waiting for further elaboration.

'The way you were with the kids, the way your focus shifted... sometimes I felt I'd lost sight of you. I needed someone around who still saw you as you used to be. It helped me.'

'I don't know what to say,' is all I can say. I've no idea how long Eric has felt this way. Does he really think I've changed so much? Am I really such a disappointment?

'Well, I'm not going to let him just do this to us,' I say, decisive where before I have not been. 'It's affecting us now too, Eric – all of us. I know it's awful, what's happened to Iris, but we can't just let Ben and Maggie ruin our lives as well.'

'I don't suppose they want that, either,' Eric says.

'Don't they? Then why are they doing this, if not to get back at us?'

'They must have been advised,' Eric says quietly. 'Maybe the doctors told them. Whoever it was probably isn't aware of the nature of the relationships between us all. Maybe they just want to do what's right by Iris.'

Christ, how can Eric be so bloody reasonable? 'And what about what's right by us?'

'We'll just have to deal with it, Isobel,' he says, his voice irritatingly measured.

'So what do we do now?'

'As I've said, we'll have to find a solicitor ourselves and get some advice,' Eric says, but we are interrupted by Gabriella, who comes down for breakfast.

'What's going on?' she asks, looking from me to Eric.

'I thought I might take the boys to Bowlplex this morning,' Eric says, though he must know as well as I do that that's not what she's asking. 'What are you up to?'

'I'm going busking with Lucy,' Gabby says.

They do this from time to time, Gabriella and her friend Lucy: head out and play a few songs on the streets of Brighton. Lucy plays guitar and sings, and Gabs plays French horn and sings harmonies. They look good together and they sound lovely, and they clean up, too. They make more money in half an hour than I could ever hope to now, having been out of the workplace for so long.

I look through the ads in the paper every now and then, wondering what I could be qualified to do and how much I might earn if I did try to start working again. It's depressingly little on both counts.

I don't regret having given up work. I wouldn't have missed out on the kids' early years, could not have handed them over to anyone else. But now they are getting older and I have a bit more time on my hands I regret slightly not doing anything to keep my options open. I wish I'd planned things a bit more, instead of letting them just happen to me.

After the initial shock of finding out I was pregnant I was in a strange phase of almost believing it was never going to happen: that, if I carried on as normal and ignored the flutters that were getting stronger ever day, it might somehow all go away. Perhaps the pregnancy would peak and reverse and my body would gradually reabsorb the growing infant inside me, returning to the point before I was pregnant.

I was thirty-two weeks pregnant, physically fine although emotionally still up and down, when it happened.

I was on a plane flying back from Krakow with a handful of colleagues. It was a fact-finding trip and we'd ended the three days of visiting various industrial areas in a restaurant in Krakow, eating dumplings. I hadn't been eating for two, but the travelling had made me hungry, and the warm dough of the stuffed *pierogi* satisfied my craving for stodge.

I'd eaten a lot, and I'd thought I was simply paying the price for overindulging when I began to feel a little queasy and my stomach began to ache as we boarded the plane. By the time we'd taken off the ache was more intense. I could only liken it to a bout of food poisoning I'd had when I was in India, and I began to curse myself for pigging out.

'I think I ate too much last night,' I said to a colleague, now a minister, edging my way down the aisle to the toilet at the back of the plane, hoping the walk might ease the pain.

'Are you OK?' Helen asked, seeing the expression on my face.

'I think I might have food poisoning. I've got terrible stomach pains.'

'How often are you having them?' She looked concerned, but even then the implication of what she was asking didn't dawn on me. 'And when did they start?'

'In the night,' I told her. 'They weren't bad at first, but they seem to be getting worse.'

My body suddenly cramped and I had to lean forward and breathe deeply to try to contain the pain. That was when Helen pushed the button to summon a member of the cabin crew.

'Isobel,' Helen said, so gently that it still makes me cry when I think of it. 'I think you're in labour.'

The maternity unit in Redhill where Gabriella was born was the closest by ambulance to Gatwick Airport. The staff there couldn't have been nicer, and the care they gave her couldn't have been better, but it was still a good hour's drive from home, and beyond the first week, when I too needed medical attention, we couldn't stay there.

That was the very worst part of it: leaving her there, in an incubator, tubes and breathing apparatus keeping her alive, having to go back to our London flat, knowing we had a baby out there in the world but not with us.

Helen came to visit and she was kind and funny in a good way. She made me laugh at myself for being so clueless, for really having had no idea that I'd been going into labour.

'I wonder what would have happened if you'd not been there,' Eric said to her. 'She might have gone and had the baby in the toilet of the aeroplane.'

I shuddered to think. Once Helen had raised the alarm, the stewardess seemed to know what to do. She was ready to deliver the baby if necessary, but thankfully it wasn't. If Gabby had actually been born before we got to hospital we wouldn't have her now.

The moment Helen said to me, 'I think you're in labour,' my mindset changed. I knew that I loved this baby more than anything in the world and that if anything happened to it I would be devastated. All that fear that I might not be able to love the child went out of the window. Seeing her tiny spoon-sized body for the first time was like falling in love ten times over. Worrying that she might not survive, while she stayed in the intensive care unit, was like the pain of losing my mother, but magnified. That sounds like a terrible thing to say, because I loved my mother and I still miss her desperately, even more so now, but I knew that I could cope and had coped with that loss. I didn't think I could cope with losing this baby.

Dad cried the first time, when he saw us both. He looked at Gabriella, lying in her little fishtank of an incubator, and he wept.

He kept apologising. 'I'm so sorry, Bel. I'm so terribly sorry.'

And I kept saying, 'Please don't say that,' because I thought he thought she wouldn't survive and he was already commiserating with me for losing her.

But he wasn't. He was sorry that I had to go through what I was having to go through. He said he couldn't bear seeing the pain I was in.

And I was. All mixed up with the joy of being a mother was the terrible pain of parenting: the almost manic desire to protect your offspring from whatever the world might throw at them, and the terrible, paralysing fear that you could not possibly do that.

Bringing her home heightened that fear. I was on my own then. I was responsible for this tiny being. I was the one that would have to make decisions that would affect her future. Suddenly all the little decisions, the sort I'd been so good at making at work, seemed huge, their implications enormous.

I didn't realise, then, just how enormous.

Ben, Sunday evening

'Tell him we're sorry we missed his fiftieth,' Maggie says.

She's painting with Iris. Creating one of those butterflies kids make when they paint on half the paper then fold it so the image duplicates.

'He wouldn't have minded. He knows the reason.'

'Well, tell him I'm sorry anyway,' Maggie repeats, as if she's getting at something. I'm unsure what.

'I won't be late.' I take a guess that she'd rather I was here on a Sunday evening. 'Anton's got an early flight in the morning.'

Maggie already knows this. He called yesterday just after our friends had gone. I picked up thinking it might be Eric again and was surprised to hear Anton's voice – I don't think he's ever called me before – but he said he was flying to a conference early from City Airport, staying in a hotel the night before, and did I fancy a drink?

And there was something in the way he said it that made me think he might be a sympathetic ear.

'I don't mind about the time,' Maggie says, although she still seems a little narked. 'It will be good for you to have a chat with him.'

'OK, well, I'll see you both later.' I kiss her and Iris.

I've got mixed feelings about meeting Anton. I haven't seen him since the holiday and I suspect Yasmin may be behind the proposed drink. I wonder if Bel put her up to it. Maybe she called to ask Yasmin for advice, after she got the letter from

Hedda, and Yasmin's dispatched Anton to find out exactly what we want from her.

Or maybe I am doing Anton a disservice and he is just offering a metaphorical shoulder to cry on. He knows, more than anyone, what it's like to discover that your child is never going to have the life you envisaged for them – that your child is different and is always going to be different.

For me, the worst part of all of this is having to tell people – having to reply to those casual staff room 'How's the baby?' questions, knowing they are expecting the answer to be 'fine'. Half of them can't remember if she's a boy or a girl, let alone her name – the younger teachers, without kids, and the men with them. The female staff who are also mothers can remember everything. It's an amazing facility, which most men don't seem to have, myself included. I know Julie Effingham, deputy head of drama, has children, because she keeps disappearing off on maternity leave and when she comes back she talks about them all the time. But, even though I see a lot of her on a daily basis, I somehow let it all flow over me – all the talk about her child, or children. None of it actually sinks in.

Maggie can't quite believe how little I really know about the people I work with. 'How many children does she have?' 'Where does she live?' 'What did she do before she worked there?' I've never had satisfactory replies to any of these questions, but within minutes of meeting her at a school play Maggie had the answers to them all, and she's retained them.

'How's Ruby getting on at her nursery now?' she'll ask if I mention Julie.

I'm not sure who Ruby is. I didn't know she went to nursery, let alone how she's getting on there.

'Fine.' I'd feign knowledge and revert to something I did know about, such as the production we were planning for the Year Tens. 'Do you think *Spring Awakening* is suitable for that age group?'

So I couldn't really mind that some of my colleagues had very little awareness of Iris. In fact I was glad of it. It meant

183

there was less chance of their asking how she was and my having to tell them.

Julie did, of course, all the time. 'How's Iris?' 'Is she sleeping though the night?' 'Has she started teething?' 'Does she crawl?' She asked on such a regular basis that I was forced to consult with Maggie about the names and ages of her children and prepare a list of questions I could ask her in return.

'How's Iris?'

Julie had been the first to ask when we went back to school after the summer holidays.

'OK now. But we had a bit of a scare,' I'd said, and filled her in on how horribly frightening it had been while she'd been ill: how we'd had to rush her to hospital and in a matter of what seemed like minutes her body went from being a bit flushed to covered in a virulent rash and her breathing from being normal to rasping and struggling.

'Is she back to full strength?' Julie kept asking during the first few weeks of term.

'Seems to be,' I'd replied, adding something about the resilience of babies, still struggling to get my head around the fact that a few weeks earlier she'd been in hospital on oxygen, being fed and medicated through tubes, and now she was home and dragging herself around the furniture in a desperate attempt to walk, as if nothing had ever happened at all.

Julie had looked concerned when I told her that Maggie was a bit worried about her, a few weeks later. 'Have you taken her to the doctor? What is she worried about?'

'Nothing specific really, just little things. She seems to be a bit more withdrawn and she's lost interest in the world around her. But I expect that's normal.'

Julie looked as if it wasn't, and when I told her that Maggie had been right to worry all along, that we'd taken her to the doctor and been referred for tests and the tests had told us she'd lost her hearing in both ears, Julie was touchingly tearful.

'Oh, Ben, I'm so sorry. You must be devastated. How badly is she affected? Or is too early to tell?'

'No, they've done tests,' I told her, feeling angry and, as usual, my stammer returning. 'She's lost the hearing in b-b-both ears. She can hear virtually nothing.'

We know this now. We don't know yet if hearing aids will make much of an impact, whether she might have cochlear implants or if we will simply have to resign ourselves to the fact that she can't hear, and learn sign language, both of us, properly.

'And yes, we are devastated,' I say to Julie, who said the right thing when she said we must be.

Not everyone does. People don't know what to say when you tell them news like this. I'm sure most of them think it's awful, but political correctness gets the better of them. We teach and have been taught to celebrate difference. It's supposed to be a wonderful thing. I have classfuls of children who remind me it's not PC to notice even. A kid the other day told me I was racist when I mentioned the Gypsy Kings.

'Sir, that's racism.'

'No, Hal, it's not. It's the name of a band.'

But he wouldn't accept this. 'You're not allowed to call people gypsies,' he insisted. 'You have to call them travellers.'

'Unless the name of the band they happen to be in is the Gypsy Kings.'

He was unswayed. I wonder what he would have said if I'd told him my daughter was deaf and I'm not cool with it. Would he tell me I was being disablist?

Maybe I am. But I don't accept that Iris's difference is a thing to be celebrated. I'm more than happy for people to bring their guide dogs into cinemas and their wheelchairs to work. I just wish my daughter was not deaf.

When I think back to my stammering schooldays, all I wanted was to be the same as everyone else – able to say my name without stumbling. That's all I want for Iris too. I want her to be the girl who can fidget while listening to her teachers and not have to concentrate to discover what they are saying. I want her to be the girl who can communicate with her friends verbally, not by waving her hands in the air and making shapes with her fingers. I want her to be the girl with her hair held back from her face with pigtails, to reveal two clichéd shell-like ears. I don't want hearing aids protruding from them.

'Of course there's a lot they can do these days,' Daniel Holland, the head, said when I told him.

He was reacting as most people do, trying to be positive. 'Look at Emma Nicholson,' they say, as if that helps. It doesn't. She comes up a lot, and Marlee Matlin, the only deaf performer to win an Academy Award, for her role in *Children of a Lesser God*. Look at these women, they say, as if plucking role models out of the air is going to assuage our grief for what we've lost: a beautiful hearing daughter. She's still beautiful but she can't hear, and, whatever anyone says, it's not a difference I see reason to celebrate.

I want people to commiserate with me. I've lost my hearing daughter. I am devastated, yes. Wouldn't they be too?

Thank God for Anton.

'When we found out Conrad was autistic, it felt as if we'd been given a life sentence,' he told me, once we were seated at a table in a pub near East Croydon railway station. That was its only real selling point. 'That's how I felt, anyway, I don't think Yasmin did. I still don't think she does.'

'And you still do?' I watch him downing his pint with a rapidity that makes me think he needs it.

'Pretty much, yes.' He lowers his voice and glances round a bit. 'It's a terrible thing to say about your own child but I really wish he was not like he is. I wish to God he was normal.'

He finishes the rest of his pint.

'Sorry.' He looks at me. 'I didn't mean to imply that having a deaf child was going to be all bad.'

'It's OK. From what I've seen, Conrad is pretty hard to cope with.'

'All I meant was – '

'It's good to hear someone actually react to their child in a negative way,' I say to him. 'Say the things you aren't supposed

186

to say. People keep saying unhelpful things like, "If they lose one sense their others become heightened – perhaps she'll be an incredible painter," and I want to say, "I don't want her to be an incredible painter, I just want her to fucking hear me speak or hear Maggie play."'

'People said the same with Conrad.' Anton has finished his drink and is looking towards the bar. 'They still do, unless they know him well and know how ridiculous it is to say it now. When we first found out he was autistic, everyone seemed to think that meant he would be some sort of *savant* or mathematical genius. He's not. He's just self-centred and crazy.'

'I know people are trying to be positive – ' I begin.

'Too soon,' Anton cuts across my sentence. 'That comes later: the picking yourself up and dusting yourself down and forging ahead.'

'What do you mean?'

'When you first get the news. You need to grieve. You've lost the child you thought you had. You can't just let go of that and adopt another one overnight and be fine about it.'

'Same again?' I ask, grateful to be sitting opposite someone who appears to have a real idea of how I'm feeling.

'The worst part,' I say, when I come back from the bar, 'is that it's all so unnecessary.'

Anton nods but says nothing. I thought he might already know, but maybe he doesn't. 'We're taking legal action. We're suing Isobel and Eric for damages.'

'I don't quite understand.'

'If they'd had Gabriella vaccinated, none of this would have happened. They knew there was every chance she had measles but they left her with Iris, knowing she was highly contagious, knowing Iris was too young to have been vaccinated yet.'

Anton says nothing. He fiddles absent-mindedly with a beer mat.

'If Isobel knew she had measles then she shouldn't have left her with Maggie and Iris. You're right,' he said, when he finally replied. 'But…'

'What?'

'I know you must be angry. I would be too, in your position. But if I'd been in Isobel's position I might have done the same.'

'You mean you wouldn't...'

'If I'd thought there was any risk of having a child like Conrad, I wouldn't have taken it. I know that's a terrible thing to say but it's how I feel. Never a day goes past when I don't wish he was normal. I hate myself for saying it but it's true. So, if I'd been in Isobel's shoes at the time, maybe I'd have done the same. That's all I'm saying. I feel terrible for you and Maggie, though, of course.'

'Do you think that's what caused Conrad to...' I wasn't quite sure how to finish the sentence.

'No. Once we found out what was wrong with Conrad, it became clear in hindsight that there'd always been something not quite right.'

'So you never thought it contributed?'

'Initially, yes, we did. But mostly because we wanted someone or something to blame. You don't want your kid to be different, I know that, Ben. I can understand why you're blaming Isobel. All I'm saying is, at the time, I might have done the same, in her shoes.'

'Does Yasmin feel the same?' I ask, my heart sinking. I don't want Yasmin to help Isobel. I want her to be on my side.

'No, I don't think so. She's always been more accepting of Conrad.'

'Maggie seems to be the same.'

'Really?'

'Yes. I mean she's upset too, obviously, but more accepting, more ready to find out what needs to be done and do it. Maybe it's a maternal thing.'

'I can see it's harder to accept something when you think it could have been avoided. We know other parents of autistic kids who were adamant that the MMR damaged their kids.'

'I thought maybe Isobel might have been in touch with Yasmin.'

'No,' Anton says. 'Not heard anything since the party, and they left that in a bit of hurry, after Isobel found out that Iris was deaf. Yasmin says she was quite upset.'

'Good,' I reply. 'Did she say anything else?'

'She felt terrible, that sort of thing.'

'And she hasn't been in touch since?'

'No,' Anton replied. 'And to be honest…'

'What?'

'Well, between you and me, Yasmin's kind of fallen out with Isobel,' Anton says, and takes a large sip of his pint.

'Since when?' I ask, and I wonder if they have fallen out over this. 'They were fine on holiday.'

'Well, that's why I say kind of,' Anton says. 'It's more in Yasmin's head really. I don't suppose Isobel is even remotely aware how she feels.'

'Which is?'

'Let down, I suppose,' Anton tells me. 'I don't know Isobel that well; we don't see much of her, even since we moved down. Yasmin told me they used to be close but she feels as if she's been, not avoiding her exactly, but giving her a wide berth, and she's hurt by that.'

'But why? Is this recent? Is there a reason?' I ask, still thinking – still hoping, if I'm honest – that it's over this business with Iris and me.

'No,' Anton replies. 'It's been going on for years, since Conrad was little, and he's the reason really. I know he's bloody difficult to be around, I know other kids don't like him, but Yasmin just expected Isobel to be there for her.'

'And she hasn't been?'

'No, to be honest, she hasn't. You really find out who your friends are when you have a disabled child, Ben.'

Isobel, Monday

Yasmin was busy when I called her earlier.

'I'm just in a meeting with a client,' she said when I was first put through. 'Can I call you back in half an hour?'

When she does, she is cautious.

'Yes,' she says, in response to my question. 'Anton had a drink with Ben, so I did know that he was thinking about taking legal action.'

'He's doing more than thinking,' I correct her. 'We've had a letter from his solicitor. That's why I'm calling. I need to find one to act for us but I don't know where to start.'

'Do you not have one?' she asks.

'No, why would we?'

'Wills, conveyancing, that sort of thing,' Yasmin replies.

'We did make a will,' I tell her. 'But that was a long time ago and this is very different. I was wondering if you could – '

'No, I'm sorry,' Yasmin replies before I've finished my sentence. 'It's not my area of expertise, and anyway…'

'What?'

'I don't think it would be a good idea for me to get involved, not since this is between you and Ben.'

'I just thought you might be able to give me a bit of advice, as a friend,' I say, feeling slightly crushed. 'And maybe point me in the right direction?'

'I'm sorry, Isobel,' she says. 'My advice would be just find a firm of local solicitors with a good reputation. There must be people there you can ask for a recommendation?'

'OK, thanks. Sorry to disturb you at work.' I end the call and feel a huge sinking feeling.

The number of good friends I thought I had is rapidly diminishing.

So I ask in the playground, when I go to pick up Vincent. One of his friends' fathers is a solicitor. I've no idea what sort of work he does but I catch sight of the mother, Rachel, and ask her, vaguely, if she knows of any good solicitors.

'For what sort of work?' she asks.

'I'm not quite sure.' I know that sounds daft, but I suddenly realise I'm not sure what kind of solicitor we need. 'It's for a friend, for some sort of civil action.'

I don't want anyone to know what's going on. I don't want to be the object of playground gossip, any more than I already am or have been. You never know what people are saying behind your back, but I know people have opinions and they air them among themselves, if not to my face.

'Oh, well, that's a relief,' Rachel replies. 'Usually when people ask me about solicitors – and it happens quite often – it's because they are getting divorced.'

'No.' I try to laugh, but it sounds hollow to myself. 'Nothing like that.'

'Well, Mark's firm specialises in divorce and conveyancing but they might be able to help your friend. Do you want his number?' she says, waving as her son emerges though the door of the school.

'No, don't worry.' I was hoping she would recommend someone else, someone less close to home than the father of a friend of Vincent. 'I'm sure they've found someone by now. I just thought I'd ask as I'd bumped into you.'

'Mum!' Vinnie's appearance diverts us from the conversation. 'Why don't bees like Marmite?'

'I've no idea.' I put my hand out to ruffle his hair, the closest he'll allow to a kiss when he comes out of school these days.

I am always thrown by Vincent's questions, never quite sure where they come from or where he's going, if anywhere, with his line of thought. 'Maybe they do like Marmite,' I suggest.

'Max says they don't. Can I put some in the garden when we get home and see? By the way, I've got a note.'

'Sure,' I say as he fishes in his pocket and pulls out a piece of paper he's folded so many times that it's about the size of a very thick fifty-pence piece.

'Have we got Marmite?'

'Yes, I think so.'

'Good.'

I started unfolding the note, far enough to see that it is about special immunisation clinics being held around the Brighton area and urging any parents whose children have not been vaccinated to attend. I fold it up again and put it in my pocket.

I turn to say goodbye to Rachel and see her looking at Vincent in a slightly odd way, the way people do who don't quite get him. I am already imagining the scene when we get home, smiling at the sense of purpose with which I can envisage him taking a jar of Marmite, spreading it on to something and taking it into the garden, conducting his experiment with energy, as if the results are of vital importance to the rest of the world, the way he does a lot of the largely pointless things he does.

I wish I had as much purpose as he does.

If I did, I might have got further with finding a solicitor than I have by the time Eric gets home, angry and spoiling for a fight.

'What have you been doing all day?' he asks.

I still find it hard to explain to Eric how my days seem to disappear before me, the way they always have since having children. I can't quite work out myself how he can travel up to London and back and do more than a full day's work in the interim, in the time that I seem to get very little done at all.

I used to pack so much into my days, before I had kids – into a day's work.

'I helped in Vincent's class this morning.' I don't mention my swim. 'And I asked a couple of parents but they weren't very helpful.'

'What about the man who made our will?'

'I'd forgotten about him.' I had, almost entirely, but now he came back to me. It had seemed slightly morbid at the time, making a will, like anticipating your own death, but after Vinnie was born we felt we needed to make one, in case something happened to us. There were adverts running on the local radio station at the time saying something like, 'If you don't have a will, you won't get to decide who becomes the legal guardian for your children.'

With three children, we thought we should make a definite plan.

I was panicky when I was pregnant with Vincent, not unlike the way I was with Gabby, wondering how I was going to cope, if I could manage with three. I wasn't a natural parent, I knew that much, and the prospect of three scared me just as much as one had done, especially as I had to keep such a close eye on Harvey because of his nut allergy.

But Vincent was the easiest, sunniest, most delightful baby and still is the easiest, most charming, delightful child. I loved the other two, with a fierceness that surprised me, but I fell in love with Vincent in a way I would never admit to anyone. Maybe it was because he was the baby. Maybe I'd have felt the same way about Harvey if we'd stopped at two and he'd have been more my baby and less Eric's boy.

Perhaps Vincent's conception was auspicious, even though all through my pregnancy it was a great source of tension between Eric and me. The pregnancy was an accident but these things are never entirely accidental, and I'd blamed my husband.

The fog had just started to lift. Gabs had started school; Harvey was going to nursery several mornings a week and loving it. Both seemed happy and had adapted well to their new surroundings. I had a little time to myself. I hadn't really done anything with it but I'd begun thinking again, which seemed like a start.

That evening, Eric came home early, with a bottle of wine and a takeaway, in time to help me bath the children and put them to bed. With no dinner to prepare, the evening stretched out ahead of us.

'Do you want to watch anything?' Eric asked as we settled on the sofa.

'I'm not bothered.' That was my usual response. I no longer actively watched television, I just sat in front of it and let it wash over me, allowed it to relax me slightly with a stream of home improvement or cookery programmes.

Eric often took my not being bothered as a chance to take in every detail of a documentary about an undercover Allied mission in Libya during the war. I am always amazed by the amount of detail men retain, with regard to world affairs, history and sport – and how little with regard to their families. I'm not sure Eric knows what the children's middle names are. But he knows the middle name of every commander in the Arab campaign, taking them in from various TV documentaries and retaining them as if they were important to his life.

But that evening Eric switched the television off.

'I'm going to look at you instead, then, Isobel,' he said, moving towards me and kissing me.

He surprised me and, as I said, the fog was beginning to lift. I felt less tired and less anxious and I was grateful to Eric for the takeaway and the wine and still finding me sexy, even though most of the time I felt anything but.

So I relaxed into his kiss, but not quite enough that I could stop myself saying, 'Not here,' when he began to undress me, there, on the sofa in the living room.

'Why not?' he said, and carried on unbuttoning my shirt, kissing me again so I could not speak.

'Because the kids might come down.'

'When do they ever come down?' Eric had undone all the buttons of my shirt now and was fumbling with the clasp of my bra.

'My period finished today,' I told him.

'I know,' he said. 'You said this morning.'

Maybe that was the reason for the early homecoming, the takeaway and the wine. I resented the planning slightly but I'd been so tired most of the time, I guess he needed to plan, and, now that we were both standing semi-clothed in the sitting room and Eric was pulling me to him, I wanted him.

It was nice until the moment Eric came, and then I was angry in an instant.

'I told you not to come inside me!'

'I thought you told me I could. I thought it was OK.'

'No, I said don't come inside me.'

'I'm sorry, Bel.' Eric was apologetic but not unduly worried. 'I wasn't really listening. I thought you said I could but it doesn't matter. You've only just finished your period.'

'I hope so, for your sake,' I said, unable to stop myself spoiling the mood, and anxious despite the fact that I knew Eric was probably right.

But he wasn't.

Two weeks later I began to feel pregnant. A few weeks afterwards, a test confirmed that I was. I resented Eric all the way through the pregnancy, blamed him for getting me pregnant, forgot that our baby had been conceived in a moment of love and passion.

And of course it meant I didn't go back to work. I'd had no definite plans to, but it was a sort of unspoken option. It was what people did: had two children, then worked again.

'Isobel just gets pregnant every time there's a danger she might have to go back to work,' Eric joked once. He was laughing as he said it, but I suspected there was an undercurrent of resentment and it triggered the guilt I felt about not working. I wanted to be at home with the children, and I did appreciate the fact that Eric never pushed me to go back. But he must have known that I felt bad about him having to shoulder the responsibility of being the sole breadwinner.

Eric was reasonably happy in his work, at the time Vinnie was conceived. He was working on the news desk at the *Guardian*. It wasn't very well paid but he liked the paper and the atmosphere and hoped it would lead to other things. But when an old colleague brought the job as a sub on the *Daily News* to Eric's attention I pushed him to apply for it. The salary was almost twice what he was getting. It wasn't a job he wanted but needs must, I argued. And he went for it, got it and took it.

And now he hates it, and he probably resents me for urging him to take it.

Ben, Monday evening

There is still a peculiar silence to our home. It always used to be otherwise. The radio would be on, one of our iPods docked and playing in the kitchen, Maggie practising or listening to music, me pontificating, both of us talking to or about Iris. Without either of us making a conscious decision to shroud the house in silence, it's crept up on us.

Why don't we still put the radio on as soon as one of us wakes up? It's what we used to do, always: first the alarm by our bed and then, whoever went downstairs to make coffee would flick the switch of the leather Roberts model in the kitchen, an original rather than one of the replicas which are everywhere these days, a legacy from Maggie's mum who, although still alive, seems determined to divest herself of all her worldly goods.

Ruth comments on the quiet when Maggie is upstairs bathing Iris. She's come to stay for a few days to look after the baby while Maggie goes for a meeting with the manager of her orchestra. There is a fairly short European tour coming up, just before Christmas. They want Maggie to rejoin them but she's not ready and hasn't practised for weeks. But she wants to talk to them, explain how things are. And the following day we have an appointment at the audiology unit. We'd rather not take Iris. So Maggie's mum being here is helpful, but she also brings with her her concerns.

'Has she played yet?' Ruth asks, when Maggie takes Iris upstairs. 'You said she'd stopped since the diagnosis.'

'I don't think so. Not while I've been here,' I tell her. 'I think it's taken away the pleasure.'

'Iris will have a sense of the music,' Ruth says to me then. 'She might not be able to hear what you will hear, but she'll feel something.'

I anticipate what she is going to say next and take a deep breath. It's another thing people have said often enough before, and they mean well when they say it but it doesn't help, and I don't want to have to keep listening to people saying it.

'Did you ever see that film about the deaf woman? I don't remember its name?'

'*Children of a Lesser God*,' I tell her. 'The one with an award-winning deaf actress?'

'If you say so.' Ruth seems undaunted by my snappy tone. 'My point is, she couldn't hear the music but she could feel it. Maybe it will be the same for Iris. Don't you think you could persuade Maggie to play some time?'

'I can't make Maggie do something she doesn't want to do,' I say, tersely.

'Well, maybe she does want to.' Ruth raises her voice to me then, not just the way she sometimes does because her hearing is beginning to fail with age, but because she's starting to get angry.

'She doesn't, Ruth. I'm not stopping her. She doesn't want to play. Why does she play? To give people pleasure from the music she makes when she does. Who would she most like to be able to hear that music? Our daughter, who can't. Therefore she doesn't want to play.'

'Or maybe she's tiptoeing around you, rather than Iris,' Ruth almost shouts.

'What do you mean?'

'It isn't only Maggie who is not playing, is it? It's you too. It's too quiet. It's as if you've decided that if Iris can't hear then no one else is going to get to listen to anything either, and that doesn't help, Ben. It doesn't help anyone.'

Ruth's never spoken to me like this before.

We both fall silent.

'I'm sorry,' she says. 'I didn't mean to speak out of turn. But you have to stop seeing Iris's deafness as a loss. Her place in the world and the way she sees it is different now, yes, but she still has a place, and she'll still see the world as something which delights her as much as everyone else. You have to accept that.'

'I can't, Ruth,' I say to her, and I can see the disappointment on her face, a look which tells me she'd thought more of me. 'You're not the first person to say what you've just said. It's not a novel idea that Iris's world is different, not necessarily worse. I've tried to make myself believe that, but I can't. I don't. It's not right. It's not what I wanted for her.'

I don't say 'it's not fair', I don't want to sound too petulant, but I think it.

'We don't always get what we want, Ben,' Ruth says more gently. 'Especially where children are concerned. You get what you are given. You have a beautiful, healthy – yes, healthy – baby daughter. So she can't hear, not like the rest of us. I know you're taking legal action and I can't say I agree with that, but it's none of my business if that's what you want to do. But Maggie is my business, and she's not happy not playing. Don't force your view of things on her.'

'I'm doing it for Maggie and Iris,' I say.

'Are you?' Ruth looks at me keenly. 'If you asked me, I would say you were doing it for yourself, Ben. I don't mean that to be critical. If it helps you come to terms with what's happened, then by all means go ahead and sue your friends. Just don't lose sight of Maggie in all of this.'

Maggie comes down then, with Iris wrapped in a towel, her sleepy face peeping out from its folds, interrupting my 'chat' with her mother.

'Everything OK?'

'Yes, fine,' Ruth replies. 'Would you mind if I put the radio on? I'd like to hear the news.'

Isobel, Monday evening

'Jesus, why is this drawer such a mess?' Eric asks.

He is rummaging through a drawer in the kitchen, the one in which you find all the stuff that has no other home: glue, Sellotape, batteries, string, duplicate keys, old camera films and instruction manuals for various household appliances.

'What do you need?' I ask, but he is still perturbed by the state of the drawer.

'There's bloody drawing pins all over everything.' He turns to show me a ball of Blu-tack with pins protruding from it. 'Why aren't they in a box or something?'

'The pot must have lost its lid,' I say, as evenly as I can.

Really, the state of the drawer is neither here nor there. I know this. Eric knows too, but for now this is what he is choosing to fight about.

'Maybe some time when you're at home all day you could sort it out so I can actually find what I'm looking for,' he snaps.

'What *are* you looking for?' I ask, refusing to rise to the bait.

'Our will,' Eric says. 'Where do we keep our will?'

'In the desk upstairs,' I tell him, and he slams the offending drawer shut and goes upstairs.

We have a desk in our bedroom. Eric sometimes uses it to work on at weekends. At some point, I'd had the vague notion that it would be my spot for doing whatever work I could do. Now, it's just a chunky oak reminder that I don't do anything.

'I'm going to take a look.'

My husband goes upstairs.

I enjoyed the will-making process when we sat down and did it. We were happy then. I was calmer after Vincent was born, entranced by his easy nature which seemed to make everything seem better and easier. Making a will felt like renewing our marriage vows, without the tacky connotations. It was a time for stocktaking, realising what we had together, not just physical assets like our house, which in reality belonged mostly to the building society, but three small children.

The solicitor, Roberto – I remember his name now, although Eric is upstairs looking for it – asked if we wanted champagne when we came in to sign it. It seemed an odd suggestion but we said yes and we celebrated, not the anticipation of our deaths, but the realisation of what we had.

'Fucking hell, Isobel!' Eric comes down the stairs again, his face like thunder.

I look around, even though I am alone in the kitchen. It's an automatic reaction when someone swears. I look out for the kids, ready to tell them to cover their ears. But they are all upstairs. Gabs in her room, the boys playing darts in Harvey's. I can hear the thud thud thud as the darts hit the board or the wall and then the floor when they don't go in. I'm listening out for screams should anything go wrong. I never wanted him to have a dartboard, it was hard enough steering Harvey clear of nuts without having to worry about darts as well, but Eric's opinion – 'You can't wrap him up in cotton wool for the rest of his life' – prevailed.

'What?' I look up as Eric enters the room, waving several pieces of paper. 'Did you find it?'

'Yes, I found it.' He spits out the words. 'And I found these.' He pushes the offending documents into my hand and it takes me a moment to realise what they are. Blue copies of documents, where the top copies have been retained by someone else. The name of the vet's surgery printed at the top.

We only had pets for a brief couple of years – two rabbits,

which Gabriella begged us to get and then took very little interest in. They were both eaten by foxes one afternoon when she let them out to play in the garden and forgot to lock them up again. She was distraught at the time, but we didn't let her have any more. Neither Eric nor I were really pet people. We'd tried it, for the sake of the children, and decided we'd failed.

I look at the documents closely, trying to decipher the handwriting that is scrawled below the address. The only thing that is really clear is that this is the copy of a bill. I wonder if it was the amount that has made Eric angry, although the date on it is nearly ten years ago, too long ago for him to be cross about, whatever I'd spent on rabbits.

'I can't quite work out what it says?' I look at Eric questioningly.

'Can't you? Can't you remember? Don't you remember why you made an appointment and took two pet rabbits to the vet?'

I look again.

The bill is for the rabbits' vaccinations against some virus which might have killed them. I remember weighing up the cost at the time, when the vet suggested they have them, thinking it was too much, but hearing only, 'It's carried by birds and if they get it they have a quite a prolonged slow death. It's not very nice,' then, seeing Gabriella's face begin to crumple in anticipation of the death of her pets, writing out a cheque.

I nod slowly.

'You had the fucking rabbits vaccinated, Isobel.'

I know Eric is not joking, the way he used to in the past when the 'fucking rabbits' were alive. I think that was why I'd taken them to the vet in the first place, to get them 'sexed' to make sure they weren't going to be fucking rabbits and leave us with more rabbits on our hands that we knew what to do with.

'You had the fucking rabbits vaccinated, but not our own children.'

202

Ben, Monday night

Maggie is asleep, and I am not tired but in bed, as Ruth is sleeping on the sofabed in the living room.

It's never easy being on the receiving end of criticism from your mother-in-law, but there is an element of truth in what she said.

OK, so it had taken a bit of head-adjusting to get used to the fact that I was going to have a baby. Not only that, I was having one with a woman I didn't really know that well and wasn't even living with.

But I had been strangely and genuinely excited by the unexpected turn my life had taken. I was going to have a child. Maggie was going to move in with me. Me, Ben, the person who'd spent the last twenty-plus years being unable to commit to a long-term relationship, largely because I thought I didn't want to have kids. I was committing to someone and I was having a child.

I was gambling on the unknown. I didn't know if Maggie and I would start rubbing each other up the wrong way if we moved in together. I didn't know if the novelty of expecting a child would begin to wear off. I didn't know what the baby would be like. But I was willing to take the gamble anyway. I surprised myself, and I kept on surprising myself.

'Shall we find out what sex it is?' Maggie had asked early on.

'No,' I said, without even thinking about it. 'Unless you want to?'

'I don't mind.' Maggie smiled at me, laughing almost. 'And you sound very certain. I guess you've already given it some thought.'

'To be honest, it hadn't even crossed my mind,' I told her. 'Until you said it, I'd forgotten you could. But I didn't have to think about it. I don't want to know. I don't care. I don't care what sex the baby is or what it's like. I just care that it's our baby.'

'Oh, Ben.' Maggie leaned over and kissed me. 'Thank you.'

'What for?' I asked.

'For being so pleased. I was terrified that I'd lose you. I was terrified that I'd lose you anyway, when I met you, because I wanted to be with you. But when I got pregnant I thought I would have to lose one of you – you or the baby. I never thought I'd get both.'

'If you'd presented pregnancy as a hypothetical situation I'd have told you I didn't want a child,' I said. 'But now that it's happened I'm ridiculously happy – not just for you – for me too. I feel as if having a child is what I always wanted, even though I thought I didn't.'

Maggie laughed.

'And what about the tests?' she asked, serious again. 'We have to decide soon whether to have those or not, and what we will do if the results aren't what we were hoping for.'

'I don't want to have them either,' I said, certain in the moment of this too.

'But I'm an older mother,' Maggie said. '"Elderly primigravida", they write on the forms, which is a bit better than "geriatric" but I know what they mean. There is a real risk of some chromosomal abnormality because of that. I'm at high risk of having a baby with Down's Syndrome and other things.'

'I don't care.' I remained resolute. 'It's a risk I'm willing to take. I didn't think I wanted a child, but now I find I do. So if a test tells us there's a chance the child might not be perfect, I might well think I don't want it, but, if I have it, I am sure it will seem perfect to me.'

'We don't know how we would feel,' Maggie persisted. 'But it might be better to know if something was wrong, don't you think?'

'Yes, hypothetically I don't want a baby with Down's. But a few months ago I never wanted a baby at all. Things change. People adapt. We will adapt.'

I really believed it at the time. I genuinely thought that I wouldn't mind if there was something wrong with our child.

I thought the same when Iris was in hospital, tubes feeding her fluids and paracetamol through her veins, an oxygen mask over her face helping her breathe. I thought to myself, I don't care what happens, as long as she lives.

She got ill not long after we came back from France. The doctor there had told us to look out for symptoms. 'It usually takes about nine days after coming into contact with someone who has the virus for them to develop.'

He was right. Exactly nine days later, Iris developed a fever and began to cough.

'It could just be a summer cold,' we said to each other, hopefully. She'd been given the triple vaccine in France, but again the doctor had warned us it might be too late. 'She has already been in contact with the virus. There's a chance she may not have picked it up, but it's unlikely.'

It came on quickly, too, from the first flush of her raised temperature to her tiny body being covered with a violent bumpy rash and her breathing becoming laboured to the point that we could no longer bear listening to it. That all seemed to happen in twenty-four hours.

'We should take her to the doctor,' I said.

Maggie had been trying to keep her temperature down with Calpol but it wasn't working. It registered at a hundred and three on our thermometer. That was too high, and her breathing was too uncomfortable to think it could possibly be normal.

They saw us immediately in the surgery, a few streets away. They're good like that, I've realised since having a child. In the past, if I'd tried to see a doctor, it often took weeks to get an appointment. But if we were worried about the baby the receptionist would usually say, 'Bring her in now.'

'You need to take her straight to hospital,' the doctor said. 'I'll phone them so you'll be admitted right away. Do you have a car?'

'Yes. At home.' I nodded, focusing on the journey rather than the reality of the situation. It seemed easier somehow to concentrate on getting Iris to hospital, rather than the fact that she needed to be admitted.

'Is that far?' the doctor asked. 'I could call an ambulance if it is.'

'No, it's just up the road,' Maggie said, and we looked at each other anxiously.

'It's not an emergency,' the doctor tried to reassure us. 'But I'd like to get her into hospital as soon as possible. Her temperature is too high and she needs intravenous analgesic and may need oxygen.'

Maggie and I looked at each other again.

'There's no need to panic,' the doctor repeated. 'But I think you should drive her straight there.'

I nodded and we raced up the hill, pushing the buggy, to where our car was parked.

'Should I go in and get some things?' Maggie asked, as we took Iris out of the pushchair and began strapping her into the car seat, trying not to upset her as she cried out in pain.

'No,' I said. 'Let's just get her there. I can come back later and pick stuff up.'

Maggie nodded. I think she was thinking the same thing. She just needed me to confirm it.

We lived in a thirty-mile-an-hour zone but I stuck my foot on the accelerator whenever I could, on the streets where the traffic was quiet. A speed camera flashed as we passed the parade of local shops but I ignored it and so did Maggie.

She didn't say, 'Slow down, Ben,' as she often did when I was driving.

It was just before midday and the roads were relatively empty, the rush-hour congestion past. But as we neared the local primary school there was a weight of traffic on the roads again, slowing as parents looked for parking spaces before picking up their children who didn't yet do whole days.

'Come on, come on, for fuck's sake,' I cursed a young mother who gave me a friendly apologetic wave as she tried to manoeuvre into a parking space unsuccessfully and was forced to pull out again and repeat the process, while I waited impatiently behind her, desperate to get on.

Again Maggie said nothing. No, 'Calm down, darling. Don't be so impatient.' She didn't even look at the woman or acknowledge her second smile and wave as we passed her, once she was halfway back into the space.

Iris was crying and coughing now, in the back of the car, and the combination of the two made it almost impossible for her to breathe. Maggie, sitting beside her, was trying to soothe her. 'It's OK, sweetheart. It's OK, darling. We're going to get you to hospital just as soon as we can.'

The roads were clearer now, away from the school, and I pressed down on the accelerator again, driving too fast to spot the woman waiting with a child in a pushchair and a toddler holding on to it by the side of the level crossing. I didn't see that the toddler had released its grasp on the buggy and was venturing across the crossing without its mother giving the signal to go.

It was too late for me to do anything other than slam on the brakes, jerking Maggie and Iris forward in the back of the car and missing the kid by an inch, or a split second, however you care to measure the narrowness of space or time by which I missed hitting him head-on. I could see the fear on the mother's face, as she left the buggy on the side of the crossing and sprang into the road to scoop up her child. I could feel the sweat beginning to prickle the back of my neck, as I allowed myself briefly to think what might have happened. And I could see the mother mouthing words, presumably obscenities, in the rear-view mirror.

But I didn't let myself think about what might have happened. Not then. I had to get Iris to hospital. She was my priority, not the kid on the crossing. If his mother knew how ill she was, she would understand, surely? She would know I could not stop.

I didn't pause to think about it then and I didn't let myself think about it later, when Iris had been admitted and 'stabilised' but was still desperately ill. My thoughts about getting her to hospital had been replaced by thoughts about getting her home again.

'Don't let her die. Please don't let her die,' I kept repeating, over and over, as Maggie and I sat by her bed, watching the tubes which were feeding and medicating her and the monitors which checked her progress. I wasn't sure who I was saying it to. I don't believe in God and wasn't calling him up in our hour of need, the way I know some people do. If anything, I was talking to myself. 'Please don't let her die,' I remember saying to myself. 'I don't care what happens, as long as she doesn't die.'

I made a pact with myself, and I hoped that, if I kept it, Iris would survive.

When your baby is lying on a hospital bed and her temperature is sky-high, she can't breathe without assistance and the doctors look worried, you have to believe in something. So I put faith in myself, in my ability not to mind what happened to Iris as long as she lived.

But I couldn't keep that promise, not when the doctor told us she was deaf. I did mind. I minded enormously. I didn't want a deaf child. I wanted the child we'd had before all this happened.

I know I've let Iris down by not not caring, and Maggie and Ruth and all the people who thought I was bigger than this. But I do care. I really do. This is not how I wanted things to be.

Isobel, Wednesday morning

I have an appointment to meet 'our solicitor'. If I think of him in quotes, it helps me distance myself from the mess we're in. I called him yesterday, after Eric unearthed his details the night before. The appointment is at ten, in town, after I've dropped Vincent off at school.

He has a school trip today and is overexcited and overprepared. They are going to an open-air museum thirty miles away – a collection of houses from different periods and places, which have all been dismantled brick by brick and reassembled on the site of the museum. It's a history trip.

'There are beds you can lie in and you get bed bugs,' Harvey told him over breakfast.

He went on this particular trip when he was in Year Six. The beds are in a Tudor house. The bedding can't be authentic but Harvey says with excitement, 'It was filthy.'

Vincent has packed an enormous backpack. He has not only a change of clothes ('It might be wet!') but a torch, compass, penknife ('You're not allowed knives at school, Vincent!'), clipboard, pens, paper and his packed lunch.

His class teacher balks at the size of his bag, as we stand on the pavement outside the school waiting for the coach. 'Are you planning on climbing Everest, Vince?' he asks.

'Yes.' Vincent is a strange mix of whimsy and literalness sometimes. 'But not till after I leave school.'

'Today?' the teacher asks.

'No, when I'm eighteen.'

The teacher shrugs and begins head-counting.

I catch sight of a blonde girl I have not seen before.

'The new girl,' Vincent says.

He has told me about her before. She is from Germany. Her father has just landed a job in Brighton. She joined their class two weeks after the start of term. Her name is Michaela. She was in a German soap opera when she was a baby, playing the baby. Her mother makes her own ice-cream. This is what I know about Michaela, and I am about to learn another thing which is of interest to me.

'Listen up, everyone,' the teacher shouts, clapping his hands to command silence from both children and parents. 'We should have sent a letter home to remind you and I'm afraid it's my fault that we didn't. But we have a child in the class with a severe nut allergy. So, if anyone has anything in their packed lunches which contains nuts, will you please take it out of your lunch bag now and give it to your parents? Or to me.'

'Does Michaela have a nut allergy?' I ask Vincent. The school has a 'no nuts' policy as standard, but they have to reiterate it on school trips.

'Yup. She's a nutter,' he replies. 'Same as Harvey.'

He uses the term affectionately for his brother. Harvey likes it, preferring to be described as 'a nutter' than as having a condition which makes him feel awkward and singled out.

The first time, I didn't even realise. It was only hindsight that made me aware that that was what it must have been. I had a sling when he was a baby. It had what Eric would have called 'a strange hippy name' like a 'huggababy' or something like that. The packaging claimed that, if you carried the baby in it, it would sleep for hours. It seemed to work and was comfortable enough to wear, and I could sit down to watch television or even to eat without disturbing my sleeping Harvey.

I laughed at the time when I looked down at him one evening. He was in the sling on my lap and Eric had brought home a Wagamama takeaway. It was some sort of noodle dish and I'd been forking my share across the sleeping Harvey, unaware that some of the noodles had dropped on to his head. When I paused to look at him, I found that my bald baby had a tiny crop of noodley curls. It looked rather sweet. I motioned Eric round to see, before I removed them and dabbed his head with my napkin.

A few hours later Harvey's head was swollen and puffy and his face red and blotchy. I didn't put the two things together at the time. I thought maybe he was getting a cold or had been crying too much, because earlier that evening he'd been very distressed and screamed for almost an hour and half, refusing to eat, before he eventually wore himself out and settled in the sling.

I only put two and two together the second time it happened and we had to call an ambulance.

He'd just started crawling and was on the floor in the kitchen watched by Gabby, who was eating a peanut butter sandwich. It all changed so quickly from happy domestic scene to disaster. One minute Gabs was eating and Harvey crawling; the next I heard this horrible rasping noise and turned round to see Harvey wheezing and struggling for breath. I thought he was choking.

I picked him up and turned him upside down. 'Did you see what happened?' I asked Gabby. 'Did he put something in his mouth?' I imagined he'd picked up one of the coloured plastic letters from the fridge that were always falling on the floor, or a stray coin.

'I gave him a bit of my sandwich.' Gabriella was in tears, as if it was all her fault.

I shook Harvey, slapped his back, tried to do a mini-Heimlich manoeuvre, but nothing seemed to help.

After I had called the ambulance, the woman on the other end of the line told me calmly that she'd dispatched the crew but continued to talk to me, asking me questions about exactly what had happened.

'Has he had any sort of reaction to nuts before?'

That was when I put the two things together. From then on my life acquired a new anxiety. I was constantly vigilant, checking the packaging of everything, telling everyone he came into contact with he must avoid nuts, sending him to nursery with a name-tag that read NUT ALLERGY – so bold and unmissable that some of the older children thought it was his name.

I smile at the blonde woman who I presume is Michaela's mother as the coach gets ready to leave, but don't introduce myself. I don't have time to stop and talk, I have to make my way to the solicitor's, but I hope to convey a feeling of solidarity with her. 'I know what it's like – always on the lookout for nuts' – that sort of look.

'Bye-bye, Mummy, Mummy, goodbye,' Vincent sings to the tune of the Bay City Rollers, as the queue he's in makes its way on to the coach.

Lucky boy, I think, not a care in the world.

Ben, Wednesday morning

'Hello, Iris!' Ruth is sitting up in the sofabed in the living room and I bring her a cup of tea. Iris crawls in after me but she takes no notice of her grandmother. She probably hasn't seen her yet, and certainly hasn't heard her name.

Reacting to hearing your own name spoken is something so natural, so instinctive, something we've all been doing from such an early age, that it seems totally bizarre that my daughter does not do this.

'Hello, Iris.' Ruth moves her hand into Iris's field of vision and waves it, another sign we all know.

Iris beams when she sees her grandmother and emits a horrid screech.

'Hello, beautiful.' Ruth opens her hand and moves it around her face, a sign I do not know. Perhaps it means beautiful.

I think the name 'Iris' is beautiful.

Maggie came up with it. She wanted a name that was 'normal' but unusual. 'There don't seem to be many Irises around these days,' she said.

'Nor Maggies!' The old joke.

'I had a great-aunt called Iris. I think it's a lovely name, and simple. People won't be able to mess with it and call her anything else.'

I agreed with her. It seemed the most apposite name for our beautiful daughter. I liked saying it, when she was born. I liked the sound of it rolling off my tongue. If I'd had specific fears for her in relation to her name they were only that she might not be able to say it, that my speech impediment gene might have been passed on to her, that perhaps she would have a lisp and struggle with the R. I never for one moment imagined that she would not be able to hear it at all.

I keep thinking about this. It's a simple, everyday thing, hearing our name spoken and reacting to it. Knowing that Iris can't do this makes me wonder all the more.

When you hear someone say your name, you get a feeling of inclusion, of the world being familiar with you, of being recognised, wanted. There's so much more to the saying of someone else's name than just trying to catch their attention. They are soliciting you, personally. I find myself reacting in the staff room differently when people say 'Morning, Ben,' as opposed to plain 'Morning.'

I was in the supermarket last weekend, wheeling Iris round in her buggy, stuffing packets of pasta into the basket beneath while Iris pulled stuff we didn't need off the shelves on her level and held them close to her. I was hoping neither of us would be arrested for shoplifting, when I heard a woman calling, 'Ben,' and instinctively turned towards her. We exchanged a look and a shrug and she pointed towards a boy who was leaning over one of the freezer cabinets, not quite tall enough to reach whatever it was he was trying to pull out. Clearly he was the Ben she was seeking out, but the hearing of my name, the looking up, the recognising of my mistake and shrugging it off created an exchange between me and the mother of the other Ben – a small, insignificant exchange but nevertheless one born out of hearing my name.

It's daft really, making things like that more significant than they are. But that's how I feel. Suddenly, hearing my name spoken seems like this huge, momentous thing, and it gets me every time someone like Ruth comes in all cheery and says, 'Hello, Iris,' and Iris takes no notice.

Julie Effingham says that when she is in a crowded place with her daughter – yes, I've been making an effort and taking in the details and I know now she's called Ruby – Ruby calls her 'Julie Effingham'! Apparently she worked out, at quite an early age, that if you called out 'Mum,' in a busy environment nearly half the women turned round.

When she told me, I had to swallow hard.

'Are you OK?' she asked.

'Yes, that's funny,' I replied, but actually her anecdote didn't make me laugh. It choked me up.

And this morning, we are going to find out about a way of maybe one day enabling Iris to hear her name spoken.

That's why Ruth is still here. That's why I've taken the morning off school and a supply teacher is taking my Shakespeare class. We are going to visit an audiology unit, and the options for Iris will be explained to us.

The audiology unit is at the top of a very tall tower block, with views over London. From the windows of the waiting area you can make out the Shard, the Gherkin and the London Eye.

'Great views for the hard of hearing!' I quip, and Maggie laughs politely, but I don't think she finds me funny. She's anxious.

'Mr and Mrs Deakin?' A young woman, a woman who looks far too young to be a professional in any field, relieves Maggie of the possibility that I might make any more jokes and introduces herself.

'I'm Claire Joiner.' She smiles and extends her hand to each of us. 'Would you like to follow me?'

She leads us down a long corridor into a room with a wall of computers along one side.

We know now that Iris's hearing loss is probably too severe to benefit from hearing aids. Claire Joiner is going to talk to us about cochlear implants.

Of course we've done our research – looked them up on the internet – but Claire Joiner has something better than that to show us.

'I'll give you both a set of headphones,' she says, tapping away on the keyboard, bringing up various files which I can see contain sound waves. 'And then I'm going to play various extracts of speech and music and you will get some idea of how things sound to someone who has a cochlear implant.'

We are both keen, Maggie and I, for Iris to be able to 'hear' again. Yes, she could learn to sign, and Maggie has already begun signing to her, but we will never both be able to learn enough to communicate with her fluently and I – well, both of us – want her to hear, something, somehow.

'It will sound quite strange to you at first,' Claire says to us. 'But what you have to understand is that the brain is very accommodating.'

'What do you mean?' I ask.

'Well, the headphones will give you a realistic impression of what your daughter might be able to hear, were you at some point to go ahead with cochlear implants. But it will sound strange to you at first. It might help if you just listened, and then I'll explain some more after.'

'OK.' Maggie and I put the headphones over our ears.

'So first of all I am going to play you an extract of speech.' Her voice sounds slightly muffled with the headphones on but is still audible.

The voice she plays sounds scratchy and jagged, like an old radio recording that is being played on damaged vinyl and broadcast on medium wave. I can make out the words, but only just. It requires a huge effort of will and concentration. I can't listen for long and I take the headphones off.

'Enough?' Claire asks, and looks from me to Maggie, who takes her headphones off too. She pushes the stop button on the screen in front of her.

'It was doing my head in,' I say, negatively.

'It's quite hard to listen to,' Maggie agrees, but as always she is more positive. 'But it's amazing if someone like Iris, who really doesn't seem able to hear anything now, might be able to pick up speech like that. Don't you think?'

She addresses this to me but I still feel disappointed. I don't know quite what I was expecting, but something better than what I just heard.

I think of Iris and wonder for the first time if maybe it would be better for her not to hear anything, to live in her own silent world, rather than to have to hear the world distorted so grotesquely.

'Do you want to hear some music now?' Claire Joiner asks.

'Is it any better?' I hear myself saying, even though, seconds before, a voice in my head had urged me to be positive for Maggie's sake.

Maggie addresses herself to the audiology specialist. 'I'm a musician,' she tells her. 'Or, rather, I was. I've not really worked since having Iris. I was on the verge of starting again, but then we found out about her deafness.'

'Deaf people can enjoy music. But I'm sure you've been told that already.'

'Yes.' Maggie nods. 'It's one of the things that made me – us – want to think seriously about implants. I know there are people in the deaf community who think it's trying to make a hearing child out of a deaf one.'

'I wouldn't put it quite like that,' Claire says.

But Maggie came across this phrase on a deaf community forum. One of the members she'd been talking to made it very clear she regarded it as butchery, almost, to force an operation on our child which she regarded as unnecessary and potentially harmful. I had no sympathy with her at the time, but now, after hearing what I've just heard, I have more.

'Music is very important to me,' Maggie continues. 'I can't imagine a world without it. I can't imagine my own daughter never being able to hear me play, never being able to enjoy a melody or a cadence. I know she might be able to pick up a beat or a rhythm but that doesn't seem enough, to me. I don't want her never to experience something that gives me so much pleasure.'

'Do you want to put the headphones on again?'

Maggie nods and places them over her ears.

I wait a little longer, watching the audiologist bringing up another file on the screen, clicking the Play button so that sound begins to seep from the phones while they are still on my lap.

Only then do I pick them up and place them over my ears.

What I hear is terrible. To say it sounds like a school orchestra tuning up would be unfair to the school orchestra, even though it's pretty bad. But that's the best way I can think to describe what I hear. It's a cacophony of screeching. It sounds as if I am listening to something underwater with the volume turned up.

I am suddenly reminded of my mother, who used to walk into my room as a teenager when I was listening to music on the stereo I'd bought with money from my Saturday job. Her disapproval used to filter across the room to me before I actually realised that she was there with it. She hated popular music; even contemporary classical was beyond her.

I'd turn it down, so she could say whatever she'd come to my room to say, but it would always be prefaced with, 'What on earth is this ghastly music?'

It used to puzzle me then – how she could hear something so completely different from what I was hearing. I know people have different musical tastes but she used literally to cringe, as if it was painful to hear it.

I think of her now saying, 'What on earth is this ghastly music?' and begin laughing out loud, probably louder than normal because of the headphones, a little hysterically too.

The audiologist looks alarmed. Maggie takes her headphones off. 'Are you OK, Ben?'

I carry on laughing, aware that I must be a ridiculous, slightly manic spectacle.

'It's unbearable,' I say, when I manage to calm myself down and stop. 'That's not music. It's just noise. Is that really the alternative to hearing nothing?'

'It's not as bad as it seems at first,' Claire Joiner says quietly.

'It's fucking terrible.' I feel angry now with everyone for having offered us hope, especially with Claire because she is sitting there in front of us, trying to be calm, trying to tell us that what she's presenting us with is a solution.

'It sounds distorted to you.' She carries on regardless of my outburst, and Maggie reaches across the space between us and puts her hand on my leg. 'But, as I said before, the brain is very accommodating. Yes, when implants are first fitted, that is what people hear. But the brain gradually adapts to the way the sound is transmitted and starts to process the information it receives in a different way. So, once people get used to it, they are able to hear more clearly.'

Maggie is looking at me anxiously, clearly disturbed by the manic laughter.

And that's when I cry, for the first time since we got the diagnosis. Maggie cried at the time, and has often cried since, muted bouts of mourning for the part of Iris we have lost, but I've simply been angry.

A part of me feels I should be embarrassed, sitting there with this young audiologist looking unsure what to do.

'Would you give us a minute?' I hear Maggie say, and Claire nods and gets up to leave the room, closing the door gently behind her.

I'm not quite sure how long we are there for, me sobbing like a baby, Maggie holding me tightly to her chest, stroking my hair, kissing the top of my head until I still, and realise Claire Joiner is back in the room with us.

'I'm sorry,' she says, quiet still. 'But I'm running late for my next appointment.'

Isobel, Wednesday, later

The solicitor is brisk and efficient – helpful, even, from a legal point of view.

'Right, well, I don't think they have much of a case,' Roberto says, looking at the letter, having listened to my account of the events that took place over the summer. 'There are several factors in your favour. There were various outbreaks of measles last summer, including one in the part of France where you were holidaying. It is quite possible that Iris Deakin caught the virus from another source. And for their case to be successful you would have to have definitely known Gabriella had measles and left her in Iris's company with the deliberate intention of infecting her with the virus, and you clearly didn't do that.'

'No,' I replied. 'Of course I didn't. The worst thing I did was not think. I knew Gabs was ill, but I didn't know it was measles. I just thought she had a cold. I even thought it might help Maggie, having her there, when we all went out for the day. I never meant any of this to happen.'

Hearing Roberto even ask me that is unnerving. It makes it seem too real. This is what they are accusing me of: deliberately harming their baby! I can't believe they really think that, but that's what they're saying.

'So what happens next?' I ask him, trying to remain calm.

'Well, I will send a letter saying that, while you are sympathetic to their plight, you have no legal responsibility. They will probably contest this. But in my opinion they don't have a case and it will be a waste of everyone's time pursuing it.'

'So you think you could make them drop the case before it gets to court?'

'I'd certainly hope to,' he replies. 'They've not laid out any specific cost yet, so they may be hoping to settle out of court anyway.'

'But how much are they likely to ask for?'

'I really can't say at this stage. But hopefully it won't come to that. I'm sure we can sort something out before it gets to court, anyway.'

'That's good.' I feel a little relieved, although even the prospect of settling out of court is daunting. We don't have any extra money. Ben knows this perfectly well.

'Indeed. So I'll send them a letter, and we can see where we go from there.'

'And how much will that cost?' I ask nervously.

'Five hundred pounds for this meeting and sending the letter.'

I gulp and wonder how we will even find the money just to pay him for his advice and letter-writing, let alone any settlements. Eric earns enough to cover the bills and the mortgage, but it's always a balancing act trying to fund the extras.

As if to reinforce this point, Harvey comes home from school later with the details of a school trip he wants to go on. No, not wants to go on – has been singled out for.

'It's a G and T trip,' he says.

This is how they refer to the pupils who've been chosen to have an eye kept on them in the huge comprehensive school that he and Gabriella attend. There are nearly sixteen hundred pupils at the school – over three hundred in every year. The numbers are so huge, it's easy for kids to get lost. So they are singled out at both ends – special needs at one end and G and

Ts at the other. Harvey is on the Gifted and Talented register for English, art, design and technology and maths.

I imagined them all being taken out for cocktails when I first heard the term being used. Gabriella is G and T in a few subjects, too, though I wonder if Vinnie will be, by the time he moves up to the school, or if he'll still be a slow reader and given extra attention on account of his special needs rather than his talents.

Harvey's G and T trip is residential – a sort of expressive Outward Bound-type week which only twenty pupils have been selected to go on. It will involve a strange combination of art and abseiling – unleashing their inner creativity though outdoor pursuits and workshops. It's a week's holiday in Wales, really, and I can see from the look on his face how much Harvey wants to go.

'I know it's a lot of money,' he says, acutely aware, in a way I wish he weren't, that our finances are limited. 'But I could put some of my savings towards it and maybe try to earn some money too. I could sell some of my stuff on eBay.'

'What stuff?' I ask, more as a delaying tactic than a question.

'My Lego.' He seems to have thought about this. 'I never really use it any more.'

This is true, but the range of multicoloured brick edifices and structures gathering dust on his shelves are testament to his creative talent. It seems a shame to get rid of them.

'And my DS games,' he continues. 'I could sell my DS too, and the Build-a-Bear stuff!'

Harvey shrugs at the latter admission. Every now and then, when I'm trying to get them all to give their rooms a bit of a clear-up, I ask Harvey if he still wants to keep it all and he has always replied with a slightly embarrassed, 'Yes.' The bear still sits on the end of his bed. I imagine he passes it off to his friends as 'ironic', the way they pass off any interest they deem too young or too uncool, but its bags of clothes and accessories are stuffed in the back of his wardrobe. They haven't actually seen the light of day for years, but until now he's been reluctant to part with them.

'Are you sure?' I ask him.

He may be willing to part with some of the trappings of his childhood, but I'm not sure I am. The Lego models he spent so many hours painstakingly assembling and then dismantling so he could have the pleasure of building them again, the bear outfits and the funny games that went with them... I am more attached to these trappings of their childhood than the kids are.

'I'll speak with Dad about it, when he gets home,' I tell him.

But I know it's not going to be easy to find the money, not on top of the five hundred pounds we need to pay the solicitor's initial fee and whatever other charges follow.

'About what?' Gabriella walks in the door and catches the last sentence.

'A school trip,' Harvey says, happy to leave it now that he's asked me if he could go. 'I'm going to watch telly.'

'What's the trip?' Gabriella asks, and I notice she is not wearing her uniform.

'It's a G and T art trip to Wales,' I tell her. 'Why are you in home clothes?'

'It was a non-uniform day,' she says, but she looks as if she's lying.

'Harvey wore his.'

'Just Year Eleven,' she says, cooler now. 'Will he be able to go? On the trip?'

'We'll have to see,' I say. 'It's a week. So there's a lot to consider.'

'Such as?' Gabriella appears to be spoiling for a fight.

'Well, how much school he will miss, and whether they can cater for his nut allergy for that period of time,' I say vaguely.

'And the cost.' She hits the nail on the head. 'Now Ben and Maggie are suing you, we won't have any money for anything, will we?'

'It's not quite like that,' I say.

'Then what is it like?'

'It's complicated.'

'Jesus Christ, Mum,' she says, and turns to leave the room but stops in her tracks. 'By the way, Dad called. He said he has to work late tonight. He won't be back until after nine.'

She says this triumphantly, as if there is some minor victory in the fact of Eric not coming home until later than usual, and I suspect she is right. We seem to have changed, over the course of a couple of weeks, from a family that was reasonably happy to one where stand-offs and petty arguments are the norm. Why would Eric rush to get home?

Ben, Thursday afternoon

'Alright, sir?'

'Hello, sir.'

'Have we missed anything, sir?'

As I'm about to go home, a group of Year Nines greet me in the car park, fresh off a minibus from somewhere.

Thursday afternoon seems to have come fast this week, I suppose because I took the day off yesterday. Nevertheless, I am anxious to be home. The kids have been getting to me today by being normal. It's not their fault. It's just the way I feel, after the trip to the audiologist yesterday. I resent them all for being regular normal kids, going on regular normal school trips.

'Good trip?' I ask, trying to hurry past towards my car.

They appear in high spirits and in the mood for passing the time of day with a teacher. I am not.

'We've been on our camping trip for the Duke of Edinburgh,' says one, indicating the rucksacks on the roof of the minibus which one of the sports teachers is unstrapping.

I say nothing.

'It was freezing, sir,' says another.

'So cold I almost wanted to get in the sleeping bag with Riley,' says someone else.

'So cold our *pain au chocolat* froze,' adds one of the girls.

'I thought it was a Duke of Edinburgh trip.'

'It was, sir,' the girl says.

'And you brought *pain au chocolat*?' I wanted to say, for fuck's sake, listen to yourself.

She looks puzzled, takes her phone out of her pocket and begins texting – a fairly typical reaction when you try to engage pupils in conversation, especially the girls. They seem to lose interest quickly and turn to their phones; either that or they find me so fascinating and funny that they're tweeting whatever I've just said. But I doubt it.

'Right.' I carry on to my car, unlock it and have just sat in the driver's seat when my phone rings. The number is withheld but I answer, just in case it's important.

'Hello.'

'Ben. It's Paddy,' I recognise his voice.

'Paddy. Your number didn't come up.'

'I'm calling from work,' he explains. 'So how are you? How are things?'

'Fine.' I don't speak to Paddy that often. 'You? And Sally?'

'Yes. We're all fine. I just wondered, are you free to talk?'

'I'm sitting in my car in the car park, about to go home, but I've got a few minutes. What's up?'

I can guess why he's calling.

'Well, we just wondered how you were doing, Sally and I, with the baby and that – whether you've got any more news or anything. Sally called last week and spoke to Maggie. She was hoping to speak to you. But I guess you've been busy.'

'Well…' I mirror his hesitancy. 'We're OK. It's not been great, though. Iris is quite fractious and irritable and it clearly frustrates her, not being able to hear, and we're not really getting very far with finding out what her future holds.'

'I see. Do you think there is anything they can do?'

'Well, there are things, but to be honest, Paddy, it's all so bloody depressing. I'd rather not talk about it, not until we know a bit more.'

'Sure.' Paddy hesitates. 'The thing is, I know you've got solicitors on board. Sally's spoken to Isobel a couple of times.'

I remain silent on my end of the line.

'She said she's in a bit of a state and really devastated, naturally, about what happened.'

'Not as devastated as we are.'

'No, but she's pretty cut up about it, Ben. It's not that she doesn't feel responsible or sorry. But what can she do now?'

'She can't do anything now,' I reply. 'That's the point. She could have done something before but she never did. So she's going to have to live with being "pretty cut up" about it.'

'I know. I know that. It's just. I just thought that if you needed help, financially, I – we... we'd be more than willing to help.'

It is, I suppose, a gesture made with good intentions, but I don't receive it as such.

'I don't want your money, Paddy. We're not a fucking charity.'

'I'm not suggesting...' Paddy flounders on the other end of the line. 'It's just that if... I mean, I realise it will be tough for you financially, and – '

'Is this to get Isobel off the hook?' I ask. 'Has she put you up to this?'

'No, of course not. I'm just trying to help, Ben,' Paddy replies.

'Well, there's nothing you or Sally can do,' I snap, irritated beyond reason. 'Iris is deaf. It's Isobel's fault, so, if anyone should pay for it, it's her.'

'They don't really have any money – ' Paddy begins, but I was not going to listen to him making excuses for her.

'As I said, I don't need your money, Paddy. Thanks for the offer, but this is between me and Isobel.'

'Right.' Paddy stalls. 'Well, the offer's always there.'

I am angry now and ready to hang up. 'If that's all.'

'Well, there was something else, actually...'

'What?'

'Look, Ben, I'm – well, we – we're worried about you. It seems...'

'*What?*'

'Look, I know it must be difficult, really difficult, coming to terms with Iris's... well, her...'

227

'Deafness.'

'Yes, her deafness. I know it's a terrible thing to have happened, but the awful thing is, it has.'

'Don't you think I know that?'

'I know – it's just, well… We're just worried for you, mate. I'm just saying, if you need to talk, I'm always around. I'll come down to Croydon after work one evening, if you want.'

'I don't need to talk, Paddy. I've been thinking and talking about nothing else for the past few weeks. I'm done with talking about it. I'm doing something about it now.'

'I'm sorry,' Paddy says.

'I've got to go,' I say, and end the call.

I put my keys in the ignition and start my car, driving it faster around the car park than is either necessary or allowed, and I have to slam my brakes on when I round a row of cars and see the *pain au chocolat* girl kneeling in the middle of the tarmac laying out the contents of her rucksack.

'For fuck's sake,' I say, winding down the window.

'Sir?' She looks up, confused.

'You're in the middle of the fucking road,' I say to her, knowing she could complain, might complain, and I don't care.

Isobel, Thursday afternoon

'I should go now,' I say to Sally as I hear the key in the lock and see Gabriella silhouetted through the glass. 'Gabs is back from school.'

'OK. Well, think about it,' Sally says.

'I will, and thank you, Sal,' I say, hanging up.

She's offered to lend us money if we need it, depending on how things develop, now we also have a solicitor on board.

I don't think we should accept – although we may have to, unless I can find a job – but I'm grateful for the offer, not least because I feel I have Paddy and Sally's support. They appear to be on our side.

'Are you OK?' I ask Gabs when she comes in. She looks upset, as if she might have been crying even. That's not like her. She usually manages her emotions. She's not like me; I wear mine on my sleeve. But Gabs, even when she is upset, often doesn't show it.

'Fine,' she replies, but her voice is slightly wobbly.

'Are you sure?' I say. I know I'm guilty of going on a bit when I think there's something up, knowing she won't tell me unless I do.

'What's it to you anyway?' Gabby snaps.

Now I know something's wrong. And she's out of uniform again, which is odd.

'You don't look very happy,' I say gently. 'I'm worried about you. Has something happened? Is something wrong?'

'There's loads of things wrong. I'll be OK,' she says.

Vincent is in his room and Harvey is playing football after school. It's just the two of us in the kitchen.

'Do you want a cup of tea and something to eat?' I ask my daughter.

'I'll get one,' she says, and goes to put the kettle on.

It's easier for her to talk that way, I recognise that. She won't sit down and talk to me, but she might let something out while she's busy doing something else.

'How was school today?' I start with all the usual questions.

'Fine,' I get monosyllabic replies, until I hit a nerve.

'How's Sam? We haven't seen him for a while.'

Usually, since they've been going out, he comes home with her after school every so often and she asks if he can stay for supper.

'If you must know, we've split up,' Gabby says, slamming the kettle down on its base so hard that the top pops off and water sloshes over the work surface. 'Bugger!'

'But when? Why? I thought you two were getting on really well,' I say, wanting to get up and go to her but sensing from her body language that a hug from me is not what she wants.

'We were,' she says.

'Then why? Did you have an argument?'

'Sort of.'

'But was it important? What was it about?'

'If you must know, it was about Iris,' she says, turning from the kettle and glaring at me. 'I told him what had happened. I told him we were being sued. I told him none of this would have happened if he hadn't got ill first.'

'It's not Sam's fault, love,' I say as gently as I can. 'Any more than it's yours.'

'I knew you'd say that,' Gabs shouts now. 'That's more or less what he said too. That seems to be all anyone is saying. It's not your fault. It's not my fault. It's not their fault. Well, that's not what Ben thinks, is it?'

'Ben's angry,' I say.

230

'Of course he's fucking angry,' Gabs screams at me. 'Wouldn't you be? I'm angry too.'

She storms past me now, bumping into me hard as she heads out of the kitchen and up the stairs. I hear her sobbing as she goes, and pause a minute, thinking I will make the tea she started and take it up with me.

She is lying on her bed, sobbing quietly, when I go up. I don't want her to be unhappy and I worry she may be more like me than Eric after all, and be more prone to upset as a result.

Eric has a greater capacity for happiness than I do. It's one of the things I love about him. He accepts whatever life throws at him and makes the best of it.

I know he doesn't like his job. It's not what he wanted to end up doing, though he says he's happy doing it. 'It's interesting enough. I deal with something different every day and the people I work with are nice. Plus, it's reasonably well paid.'

He sees all the advantages and forgets the disadvantages – the long hours, the inflexible management, the fact that he hates the politics of the paper. At least he does when things are good between us. But when they become strained, so too does his ability to be happy, and resentments about his work seem to surface.

And it's not the first time.

I was lucky when we first left university. I landed a job I wanted before we'd even left: I was assistant to Dinah Cohen. Her constituency was in north London and her profile was high. The job description was mainly office work – answering letters, taking calls, that sort of thing. But I knew from the interview that she was looking for someone who could do more than that: help with research, speech-writing, event-planning – and within weeks the job was so much more than it said on the tin.

I loved it. Dinah seemed to love me. When she was given a job in the shadow cabinet I spent more time in Westminster, less in the constituency. I was happy. I loved doing what I was doing and I knew that, if I kept doing it well, I would end up where I wanted.

But it was different for Eric. He wanted a career in investigative journalism and he had to start somewhere. For a while he was happy with his job on the *Hampstead and Highgate Reporter*. I occasionally fed him stories from Dinah's office. He happily ran with them, but he was less happy with the daily round of stories about planning applications and parking restrictions. He was regularly disappointed, not just by the job but the people he was dealing with too.

I remember one day he came home in a particularly low mood.

'What's up?' I asked him as took a beer from the fridge and slumped in front of the TV.

'I went to interview Frank Carey today,' he told me.

'Frank Carey? But you're always loved Frank Carey. It must have been great to meet him.'

Frank Carey was – still is – an artist with a cult following among students. When we were at university he was in South Africa, living with the ANC and producing rather lovely Impressionist-style paintings of meetings and townships which adorned mugs and T-shirts in student halls up and down the country. I had one of each. He was the sort of person everyone we knew would have been excited to meet.

'What was he like?'

'Charming, polite,' Eric said. 'But disappointingly outraged over the introduction of parking charges in the lovely leafy street where he lives.'

I laughed, but Eric was genuinely feeling let down.

'He's Frank Carey, Isobel. I was so excited about meeting him, and all we talked about was the difficulty of parking in Highgate. It's depressing.'

By contrast, work for me was exciting. I had what I wanted: good job, nice flat, lovely boyfriend whom I presumed I would one day marry or, if not marry, who would be my life partner.

And Eric had two of those things, but it wasn't enough, not then.

I thought that sooner or later he would apply for a job at one of the nationals, or a training scheme at the BBC. I thought he would look for a better job in London. I didn't realise he was thinking of moving elsewhere, not until a month or so later when he told me he had an interview and would be away for a night as the interview process lasted two days.

'But can't you come home in the evening?' I asked.

'It would be difficult.'

We were having dinner in our flat, and he got up and went to get some bread when he told me, as if he didn't quite want to face me, just as Gabriella had done earlier.

'It's in Glasgow.'

'Glasgow?'

'Yes, Glasgow. BBC Scotland, which is based in Glasgow.'

There. It was out there.

'So you're going to leave me?'

'I'm not going to leave you, Isobel. I am just applying for a job, a good job, a job I'd really like to get, in Glasgow.'

'And if you get it?'

'Then I'll go and live in Glasgow for a while.'

'So you would leave me?'

'I may not even get the job,' Eric said. 'They may not want me. But I should at least go for the interview.'

'And if you get it?'

'We'll cross that bridge when we come to it.'

I hated myself for not being more supportive, for making him feel bad about following his dream, but I couldn't seem to stop myself doing it.

We were hardly speaking by the time he went up for the interview, had a huge row the night before, and while he was away something happened which made me check myself, calm down a bit, take stock, look at the way I was behaving and try to behave better.

'How did it go?' I asked, when he came back.

233

'Yes, really well.' There was a polite guardedness to our exchange. 'Thank you.'

'And when will you hear?' I asked.

'It should be in the next couple of days. Is there anything to eat?'

'I've got a couple of steaks. I'll cook them in a minute.'

Eric loved steak. We hardly ever ate it. I didn't eat a great deal of meat, for no reason other than that I didn't really like it that much. Steak was my peace offering.

'Great.' Eric appeared to accept it as such. 'Thanks, Isobel.'

'So how did you feel about being there?' I felt calmer now. His going for the interview had forced me to accept that there was a real possibility he might take the job, if he got it, and the thing that had happened in his absence had left me subdued and ashamed for being so selfish.

'It was good.' Eric took a bottle of wine out of his bag. 'Want some? It was exciting. It's quite a big centre and there's lots going on there. It would be a great opportunity for me. But we'll have to wait and see.'

'Listen, Eric,' I said, 'I know I've been behaving selfishly for the past few weeks and I'm really sorry. If it's what you really want then you must take it. I will miss you, of course, but I couldn't live with myself if I stopped you doing something you really wanted to do.'

'I'm not sure that I do,' Eric said then, pouring us both a glass of wine and taking a large swig of his.

'What do you mean?'

'I've been thinking about what it would mean if I got it. I've been thinking of nothing else. I was torn, Bel, over even whether to go to the interview or not, but I thought it would become clearer if I went.'

'And did it?'

'In a way, yes. If I got the job, I'd have a great job but I'd be away from you, away from our friends, away from my family. Having spent just the one night in a hotel in Glasgow by myself, I'm not sure that a great job would be enough. I'd miss all the other things in my life too much.'

I turned away, unable to look at him, feeling even worse for the way I'd behaved. I almost wanted him to take it now, to punish me, if nothing else.

'I don't know what to say,' I said. 'I feel I've taken the edge off your excitement. If you get it and you want it, you should take it.'

'I don't think I do, Bel,' he said, and he came over and put his glass of wine down and kissed me. 'I want to stay with you, more than I want the job. I realised that before I went up there.'

'Even though I've been a selfish bitch for the past few weeks?'

'Even though you've been a selfish bitch,' he said, taking me in his arms and kissing me. 'Don't cry. It's OK. I'm not going anywhere.'

But that wasn't why I was crying. I was crying because of the way I'd behaved in his absence.

Eric was offered the job and he turned it down. A few months later he landed a job as a trainee on the *Guardian* news desk. It looked better on paper than it was but he was happy, using the capacity he has to be so.

He asked me to marry him not long after. It was what I wanted but I didn't think I deserved him, not then. I wasn't the sort of woman for whom someone should give up something that would have made them happy.

And now my daughter's given up some*one* that seemed to make her happy, and I don't really understand why or what good it will do. I just have a sinking feeling that things are going to keep on coming. Finding out Iris was deaf was just the tip of the iceberg. Who knows what else is going to be affected?

Ben, Friday morning

I have a missed call on my mobile when I finish my Year Eight lesson and I listen to it as the Year Elevens begin to file in. The longer the kids have been at the school, the slower they are to get to their lessons. I suppose I was the same but it annoys me. These are the boys and girls who are taking their GCSEs next summer. Most of them need all the help they can get. Every second counts.

So I barely look up as they come in. Two can play at nonchalant. I'm in a bad mood, obviously. There's no particular reason for it. Iris woke in the early hours and cried a bit, but Maggie got up and went to her and I went back to sleep. It's just one of those days.

'Hello, Mr Deakin?' The speaker on my voicemail has a trace of an accent. It is Hedda. 'I am just calling to tell you we have had a response from the Jordans' solicitor and I need to speak to you before we proceed. If you can call me this morning, please.'

'Sir, how long is a Pinter pause?' Josh Foley is sitting in the desk nearest to me, watching me, waiting for me to finish listening to my message.

'What do you mean?' I say, pressing the End Call button and checking the time on my phone. The class should have started five minutes ago.

'Well, Mr Poole says you should count five seconds when Pinter writes "pause" in the script and ten seconds when he writes "silence". But that sounds a bit long to me. Is he right?'

If we were studying *Who's Afraid of Virginia Woolf?*, which we are not, I'd say we were playing 'Get the Teacher'. It's a favourite game amongst the pupils in the upper half of the school, to pit a teacher's opinions against those of their colleagues. 'Sir, so and so says this. What do you think of that?' Half the time I think they make up what the other teacher has said. They're aware it goes against some innate code of teaching practice to undermine your colleagues, but also aware that each of us has our own opinions and, with a little stirring, they wind up one of their teachers to a pleasingly satisfactory degree.

I don't answer Josh immediately. I continue to stare at my phone.

'Sir?' Josh asks again.

'What was that?'

'I was asking how long a Pinter pause should be. And a silence.'

'I know you were.' Two can play at Year Eleven games too. 'And I paused before replying. Or was there a silence before I replied. Which do you think it was?'

The rest of the class are taking their seats now and have heard this exchange; some of them laugh. Round one of 'Get the Teacher': one nil to Mr Deakin, I think, and I wonder who will be the winner of round one of 'Sue your Friends'.

I call Hedda at break.

'We have had a response from the Jordans' solicitor,' she tells me again.

'And?'

'They deny responsibility, which we thought they would at this stage.'

'So what happens next?'

'I will write to them saying we hold them liable for the costs of ongoing treatment, specialist equipment, education, etcetera, and we will invite them to attend a meeting before we issue proceedings.'

'OK.'

'I am just calling to check you are still happy with this and wish to me to go ahead?'

'Yes,' I say.

'OK, then I will do that, and also start working on the details of the damages we are seeking. I need to seek advice but realistically we are looking at a six-figure sum.'

'Yes,' I say, and I feel a little sick, but I know Hedda would not be taking on the case, it wouldn't be worth her while to take it on, unless she thought she could get substantial damages.

I also know that, unless they sell their house, Isobel and Eric don't have access to that sort of money. But that's beside the point.

I've no idea how much Eric earns. He has told me his job is 'well paid'. That was the reason he cited for taking it, this job that was peculiarly unsuited to his talents or ambitions. 'I've got three kids to support now,' he said, when he told me about it.

'Seriously, you're going to work on the *Daily News*?' I was a little incredulous.

It wasn't the first time I'd felt a little angry on his behalf. Vincent had just started school when he took the job. Isobel could, if she'd chosen to, have thought about going back to work in some capacity, but she'd clearly decided not to. So Eric, rather than staying at the *Guardian* a little longer, waiting for the promotion he hoped would come his way, had taken a sideways step, out of writing into sub-editing, on a paper which typified everything he hated about tabloid newspapers.

I felt miffed on his behalf, that he had to take a job that would close more doors than it opened. But it wasn't the first time he'd sacrificed his own ambitions because of Isobel.

My loyalties had been divided at the time Eric applied for a job with the BBC in Glasgow. It would have been a great opportunity for him, and a job he'd have loved. It could have led to great things. He'd probably be gracing our TV screens nightly, reporting from somewhere exotic, if he'd taken it rather than staying put and then getting the job at the *Guardian*. But

Isobel got herself in such a state about him going that he turned it down, decided to stay in London and marry her instead of following his dreams.

I hated her for doing that to him then, and I hated myself for being unsure which way to turn when they both approached me, asking what they should do.

I ended up taking a wrong turn.

Eric called me first in the week before his interview, told me his dilemma and asked if we could go for a drink. I couldn't see the problem really. People had long-distance relationships these days. If he was really serious about Isobel then surely they could weather the couple of years that he might be in Glasgow?

I said as much to him.

Then Bel called and asked if I could go round, the night he was away for the interview.

She was in such a state when I got there, tearful, angry, beating herself up about being tearful and angry. I didn't really know what to do so I suggested we go for a walk.

We drove to Hampstead Heath and we walked and talked. I told her what I'd told Eric – that they could weather a temporary separation – and she seemed to calm down a lot.

Then we went back to their flat for dinner. Bel cooked and she seemed happier, but then, just as I was about to go and get the tube, she got tearful again.

'You've got to stop now, Bel,' I said, putting my arms around her before I left. 'You and Eric will be fine.'

'Maybe,' she said, holding me so that it was hard to extricate myself. 'But I'll miss him. I miss you too.'

'What do you mean?' I asked, trying to pull away.

But she held on to me. 'You know what I mean,' she said. 'It's hard to let go of someone you've been close to, even if it's the right thing to do, for their sake.'

'We're still close,' I said. I was standing a few inches away from her now. 'I really need to go now, Bel, or I'll miss the last tube. You'll be OK. Shall I call you when I get home?'

'You could stay,' she said, and she looked away as she said it, as if embarrassed by her suggestion.

'I don't think I should,' I said.

But I'd taken a step closer. Even then, even though she was living with my best friend, I still couldn't quite let her go, couldn't quite pass up an opportunity to be close to her – if that was what she was suggesting; I wasn't quite sure.

'No one will know,' she said, taking a step closer herself, looking at me directly now, our faces only inches apart so that there was no mistaking what she was suggesting.

I held her face in my hands then and kissed her. And I didn't think about Eric once, not even when I was lying on his side of the bed curled around his girlfriend, falling asleep having fucked her.

It wasn't until I woke up in the morning, in the cold light of day, that the realisation of what we'd done dawned on me.

I got up awkwardly, and headed off with only a few words. I think I tried to reassure her that everything would be fine, with Eric's job. Though, bearing in mind how we'd spent the night, it seemed unlikely that it would be, if he got it and took it.

But he didn't. He turned it down to be with her and they decided to get married.

I was their best man, for fuck's sake. I told Bel to ask Eric not to ask me. Why didn't he ask his brother or anyone other than me? How could I be his best man?

But it was easier than I thought, when it happened.

Maybe that final night helped them in some way decide their future. Anwyay, it wouldn't happen again, not now they were getting married. But maybe it happening that 'one last time' helped Bel sort herself out. Or maybe it just helped me feel better, to tell myself that.

WEEK THREE

Isobel, Tuesday morning

It had to be today that the next letter arrived.

It's Vincent's birthday and he's been excited for days, days in which I've been quietly dreading whatever happens next and at the same time anticipating that something will. I knew our solicitor had sent a reply to Ben's. I had no idea what reaction it would prompt, but I have been expecting something.

'Can I have waffles with Nutella, Coke and squeezy yoghurt for breakfast?' Vincent asks.

'Not Coke.' I am indulging him a little but there are lines to be drawn. 'You'll be completely hyper.'

'But they won't mind at school. I can just work with the ADHD group today.'

'No, Vinnie.'

I feel a bit mean. It's not been much of a birthday so far. Eric left for work before Vincent was up, Harvey overslept and had to be reminded, by Vincent, that it was his birthday, and Gabs has just come down to breakfast and told him the present she ordered on Amazon hasn't arrived yet.

I almost feel like conceding over the Coke, just to inject a bit of life into the day. 'Well, anyway, do I have to go to school today?' Vincent tries another tack. 'I could not go because it's my birthday.'

'No, Vincent. You have to go.'

'You're such a pushy parent!'

'This is from me.' Harvey is still a bit of an overslept grump but he hands over a package. 'Happy birthday.'

'What is it?' Vincent feels the package, which is about a foot long and misshapen.

'Open it,' Harvey and I say in unison. I am as curious as Vincent to know what the parcel contains. All Harvey has told me is that he's been making him something.

'Oh, wow!' Vincent unwraps what appears to be a stick. He is clearly a little bemused but too polite to say so. 'What is it?'

'It's an elastic band gun.' Harvey takes the object, which on closer inspection reveals itself indeed to be a stick, stuck to another stick to form the shape of a gun, with a clothes peg fixed to the top and a groove carved into the end.

'You stretch the elastic band across the end. Then push the peg, like a trigger, and it shoots it.' He demonstrates.

The band disappears across the room. In fact the band seems to disappear entirely. Vincent cannot find it and is disappointed, as he wants to have a go.

'There might be some in the drawer.' I nod to the drawer that offended Eric so much last week, and Vincent starts rummaging through it. 'That's brilliant, Harvey,' I say. 'Well done.'

Harvey shrugs.

'You'll have to show Dad later.'

'I can't find any,' Vincent shouts, but he is distracted by the sound of the letterbox clanging as the postman struggles to push something through it. Vincent leaps up and races into the hallway, coming back with a small packet and a big grin and a handful of other envelopes.

'That's for you and Dad,' he says, handing a manila envelope to me, and my heart sinks. It has the hallmarks of being from a solicitor and I don't know if I can face opening it. Not today. I want to enjoy Vincent's birthday. I want to go out and shop for pizza and make a cake, without having to worry about whatever it says. I want to start thinking about what I need to do before his party, which is not till the weekend.

It's a Space Hopper jousting party. Vinnie came up with the idea, and I need to borrow some more Space Hoppers from friends and brooms to use as jousting poles.

'You can wrap them in towels or something so they don't prick people,' Vincent had suggested.

'Have you played this before somewhere?'

'No, I invented it,' he'd replied. 'But I did see elephant polo on the telly. I sort of copied that a bit.'

I put the letter aside and watch him flicking through the others now, putting the coloured envelopes with his name on them on the table next to the packet.

'This one's from Grandad,' he says, tearing open a blue envelope from which flutters a fifty-pound note. 'Wow, that's amazing. And I think this is from Sally and Paddy.'

I know Sally's writing but I'm surprised Vince does, and say so. 'I think it's because they always remember,' he says. 'And I think I know what this one is.' He picks up the parcel and begins squashing it excitedly. 'Can I open it now?'

'Of course.' I suspect it's from Eric's brother, but whatever it is will have been chosen by his wife, Natasha.

'Oh.'

Vincent shakes out a blue T-shirt from its wrapping. On the front a series of baked bean transfers snake across the front to form the words 'Full of Beans'. Vincent loves blue. 'Why do people say they feel blue when they feel sad? I like feeling blue, it's tickly.' And he loves baked beans. It's a perfect present for him. But he looks disappointed.

'Don't you like it? I ask.

'Yes, I love it,' he says, looking slightly put out.

'You can wear it after school.'

'Yes,' he says, and hangs it over the back of his chair. 'Mum?'

'Yes.'

'Do you think Ben will send my present before my party?'

'Oh...' I'm not sure what to say. 'He doesn't always remember your birthday, does he?'

'You won't get a birthday present from Ben this year,' Gabriella says.

'Gabs,' I say, warningly.

'Well, he won't, will he?'

'Why not?' Vincent looks anxious, as if he's done something wrong. 'He said he was going to try to get me a straitjacket.'

'He's not going to get you a straitjacket, Vincent,' Gabriella says to him, but it's me she's looking at and daring to contradict her.

'Do you think he couldn't get one?' Vincent looks from his older sister to me.

'I don't know if he could get one or not, Vinnie,' I say. 'Let's wait and see, shall we?'

'He won't send you a present this year because he hates us,' Gabriella tells him.

'But why?' Vincent looks confused and upset.

'He doesn't hate *you*, Vincent,' I say quickly.

'Well, he hates Mum and he hates me,' she says. 'So he probably doesn't like anyone else in our family much either.'

'Did I do something wrong?' Vincent's lip is quivery now.

'Gabriella, that's enough,' I say sharply, and she busies herself making toast, admonished but not placated.

'Listen, Vincent,' I try to explain, 'Ben doesn't hate you. He thinks you are fantastic, which you are, but, well, the thing is, Iris hasn't been very well, and Ben and Maggie have been very busy trying to deal with that and they probably haven't had much time to think about what they were going to get you for your birthday.'

'But why did Gabriella say he hates us?'

'Gabriella says things that are not always right,' is the best I can come up with.

'Like when she told me jamlee was the worst swear word in the world?' Vinnie asked.

'Yes, a bit like that.'

Jamlee was a word I'd invented to try to stop Vincent using the bad language he'd started to pick up at school.

246

'Vincent, don't say shit,' I'd admonished him when he dropped something after school one day.

'Everyone says it,' he'd replied.

'That doesn't mean you have to.'

'Connor uses the F word too.'

'Well, I hope you don't?'

He didn't answer, which suggested that he did. It was one of those parental battles you feel you can only lose. You tell your children not to use certain words but all their peers do, so you know they probably will as well.

So I offered him an alternative.

'Well, as long as you never say...' I looked around the kitchen, searching for inspiration and hit upon a pot of jam '... jamlee!'

He believed it was the worst thing anyone could say, right up until a few months ago when Harvey put him straight.

'So Ben doesn't hate us. He just forgot my birthday because Iris hasn't been very well?'

'Yes,' I said. 'Maybe he'll remember before the weekend.'

'And you remember that Jack's coming home after school today?'

'Yes, of course,' I say. 'And I've not forgotten that you want cake, crisps and popcorn for tea and pizza, chocolate biscuits and ice-cream for dinner.'

'Yeah.'

'Is Jack still a vegetarian?' I ask.

'No, he eats meat now,' Vincent fills me in. 'But only orgasmic meat.'

'Organic,' Harvey corrects him, and smirks.

'That's what I said.' Vincent looks peeved, clearly aware he's said something wrong but not quite sure what. 'He says that kind of meat is better 'cos the animals have had happy lives so it's OK to eat them.'

'I think it's worse,' Harvey retorts. 'If I'd had a happy organismic life – '

'You wish,' said Gabriella.

'If I'd had a happy life,' he continued, 'I'd want to carry on living it, not be killed and eaten. But if I'd had a miserable life, I'd probably want to end it and end up in a burger.'

Harvey could be a lawyer if the industrial design idea founders. Maybe I should tell him about the mess we're in now. Maybe he could come up with a better defence than the solicitor I paid five hundred quid to, to send a letter to Ben's.

I wonder if Harvey is aware that something is going on. Gabs knows, and I am sure Vincent has no idea, but maybe in his quiet way Harvey has absorbed some of the tension in our house, and is just as confused as Gabriella but hasn't said anything.

I look at the letter in the manila envelope lying on the side. I am almost certain it's a response from Ben's solicitor. I tell myself I'll open it in the evening, when Eric is home, after the kids have gone to bed. I don't want to spoil Vincent's birthday if I can help it. The letter can wait.

Ben, Tuesday morning

'What time do you have to leave?' Maggie asks, as I bring her tea in bed.

It's seven-thirty and Iris is still asleep. Maggie could have slept in a little longer, but she woke when my alarm went off. I'm taking a Year Nine group on a trip today, to the Globe Theatre, and my needing to be at school by eight has blown Maggie's chance of a lie-in. I can make up for it, a little, by bringing her tea. She can sit and think her own thoughts for however long before Iris wakes.

'I'm going in a minute,' I say, putting her cuppa on the bedside table and sitting on the edge of the bed. 'And I'll be back a bit later than usual.'

I love the Globe but I've already decided I'm not going to enjoy the trip. It's never easy having fifty-plus kids on the loose anywhere other than school. I know there are a few who are liable to wander off and I won't relax until we are back at school again.

And then, as soon as I get home, we have to go out again.

'Don't forget we're going out this evening,' Maggie reminds me now.

'I hadn't,' I say, in as even a tone as I can muster.

Maggie has arranged for us to meet a couple of young deaf adults, adults without hearing aids or cochlear implants, who communicate only by signing. It's the latest stage of her mission to find out as much as possible about what the future might hold for Iris. But she's going too fast for me. I'm still slowly getting used to the fact that Iris is deaf. I'm not ready to fast-forward to what she might be like when she's a twenty-something deaf adult.

But Maggie has her way and I have mine.

'It will be fine,' Maggie says.

'It's not that,' I reply. 'I'm not really looking forward to this trip.'

I have a strange relationship with theatre these days. The older I get, and the more jaded I become with teaching, the more irritated I get with the young actors plying their Romeos and Hamlets on stage, when I never got the chance.

You think I'd be over it by now, the being a failed actor, and sometimes I think I am. But at other times, especially when life seems a bit shit all round, which it does right now, I still wish I'd had a break, wish I'd had a different life.

'It'll be fine,' Maggie says again, kindly.

Iris starts to holler.

'Shall I get her?' I ask Maggie.

'No, leave her a bit longer,' she says. 'She's not distressed yet. She's just talking to herself.'

'Talking?'

I can't help myself. I know it doesn't help Maggie, I know she's trying to come to terms with how Iris is, and my pointing out how she isn't doesn't make it easy, but I still can't help myself.

'Ben, please,' she says.

'I'm sorry.' I kiss her and get up to go. 'Can't I bring her in now? I won't see her before I go if I don't.'

'OK.' Maggie smiles. My wanting to see her is at least an admission of something, that I do love her, even though I've not yet accepted the way she is, or the way she is going to be.

'Hey!' I say, popping my head round the door of Iris's room, and she looks up, sensing the motion of the door and me coming through it.

'Ork.' She makes a peculiar noise, which sounds more like a dolphin than a human being.

'Hello, bottlenose,' I say, going to her cot.

I know it's a cruel thing to say and, although she can't hear me, I wish I had not said it.

'Ork, ork,' Iris says as I carry her along the corridor to her mother.

'Don't worry, sweetheart,' I tell her, kissing the top of her head. 'We have our own way of dealing with things.'

And I think of the letter Hedda should have sent to Isobel and Eric and wonder if they've got it.

'Here's Mum,' I say, putting Iris down on the bed next to Maggie.

'Hello, lovely girl.' Maggie smiles and coos and carries on chatting to her, the way she always did. Neither of us is used to the fact she can't hear us, so we carry on talking to her, as if she can.

I remember doing the same to my grandfather before he died. He'd come to stay with us for a few days at a time and spent most of his time sitting in a chair, reading or staring into space. 'Why don't you go and talk to Pops?' my mum would ask. And I would. I'd go and sit next to him and chat away, tell him about my day. Strangely, he was one of the few people I could speak to with perfect fluency. It was as if there was some trip in my brain which flicked my stammer off if the person I was talking to couldn't hear me. He was aware I was there, chatting away, and he smiled at me benignly from time to time. But I don't think he ever heard a word, not at that stage of his life, just as Iris clearly hears nothing her mother is saying now.

'By the way, Ben,' Maggie says as I'm about to go, 'you know it's Vincent's birthday today?'

Naturally, I do not know that. I can barely remember the date of Maggie's birthday (actually I have recorded it in my phone so that I don't forget and have an alarm set to remind me a month, a fortnight and a week before). I realise birthdays are important to people and forgetting them is a terrible slight, especially if it is your partner's. But until Maggie came on the scene I hadn't taken note of when Vincent's birthday was, and I should have, because he is my godson.

'Men don't really do birthdays,' I'd told Maggie once when she asked me if I'd remembered Eric's. 'They have homosexual overtones!'

Eric wouldn't care that I'd forgotten his and he'd appreciate the joke, but I ought to remember Vincent's.

It had kind of annoyed me, before I was finally given the job, that I'd not been asked to be a godparent to any of Eric and Isobel's children. I'd thought I was the obvious choice, when they announced that they were having a bit of do 'to celebrate Gabriella's birth'. Bel told me she wasn't being christened but they were going to have godparents and they'd be at the party, with a few other close friends.

'Will you come?' Bel had asked.

'I'd love to,' I'd replied, but I'd felt a bit miffed. Who the fuck was the godfather?

It was Eric's brother, which I suppose was fair enough but a bit of waste if you ask me. Eric's brother was already his uncle, so Gabs was missing out on another present at Christmas.

And for Harvey they chose Paddy, which also pissed me off a bit. I mean, I was a closer friend, surely? Why did they never ask me? Was it because I'd already had the best man role? Or because they thought I'd be crap at it?

If that was what they thought, they were right.

Beyond the first formal-ish get-together when I presented Vincent with a silver chip fork – a perfect present given that they lived in Brighton, I thought – I'd failed to remember a single birthday, and sent him unimaginative notes of varying denominations tucked inside a Christmas card for years. It was only when Maggie arrived on the scene that the presents became a bit more inspired and I/we/she endeavoured to get him something he actually wanted.

This year he'd given me the heads-up on ideas.

'What do you want for your birthday this year, Vincent?' I'd thought to ask him while we were in France. The two of us were cooling off in the pool, one afternoon. 'Have you got any ideas?'

'A straitjacket,' he said, splashing around in the shallow end.

I thought I had misheard him. 'A life jacket?'

'No a straitjacket. So that I can learn to escape. I really want one.'

'Right.'

I quizzed Eric about this later.

'He really does want one. He's into magic and all sorts at the moment,' he told me. 'He'd be made up if you remembered.'

I did remember, and when we got home I searched for straitjackets online. But the only things that came up were in online sex shops and I knew Bel wouldn't be entirely happy if I gave him anything made from black rubber.

So I abandoned that idea and forgot all about Vincent and his birthday until now, when Maggie brings it up.

'What do you want to do about it?' she asks.

'I don't know.'

'We shouldn't involve him in all of this,' Maggie says.

'I'll have a think,' I reply, as I make for the door.

Maybe I'd pick something up in the gift shop at the Globe. There must be something there that would appeal to him. I could buy something, even if I never gave it to him.

'We need to leave by five-thirty tonight,' Maggie reminds me about this drink again. 'Have a good day.'

Isobel, Tuesday evening

Vincent is happy. Eric is home early and also seems happy. In fact, everyone has relaxed into Vinnie's birthday, and the atmosphere in our house is normal to good.

I know it won't last. But I don't yet know how stressed things will become, or that, when they do, that will feel almost normal too.

Jack has gone home and Vincent is buzzing from the day.

'We had music and Miss Rusbatch played "Happy Birthday" to me on the piano,' he tells Eric.

'So you're glad you went?'

'Yes, but you are still a pushy parent for making me!' This is aimed at me. 'And Max gave me a packet of Maltesers at school. Can I put them on my ice-cream?'

'You've already had ice-cream, Vincent, when Jack was here.'

'But it is my birthday!'

'Oh, go on, then,' I say. 'Ask Harvey if he wants some too.'

'Harvey, do you want ice-cream with Maltesers?' Vincent shouts in the direction of the sitting room where his brother is watching *Dragon's Den*. He's decided he wants to go on it. He wants to show them the full range of his inventions: the trolley chairs, the vinyl bowls, the fruit carton spectacle cases, the band shooter and more. He thinks he might be able to persuade them to invest in him, if he gets his pitch and presentation right.

'OK,' comes the reply to the ice-cream offer, as if he's doing him a favour.

'I'll get it,' Vincent says, pulling out the bottom drawer of the freezer and taking a tub of vanilla ice-cream over to the work surface, spooning it out. 'The Maltesers are in the sitting room,' he says as he carries the two bowls out of the kitchen.

I wonder if he will be sick tonight, but after eating his second pudding he goes into the garden to kick a ball around with Eric and then suddenly zonks out, sits on the sofa and looks as if he might fall asleep.

'Why don't you go and get a shower now, Vinnie? You look shattered.'

Any other day he would resist tiredness, but today he accepts it. 'Will you come up with me?' he asks, which means he wants me to accompany him to the top of the stairs, but part company as soon as he enters the bathroom.

'Of course I will, birthday boy.' I get up and ruffle his hair as he drags himself slowly up the steps and I put the bathmat on the floor while he hovers, unwilling to undress in front of me any more.

'I'll shout when I'm done,' he says, as I exit the bathroom.

A few minutes later he shouts down that he's ready. Eric and I both go up to tuck him into bed.

'I had a really good day, thank you,' he says, looking much younger the instant his face touches the pillow, as if the state of unconsciousness wipes some of the knowingness off his face. Eric too, when he is asleep, looks more boyish, but today he looks tired as he kisses Vincent, and I don't know whether to tell him about the still unopened letter.

'Well done, Bel,' he says to me, kindly, as we go back down and into the kitchen to clear up after dinner. Gabs is sitting at the table, looking through Vincent's birthday cards.

'What for?' I ask Eric.

'For raising such a great kid and giving him such a good day today.'

He often says something like this on their birthdays: expresses some sense that he thinks I've done a good job of bringing them up.

'Thank you,' I reply, and I touch his arm.

He doesn't pull away, the way he has been recently if I try to make any sort of physical contact. It's not much, but it's a start, and I am loath to do anything which will destroy the mood.

Gabriella does it for me.

'What about that other letter that came this morning?' she says, putting Vincent's cards down and looking at me.

'What was that?' Eric asks, more as a reflex than a question.

'Another letter came this morning,' I say, as we stack the dishwasher together. 'I think it's from the solicitor.'

'Didn't you open it?'

'Not yet. I had a lot to do and I thought I'd wait for you to come home.'

'I'm going to have a coffee,' Eric says, going to put the kettle on. 'Do you want one?'

I nod. Coffee will be the accompaniment to us finding out whatever the latest development is. I fear we may need something stronger.

'Do you have any homework?' I ask Gabriella.

I want her to leave but I don't want to tell her to.

'She might as well stay,' Eric says. 'She knows what's going on.'

'It might be better – ' I begin, but Gabs interrupts me.

'I've a right to know what's happening too.'

I take the letter from the side, where I put it earlier, while Eric fills a cafetiere with grinds and hot water and brings it over to the table. 'Open it, then,' he says, standing behind me so he can read its contents over my shoulder.

There's legalese to start with: a few paragraphs before it gets to the point. Ben's solicitor doesn't accept that we are not responsible for Iris's deafness. She says they have evidence that we are responsible for causing it and are inviting us in for a meeting to discuss the damages they intend to pursue, in court, if we cannot agree out of it.

There is a figure, and I am thankful I am sitting down when I read it. It's a six-figure sum, way in excess of anything we could possibly afford. Ben knows we don't have that sort of money and could never find it.

'Jesus Christ.' Eric sits down too.

We look at each other, unsure what to say.

'What does it say?' Gabriella asks.

'They're asking for a lot of money,' Eric tells her.

'How much?'

'A lot more than we could afford,' Eric says and begins folding the letter.

I am thankful that he does not show it to Gabs. He may think she has a right to know what's going on, but I don't want to worry her any more than necessary.

'Why won't you tell me?' she persists.

'Actually, Gabs,' Eric says, 'I'm sorry but maybe it's best if Mum and I discuss this together first. I'm sorry, love. Do you mind leaving us for a bit?'

Gabriella looks put out, but she goes.

'What are we going to do?' I ask, and for a while Eric says nothing.

'The whole thing is ridiculous,' he says, eventually. 'Ben knows we don't have that sort of money, unless we sell the house.'

'You don't think we'd have to, do you?'

'I don't know. I don't think they could make us. We'd need to ask our solicitor. Jesus Christ,' he says again. 'What a fucking mess.'

'Why are they doing this to us, Eric?'

'Maybe it's not personal,' he says, ever the optimist.

'How can it not be? We are their friends. Ben's friends, anyway. It's ridiculous.'

I am almost certain Maggie is behind this now, and am about to say so, but we are interrupted.

'Mum!' I hear Gabs shouting from the living room. There's an urgency to her voice I can't ignore, so I get up and follow it.

Harvey is slumped on the sofa. His face is red and he is struggling for breath. 'I think there must have been nuts in those chocolates,' he says, wheezing terribly.

'Where's your pen?' I ask. 'Is it in your school bag?'

'I think so.'

'Gabriella, go upstairs and get the one from the bathroom cabinet,' I tell her. We have several epipens for such an eventuality.

'I feel sick,' Harvey says, as I rummage in his school bag.

I can't find his pen.

'Gabriella!' I shout.

I don't know if she can hear me from upstairs, but she comes back down with the pen in her hand and thrusts it over. 'Here.'

I know what to do, I've been shown, I've watched the video a thousand times, but still I hesitate. There's something about thrusting a needle into your child's thigh which you instinctively recoil from, even if you know it will save his life.

'Just do it, Bel,' Eric says. 'Or let me.'

But I do it myself. I pull the safety catch of the pen and push it against the fabric of Harvey's trousers, so that the needle releases and pierces through them and into his outer thigh.

I wait and remove it, check the window to make sure the drug has been released, and begin massaging the spot where the needle went in, as instructed.

It works quickly. Within minutes, Harvey's breathing is steady again and the red swelling around his mouth has subsided.

'I think I'm going to be sick,' he says again, and Eric thrusts the washing-up bowl under his chin just as he throws up.

'What did you eat, Harvey?' I ask, looking at the contents for something to give me a clue.

'It must have been those sweets of Vincent's we had with the ice-cream,' he says, looking shamefaced.

'I thought they were Maltesers. You're fine with Maltesers,' I say.

'No, they were just similar to Maltesers,' Gabriella says, holding up the packaging. It's red, but they are some sort of cheap supermarket own brand version called 'Chocolate-Coated Crunchy Balls'. Neither of the boys had stopped to read the packaging, let alone the allergy guidelines.

I screw up my eyes to look now and there it is, clear enough. 'May contain nuts'.

'Oh, Jesus, Harvey,' I say angrily now, but my anger stems from relief. 'Why didn't you check what was in them?'

'I didn't think,' he says. 'I just thought they were Maltesers and they're OK. I'm sorry, Mum.'

'Leave him, Bel,' Eric says.

'But he could have...'

I don't finish the sentence. We all know what could have happened.

Ben, Tuesday evening

I was knackered after the theatre trip. By the time I got home all I wanted to do was slump in front of the TV, but Maggie was keen to get me straight out again.

'You've just about got time for a cup of tea but I don't want to be late. We don't want to keep them waiting.'

'They can wait a few minutes, surely?' I said, grumpily. Really, this was the last thing I wanted to do now. I thought it would depress me further, meeting adults who cannot hear or speak.

'They can speak,' Maggie persisted in saying. 'They just have a different way of doing it.'

'Do you really need me there?' I said, petulant. 'Maybe you could chat to them first and I could join you a bit later?'

'No.' Maggie puts her foot down. 'These people have lives themselves and they've arranged to meet us out of kindness, to give us an idea of what life might be like for Iris if she doesn't have cochlear implants – and I know you don't like that idea much any more.'

I kept quiet and Maggie continued.

'You might not be keen, but I wasn't keen for you to start involving solicitors in our lives. But I let you talk me round, because it seemed important to you. So do this for me. Please.'

I could not argue, and now that I am here sitting in a pub, with these two young adults talking in sign language, I realise I haven't been listening to the translator. Instead I have become slightly mesmerised by the gestures and hand movements and am being drawn into the world which I have been resisting.

Maggie would be pleased if she could read the thoughts that are going through my mind. They go something like this: *This is amazing, actually. They can say all this, just by waving their hands about in the air. These people are brilliant. It's like acting, almost. I could get into this...*

But she can't read my mind, and she misreads the look on my face as indicating that my mind is wandering, rather than rapt.

'Ben!' she says, with a slight shrillness that makes me wince.

'Yes?' I look up, half expecting her to begin making hand gestures to accompany her question. But her hands are folded in her lap as she speaks.

'Rachel was asking if you knew any sign language.'

'Oh, right.' I shake my head and look at Rachel, a twenty-something profoundly deaf woman seated on the opposite side of the pub table. She's very beautiful: long dark wavy hair, pale skin and big blue eyes. She could be Irish, but of course sign language has no accent, so I can't tell.

'A little,' I say, looking at Rachel as I hold my thumb and forefingers in L shapes, making the sign for 'little'. I only know it because Maggie has been signing 'Twinkle, Twinkle, Little, Star' to Iris before she goes to bed each night. She sings and signs, twitching her fingers in the air to represent twinkles as Iris lies in her cot, lulled to sleep by hand movements rather than sound.

Rachel makes a movement, which looks as if she is blowing me a kiss.

'Good!' the sign language interpreter translates the sign for me, and I laugh.

It was the National Deaf Children's Society that suggested this meeting we are having in a pub in Clapham. They didn't suggest we have it in a pub. I think that idea actually came from Rachel, which was a brilliant one, given we were all bound to feel a bit less tense with a beer close to hand.

I wonder if Rachel and Darren, the young man sitting next to her, felt as uncomfortable about the whole meeting as I did. It felt forced and unnatural. 'Let's meet up with these two people we have never met before and have nothing in common with, other than that they are deaf and so is our daughter, shall we?' That's not exactly a comfortable proposition for any of us, but I suppose Rachel and Darren must have been up for it or they wouldn't have agreed.

Maybe they do it a lot. Maybe they are on a list of deaf people willing to talk to parents of newly diagnosed deaf children and tell them how great it is.

I'm becoming cynical again, but I do also want to know.

'Will you ask Rachel if she does this a lot?' I say to Sylvie.

Sylvie had put out a hand, when we arrived in the pub and introduced herself as 'your translator for the day'.

They were easy enough to spot, when we walked into the bar. Three people sitting round a table, all signing to each other. It had to be them. And we probably had to be us too, the quite-old-to-have-a-baby couple with said baby fast asleep in a buggy, a state she remains in for the duration of the meeting. It's almost as if she's decided to leave any decisions about her future up to us.

'Does what?' Sylvie asks me before translating my spoken words.

'Meets up with anxious parents,' I say, smiling to Rachel as I say it.

She smiles back, unaware yet what I am asking her.

Sylvie makes the signs and Rachel mimes back.

'We are happy to meet with people and talk if they think it will help,' Sylvie says.

Rachel and Darren look together-ish, squashed up on a bench seat close to each other, mirroring body language and being tactile towards each other. But then I guess, if body language is your language, you mirror it. And, if neither of you can hear, then touch is a good way of getting the other's attention.

'How did you two meet?'

Sylvie signs my question and Darren and Rachel both begin making the same signs together at the same time. Then they both shrug, also in unison. Rachel makes a familiar enough hand gesture, which I know means 'you speak', and sits quietly while Darren explains in a way that ends with him clapping his hands together.

'They met at a school for the deaf,' Sylvie tells me, and I feel my heart sinking slightly. I like these two young people, from what I've seen, I really do. They seem open and friendly, and they are here because they think it might help us, but the 'I did not want this' part of my brain is fast-forwarding and thinking negative thoughts.

I wonder if they are a couple. They don't look like a couple because she is more attractive than he is. Much more. That's not unusual – you see that a lot, I know – but I can't help thinking that if the place you are most likely to meet a boyfriend is at deaf school then your options are limited. I don't want my daughter to end up with a bloke who is nice enough, if a few features short of ugly, just because he speaks the same language. I don't want that for her.

'We're also thinking about cochlear implants. Aren't we, Ben?' Maggie is saying to Sylvie. 'We'd like her to be able to hear a little, if it was possible.'

I nod, but Maggie knows that since we had our trip to the audiology unit cochlear implants no longer seem like the miracles I once hoped they would be.

There's intensity to the signing now going on between Rachel, Darren and Sylvie, which hints at 'discussion'.

I look to Sylvie for explanation, when they come to the end of the frenzied flurry of hands.

'Rachel thinks it is unfair of parents to try to force their children to hear,' she says. 'She says deafness is not a disability. It is a difference.'

'I know...' Maggie begins, but she is clearly flustered.

'Maggie is a musician,' I try to interpret for her. 'Hearing is very integral to her world. Of course we want our daughter to be a part of that, if it was at all possible.'

Sylvie signs and Rachel, obviously sensing that Maggie is a bit upset by her outburst, begins rubbing her fist around her chest in a circular motion – another sign I realise I am familiar with. I must be picking it up by proxy because Maggie has been making such an effort, even though I've made very little.

It means 'sorry'.

Darren speaks now. His movements are slower and more expressive than the two women's. Perhaps this says something about him. Perhaps I am wrong in my assumption that Rachel is too good for him. Perhaps he is the one who is thoughtful and highly intelligent and Rachel was drawn to him for those qualities.

I've no idea what he is saying, but I find myself mesmerised again in a way I had not expected to be.

Maybe I should have expected it.

I remember going to see the comedian Eddie Izzard once and that particular show had a sign language interpreter, who stood on one side of the stage throughout. Even though Izzard's own performance was full of mime and theatricality, and mesmerising because of it, I found my attention kept being diverted from him to the guy doing the signing. The way he morphed the comic's words into actions, which seemed to speak louder than the words themselves, was amazing. I remember being impressed, at the time.

I'd just forgotten.

'Darren says Rachel was born deaf so, for her, life has always been this way, but he lost his hearing after getting meningitis as a child,' Sylvie interprets Darren's hand signals. 'He's asking if your daughter was born deaf?'

'No.' I shake my head. 'She had measles and became deaf as a result.'

'That's bad,' Sylvie says, as Darren makes a sign which is like blowing a kiss but, rather than blowing it, he appears to slap it down on an imaginary surface.

'She caught it from the daughter of a friend who had not been vaccinated,' I add, wanting them to understand the full picture.

I hope that perhaps this will make Rachel more sympathetic towards Maggie, for wanting her to be able to hear a bit. If she understands how unnecessary Iris's deafness is, I hope that perhaps she will understand us better.

Rachel puts both her palms flat in the air then bends her fingers, turning them into claws and scraping them back towards her.

'Selfish,' Sylvie translates.

'Yes,' I say and nod and repeat what she has just said. 'Selfish.'

As I say it, I put my palms flat, then bend my fingers and draw the claws back towards myself. It feels strangely liberating.

Isobel, Friday

'The police?' I can't quite believe what I am hearing, although half of me is hardly surprised. Our friends' baby is deaf, solicitors are involved – why shouldn't the police be mixed up in our lives too?

Gabriella has never been in any sort of trouble with anyone before.

'But why wasn't she at school?'

I am in the foam shop when I get the call. It's one of those shops that never seems to have any customers to keep it going. All the other shops in the street are busy, doing a good trade in 'vintage' clothes, or homewares, or what Eric calls 'ifty wifty' shops, i.e. shops that sell stuff no one really needs. There's a huge market for all of that. People always have the money to buy things they don't really need. Even in the midst of a recession, unnecessary stuff still seems to sell well – here, anyway. But foam is the possible exception.

Nevertheless there is a shop, stuck between an 'ifty wifty' shop and a retro café, which is stacked with foam strips of varying size and thickness. Most of it is that off-yellow spongy colour, but there are a few shelves of green and grey too. I need some to cover the ends of broom handles, to make them safer to use as lances for Vinnie's Space Hopper jousting party.

'Why bother?' Gabriella said, when I was discussing it with Vincent, keen to use any opportunity to highlight my casual neglect of other people's children's welfare.

I caught myself reflected in the glass of the foam shop door, as I went in. Even though I didn't have any of the children with me, I recognise that there is something about me which makes me look like a mother. I look like someone who would be buying foam for some ridiculous project which only she has time for because she does not work.

I'm not quite sure what it is about my appearance that gives me away. I'm dressed casually, but so is everyone these days.

I remember when Gabs was little she saw a group of men standing outside a bank. 'Are they prime ministers?' she asked.

'No, love. They work in the bank, I think.'

'They look like prime ministers,' she said. 'They're wearing prime minister's outfits.' By this she meant suits. In her three-year-old life, she'd so rarely encountered anyone wearing a suit that she thought these men having a cigarette on the pavement outside their place of work must all be having a break from running the country.

So I don't know what it is that makes me appear so definitely someone who is a mother who does not work.

Eric came home last night telling me he'd bumped into an old colleague of mine.

'You'll never guess who I came across today.'

I hate having to guess. 'Tell me.'

'Emma Dunlop!'

I struggled at first to place the name. Then I remembered: she had joined my team a few months before I left work. As far as I knew, Eric had never met her.

'Oh, yes? Where was that, then?'

'She came into the office to give a briefing to someone on the politics desk. We got in the same lift.'

'And got chatting?'

Emma Dunlop was, if I remembered rightly, very beautiful.

I wondered how, in the short space of time it took a lift to go to the fifth floor of the building where Eric worked, he had elicited enough information not only to discover who Emma Dunlop was but also to make the connection with me.

'She asked if there was a coffee bar anywhere in the building,' Eric told me. 'She said she had a meeting with Roger Palin but she was twenty minutes early and needed a coffee. So I went with her, as I was going there anyway. I can't quite remember how it came up that she used to work in your old office but she remembered you and said to send you her best.'

'What does she do now, then?' I asked, and began to feel a huge and unreasonable resentment towards this woman I barely knew but who definitely did something impressive these days, if she was stalking the corridors of the *Daily News* ready to brief its chief political correspondent.

'She's the mayor's campaign director now.'

She would be.

'She did your old job for several years after you left, had a couple of children and worked as a consultant for a few years while they were young, and now she's back working full-time for the mayor.'

His words were delivered casually but I was super-sensitive to them. Emma Dunlop had done all that and managed to fit two children in too. Well, bully for her. And no doubt when *she* caught sight of herself reflected in shop doorways she looked like a high-powered career woman.

'Can I help you?' the woman who ran the foam shop asked, and I was about to tell her what I needed when I heard my phone ringing inside my bag.

I go straight up to the school after I've hung up. I take a taxi from the rank by the Royal Pavilion. I want to get there quickly, even though the school said it was unnecessary.

'We'd just like to speak to you and Gabriella after school,' Mr Collins, the head of Gabriella's year, said to me on the telephone. 'If you could be here by three-thirty, that will be fine.'

But I want to get there sooner. I need to speak to Gabriella and find out what is going on. The police are involved, for goodness' sake. Surely that makes speaking to one of her parents a matter of urgency.

'I'll come straight up,' I said to Mr Collins on the phone. 'Should I go straight to reception and ask for you?'

'Yes, if you like.' He sounded almost weary, annoyed by my insistence that I come straight to see him. He seems to think this can wait until after school. I don't.

I phone Eric from the taxi.

'I'm in a meeting.' He is brusque and to the point when he answers the phone. It's the second time I've called; my first went to voicemail.

'Something's happened,' I tell him. 'Can you leave it for a minute?'

'Sure.' His voice becomes softer, picking up on the anxiety in mine. 'I'll call you back in a minute. Are you at home?'

'No. I'm on my way to Gabs's school. Call me back as soon as you can.'

He must have made his excuses quickly, because I am still holding my phone after ending the call when it rings again and Eric's number appears on the screen.

'What's up?' he says as I press the Answer button. 'What's happened? Have you heard something more from the solicitor?'

'No, it's not that.'

In the time between getting the call and taking Eric's now, I had, for the first time in ages, forgotten completely about the solicitors. I am supposed to be calling ours later. I need to tell him about the letter we received yesterday. I need to ask how Ben and Maggie can possibly expect us to raise the sort of money they're asking for.

I should have done it first thing really. The foam shop trip was part delaying tactic and part coping mechanism. If I carry on as normal, at least with some aspects of my life, then I can, at least some of the time, pretend that it still is.

But it's unravelling further still.

'No, it's not that. It's Gabriella,' I tell Eric. 'I got a call from the school earlier. They said she'd been picked up by the police earlier and they wanted me to go in.'

'The police? Where? Why? That's not like Gabs? What was she doing?'

'I'm not quite sure, Eric,' I say to him. 'I spoke to her head of year, Mr Collins. He didn't sound very concerned; he just asked me to be there at the end of school so we could have a talk.'

'And he didn't say why? He didn't tell you any more?'

'He said he'd rather discuss it in person, with Gabriella present,' I tell him. 'He told me not to worry. But, of course, I am.'

I don't have any reserves left to deal with this, not after everything else.

'I'll try and get back a bit early tonight,' Eric says, and despite the reason I feel a huge relief. 'I've got a few things that I have to do, but I should be able to get away.'

'Thank you,' I say. 'I'm just coming up to the school now, Eric. I'd better go.'

'OK,' Eric says. 'And Bel...'

'Yes.'

'Try not to worry too much, love.'

Ben, Friday afternoon

'Why do you have to go in?' Maggie asks. 'Can't they just tell you whatever it is over the phone?'

'Hedda said she needed to discuss something with me – us,' I correct myself. 'In person?'

'You see, this is just the reason...' Maggie stops, but I know she is angry.

She's had a difficult day, she's already told me, at length, as soon as I got in from school. Iris has been fractious and upset for much of it. She took a tumble when Maggie took her to the park before lunch, tried to stand on some sort of roundabout thing and fell off – not far, just far enough to cause a slight bruise to her cheek, and far enough for her to howl all the way home.

Then she slept, but too long for Maggie to relax. She was worried she was not just sleeping off the shock but maybe had some sort of concussion. And of course Maggie worries more about the effects of things on Iris than she used to.

Iris is sitting in her high chair now, with a plate of chicken, potatoes and vegetables in front of her. She's flicking most of it on the floor, not actually eating it. She still doesn't look happy and Maggie has clearly had enough.

'Just the reason for what?' I ask.

'Why I never wanted you to go ahead with this bloody legal action,' Maggie snaps angrily, picking up a piece of chicken and putting it back on Iris's plate. The two-second rule applies. This is one of the rules I've learned as a parent. If food hits the floor, ground – anywhere vaguely dirty, basically – as long as it doesn't stay there longer than two seconds, it's OK to pick it up and hand it back to your child to eat.

I don't imagine Isobel ever applied that rule to her precious children. But there's sense in the rule, if not much logic. Why waste perfectly good food just because children are particularly inept at the business of moving it a few inches from their plate to their mouth?

'But we discussed this.' I don't feel good about going again, but Hedda said it was urgent.

'When you say discussion you mean monologue,' Maggie snaps.

'That's not fair. I know you weren't keen to begin with, but we talked about it.'

Iris is looking increasingly agitated. She can't hear that our voices are raised, obviously, but some other sense kicks in and she begins shifting around in her high chair looking from her mother to me.

'I'm really sorry, Maggie. She said it was important.'

'What's important is that Iris needs more attention than a normal baby. What's important is that I sometimes need more help than I otherwise might because of that. What's important is that we need to sit down and talk properly about cochlear implants, or the implications for her future if she doesn't have them.'

'I know that's important too, but...'

'But what?'

'But if the legal action is successful – '

'If!' Maggie screams. 'It's a big "if", Ben, and you know that. Meantime, you spending every five minutes on the phone to that solicitor or going to see her isn't helping.'

'I'm only talking to her because she's trying to help us!'

'Is she? Is she trying to help us, or is she trying to further her career with an interesting case?'

'Maggie...' I'm not sure what I'm going to say next. There's no point telling her we've discussed this and she agreed with me. I know we'll end up having a 'nonversation', one in which we both stick to our points of view at that particular moment and get nowhere.

I know, or at least I think I do, that Maggie is only saying all this now because she's had a bad day and doesn't want me to go out again. And, while I try to think of something there would be a point in saying, Iris throws her plate of food on to the floor and begins screaming.

'Now look what you've done.' Maggie leaves the food and goes to lift Iris out of her high chair. 'Leave that,' she says to me, as I move to clear up the food-splattered floor. 'Just go.'

'Maggie.'

'Just go, Ben. I don't want to talk about it now. The sooner you go, the sooner you'll be back.'

In Hedda's office I am given a cup of tea, in a lime-green cup, with a plate of biscuits – a grey plate of biscuits. I can't quite take it seriously, this colour co-ordination. But Hedda seems to know what she's doing.

'So,' I begin. 'You said there'd been a development. Has there been a response from Isobel's solicitors?'

'Not exactly,' Hedda replies.

I wait for further clarification, thinking they either have responded or they haven't. But I suppose that's what solicitors do – ask each other questions, seek further clarification, go round the houses playing legal games with each other for as long as possible.

There's a brief tap on the door and a man who looks about my age sticks his head around it. 'Is this Mr Deakin?' he asks.

Hedda nods and he walks in, a striking man with a very full head of very dark hair and very dark eyes to match.

'Angus McDonald,' he introduces himself, and I presume he is the McDonald in the practice name – the senior partner, probably. I wonder what he's doing here.

'Pleased to meet you.'

He pulls up another chair and sits down.

Hedda looks suddenly nervous. She's shuffling stuff around on her desk for no apparent reason. Her Nordic composure is ruffled.

'I don't know if Hedda has filled you in – ' Angus McDonald starts to say.

'Mr Deakin has only just arrived,' she cuts in.

'Right.' He looks from me to her and I sense a problem.

'Do you want a tea or anything, Angus?' Hedda asks him.

'No, thank you,' he says, looking at his watch,

It's five forty-five. Probably too late for tea for Angus McDonald, more like whisky time. I wouldn't be surprised if he has a bottle of scotch in his office, ready to offer some of his clients, the ones that come later in the day, or perhaps the more distraught ones – or the richer ones.

'The thing is,' Angus McDonald says to me, 'I wasn't aware, until we had a meeting yesterday, that we had taken this case on.'

'Right.' I don't know if this is normal or not, and therefore whether or not it is a problem. I sense the latter.

'Your position is very unusual,' he says. 'Not to say very difficult for you and your wife and child. I'm very sorry for what's happened to your daughter.'

'That's OK.'

It's hard to know what the appropriate response is, when people say they are sorry. It's not their fault. The only person who could say she was fucking sorry hasn't. That's why we are here.

'I'll get to the point,' he continues. 'It's a very unusual position that you find yourselves in and it's very interesting from a legal point of view. There are no comparable cases in the UK, although there are examples of people successfully suing others for knowingly infecting them with AIDS.'

'Yes, Hedda mentioned those.' I look at her, but she is surprisingly quiet. Silent, in fact.

'As I said,' he repeats himself, 'I wasn't aware until recently that this case had been taken on and, now that I am, we've discussed it in some detail and I have to tell you, I think there is very little chance of it succeeding.'

'But Hedda was very optimistic about its chances of success.' I look at her now for explanation.

'I am sorry, Ben,' she says, and her accent is suddenly stronger, as if nerves or being on the back foot make it more pronounced. 'I thought we had a good case.'

'But?'

'Hedda is a very competent solicitor and I have the utmost faith in her ability to handle the law,' Angus McDonald continues. 'And with a little bit more proof and evidence this could be a very prominent, groundbreaking case. I can see why she was attracted to it.'

'You make it sound like some sort of dating choice!' I try to sound breezy, to mask my growing concern, but I don't think I pull it off.

'The point I am trying to make is that with a little bit more body of proof the case could be exceedingly high-profile and possibly set a precedent. And, because of that, I recognise the reasons for Hedda deciding to take it on.'

'But she shouldn't have?' I try to get to the point on his behalf.

'What we have to decide is where we go from here,' he says, avoiding my direct question. 'And whether you wish to proceed with the case or not.'

'That's why I'm here,' I state the obvious.

'Yes,' he says. 'But we also have the right to terminate our agreement to act on your behalf if we don't think the case is likely to succeed.'

'And you don't?'

'No, to be honest, I don't. I think you have strong reason for directing the blame for your daughter's condition towards Ms Blake. But I think that laying that blame definitively at her feet will prove very difficult.'

'I thought you said we could.' I look at Hedda again.

'I am sorry,' she says, for the first time. 'It seems I may have been too optimistic.'

I feel angry with Hedda but I can tell she's had her knuckles rapped, in private, prior to my being called in to talk. And, as it begins to dawn on me that they are about to tell me they won't take the case after all, I think back to my argument with Maggie, before I left.

Things are getting more difficult now with Iris. If we could win this case then of course it would make a difference, but if we have to spend time fighting it and it all comes to nothing, then perhaps the difference I could have made by being around more instead of fighting it would be the important one.

'There are two areas of concern,' Angus McDonald continues. 'Unless Ms Blake actually admits that she was one hundred per cent certain that her daughter had measles when she left your daughter with her for the day, it is very difficult to prove that there was any deliberate intention to harm, on her part.'

'She must've known,' I say.

'Must have is not going to stand up in a court of law, I'm afraid.'

'But she knew Gabriella was ill. She knew that her boyfriend had measles and that she'd been in close contact with him before the holiday. And she knew she had not been vaccinated.'

'But I'm afraid, Mr Deakin, that, until the doctor confirmed that...' he looks at his notes '...that Gabriella had measles, she did not actually know.'

'She knew,' I repeated.

'A judge won't see it that way, I'm afraid.'

'But what if they settle out of court?' I look at Hedda again. 'You said that was a possibility. No, you said it was likely they would do everything possible to avoid the additional costs that taking the case to court would incur.'

'That is my other area of concern,' Angus McDonald takes over again. 'From what the Jordans' solicitor has told us, and from what Hedda has told me about your discussion with her, the Jordans actually have very little means of paying damages. I believe they have three children, that Ms Blake is not in employment and that the salary Mr Jordan earns is not sufficient to pay damages at the level we would be seeking.'

'Couldn't we ask for less?' I clutch at straws.

'It would then not be worth our while taking on the case on the basis my colleague agreed to,' he says. 'If you wanted to pursue it further there would be costs to yourself involved, costs which I would advise you against incurring as I really don't believe you have a realistic chance of recovery at any stage in the future.'

'So you're saying we should drop the case?'

They both nod. 'I am very sorry, Ben,' Hedda says again.

'What were you thinking?' I'm furious with her now. 'This is my life, our lives, we were talking about. This is about our daughter being deaf. You told me you could do something to help her.'

'I thought I could. I really, genuinely thought we had a chance of making this case work.'

'Did you?' I ask. 'Or did you think you had a chance of making a name for yourself. Of getting yourself talked about a bit and sod what happened to us?'

'No, I thought...' She looks to Angus McDonald for support.

'I'm sure my colleague had your best interests at heart when she took on the case – ' he begins.

'But when you decided there wasn't enough money in it...' I cut in.

'Yes,' he says, bluntly. 'That is what it comes down to. Money, for you and for us. That is what you wanted, isn't it?'

'Yes, but...' I begin.

'But?'

'It doesn't matter,' I say.

I could make a speech about how it's more about the principle, about making Isobel take responsibility for the thing which caused Iris's deafness, about alerting others to the consequences of not having their kids immunised. But that wouldn't really be true.

It isn't about the money, not really, nor the principle. It's about me getting back at Isobel for this and for other things too, for somehow always making me feel belittled and unimportant. Just as Hedda has.

'Maybe next time you tell someone you can help them you should think about them first and the effect it will have on them, if actually you can't,' I say to her.

'I am sorry,' Hedda says, but she doesn't look sorry at all. She just looks as if she wants me out of the office. All that chat and sympathy before... I don't think any of it was genuine. Well, fuck her. Fuck the lot of them.

'So what happens now?' I address my question to Angus McDonald. I am not going to give Hedda the satisfaction of any further explanations.

'We will write to Ms Blake's solicitor and tell him that we've taken instructions from you and you have decided not to go ahead with the case.'

'You'll tell them I've given up. Great.'

'I can discuss the phrasing of the letter with you, if you wish,' he says.

I shrug. I want to leave now. I'm fed up with this. I suppose there may be a way of phrasing the letter so that I still retain the moral high ground. I suppose they could make it look as if I was being magnanimous and maybe that would make Isobel feel bad, which is what I want, mostly. Maybe in fact she will feel even worse if we let her off the hook.

'I'll draft it on Monday and send you a copy for approval before I send it out?'

'OK,' I say, and I nod to them both as I leave the office.

I feel deflated and mightily pissed off, and I'm going to have to go home to Maggie and tell her she was right after all and I should have been concentrating on Iris all along and not wasting my energies on some wild goose chase.

And, however they phrase their fucking letter, I feel furious that ultimately Isobel will get off scot-free. I wanted her to suffer the consequences. She should be made to – somehow.

Isobel, Friday evening

It ought to be nice that Eric is home early. It should be lovely
that the two of us are alone, seated at our kitchen table with
a bottle of white open, knowing we have at least half an hour
before Harvey and Vincent get back from the chippy with
dinner. It would be, if the reason for all of this weren't what
happened with Gabs today. She's in her room, keeping a low
profile, not wanting to talk – not to me anyway.

Wouldn't it be nice, I think, if Eric were just home early
so that he could help me prepare for Vincent's party, and had
given Harvey the money to go and buy fish and chips just so
that we could have a bit of time to ourselves? How rare that
we have half an hour in which we can just sit with a drink
and talk. But the scene is not set for enjoyment. It's set for
explanations and, I fear, recriminations too. They have been the
backdrop to my life these past few weeks.

'So is she OK?' Eric asks. 'Is she upset?'

'I don't know. She's barely said anything since I picked her
up. She went straight up to her room, and I took her up a cup
of tea, but she just took it and closed the door again.'

'Maybe she's embarrassed,' Eric says. 'There's no reason
she should be, but you know how she likes to toe the line. She
doesn't do trouble, does she?'

'No.' I nod in agreement. Gabs has always been one,
almost pathologically, to abide by the rules. She used to panic,
as soon as she could read, if I parked without paying five
minutes before free parking kicked in, or used food that was

fine but past its sell-by date. When she first started cooking, she'd burn biscuits rather than take them out of the oven before the time stated in the recipe was up, even if she could smell the smoke.

And when she was at junior school, throughout her entire seven years, she only lost Golden Time once, and that was for carrying on working when she was supposed to be tidying up!

She's never transgressed at secondary school until now, either – never been reprimanded for a lapse in uniform, never had a detention, never handed in homework late. The only time I've had cause to be angry with her was when she went up to London with a friend, without telling me the friend's parents were not going with them too. And, even then, the purpose of their trip was to visit the Royal Academy.

So playing truant and being brought back to school in the back of a police car is a spectacular way to start. It would be funny if it was just youthful rebellion, but even Gabs bunking off school is underpinned by serious motives.

And of course I worry that this is my fault too – her lack of rebelliousness.

'Maybe she'll go off the rails when she goes to college,' Eric said once, and he was joking, but I think, when he said it, he actually wanted to see her doing something a bit out of character.

Well, now she has.

'So tell me what exactly happened,' Eric says now. His voice is calm and practical and tinged with concern for Gabs. I'd given him a brief outline on the phone, once I was home this afternoon, but he wants filling in.

'Well, it seems she hadn't been at school at all today. She wasn't even wearing her uniform when I picked her up, although I'm sure she was when she left this morning.'

'She probably changed somewhere,' Eric says.

I nod. 'She must have thought it all out.'

'Except what would happen if the police stopped her and questioned her.'

'Poor Gabs,' I say. I can imagine how humiliated she must have felt, being bundled into the back of the car and driven to school.

'It wasn't the first time,' I tell Eric after a pause. 'I noticed she'd not been wearing uniform a few times, but I didn't really think anything of it.'

'So, go on.'

'Well, she'd gone into Hove. I think she must have thought there'd be less chance there of being seen by anyone she knew. She was busking outside the town hall.'

'And the school didn't notice she wasn't there?' Eric asks.

'She told me her form tutor doesn't really bother with the register. So I think she thought no one at school would actually notice.'

'And did they?'

'No. I don't think they had a clue she wasn't there, until the police brought her back.'

'That's reassuring,' Eric says.

'I know. They're supposed to let us know if our kids don't turn up, in case anything has happened to them!' Gabs is fine, but scenarios start playing out in my mind anyway. 'She could have been run over or abducted on the way to school and we'd never have known until it was too late.'

'But she wasn't, Bel. She's OK,' Eric says, and there is a hint of his old kindness in his tone. It makes me want to cry. 'She just got into a bit of trouble. It's about time she did.'

'I knew you'd say that,' I say, and smile despite myself. 'And I know she's OK. It's just so out of character, and I'm really worried now about how everything is starting to affect her.'

'She told you and the school that she needed to make money,' Eric says. 'Is she in some kind of trouble?'

'No, Eric. We are,' I say.

I thought he would have put two and two together by now. But I suppose the fact that we've been avoiding talking to each other means he's not as aware of how Gabs has been feeling as I have been.

'It's not her that's in trouble. It's us. She's been trying to raise money for Ben and Maggie. She knows they're suing us. She thinks it's her fault. She was trying to do something about it herself.'

'But she can't possibly hope to raise that amount of money by skipping school and busking,' Eric says.

'I know. Although she doesn't know how much they're asking. But I don't think that's the point. She made quite a bit the last couple of weekends too, when she went out with Lucy, and she's not been spending her allowance.' Gabs had told me all this on the way home.

'But that still hardly adds up.'

'She says she just wanted to do something. She was planning to take the money round to Ben and Maggie herself. She was thinking of getting the train up to Croydon tomorrow and knocking on their door.'

'But we haven't been to their house for ages. She doesn't know how to get there.'

'She's a resourceful girl. She could have worked it out.'

'And what did she think that would achieve?'

'I don't know. Realistically, I think she thought that if she did something they might drop the legal action. Gabs really liked Maggie, once she got to know her a bit, and she adored Iris too.'

'But did she really think showing up on the doorstep with a few handfuls of coppers would be the answer?'

'I've no idea, Eric. The point is, she was doing something. That's what she said to me earlier. She said someone had to do something. She said you and I – but I know she meant me really – were just letting things happen. And she's right. I know that.'

'What did you say to her?'

'I told her I'd call Ben. I told her I'd try and speak to him. I told her I'd try to find a way to sort this mess out for all our sakes.'

'And have you?' Eric asks.

'I'll do it after dinner,' I say, as the door of the kitchen opens and Harvey comes in with a big bag of fish and chips, which he plonks on the table.

'What?' he says, looking from Eric to me, aware that he's caught us in the middle of something important.

'Do you want to get some plates?' Eric says. 'And get the vinegar out as well, will you?'

Ben, Friday evening

Maggie is upstairs bathing Iris when I get back from my meeting with Hedda and Angus McDonald. I sit on the chair we've put by the bath for whichever of us isn't bathing Iris to sit and watch. I never fully understood, before having Iris, how people like Isobel could watch their offspring with such rapt attention when they were doing so very little to merit it. I get it now, and I keep wondering how long it will last.

'She looks a bit happier now,' I say, sitting down, feeling my heart lurch as Iris looks up, her face covered in bubbles, and smiles at me. 'I'm sorry I had to go out again, Mags.'

'She's been OK,' Maggie replies, scooping up a cupful of water and letting it cascade into the bath a few inches in front of Iris. She sticks her hands forward, trying to catch the water as it flows, cackling a bit with pleasure at the sensation.

'How was your urgent meeting?' There is a barb in the word 'urgent' but I ignore it.

'It was – well, I don't know how to describe it exactly. It's probably best if I wait until we have dinner to tell you about it.'

'Yes, we don't want to upset Iris now that she's happy.'

'Should I go and make a start? Did you have anything planned?' I try to placate her.

'I haven't even thought about it,' Maggie says. 'So yes, why don't you go and see what you can find for us to eat? I'm hungry and I'm sure you are too.'

'Sure.' I stand up to go.

Maggie focuses all her attention back on Iris. She takes a rubber duck from a basket of toys fixed with suction cups on the tiles. 'Here's the duck,' she says, smiling and pushing it along the surface of the water towards Iris. 'Quack, quack. Quack, quack!'

I turn to look at them both and, as I do, Iris picks up the duck and makes a bizarre and heart-wrenching sound.

'Cwar cwar,' she says.

At least that is what it sounds like, to me anyway. I hear the sounds as if they are crystal-clear words. 'Cwar cwar.'

'Did you hear that?' I say to Maggie, tingling with excitement.

'What?' Maggie says, giving me the cold shoulder still.

'She said quack quack!' I say excitedly. 'Didn't you hear her? It sounded like cwar cwar, but she must have been repeating what you just said. Didn't you hear her, Maggie?'

I need Maggie to have heard this too. I need Maggie to confirm what I just heard. I need Maggie also to have witnessed that some miracle has just happened and that Iris isn't deaf after all, that she heard her mother say 'quack, quack' and repeated it, like any normal child.

But she didn't. She hadn't.

'She didn't say anything, Ben,' Maggie turns to me with a look that I can't quite interpret. She sounds a little more forgiving when she speaks again. 'She just made one of her noises. That was all it was.'

'Yes, of course.'

I'm disappointed, of course, hugely, and I feel slightly ridiculous, too, for daring to hope when we know perfectly well that she couldn't hear.

'I'll go and make a start on dinner.'

'Is she asleep?' I ask, as Maggie comes into the kitchen. I'm sautéing two pork fillets and waiting for some rice to cook. 'Dinner won't be long.'

'Yes,' Maggie says wearily, going to the fridge and taking out a bottle of white wine from which she pours herself a large glass. 'Finally.'

She doesn't look to see or ask if I already have a drink. I am clearly still out of favour.

'I'll go up and kiss her,' I say, brushing past Maggie.

'No.' She steps back from the fridge, blocking my path. 'You might wake her again. I've had enough for one day. I can't cope if she wakes up again just now.'

'Maggie, I'm sorry,' I say, stepping towards her.

'Don't,' she replies, moving away, shunning any sympathy or support I might be able to give her. 'Just tell me why your solicitor needed to see you so urgently.'

'Our solicitor,' I say.

We fall silent and I anticipate admitting defeat.

'The meeting was with the senior partner,' I tell her.

'Why? Has there been a development?'

We are both standing in the space between the fridge and the dining table. I move away from Maggie, towards the stove, where I busy myself with the pork and rice. Maggie sits at the table, sipping her wine, waiting.

'There has,' I say, spooning out rice and pouring a little cream into the sautéed pork before sliding a chop on to each plate. I take them over to the table and sit at a right angle to my partner.

'Apparently I was being taken for a ride,' I say, looking at her, wondering if she will be secretly pleased.

'What do you mean?'

'The senior partner asked me to come in because, until today, he was unaware that Hedda had taken on the case, and when he found out he told her to drop it.'

'Oh, Ben.' Maggie slides her hand across the table and puts it over mine. 'I'm sorry.'

'Why should you be sorry?' I pull my hand away. 'That's it. That's the end of it. He said he didn't think we had a hope in hell of winning the case. So unless we can pay the costs of pursuing it ourselves, which he's well aware we can't, then Hedda has to stop acting on our behalf.'

'I'm sorry because I know you thought it might help,' Maggie says simply.

'You were never keen. So I guess you're happy,' I reply.

'No, I wasn't keen because I thought it would divert your attention away from me and Iris, which it has. But I agreed that you should go ahead because I thought it might help you. I thought if it helped you get something out of your system, maybe it would ultimately help us all. Somehow.'

'I'm sorry, Maggie.' I wonder at her understanding. 'I'm sorry I've been so rubbish at dealing with all of this. I was just – no, I still am so angry, so frustrated by the unnecessariness of it all. I was just trying to do something.'

'Ben...' Maggie puts her hand out again and holds mine, and this time I let her. 'Don't think I don't feel the same. I just have a different way of dealing with it. We have to accept what's happened and deal with that.'

'I know,' I say. 'And I do. It's just – '

'No,' she interrupts me. 'You don't. You haven't. Not yet. You're railing against it all the time in different ways. Like up there in the bathroom just now, thinking you heard Iris speaking. You know she can't speak. You know we have to learn to sign to her. You know that's the case but you keep ignoring it. You keep hoping you can do something to change the way Iris is. But you can't, Ben; neither of us can.'

I know Maggie is right.

'We have to be there for her,' Maggie continues. 'We can't be off fighting other people, when she needs us more than ever now.'

I try to say 'but', but the word won't come out. I'm back where I was thirty years ago, trying to speak but unable.

'The trouble is,' I say instead, as Maggie watches my face twisting in the strange way it used to when I tried to speak, 'you're right. I loved her so much when she was born. I still do. But I don't want her to be deaf. I want her to be normal, like everyone else. And I can't make her normal. I can't do anything to change what's happened but I can't simply accept it, the way you seem to. Does that make me a terrible person?'

'No, Ben,' Maggie says gently. 'It doesn't make you a terrible person. It makes you the person you are, the person I love. But we can't fight this. We have to accept it.'

'You're so much better than me.'

'No, I'm not,' Maggie replies, taking her hand away now. 'I'm not better. I'm just different.' She pauses to cut the piece of meat on the plate in front of her. 'So what happens now?'

'With the solicitor?'

'Yes.' She takes a mouthful. 'This is good. Thanks.'

I am about to tell her when the phone rings.

'I'd better get it,' Maggie says. 'It might be Mum. She said she'd call this evening.'

She gets up, perhaps glad of the diversion, and picks the phone out of its cradle on the wall by the doorway. 'Hello,' I hear her say, relaxed and easy the way she is when she talks to her mother. But her tone changes. 'Yes. It is.'

A pause.

'Well, you know. We're OK, in the circumstances.'

I strain to try to hear who is on the other end of the line.

'Yes, he's right here. I'll get him.'

She takes the two steps to where I'm sitting, her arm outstretched, ostensibly to hand me the phone but also looking as if she wants it as far away from her as possible.

'Who is it?' I mouth, but the phone is in my hand and I have to find out for myself.

'Hello, Ben speaking,' I say.

'Ben.' A familiar voice speaks down the line. 'It's Isobel.'

After I finish talking to her and arranging to go down and see her next Monday, I feel strangely alone. I have no idea what meeting up with Isobel is going to achieve but, as Hedda has let me down, I feel I have no choice.

289

'If it makes you feel better,' Maggie says when I tell her I'm going.

'Do you mind?'

'No, I don't mind. I just want the whole thing over. I want to get on with our lives. If you need to have it out with Isobel, well and good.'

But she doesn't sound happy and, when I get into bed later that evening, she rolls over and turns her back to me.

'Mags?' I think she might be sleeping.

'What?'

'Are you OK?'

'Yes. I'm just tired.'

'I'm sorry,' I say, rolling towards her and putting my hand on her stomach. I know I haven't been being the person she wanted me to be over the past few weeks, but I'm going to make it up to her. I begin moving my hand across her stomach, stroking, soothing.

'I need to go to sleep now, Ben,' Maggie says, pushing my hand away.

WEEK FOUR

Isobel, Monday morning

'You're a bum-bailey!'

  'And you're a foot-licker!'

  'Bum-bailey!' retorts Vincent

  'Foot-licker!' repeats Harvey.

  I'm only half listening, as I clear away the breakfast debris and wipe down kitchen surfaces with a zeal born out of anxiety. I unplug the toaster from its socket in the wall and hold it upside-down over the sink, tapping it furiously against the ceramic edge so that the lumps of burnt toast shower into the washing-up bowl. For some reason, I believe the huge anxiety I feel about meeting Ben later this morning will somehow be eased if the toaster is crumb-free and the kitchen is gleaming.

  There is no logic to my thoughts, but there is less logic to psychology than our next-door neighbour, who is a psycho-therapist, would have us believe. I wonder if he can hear the boys now, their argument crescendoing around the kitchen, seeping through the party wall and disturbing his breakfast.

  'Clotpol!' Vincent shouts

  'Codpiece!' Harvey appears to trump him again.

  'Boys, that's *enough*!' I raise my voice higher than theirs, slamming the toaster so hard against the side of the sink at the same time that the shock of the combined sounds stuns them both, momentarily, into silence.

  Vincent looks upset but Harvey just gives me his 'you're being totally unreasonable' look, one perfected over the years of me being totally unreasonable.

I take a deep breath.

'We're not arguing,' he says.

'No, we're practising.' Vincent is emboldened by his brother's defiance. 'You're so gorbellied, Mum.'

'What does that mean?'

'I don't know,' Harvey says. 'It's Elizabethan swearing. We're doing it in English, for Shakespeare.'

'Oh, I see,' I say as Harvey puts his thumb in his mouth, nibbling the edge of a nail or loose skin or something, and pulls it out again. 'Harvey, don't bite your nails.'

'I'm not!' He triumphs over me this time. 'I am biting my thumb at you. *Romeo and Juliet*!'

'Well, whatever it is,' I say, returning to the toaster, irritated now, not with them, but with myself for feeling so wound up about Ben's impending arrival, 'it's time you two went to school.'

'Stressy,' Harvey mutters under his breath and he picks up his bag.

'Dankish,' Vincent mutters under his.

I have no idea what it means, but no doubt it's apposite.

I continue my cleaning frenzy after the boys have gone. Vinnie's bedroom is still a mass of camping mats, sleeping bags and sweet wrappers. He had several friends to stay, after his party on Saturday, and I didn't get round to tidying up yesterday.

I still don't know what I'm going to say, and every time I try to think about it, or try to rehearse a speech, I don't get very far. I begin by saying I'm sorry. I try to explain things from my point of view. I try to defend myself against the accusations I anticipate Ben will make. I try to ask him how involving solicitors can possibly help. Maybe I'll get angry. I'll tell him not to forget the actual people involved in all of this. It's us. Eric and me and Ben. We are a triumvirate.

And then the imaginary encounter stalls and I can't get any further. So, instead, I shake out a sleeping bag, turn it inside out and hang it over the edge of the banisters to air, roll up a camping mat, and scrunch sweet wrappers into the pocket of my jeans.

Vincent's room begins to return to its former state, not immaculate but not quite such a bomb site as it was half an hour previously. I drag the last mattress from the floor down the corridor to Harvey's room. He has a futon base tucked in an alcove next to the chimneybreast in his. The mattress belongs with it.

Before I put it back, I drag the wooden frame away from its position against the wall to retrieve some of the things that have become lodged underneath: loose change, CDs, various bits of junk which could either be rubbish or vital components of something Harvey plans to make. I don't know which and therefore daren't get rid of it.

'EDF' is under there too, a toy which belongs to Vincent and which I suspect may have been hidden there by Harvey after an argument more heated than the one they were having this morning.

EDF is one of the energy suppliers to the area. They have adverts, which feature an animated gas flame. When he was younger, Vincent found it hilarious. He'd double up with laughter watching the black-eyed orange flame shimmying around a show home. He laughed so much that Gabriella decided to make him his very own EDF, out of felt, with buttons for eyes. Vincent became ridiculously attached to it for a time. He couldn't sleep without it, resulting in lengthy searches of the house at bedtime.

I pick it up, intending to return it to his bedroom, but underneath I find an epipen.

Is this the one Harvey is supposed to keep in his school bag at all times, just in case? I look at my watch and think that I don't have time to jump in the car and run it up to the school before Ben arrives, but I start to feel anxious. What if he doesn't have another one in his bag, and what if he has something to eat at school? He should be being extra-vigilant after last week, but he's a twelve-year-old boy and the fact that he ate Vinnie's chocolates, without checking, shows he's not really taking his condition seriously.

I push the futon base back into its space, folding the mattress on top before heading downstairs.

I am almost certain Harvey has another epipen with him, but it would be sod's law, if I don't check just because I'm expecting Ben, that he doesn't, and someone will offer him something he should not eat.

So I phone the school, glad of something to distract me.

'Hello, it's Isobel Jordan.' I use Eric's name to avoid confusion as the kids have it too. 'Harvey's mother. He has a nut allergy and I've found an epipen in his bedroom. I just wanted to make sure it's not the one he should have in his school bag.'

The woman in the office asks which class he is in and I tell her.

'I'm sure he has one, but he had a reaction a few days ago so I just wanted to double-check.'

The woman says she will find out what lesson he is having, go and check, and call me back.

I put the kettle on and realise that after my cleaning blitz there is not much for me to do, other than wait for it to boil and think more about what I'm going to say to Ben.

The phone rings before I have put my thoughts into any sort of order (which maybe just isn't going to happen) and the woman from the school office tells me she dug Harvey out of science and he showed her he had an epipen in his bag.

I'm thanking her when the doorbell rings and it flusters me. I'd thought I had ten minutes in which to change the top I'd been cleaning in, tidy myself up a bit, and brush my hair at least. Instead I open the door, feeling caught on the hop, and Ben looks at me strangely, taking me in in a slightly unnerving way.

'Come in,' I say, and I head for the kitchen.

Ben follows, dropping his backpack from his shoulder into his hand and knocking the neat row of post-party Space

Hoppers I have lined up in the hallway, ready to return to the various people who lent them.

'Vincent's birthday,' I explain. 'Coffee?'

'Yes, please,' Ben says, and he surprises me by producing a present from his rucksack.

'Oh. How kind. I didn't think you'd remember.'

'I didn't. Maggie did,' he says, and I smile, momentarily reassured that in the midst of all of this Maggie still remembers Vincent's birthday. Maybe things aren't as bad as they seem. Maybe, because we haven't talked, I've built up the antipathy I think Ben and Maggie must feel towards me, to a level it may not actually have reached, not personally anyway. Maybe the legal action is separate. It's devastating for us, obviously, but, for them, perhaps it's just what they need to do for Iris.

'I'm afraid it's not what he asked for,' Ben says.

'What was that?'

'A straitjacket. He told me that was what he wanted, in France.'

I wince at the mention of France but Ben seems not to notice. 'I tried the children's section of Ann Summers,' he continues, 'but I couldn't find one.'

I laugh despite myself as I make coffee. It feels almost normal until Ben's face clouds, as if he's just remembered something.

'Sit down,' he says, when I bring the coffee over and hover, unsure.

I sit, but neither of us says anything.

I start.

I begin the apology I've half rehearsed, but it's harder saying it out loud to Ben than rehearsing it upstairs.

'Ben... I'm so sorry,' I begin. 'For everything that's happened. You've no idea how bad I feel. If there was anything I could do to turn the clock back, I'd do it. I'd never have left Gabs with Iris. I'd have had the kids vaccinated. I'd have been in touch with you before now; I'd have done something, anything to try to make things different...'

I can hear myself gabbling. My voice is racing, too fast for me to keep up with the words, and then it falters. I feel a bit detached from myself, but I recognise the faltering sounds as upset.

I said I would not cry. I am not going to cry, but it's so difficult.

I don't even get to the point where I get stuck. Ben interrupts me.

'Why now?' he asks, and his voice has a harsh edge I don't think I've ever heard before. 'Why after all this time?' It's his turn to stream thoughts and questions now. 'Why didn't you get in touch with us b-before, when you heard that Iris was deaf? Why didn't you call and apologise or do something? How could you live with yourself, knowing you were responsible, knowing you were to b-blame?'

I have not heard Ben falter over his words for years. He'd told me he used to have a stammer, when I first met him, but I hadn't believed him, he had it so well under control. Only very occasionally, when he'd been flustered, had I heard him pause slightly before getting a word out.

'You fucking forced me to take legal action, Isobel, by sitting at home and refusing to face up to the consequences of your decision. My daughter is deaf. She can't hear a fucking thing. Maggie's a musician. I'm a fucking drama teacher. Our worlds are full of sounds and words. Our kid will never be part of that world. Have you got any idea how that feels?'

'I know it can't be easy,' I begin. 'I know it's not the same, having a child with a disability.'

'But you don't know, do you?' Ben interrupts me. 'You've got no idea. You've got your three perfect children and you're not really interested in anyone else's, especially if they're not perfect themselves.'

'What's that supposed to mean?'

'You know what I mean. You're so wrapped up in your own life that you don't really care about anyone else's, not even your oldest friends.'

'Of course I care about you,' I begin.

'I'm not talking about me,' Ben says. 'I'm talking about Yasmin. I saw what you were like with her on holiday, irritated every time Conrad upset your children, and I know she feels you've let her down.'

'I haven't let her down. I hardly see her!'

'Exactly,' Ben says triumphantly.

'Did Yasmin say something?' I ask.

'She didn't have to,' Ben says, but I suspect something has been said and I know it's partly true, whatever it is that Ben is accusing me of.

I say nothing. I can't think of anything to say. All those rehearsed words escape me.

'If it had been anyone else. Anyone other than you!' he carries on shouting.

'What do you mean?' I say this quietly.

'You know what I mean!' He is screaming at me now.

The cafetiere sits between us, its plunger still up. The social niceties we intended to perform, to keep this civilised, are abandoned. It seems we are going to have a good old-fashioned screaming match instead. Maybe this is good. Maybe Ben needs to scream at me. Maybe it will make him feel better.

'You know why.' He spits the words out. 'You know why it's worse because it's you. You've got fucking everything, Isobel. You're married to fucking perfect Eric. You've got three fucking perfect kids. A lovely house by the fucking seaside. You don't have to work. But that wasn't enough, was it? It wasn't enough for you to have it all. You couldn't let me have a tiny bit of that too. Why couldn't you just be happy that I was happy?'

'Ben, that's not fair,' I try to interject, but Ben doesn't stop.

'Me,' he says. 'Why have I always been the stooge in your life? It's always been me. Isobel arrives at uni, nursing a broken heart, and who does she use to help her get over it? Me. Ben, who can always be trusted to be there, no matter what I do to him. Ben, who comes running every time things aren't going your way. Ben who can always be relied upon to care for you, even though you hurt him again and again. And the first time, the first fucking time I am really happy, you have to go and ruin it all. You just had to, didn't you?'

All the while, he's moving his face closer to mine. And the closer he gets, the more I can feel his anger, in the contortions of his face and the volume of his words, and I don't think I can soak it up any more. I'm going to crack. One way or another, I am going to crack. I'm not sure if I'm going to start yelling too, scream back at him, or if I'm going to cry. Maybe that's what he wants.

'I'm so sorry,' I say. 'Really, truly. If I could change things, I would. If I can do anything now, anything at all, I'll do it.'

I start to cry and Ben stops shouting, but his face is still up close, intent on something. I don't know what. It's as if he's looking for something. Fear? Contrition? Some sort of resolution?

I hold his look, even though he's scaring me slightly. But it feels important that I don't turn away. I have to face him, whatever he does next. I have to face up to it. That's why he's here.

For a second I think he might be going to strike me and I flinch slightly in anticipation.

And then he kisses me. He takes my face in his hands and I know what he's going to do and, when he does, it's not gentle or tender, it's urgent and necessary and it doesn't make sense. He's been sitting there yelling at me, as if he hates me more than anyone.

And now we are kissing.

It feels as if Ben might swallow me up. And, despite the sudden transition, I find myself responding. I have to stand up from my chair, because the corner of the table is digging into my rib, and when I do Ben reaches up and grabs my breast and his other hand is on my buttocks, pulling me towards him.

Is this it? I think. Is this how we resolve this one?

Ben stands up and pushes himself against me and I can feel him hardening and there's a sense of illogical inevitability to this.

We are going to sleep together again, and I don't know if it will help or not but I think I am going to do it, if it's what Ben wants.

And then the doorbell rings and we spring apart, shocked and repulsed. And I tidy my hair a bit and look at the clock. I don't know why. I'm not expecting anyone.

I'm not expecting anything either, but I can see the red of a postman and his van through the glass on the door.

'Would you mind signing for this for your neighbour?'

'Sure,' I say, and I take the pen the postman offers and make a shape that bears little resemblance to my signature on the screen thing.

'A parcel for one of the neighbours,' I say to Ben, returning to the kitchen.

'Saved by the bell, Bel,' he says, and we are awkward now, unsure what to say to each other.

'The thing is…' I begin, but I don't actually know what the thing is. I'm starting to lose the plot.

'I'm going to drop the legal action,' Ben says, suddenly, in such a way that I can't tell if this is what he came to tell me or if he just made a spur-of-the-moment decision.

'Really?' I say.

It would be wonderful it were true. I feel relief begin to creep over me but I don't feel I should give in to it. He might change his mind.

'I know you're angry with us, with me, and I can understand that, but it was affecting all of us and…' I don't finish my sentence.

'Not because of you,' Ben says. 'Because of Maggie. And Iris. I'm not dropping it for your benefit, or Eric's or anyone else's. I'm doing it for Maggie and Iris. Because I love them both, more than anything in this world, more than I ever loved

301

you. No, more than I ever could have loved you, even if you'd given me a chance.'

'I know that,' I say.

'I hate you because of what's happened but not as much as I love them, and my trying to fight you, trying to force you out of your cosy world to face reality, was upsetting Maggie and not helping Iris and I can't do that any more, to either of them.'

'Have you told her?'

'Maggie knows,' is all he says. 'Just as she knows that I love her and Iris more than anyone.'

'I know,' I repeat. 'And I know I can't change things, but, if there is anything I can do, I'll do it. I know things won't be easy for you and Maggie. I'd like to help.'

'I have to go now,' Ben says, looking round the kitchen and catching sight of the parcel he brought with him. 'Wish Vincent a happy birthday from us.'

'I will. Thank you.' It feels almost normal.

I walk behind Ben to the door and close it behind him when he's gone. Then I go into the sitting room and watch from the window as he walks down the front path.

Our next-door neighbour, the psychotherapist, is walking up the path to his house. 'Nearly everyone in Brighton's a psycho-something,' Eric always jokes. 'There's a psychologist living on the other side and the guy opposite is a psychopath!' I see Ben nod to the psychotherapist now, catching his eye as he approaches his door, and I wonder if he could tell us why the exchange that just took place between Ben and me feels like some sort of strange resolution.

Ben is standing on the pavement now, taking something out of his rucksack. It's his phone. He's paused on the street and is talking to someone.

I presume it is Maggie he is talking to, reassuring her that he's sorted everything out and is on his way home again.

And I decide to reassure Eric too. I text him.

'Ben been and gone. Legal action dropped. Speak later.'

I wonder if he will call when he gets the message, but he doesn't and I'm glad. I want a bit of time to myself first, before I have to relay a version of events to Eric.

When Eric comes home we are wary of each other, as people are who've had an argument and decided to stop having it, rather than resolving it.

'How did it go?' he asks.

'I let Ben shout and scream at me. It seemed to help,' I say.

'Help who? You, or him?'

'Both of us,' I say, half laughing, almost tearful, but relieved that at least one dark cloud has been removed.

'What did he say?' Eric asks.

'He said I was selfish, self-obsessed, wrapped up in my perfect world,' I begin.

'That's harsh,' Eric says quietly, not as if he really means it.

'Is it? It's what you've been saying for the past few weeks,' I remind him.

'I was angry, Bel,' he says, resigned to the tension that remains between us. 'It was all such a fucking mess.'

'He was angry too,' I say. 'Furious – that Iris is deaf, that it's all so unnecessary, that neither of us got in touch.'

'I did get in touch,' Eric says, but has the grace to catch himself.

'Well, he didn't think either of us had done enough. But especially me. You and he were in accord there,' I say.

'Why you particularly?' Eric asks, and he's looking at me so intently now that I try not to squirm under his gaze.

'I suppose because, like you, he thinks I am to blame, that it was my decision not to have the kids vaccinated that caused all this trouble.'

'Is that all?' Eric is still looking at me, and I try not to give anything away by reacting.

'Not exactly,' I say, looking away now.

'What do you mean?'

'I don't know exactly. I can't quite remember what he said,' I tell him. 'The atmosphere felt so loaded.'

'With what exactly?' Eric is aware of my discomfort but he won't let it go.

'Anger, tensions, issues. You name it. It's complicated,' is the best I can manage.

'What is, Isobel?'

'You and Ben, Ben and I. It's like you said. He probably was a bit hung up on me and maybe I didn't tread carefully enough. I don't know. It sometimes feels as if Ben is hostile towards me for being with you. You are his best friend and he doesn't know which way his loyalties lie.'

'But he's always been loyal to both of us, hasn't he?' Eric is chipping away, trying to get at something, and I won't let him.

'Yes, but I used to think Ben might have preferred it if you'd married someone else. Maybe he didn't want to have to drag me round with him for the rest of his life, but he had to, didn't he, because I married you.'

'Is that why you say he was angrier with you?'

I wonder, not for the first time in my adult life, if Eric knows more than he lets on. If it is the great unspoken between us – unspoken because, if it was raised, it would be so much more damaging than just letting it lie.

'Maybe if you'd married someone else his daughter wouldn't be deaf,' I tell him.

'But that's just one of many "what if"s, Bel,' Eric says, more gently. 'Things don't always turn out the way you want or expect.'

'Like me,' I say, deflecting the attention away from my relationship with Ben and back to one of the issues that remains unsolved.

'What does that mean?' Eric asks, but I suspect he knows full well.

'Oh, come off it, Eric,' I say, taking a deep breath because really I am too tired for another argument. 'You've been saying it in your every reaction to me these past few weeks. I'm not the person you thought I was. I'm a disappointment. I'm a boring stay-at-home mother who made a mistake that came back to haunt us in a terrible way. Why wouldn't you be disappointed? Maybe that's why Ben was more angry with me. He also saw me for what I've become, whereas you are still the wonderful Eric Jordan.'

'I'm hardly that, am I?' Eric says, and his tone is accusing, yet again. 'My life didn't turn out exactly as I wanted it to, either.'

'Well, I'm sorry if that's down to me too,' I say, the sarcasm all too clear in my tone.

'That's not what I meant, Isobel,' Eric says. 'But look at us. Look at the way we've been for the past few weeks. That didn't spring from nowhere; it just got exposed.'

'Jesus, Eric, what are you saying?' I begin to feel panicky now. Hours earlier I'd thought one crisis had been averted, then another one narrowly avoided just now, and now a third appears to be looming.

'I'm not saying anything,' he says, his tone calmer. I wouldn't go as far as to say it's understanding, but it's gentler at least.

'Eric, we can't let this...' I hesitate, unsure what exactly to say. 'We can't let this destroy us. I know I made a mistake, and I've been paying for it, not just because of what's happened to Iris but because of the way you've been acting towards me. We used to be a team, I thought we'd always be a team, but, as soon as you found out, you made it very clear that I was on my own in this. You're still doing it and I can't stand it. Why can't you just stop?'

'It's not that easy,' Eric says. 'I know I haven't handled all of this well. I didn't mean to make you feel that you were on your own.'

'Well, you did,' I say, flatly. 'I've never felt quite so isolated from you as I have these past few weeks. It's unforgivable, the way you've been treating me.'

'Then, clearly, we've both disappointed each other,' he says.

This is not the reaction I want. I want to shake him out of this distant, recriminatory stance and back into taking notice of me, of my needs, of the fact that I need something from him.

'Is that all you've got to say?' I try to push him into something more.

'I'm sorry. Is that what you want me to say?' he asks. 'I'm sorry, Isobel, I really am. I wish I could have found a better way through all this, but I didn't. I played it all wrong and I'm sorry if I hurt you in the process. I didn't intend to.'

'I'm sorry too,' I say.

I still want to be angry with him but I'm treading carefully, the memory of Ben, here in the kitchen and what might have been, too fresh not to, and Eric's earlier words, 'Look at the way we've been for the past few weeks. That didn't spring from nowhere,' ringing in my ears still. Does he really believe that? Does he think things were wrong between us even before this happened? I've been scared these past few weeks about what would happen if Ben carried on with the legal action and, now that he's dropped it, I'm even more scared.

'I haven't always found it easy, looking after the kids,' I say to him. 'I've always wanted to, and I love them all to bits, but it's not always easy.'

'I know that, Bel,' he says again, and looks at me directly now. 'And they're great kids.'

'We're lucky,' I say. 'We've been very lucky.'

'It's not all down to luck – ' he begins.

'Don't start, Eric, not now, please,' I interrupt him. 'Can't we just try to move on?'

'What?'

'I know my actions led to Iris being…' I pause. It's still hard to say 'deaf'.

'I was going to say that you've done a good job,' he says. 'With the kids.'

'Oh. Thank you.'

It's something.

'I know I haven't always got everything right,' I say. 'But, as I said, it's not always been easy. I need someone to be there for me, Eric.'

'I tried to be there for you,' Eric replies.

'Not enough.' I say. 'And not at all recently.'

'Sorry,' Eric says again. Then he changes tack slightly. 'Did Ben say why they've decided to drop the legal action? Did he just want to force an apology out of us?'

'I don't know. I don't know if they'd already decided, before he came down, or if he just realised that arguing was getting us all nowhere,' I say. 'But I think he just needs to concentrate on Iris.'

That is pretty much the truth of it, and Eric seems to accept it, for the time being. 'I'll go and see the kids,' he says. 'Are they are all home?'

'Gabs went to see Megan after school and she's staying the night,' I tell him. 'The boys are in the living room, I think.'

I take a deep breath as he walks out of the kitchen, and slowly exhale before I begin the evening meal preparations.

When dinner is ready I head to the living room, but I pause before going in. Everyone is laughing. I can't hear what they are laughing at, just overlapping peals of riotous laughter interspersed with bouts of speech. My two boys and my husband, laughing loud, full, deep laughs – joys-of-family-life laughs.

If I go in and ask, 'What's the joke?' I fear they may stop, so I wait at the threshold of the living room and listen.

'The Koran?' Harvey repeats in a high-pitched voice.

'No, Mum,' he says in an exaggerated version of his own. '*Kerrang!* It's a heavy metal magazine.'

So that's what's got them going. I smile to myself. Harvey is repeating a conversation I had with him earlier in the week. 'Can you ask if they've got a copy of *Kerrang!* in the newsagent?' he'd asked me. 'I want to get it.' But, not being a teenage fan of heavy metal, I'd had no idea what he was talking about and replied, surprised, 'The Koran?'

I'm about to go in but I hesitate, long enough to hear Eric say, 'And how did she react when she thought you wanted a copy of the Koran? I'd love to have seen her face.'

'*Oh, no, Harvey, you can't become a muslin,*' Vinnie says in a high voice. '*They make women wear nose-warmers!*'

'Muslim, eejit,' Harvey says, but his tone is friendly enough. 'And they're called burqas, not nose-warmers.'

'Can you imagine?' Eric says, and he's not really laughing any more. 'That would have been a real slap in the face for your mother.'

'*Oh, no, you must be liberal activists and not Muslims,*' Harvey says in his high-pitched 'me' voice again, and they laugh.

But I can't find it in myself to find any of it funny, not now. The three of them laughing at me, Eric colluding in their joke, insinuating that I'm so controlling I couldn't handle it if one of my children wanted to convert.

That's the real slap in the face.

And my face is still stinging.

A FEW
MONTHS LATER

Ben, Saturday

It's the first time I'll have seen Isobel since I went to their house. It's the first time Maggie's seen her since we went to France – and Eric and the kids. I'm feeling a little apprehensive, naturally.

But Maggie won't be drawn.

If I ask her how she feels about everyone coming she says, 'Fine.' But she says it in a way that suggests she's anxious and trying not to let it show, trying just to get on with the preparations.

Iris is not being christened but we decided to have a party to celebrate – not a naming ceremony or anything official, just a party.

Maggie wasn't that keen, when I first suggested it, but I wanted to do something. We're not married, our daughter's not christened, and we've never had an occasion to mark the fact that we are together and a family. We won't have any photographs to show Iris when she's older, or any memories of starting out as a family – not good ones, anyway. I want a good one, after the past few months of crap.

I want to celebrate Maggie and me being together and having a beautiful daughter who won't grow up to be like other children but will be uniquely herself. I get that now. It's not just accepting it, like a bad thing that I have to accept and get on with; I really think Iris is amazing, the way she is.

She's started to walk and she's signing quite a lot. We do communicate, probably as much as any parents of kids this age.

Bel once told me that Yasmin described finding out Conrad was autistic was like thinking they'd booked a holiday to Italy and finding out they were actually going to Holland. It's a good analogy. So we're not going to Tuscany any more, we're going to the Zuiderzee. Tuscany's too hot and it gets really crowded with Brits and politicians in summer. Holland is flat and emptier and great for cycling, and that's where we're going with Iris.

I'm glad now that the travel agent got the bookings muddled up. Life never turns out the way you expected. A year ago, I was a disenchanted drama teacher with a healthy new baby. Now I've got a deaf daughter and I'm looking into training to teach in a deaf school, and I'm excited by the prospect, really excited actually, more excited than I have been about anything for a while.

And I'm happy too, even if just now I am not exactly looking forward to seeing Isobel. But she's only one of fifty guests. I'm not going to have to spend much time talking to her. I can be civilised because I feel kind of free of her now. Finally, I really don't care what Isobel does or thinks.

So I have spent the morning at the park with Iris while Maggie was preparing food. Everyone is invited for two o'clock, for a late buffet lunch, followed by tea and cake.

The timing has confused Ruth, Maggie's mother, but we wanted to fit the guests around Iris's routine. She naps early afternoon and usually wakes up happier for it. So she will be sleeping while everyone has lunch and then, when she wakes, we can have cake.

'Do we need cake, if we'll have had a late lunch?' I had asked Maggie. She seemed to have been fretting about it more than it warranted – looking up various different recipes, trying to find a cake that would appeal to everyone.

'It's a celebration. We need a cake.'

'I could order one somewhere, if you don't want to have to make one on top of lunch,' I'd suggested. 'There's that pâtisserie just off the high street. I am sure they could do us a cake.'

'No, I want to make it. It needs to be perfect for Iris,' Maggie had said.

But in the event she didn't quite get around to it. 'I'll buy something from the supermarket and ice it myself,' she said when I asked yesterday if she was still planning to make one.

I love the fact that Maggie doesn't try too hard to be perfect. She wants Iris to be excited by the look of the cake. She knows no one will really care if she made it herself or bought it from Sainsbury's.

So Maggie is in the kitchen now, taking two shop-bought sponge cakes out of their packaging and laying them on a large foil-covered chopping board, only just starting the assembling and icing, even though nearly everyone has arrived, including Eric and Isobel and the kids.

I've exchanged a few words with Isobel – pleasantries on arrival, nothing more. But she comes over now, as I am about to go and drag Maggie out of the kitchen.

'Where are Maggie and Iris, Ben?' she asks. 'I haven't seen either of them yet.'

'Iris is asleep,' I tell her. 'And I think Maggie's in the kitchen. I was just going to go and tell her to leave what she's doing and come and join us.'

'Can I come with you?' Isobel asks, and she follows me, even though I only shrug by way of reply.

Maggie has almost finished the icing now.

'That looks good,' I say, half wanting to make Isobel think she has baked it herself.

'Lemon cake,' Maggie says, although I know this. I've seen the now discarded packaging. 'And a cream cheese icing.'

'It sounds delicious,' Isobel says, and Maggie looks up, as if registering her for the first time.

'Iris loves it,' she says. Her expression gives nothing away.

'Can I do anything to help?' Isobel asks.

'No, thank you,' Maggie says, politely enough. 'It's all under control.'

'Are you going to come and join everyone?' I ask.

'I'll be there in two minutes,' Maggie says.

'OK.' I pause, not sure whether I should leave Maggie on her own with Isobel.

'I'll be out in a second, Ben, really,' she repeats, as if she wants to me to leave.

So I turn to go, but I move slowly enough to hear Isobel saying, 'Maggie, I know it's not the time or the place. But I just wanted to say I'm sorry. I know I should have said it before, to you, and I'm sorry I haven't.'

I don't hear the rest of the conversation. Julie Effingham comes over to me. 'Lovely house, Ben,' she says. 'Where's the lovely guest of honour?'

'Asleep,' I say. 'She's a princess. She needs a lot of sleep.'

'Ha – don't we all?' Julie replies, and then Maggie comes to join us.

'Hi, Julie. How lovely you could come! Have you got a drink?'

And so it goes on. People come and go. I top up their glasses. Maggie invites them to help themselves to food. Everyone seems happy. I kind of wish Iris were here too. It's in her honour after all, this party; it seems a shame for her to miss it. But Maggie's right, it's easier to get all the eating out of the way while she's still asleep. It's easier for Maggie to deal with the guests if she's not having to pick Iris up or try to sign to her.

'When are we having the cake?' Vincent asks, rushing up with purpose, the way he does.

'Not till Iris wakes,' I tell him – and right on cue the baby monitor on the mantelpiece squawks.

'She's awake!' Vincent says triumphantly, as if he made this happen.

'OK,' I say. 'I'll go and get her. Will you find Maggie and tell her?'

People clap when I come down the stairs carrying Iris. She'd probably cry if she could hear the rumble of applause. But of course she can't. She simply takes in the smiley faces and beams back, half aware perhaps that this party is for her.

'I'll get the cake,' Maggie says, and she goes to the kitchen and returns with it, iced now and decorated with a butterfly shaped out of Smarties, with two candles for antennae.

The spectacle makes Iris squirm and clap.

I put her down and say a few words. Not much, just stuff about how happy we are to have a baby and how happy I am to have met Maggie.

I catch Isobel watching, out of the corner of my eye, and I can't quite interpret the way she is looking.

Maggie cuts the cake.

Vincent and Harvey are nearest, Harvey wiping crumbs of what he's already eaten off his jumper in preparation for cake. Maggie hands them the first slices. Then she keeps cutting, handing out plates with thick triangles of lemon cake.

Iris has the biggest slice. She's kneeling on the floor with her plate on the coffee table, smearing her face with the cream cheese icing, happy. Ruth has brought extra teapots from her home and has been filling them valiantly, ready for people to serve themselves. When she's done cutting cake, Maggie sits down, maybe for the first time during the day.

'Well done, love,' I say going over to her. 'Do you want a cup of tea?'

'Thank you,' she replies, and I go to pour some from one of pots Ruth has lined up along the dining table.

And that's when the commotion begins.

'Eric!' I can hear Isobel's voice cut sharply across the general babble in the room.

'*Eric!*' There's a note of panic. 'Eric, can you get my bag? Harvey's having a reaction.'

'Where is it?' Eric asks.

'All the bags and coats are in our bedroom,' I say to him. 'But I don't know which is Isobel's. Can I do anything?'

I know Harvey has a nut allergy, of course, but I've never witnessed him have a reaction. It's a little scary. He was fine one minute and now his face is red and he seems to be struggling to breathe.

315

'I'll go and get it.' Eric bounds up our stairs and a little space is beginning to clear around Isobel and Harvey.

Maggie is, strangely, still in her seat. I'm not quite sure what to do but I feel, as hosts, we should be doing something as Harvey gasps for breath.

'Breathe slowly,' Isobel is saying to him. 'Dad's just gone to get my bag. Your epipen is in it. Just keep calm.'

Harvey is beginning to look terrible. His face is getting redder and his lips are swollen.

'Gabriella, will you go and help Dad find the bag?' There's urgency in Isobel's question and Gabs rushes upstairs without further prompting.

'Shall I get him some water?'

'Is he choking?'

'Is he asthmatic?'

'No,' Isobel says, looking towards the stairs. 'He's got a nut allergy. Harvey, what have you eaten?'

'Nothing,' Harvey gasps.

But he's had lunch, like everyone else, and finished his cake before half the other guests had even been given a slice.

Eric seems to be taking his time, but he finally returns with Isobel's bag. 'Sorry,' he gasps. 'It had fallen off the bed on to the floor. It took me a while to find it.'

Isobel yanks at the bag to open the drawstring. There's a single compartment and it's clearly not easy to find anything in it.

'It's not in here.' Isobel is rummaging through her bag. 'It's not here! I know I had one in here. Where is it?'

'Tip it out,' Eric says, picking the bag up and turning it upside down. A cascade of lipsticks, keys and tampons spills across the floor.

There is no epipen. I know what they look like. There've been enough kids over the years with nut allergies at school and enough times I've been asked to look after the epipens on school trips. Thankfully I've never had to use one, never had to deal with the situation that is unfolding in my own living room.

'It must have fallen out upstairs!' Isobel says. 'I know I had it in here. Will you go and see if you can find it.'

'Gabs, you look,' Eric says, and then to Isobel. 'I think we need to call an ambulance.'

'I'll call one, ' I say and I go to the base station on a table by the door, but the phone isn't there.

'I think it's in the kitchen. Here, use this.' Maggie produces her mobile from somewhere and hands it to me. I dial 999.

'Emergency. Which service?' a woman's voice asks.

'Ambulance,' I say. 'We're having a party and there's a boy who has a nut allergy and seems to be having a reaction.'

'What's the address?' I tell her. 'Right, the ambulance is on its way and should be with you very soon,' the operator says. 'Are you near the casualty?'

'No,' I say, but I begin to move across the sitting room. 'I'll hand you over to the boy's father.'

I hand the phone to Eric.

'Yes, he's still breathing, but with difficulty,' Eric says. Then to Isobel. 'They say to lie him on the floor and put his legs up.'

People move back as Isobel moves Harvey off the chair he was sitting on and on to the floor.

'What's happening?' Vincent, who had disappeared momentarily, rematerialises and looks anxiously towards his older brother. 'Is Harvey OK?'

'It's OK, Vinnie. An ambulance is on its way,' Gabriella tries to reassure him.

'You need to keep his airways open,' Eric is saying to Isobel. 'Open his mouth and make sure his nostrils are clear.'

Isobel is already doing this and checking his pulse. She looks alarmed. 'Eric…'

There is fear in her voice, but we can hear the wail of an ambulance siren and a flash of blue strobes through the window and across the room.

'The ambulance is here now, Harvey,' Isobel says and then, with a look of horror on her face, 'Eric, he's stopped breathing.'

317

'Harvey!' Eric drops the phone and kneels beside the boy, as the paramedics come into the room and begin ministering to him. One of them takes out a syringe and injects something into Harvey's leg.

He doesn't respond.

They lift him on to a stretcher and carry him out of the living room to the ambulance. Isobel and Eric follow.

'Only one of you can come in the ambulance,' the paramedic says.

'Bel, you go with him,' Eric says.

'I'll drive the rest of you up to the hospital,' Paddy volunteers.

The party is over. Everyone is shocked. People begin to get their coats and thank us. Some offer to stay and help clear up, but we decline.

'That came on suddenly,' I say when everyone has gone. 'I wonder what caused it.'

'I can't think it was anything he ate here,' Maggie says. 'There was nothing with nuts in.'

'Did you check all the packaging?' I ask.

'Not every single thing,' Maggie says, dismayed. 'But I didn't buy anything that was going to contain nuts.'

'It's not your fault,' I say. 'It's Isobel's responsibility to check or ask, and I'm surprised she doesn't keep the epipen with her all the time, if that's how bad his reactions are.'

'Yes, that's odd,' Maggie says, and she starts picking up plates with half-eaten slices of cake and carrying them into the kitchen. She puts her foot on the pedal of the bin, but pauses before scraping the leftovers onto packaging that is already in there 'You'd think they'd all be aware of anything that might trigger one.'

She goes ahead and tips half-eaten slices of cake on to the rest of the detritus.

'I'm sure he'll be OK,' I say, as I stack the plates in the dishwasher.

'I hope so,' Maggie replies, and we both look up as Iris toddles into the kitchen, her face covered in cake icing, smiling, and makes one of her strange noises.

It's a happy noise though. Iris is blissfully unaware of the drama which is now playing out in an ambulance, racing to hospital through the streets of London.

Acknowledgements

On the off-chance that they're reading this, I have to thank the burglars (or maybe it was just one burglar) who broke into my house at the end of 2012 and left with my computers and the memory sticks containing the first draft of this novel. You forced me to start again from scratch and, while I'm still a bit miffed about the muddy footprints, in the end you did me a favour. This is a better book because of it.

But breaking in is easy. The real hard work was done by my editor and friend, Candida Lacey, to whom I am hugely indebted for her insight, patience, humour, kindness, and an almost unlimited supply of tea and prosecco. I can't thank the whole Myriad team enough for putting their faith in me and for all their boundless energy and hard work and general very-niceness; it has been a real pleasure. Enormous thanks to Linda McQueen, who is quite the best copy-editor ever, and hilarious too. And to Emma Dowson for doing the press stuff. (I know journalists and editors can be a real pain!)

Thank you, too, to my agent Peter Straus at RCW for his continued support.

At the risk of repeating thanks too often, it also goes to Anna Galandzij at the National Deaf Children's Society and Mark Chacksfield for help and advice on deafness, and Dino Skinner for the same with legal stuff.

And for support from all my writer friends, especially Araminta Hall, Richard Bingham, Craig Melvin, Martine McDonagh, Stephen May and Colin Grant who have borne the brunt of the insecurity, paranoia and endless going on – thank you.

Plus my friends and family who also have to live with it (and me) and never let on, if they mind, especially my three children who are inspirational in so many ways. For all sorts of reasons, I could not have written this without the support, love and friendship of so many people. You know who you are and I know I owe you all.

And because the book deals with the highs and lows of bringing up children, a special mention goes to Esther, Hannah, Helen, Jo and Nicola: you've been there for me throughout. And I've borrowed your surnames as well as various anecdotes and incidents from your lives – you know I do this and you don't object. Apologies and thanks in equal measure.

1. How do your sympathies with Isobel and Ben change over the course of the novel?

2. Isobel's experience suggests there are times when the parental desire to protect one's own children conflicts with one's responsibilities to a wider community. In what other situations might this apply?

3. Could you understand Eric's reaction to the news of Iris's deafness?

4. How do the reactions of Isobel's three children, in the novel, reflect your own response to the hesitation, denial and conflict of the adults around them?

5. To what extent do you sympathise with the divided loyalties of Isobel and Ben's mutual friends?

6. The novel explores different kinds of disappointment. Which characters cope best with their changed circumstances and why?

7. Is Ben right to feel that Maggie is a better person than him?

8. Eric says, about Ben, that he needs someone around who still sees Isobel as she used to be. Is the Isobel of the university flashbacks as distant from the Isobel of today as Isobel and Eric and Ben believe, or are there threads still linking past and present?

9. Eric says that the situation with Iris didn't cause the problems in his and Isobel's marriage, it simply exposed them. Is he right? And is there hope for them, for the future?

10. How would the novel be different if it had been Eric and Maggie telling the story, not Isobel and Ben? Or if it were written in the third person, from an outside perspective?

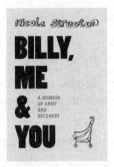

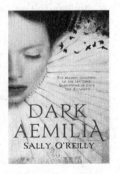

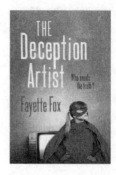

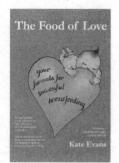

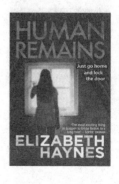

MORE FROM MYRIAD EDITIONS

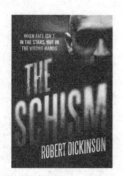

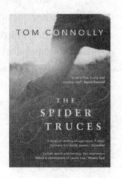

Lizzie Enfield is a journalist and the author of two previous novels, *What You Don't Know* and *Uncoupled*. Her short stories have been broadcast on BBC Radio 4 and published in various magazines, and her articles regularly appear in national newspapers. She lives in Brighton with her husband and three children.